The Brethren

Centennial Edition 1904-2004

The Brethren was originally published in 1904 and has for one hundred years led a relatively obscure existence compared to Haggard's other more celebrated works; among them, *King Solomon's Mines*. Now, through this new Centennial Edition, the publisher hopes to reintroduce this little known classic to a whole new audience.

Also published by Christian Liberty Press

Pearl Maiden
by H. Rider Haggard

Lysbeth
by H. Rider Haggard

In Freedom's Cause
by G. A. Henty

A Tale of the Crusades

H. Rider Haggard

Revised and Edited
by
Michael J. McHugh

Christian Liberty Press
Arlington Heights, Illinois

Revised Edition

Originally by: McClure, Philips, and Co., 1904

Revised and edited by Michael J. McHugh
Copyediting by Diane Olson
Cover painting by Timothy Kou
Original book illustrations by H. R. Millar

A publication of
Christian Liberty Press
502 West Euclid Avenue
Arlington Heights, IL 60004
www.christianlibertypress.com

ISBN 1-930367-97-X

Printed in The United States of America

Contents

Two lovers by the maiden sate,
without a glace of jealous hate;
the maid her lovers sat between,
with open brow and equal mien;
it is a sight but rarely spied,
thanks to man's wrath and woman's pride.

Scott

About the Author

Sir Henry Rider Haggard was born in England on June 22, 1856. He was the eighth of ten children and received most of his primary and elementary education at home through private tutors and occasionally at a local grammar school. His parents took him on frequent trips to the Continent during childhood days.

In 1875, when Haggard was nineteen, he traveled to South Africa to work as a secretary for the newly appointed governor of Natal. Three years later, the young Englishman resigned his post at the high court of Pretoria to take up ostrich farming in Natal.

Haggard visited England in 1880 and was married on August 11 to Mariana L. Margitson. The newlyweds soon returned to their farm in Natal to resume the business of farming. In his spare time, Haggard began to work on his first book project and also began to take up the study of law. In 1882, the Haggard family sold their farm in Natal and returned to England.

Henry Haggard completed his law studies in 1884 and accepted a call to the bar of attorneys in London where he worked as an assistant to a chief judge. It was during this time that he made use of what he describes as his "somewhat ample leisure time in chambers" to write his first successful novel, *King Solomon's Mines*. This book, as he put it, "finally settled the question of whether to pursue a legal or literary career." Henry Haggard proceeded to write over sixty-six novels and numerous papers, producing nearly one book for each year of his life.

Haggard traveled extensively throughout the world during much of his married life. His knowledge of the culture and terrain of Europe and the Middle East enabled him to complete one of his grandest novels, *The Brethren*, in 1904. The recognitions of his contributions as a writer were crowned in the year 1912 when Henry Rider Haggard was knighted.

Sir Haggard died in London on May 14, 1925, at the age of sixty-eight.

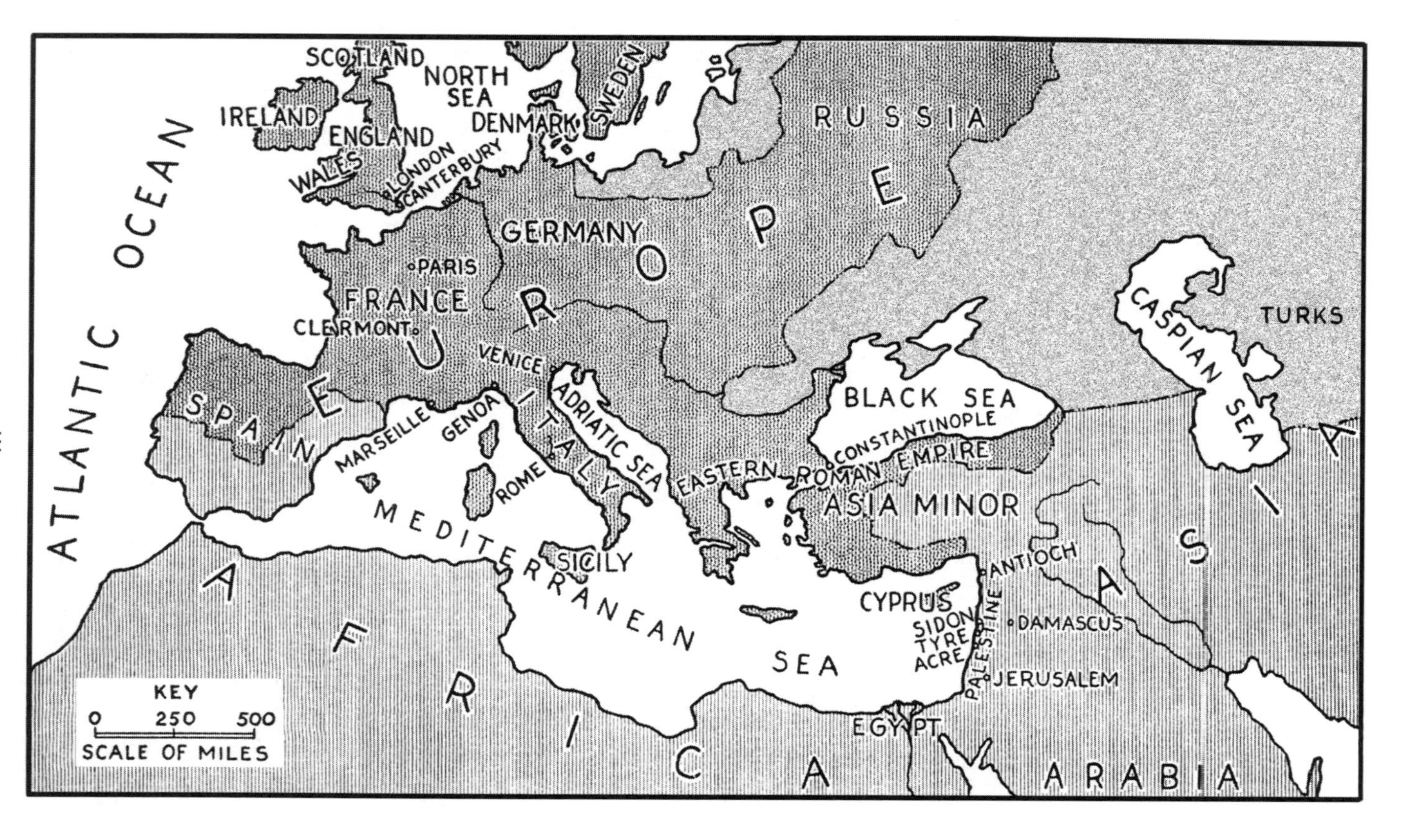
ATLANTIC OCEAN
IRELAND
SCOTLAND
ENGLAND
WALES
LONDON
CANTERBURY
NORTH SEA
DENMARK
SWEDEN
RUSSIA
EUROPE
GERMANY
FRANCE
PARIS
CLERMONT
VENICE
GENOA
MARSEILLE
SPAIN
ITALY
ROME
SICILY
ADRIATIC SEA
MEDITERRANEAN SEA
EASTERN ROMAN EMPIRE
CONSTANTINOPLE
BLACK SEA
ASIA MINOR
CYPRUS
ANTIOCH
DAMASCUS
PALESTINE
JERUSALEM
SIDON
TYRE
ACRE
EGYPT
AFRICA
ARABIA
ASIA
CASPIAN SEA
TURKS
KEY
0 250 500
SCALE OF MILES

PREFACE

The novel you are about to read is set within the years that preceded the Third Crusade. The climactic events described at the close of the book center upon the Battle of Hattin in 1187, in which the Muslim general, Saladin (1138–1193), swept through Palestine, taking Jerusalem and capturing thousands of crusaders. It was the military successes of Saladin that sparked the Third Crusade, which historians often refer to as the Kings' Crusade (1188–1191).

It has become quite popular for modern historians to ridicule, or at least to soundly criticize, the efforts of the crusaders. In some respects, this criticism is quite valid, for too often popes and bishops were so eager to put down violent pagans that they undermined the Gospel of Christ by pronouncing that those who fought with the sword could, by their own human efforts, gain remission for all sins—past and present! Despite the unbiblical excesses, there is still much in the crusades which can be thought of as virtuous and honorable.

How easy it is to forget that, thanks to the aggressive actions of the crusaders in taking the fight to Muslim strongholds in the East, the followers of Mohammed were forced to curtail their efforts to pursue further military conquest in the West. God was, indeed, using the imperfect actions of men to accomplish His perfect will by preserving Europe from Muslim domination, thereby setting the stage for the glorious Protestant Reformation.

In the exciting story that follows, H. Rider Haggard presents an inspiring array of chivalrous knights and fair maidens who strive in their zeal to do what is noble. What a blessing it would be if the Christian Church in the twenty-first century could emulate the zeal and dedication possessed by so many ordinary believers in the eleventh and twelfth centuries. What would be even more blessed, however, is for all believers to be led by the Holy Spirit to be not only filled with zeal to pull down the strongholds of Satan, but to do so with its most powerful weapon, the Sword of the Spirit, which is the Word of God.

As Paul the Apostle stated to the Church at Corinth:

> For though we walk in the flesh, we do not war after the flesh: (For the weapons of our warfare are not carnal, but mighty through God to the pulling down of strong holds;) Casting down imaginations, and every high thing that exalteth itself against the knowledge of God, and bringing into captivity every thought to the obedience of Christ; And having in a readiness to revenge all disobedience, when your obedience is fulfilled.
>
> *2 Corinthians 10:3-6*

May the Lord of the whole earth, the only wise God, Jesus Christ, be pleased to raise up a whole new and more perfect generation of "crusaders" for King Jesus.

Michael J. McHugh
2004

Prologue

Saladin (săl'ə•dĭn, *Ar.* să•lă'əd•dēn'), Commander of the Faithful, the King Strong to Aid, Sovereign of the East, sat at night in his palace at Damascus and brooded on the wonderful ways of Allah (äl'lə, *Ar.* ăl•lăh'), by whom he had been lifted to his high estate. He remembered how, when he was but small in the eyes of men, Nour-ed-din (nūr'əd•dēn'), king of Syria, forced him to accompany his uncle, Shirkuh (shîr'kə), to Egypt, whither he went, "like one driven to his death," and how, against his own will, there he rose to greatness. He thought of his father, the wise Ayoub (ă•yūb'), and the brethren with whom he was brought up, all of them dead now, save one; and of his sisters, whom he had cherished. Most of all did he think of her, Zobeide (zū•bā'•də), who had been stolen away by the knight whom she loved, even to the loss of her own soul—yes, by the English friend of his youth, his father's prisoner, Sir Andrew D'Arcy, who, led astray by passion, had done him and his house this grievous wrong. He had sworn, he remembered, that he would bring his sister back, even from England, and already had planned to kill her husband and capture her when he learned of her death. She had left a child, or so his spies told him, who, if she still lived, must be a woman now—his own niece, though half of noble English blood.

Then his mind wandered from this old, half-forgotten story to the woe and blood in which his days were set, and to the great struggle between the followers of the prophets Jesus and Mahomet (mə•hŏm'ĭt), that Jihad (jĭ•hăd', or Holy War) for which he made ready. He sighed, for he was weary of battle and loved not slaughter, although his fierce faith drove him on from war to war.

Saladin slept and dreamed of victory. In his dream, a maiden stood before him. Presently, when she lifted her veil, he saw that she was beautiful, with features like his own, but fairer, and knew her surely for the daughter of his sister who had fled with the English knight. Now he wondered why she visited him after this manner. Moments later, he saw this same woman standing before him on a Syrian plain, and on either side of her a countless host of Saracens (sâr′ə•səns, or Arabs) and Franks, of whom thousands and tens of thousands were appointed to death. Lo! He, Saladin, charged at the head of his squadrons, scimitar (sĭm′ə•tär) aloft, but she held up her hand and stayed him.

"What are you doing here, my niece?" he asked.

"I am come to save the lives of men through you," she answered; "therefore was I born of your blood, and therefore I am sent to you. Put up your sword, King, and spare them."

"Say, maiden, what ransom do you bring to buy this multitude from doom? What ransom, and what gift?"

"The ransom of my own life freely offered, and the gift of temporal peace for your sinful soul, O King." And, with that outstretched hand, she drew down his keen-edged scimitar until it rested on her chest.

Saladin awoke, and marveled on his dream, but said nothing of it to any man. The next night, a new dream came before him, and he heard a voice saying, "The oath you made to rescue your sister now binds itself to her daughter. Arise, and atone for your sins of the past."

The next night, the same dream returned to him for the third time, and the memory of it went with him all the following day.

Saladin was now persuaded that he had the duty to bring his niece from England to his own royal house. So he summoned a certain false knight who bore the Cross upon his chest, but in secret had accepted the Koran (kôr′än), a Frankish spy of his, who came from that country where dwelt the maiden, his niece. From this traitor and spy he learned about her, her father, and her home. With him and another spy who passed as a Christian, by the aid of Prince Hassan (hă′săhn), one of the greatest and most trusted of his emirs (ĭ•mîrs′, princes), he made a cunning plan for the capture of the maiden if she would not come willingly, and for her bearing away to Syria.

Moreover—that in the eyes of all men, her dignity might be worthy of her high blood and fate—by his decree he created her, the niece whom he had never seen, Princess of Baalbec (bā′əl•bĕk′). He endowed her with great possessions and a rule that her grandfather, Ayoub, and her uncle, Izzeddin (ĭz′əd•dēn′), had held before her. Also, he purchased a stout galley of war, manning it with proved sailors and with chosen men-at-arms, under the command of the prince Hassan. He then wrote a letter to the English lord, Sir Andrew D'Arcy, and to his daughter, and prepared a royal gift of jewels, and sent them to the lady, his niece, far away in England. Saladin commanded this company to win her by peace, or force, or fraud, as best they might; but that without her, not one of them should dare to look upon his face again. And with these he sent the two Frankish spies, who knew the place where the lady lived, one of whom, the false knight, was a skilled mariner and the captain of the ship.

These things did Saladin, Yusuf ibn Ayoub (yū′səf ibn ă•yūb′, Joseph son of Job), and waited patiently till it should please Allah to permit him to accomplish the mission which he had been given while his soul was filled with sleep.

H R MILLAR '903

Chapter I
By the Waters of Death Creek

FROM the sea wall on the coast of Essex, Rosamund looked out across the ocean eastwards. To the right and to the left, but a little behind her, like guards attending the person of their sovereign, stood her cousins, the twin brethren, Godwin and Wulf, tall and stout men. Godwin stood as still as a statue, his hands folded over the hilt of the long, scabbarded sword, of which the point was set on the ground before him. His brother Wulf, however, moved restlessly and, at length, yawned aloud. They were handsome to look at, all three of them, as they appeared in the splendor of their youth and health—the imperial Rosamund, dark-haired and dark-eyed, ivory skinned and slender-waisted, with a posy of marsh flowers in her hand; the pale, stately Godwin, with his dreaming face; and the bold-faced, blue-eyed warrior, Wulf, Saxon to his fingertips—notwithstanding his father's Norman blood.

At the sound of that unstifled yawn, Rosamund turned her head with the slow grace that marked her every movement.

"Would you sleep already, Wulf, and the sun not yet down?" she asked in her rich, low voice, which, perhaps because of its foreign accent, seemed quite different from that of any other woman.

"I think so, Rosamund," he answered. "It would serve to pass the time, and now that you have finished gathering those yellow flowers which we rode so far to seek, the time—is somewhat long."

"Shame on you, Wulf," she said, smiling. "Look upon yonder sea and sky, at that sheet of bloom all gold and purple—"

"I have looked for hard on half an hour, Cousin Rosamund; also at your back and at Godwin's left arm and side-face, till in truth I thought myself kneeling in Stangate Priory staring at my father's effigy upon his tomb, while Prior John performed the Mass. Why, if you stood it on its feet, it is Godwin, the same crossed hands resting on the sword, the same cold, silent face staring at the sky."

"Godwin, as Godwin will no doubt one day be, or so he hopes—that is, if the saints give him grace to do such deeds as did our sire," interrupted his brother.

Wulf looked at him, and a curious flash of inspiration shone in his blue eyes.

"No, I think not," he answered; "the deeds you may do, and greater, but surely you will lie wrapped not in a shirt of mail, but with a monk's cowl at the last—unless a woman robs you of it and the quickest road to heaven. Tell me now, what are you thinking of, you two—for I have been wondering in my dull way, and am curious to learn how far I stand from truth? Rosamund, speak first. Nay, not all the truth—a maid's thoughts are her own—but just the cream of it, that which rises to the top and should be skimmed."

Rosamund sighed.

"I was thinking of the East, where the sun shines ever and the seas are blue as my girdle stones, and men are full of strange learning—"

"And women are men's slaves!" interrupted Wulf. "Still, it is natural that you should think of the East who have that blood in your veins, and high blood, if all tales be true. Say, princess"—and he bowed the knee to her with an affectation of mockery which could not hide his earnest reverence—"say, princess, my cousin, granddaughter of Ayoub and niece of the mighty monarch, Yusuf Saladin, do you wish to leave this pale land and visit your dominions in Egypt and in Syria?"

She listened, and at his words her eyes seemed to take fire, the stately form to erect itself, and the thin nostrils to grow wider as though they scented some sweet, remembered perfume. Indeed, at that moment, standing there on the promontory above the seas, Rosamund looked a very queen.

Presently, she answered him with another question.

"And how would they greet me there, Wulf, who am a Norman D'Arcy and a Christian maid?"

"The first they would forgive you, since that blood is none so ill either, and for the second—why, faiths can be changed."

Then it was that Godwin spoke for the first time.

"Wulf, Wulf," he said sternly, "keep watch upon your tongue, for there are things that should not be said even as a silly jest. See you, I love my cousin here better than aught else upon the earth—"

"There, at least, we agree," broke in Wulf.

"Better than aught else on the earth," repeated Godwin; "but, by the Holy Blood and by St. Peter, at whose shrine we are, I would kill her

with my own hand before her lips kissed the book of the false prophet."

"Or any of his followers," muttered Wulf to himself, but fortunately, perhaps, too low for either of his companions to hear. Aloud he said, "You understand, Rosamund, you must be careful, for Godwin ever keeps his word, and that would be but a poor end for so much birth and beauty and wisdom."

"Oh, cease mocking, Wulf," she answered, laying her hand lightly on the tunic that hid his shirt of mail. "Cease mocking, and pray St. Chad, the builder of this church, that no such dreadful choice may ever be forced upon you, or me, or your beloved brother—who, indeed, in such a case would do right to slay me."

"Well, if we were forced to choose," answered Wulf, and his fair face flushed as he spoke, "I trust that we should know how to meet it. After all, is it so very hard to choose between death and duty?"

"I know not," she replied; "but oft-times sacrifice seems easy when seen from far away; also, things may be lost that are more prized than life."

"What things? Do you mean place, or wealth, or love?"

"Tell me," said Rosamund, changing her tone, "what is that boat rowing round the river's mouth? A while ago it hung upon its oars as though those within it watched us."

"Fisher-folk," answered Wulf carelessly. "I saw their nets."

"Yes; but beneath them something gleamed bright, like swords."

"Fish," said Wulf; "we are at peace in Essex." Although Rosamund did not look convinced, he went on: "Now for Godwin's thoughts—what were they?"

"Brother, if you would know, I was thinking of the East also—the East and its wars."

"The Crusades continue and our costs mount," answered Wulf, "seeing that our dear father was slain in them and naught of him came home again save his heart, which lies at Stangate yonder."

"How better could he die," asked Godwin, "than fighting for the Cross of Christ? Is not that death of his at Harenc told of to this day? By our Lady, I pray for one but half as glorious!"

"Aye, he died well—he died well," said Wulf, his blue eyes flashing and his hand creeping to his sword hilt.

"But, Brother, there is peace at Jerusalem, as in Essex."

"Peace? Yes; but soon there will be war again. The monk Peter—he whom we saw at Stangate last Sunday, and who left Syria but six months gone—told me that it was coming fast. Even now the Sultan Saladin, sitting at Damascus, summons his hosts from far and wide, while his priests preach battle amongst the tribes and barons of the East. And when it comes, Brother, shall we not be there to share it, as were our grandfather, our father, our uncle, and so many of our kin? Shall we rot here in this dull land, as by our uncle's wish we have done these many years, yes, ever since we were home from the Scottish war? Is it our destiny to count cows and plough fields like peasants, while our peers are charging on the pagan, with cross and banner, as their blood runs red upon the holy sands of Palestine?"

Now it was Wulf's turn to take fire.

"By our Lady in Heaven, and our lady here!"—and he looked at Rosamund, who was watching the pair of them with her quiet, thoughtful eyes—"go when you will, Godwin, and I go with you, and as our birth was one birth, so, if it is decreed, let our death be one death." And suddenly his hand that had been playing with the sword-hilt gripped it fast and tore the long, lean blade from its scabbard and cast it high into the air, flashing in the sunlight, to catch it as it fell again, while in a voice that caused the wild fowl to rise in thunder from the saltings beneath, Wulf shouted the old war-cry that had rung on so many a field—"A D'Arcy! A D'Arcy! Meet D'Arcy, meet Death!" Then he sheathed his sword again and added in a shamed voice, "Are we children that we fight where no foe is? Still, Brother, may we find him soon!"

Godwin smiled grimly, but answered nothing; only Rosamund said: "So, my cousins, you would be away, perhaps to return no more, and that will part us. But"—and her voice broke somewhat—"such is the woman's lot, since men like you ever love the bare sword best of all, nor should I think well of you were it otherwise. Yet, Cousins, I know not why"—and she shivered a little—"it comes into my heart that Heaven often answers such prayers swiftly. Oh, Wulf! Your sword looked very red in the sunlight, and I am afraid of I know not what. Well, we must be going, for we have nine miles to ride, and the day is far spent. But first, my cousins, come with me into this shrine, and let us pray St. Peter and St. Chad to guard us on our journey home."

"Our journey," said Wulf anxiously. "What is there for you to fear in a nine-mile ride along the shores of the Blackwater?"

"I said our journey home, Wulf; and home is not in the hall at Steeple, but yonder in Heaven," and she pointed to the quiet, brooding sky.

"Well answered," said Godwin, "in this ancient place, whence so many have journeyed home; all the Romans who are dead, when it was their fortress, and the Saxons who came after them, and others without count."

Then they turned and entered the old church—one of the first that ever was in Britain, rough-built of Roman stone by the very hands of Chad, the Saxon saint, more than five hundred years before their day. Here they knelt a while at the rude altar and prayed, each of them in his or her own fashion, then crossed themselves and rose to seek their horses, which were tied in the shed nearby.

Now there were two roads, or rather tracks, back to the hall at Steeple—one a mile or so inland, that ran through the village of Bradwell, and the other, the shorter way, along the edge of the saltings to the narrow water known as Death Creek, at the head of which the traveler to Steeple must strike inland, leaving the Priory of Stangate on his right. It was this latter path they chose, since at low tide the going there is good for horses—which, even in the summer, that of the inland track was not. Also, they wished to be at home by supper-time, lest the old knight, Sir Andrew D'Arcy, the father of Rosamund and the uncle of the orphan brethren, should grow anxious, and perhaps come out to seek them.

For half an hour or more they rode along the edge of the saltings, for the most part in silence that was broken only by the cry of curlew and the lap of the turning tide. No human being did they see, indeed, for this place was very desolate and unvisited, save now and again by fishermen. At length, just as the sun began to sink, they approached the shore of Death Creek—a sheet of tidal water that ran a mile or more inland, growing ever narrower, but was here some three hundred yards in breadth. They were well mounted, all three of them. Indeed, Rosamund's horse, a great gray, her father's gift to her, was famous in that countryside for its swiftness and power, also because it was so docile that a child could ride it; while those of the brethren were heavy-built but well-trained war steeds, taught to stand where they were left, and to charge when they were urged, without fear of shouting men or flashing steel.

Some seventy yards from the shore of Death Creek and parallel to it, lay a tongue of land, covered with scrub and a few oaks. It ran down into the saltings, its point ending on their path, beyond which were a swamp and the broad river. Between this tongue and the shore of the creek the track wound its way to the uplands. It was an ancient track; indeed, the reason for its existence was that here the Romans or some other long dead hands had built a narrow mole or wharf of rough stone, forty or fifty yards in length, out into the water of the creek, doubtless to serve as a convenience for fisher boats, which could lie alongside it even at low tide. This mole had been much destroyed by centuries of washing, so that the end of it lay below water, although the landward part was still almost sound and level.

Coming over the little rise at the tip of the wooded tongue, the quick eyes of Wulf, who rode first—for here the path along the border of the swamp was so narrow that they must go in single file—caught sight of a large, empty boat moored to an iron ring set in the wall of the mole.

"Your fishermen have landed, Rosamund," he said, "and doubtless gone up to Bradwell."

"That is strange," she answered anxiously, "since here no fishermen ever come." And she checked her horse as though to turn.

"Whether they come or not, certainly they have gone," said Godwin, craning forward to look about him. "So, as we have nothing to fear from an empty boat, let us push on."

On they rode accordingly, until they came to the base of the stone wharf or pier, when a sound behind them caused them to look back. Then they saw a sight that sent the blood to their hearts, for there behind them, leaping down one by one onto that narrow footway, were men, armed with naked swords, six or eight of them, all of whom, they noted, had strips of linen pierced with eyelet holes tied beneath their helms or leather caps, so as to conceal their faces.

"A snare! A snare!" cried Wulf, drawing his sword. "Swift! Follow me up the Bradwell path!" and he struck the spurs into his horse. It bounded forward, as Wulf quickly pulled the reins with all the weight of his powerful arm almost to its haunches. "God's mercy!" he cried, "there are more of them!"

And more there were, for another band of men, armed and linen-hooded like the first, had leapt down onto that Bradwell path. Among this group was a stout man, who seemed to be unarmed, except for a long, crooked knife at his girdle and a coat of ringed mail, which showed through the opening of his loose tunic.

"To the boat!" shouted Godwin, whereat the stout man laughed—a light, penetrating laugh, which even then all three of them heard and noted.

Along the wharf they rode, since there was nowhere else that they could go, with both paths barred, and swamp and water on one side of them, and a steep, wooded bank upon the other. When they reached it, they found why the man had laughed, for the boat was secured with a strong chain that could not be cut; still more, her sail and oars were gone.

"Get into it," mocked a voice; "or, at least, let the lady get in; it will save us the trouble of carrying her there."

Now Rosamund turned very pale, while the face of Wulf went red and white, as he gripped his sword-hilt. But Godwin, calm as ever, rode forward a few paces, and said quietly, "Of your courtesy, say what you need of us. If it be money, we have none—nothing but our arms and horses, which I think may cost you dear."

Now the man with the crooked knife advanced a little, accompanied by another man, a tall, supple-looking knave, into whose ear he whispered.

"My master says," answered the tall man, "that you have with you that which is of more value than all the king's gold—a very fair lady, of whom someone has urgent need. Give her up now, and go your way with your arms and horses, for you are gallant young men, whose blood we do not wish to shed."

At this it was the turn of the brethren to laugh, which both of them did together.

"Give her up," answered Godwin, "and go our ways dishonored? Aye, with our breath, but not before. Who then has such urgent need of the lady Rosamund?"

Again there was whispering between the pair.

"My master says," was the answer, "he thinks that all who see her will have need of her, since such loveliness is rare. But if you wish a name, well, one comes into his mind; the name of the knight Lozelle."

"The knight Lozelle!" murmured Rosamund, turning even paler than before, as well she might. For this Lozelle was a powerful man and Essex-born. He owned ships of whose doings upon the seas and in the East evil tales were told, and once had sought Rosamund's hand in marriage, but being rejected, uttered threats for which Godwin, as the elder of the twins, had fought and wounded him. Then he vanished—none knew where.

"Is Sir Hugh Lozelle here then?" asked Godwin, "masked like you common cowards? If so, I desire to meet him, to finish the work I began in the snow last Christmas."

"Find that out if you can," answered the tall man.

But Wulf said, speaking low between his clenched teeth: "Brother, I see but one chance. We must place Rosamund between us and charge them."

The captain of the band seemed to read their thoughts, for again he whispered into the ear of his companion, who called out: "My master says that if you try to charge, you will be fools, since we shall stab and hamstring your horses, which are too good to waste, and take you quite easily as you fall. Come then, yield, as you can do without shame, seeing there is no escape, and that two men, however brave, cannot stand against a crowd. He gives you one minute to surrender."

Now Rosamund spoke for the first time.

"My cousins," she said, "I pray you not to let me fall living into the hands of Sir Hugh Lozelle, or of yonder men, to be taken to what fate I know not. Let Godwin kill me, then, to save my honor, as but now he said he would to save my soul. Strive to cut your way through, and live to avenge me."

The brethren made no answer, only they looked at the water and then at one another, and nodded. It was Godwin who spoke again, for now that it had come to this struggle for life and their lady, Wulf, whose tongue was commonly so ready, had grown strangely silent, and fierce-faced also.

"Listen, Rosamund, and do not turn your eyes," said Godwin. "There is but one chance for you, and, poor as it is, you must choose between it and capture, since we cannot kill you. The gray horse you ride is strong and true. Turn him now, and spur into the water of Death Creek and swim it. It is broad, but the incoming tide will help you, and perchance you will not drown."

Rosamund listened and moved her head backwards towards the boat. Then Wulf spoke—few words and sharp, "Be gone, girl! We guard the boat."

She heard, and her dark eyes filled with tears, and her stately head sank for a moment almost to her horse's mane.

"Oh, my knights! My knights! And would you die for me? Well, if God wills it, so it must be. But I swear that if you die, that no man shall be aught to me who have your memory, and if you live—" And she looked at them confusedly, then stopped.

"Bless us, and be gone," said Godwin.

So she blessed them in words low and holy; then quickly wheeled round the great gray horse and, striking the spur into

its flank, drove straight at the deep water. The stallion hung for a moment, and then from the low wharf-end sprang out wide and clear. Deep it sank, but not for long, for soon its rider's head rose above the water. Rosamund regained the saddle, from which she had floated, and headed the horse straight for the distant bank.

Now a shout of wonderment went up from the woman thieves, for this was a deed that they had never thought a girl would dare. But the brethren laughed as they saw that the gray swam well, and, leaping from their saddles, ran forward a few paces—eight or ten—along the mole to where it was narrowest. As they went they tore the cloaks from their shoulders, and, since they had none, threw them over their left arms to serve as bucklers.

The bandits cursed aloud, then their captain gave an order to his spokesman, who cried aloud:

"Cut them down, and to the boat! We shall take her before she reaches shore or drowns."

For a moment they wavered, for the tall twin warriors who barred the way had eyes that told of wounds and death. Then with a rush they came, scrambling over the rough stones. But here the causeway was so narrow that, while their strength lasted, two men were as good as twenty, nor, because of the mud and water, could they be attacked from either side. So after all it was but two to two, and the brethren were the better two. Their long swords flashed and smote, and when Wulf's was lifted again, once more it shone red as it had been when he tossed it high in the sunlight. A man soon fell with a heavy splash into the waters of the creek, and wallowed there till he died. Godwin's foe was down also, and, as it seemed, finished.

Then, at a signal, not waiting to be attacked by others, the brethren sprang forward. The huddled mob in front of them saw them come, and shrank back, but before they had gone a yard, the swords were at work once again. They swore strange oaths; they caught their feet among the rocks, and rolled upon their faces. In their confusion three of them were pushed into the water, where two sank in the mud and were drowned, the third only dragging himself ashore, while the rest made good their escape from the causeway. But two had been cut down, and three had fallen, for whom there was no escape. They strove to rise and fight, but the linen masks flapped about their eyes, so that their blows went wide, while the long swords of the brothers smote and smote again upon their helms and harness as the hammers of smiths smite upon an anvil, until they rolled over silent and stirless.

"Back!" said Godwin; "for here the road is wide, and they will get behind us."

So back they moved slowly, with their faces to the foe, stopping just in front of the first man whom Godwin had seemed to kill, and who lay face upwards with arms outstretched.

"So far we have done well," said Wulf, with a short laugh. "Are you hurt?"

"Nay," answered his brother, "but do not boast till the battle is over, for many are left, and they will come on thus no more. Pray God they have no spears or bows."

Then he turned and looked behind him, and there, far from the shore now, swam the gray horse steadily, and there upon its back sat Rosamund. Yes, and she had seen the combat, since the horse swam somewhat sideways with the tide, for look; she took the kerchief from her throat and waved it to them. Then the brethren knew that she was proud of their great deeds and thanked the saints that they had lived to do even so much as this for her dear sake.

Godwin was right. Although their leader commanded them in a stern voice, the band sank from the reach of those awful swords, and, instead, sought for stones to hurl at them. But here lay more mud than pebbles, and the rocks of which the causeway was built were too heavy for them to lift, so that they found but few, which when thrown either missed the brethren or did them little hurt. Now, after some while, the man called "master" spoke through his lieutenant, and certain of them ran into the thorn thicket and soon appeared again bearing the long oars of the boat.

"Their counsel is to batter us down with the oars. What shall we do now, Brother?" asked Godwin.

"What we can," answered Wulf. "It matters little if Rosamund is slowed by the waters, for they will scarcely take her now, for they must loose the boat and man it after we are dead."

As he spoke, Wulf heard a sound behind him, and suddenly Godwin threw up his arms and sank to his knees. Round he sprang, and there upon his feet stood that man whom they thought was dead, and in his hand a bloody sword. At him leapt Wulf, and so fierce were the blows he smote that the first severed his sword arm and the second shore through cloak and mail deep into the thief's side; so that this time he fell, never to stir again. Then he looked at his brother and saw that the blood was running down his face and blinding him.

"Save yourself, Wulf, for I am spent," uttered Godwin.

"Nay, or you could not speak." And he cast his arm round him and kissed him on the brow.

Then a thought came into his mind and, lifting Godwin as though he were a child, he ran back to where the horses stood, and heaved him onto the saddle.

"Hold fast!" he cried, "by mane and pommel. Keep your mind, and hold fast, and I will save you yet."

Passing the reins over his left arm, Wulf leapt upon the back of his own horse and turned it. Ten seconds more and the pirates, who were gathering with the oars where the paths joined at the root of the causeway, saw the two great horses thundering down upon them. On one horse sat a sore wounded man, his bright hair dabbled with blood, his hands gripping mane and saddle, and on the other the warrior Wulf, with starting eyes and a face like the face of a flame, shaking his red sword and, for the second time that day, shouting aloud: "A D'Arcy! A D'Arcy! Contre D'Arcy, contre Mort!"

They saw, they shouted, they massed themselves together and held up the oars to meet them. But Wulf spurred fiercely, and, short as was the way, the heavy horses, trained to combat, gathered their speed. Now they were on them. The oars were swept aside like reeds; all round them flashed the swords, and Wulf felt that he was hurt, he knew not where. But his sword flashed also,

one blow—there was no time for more—yet the man beneath it sank like an empty sack.

By St. Peter! They were through, as Godwin still swayed upon his saddle, and yonder, nearing the further shore, the gray horse with its burden still battled in the tide. They were through! They were through! To Wulf's eyes the air swam red, the earth seemed as though it rose up to meet them, and everywhere was flaming fire.

But the shouts had died away behind them, and the only sound was the sound of the galloping of their horses' hoofs. Then that also grew faint and died away, and silence and darkness fell upon the mind of Wulf.

Chapter II
Sir Andrew D'Arcy

Godwin dreamed that he was dead, and that beneath him floated the world, a glowing ball, while he was carried to and fro through the blackness, stretched upon a couch of ebony. Also, there were bright watchers by his couch, two of them, and he knew them as his guardian angels, given him at birth. Moreover, now and again presences would come and question the watchers who sat at his head and foot.

One such visitor was his father—the warrior sire whom he had never seen, who fell in Syria. Godwin knew him well, for the face was the face carved on the tomb in Stangate Church, and he wore the blood-red cross upon his mail, and the D'Arcy death's-head was on his shield, and in his hand shone a naked sword.

"Is this the soul of my son?" he asked of the white-robed watchers. "If so, how died he?"

Then the angel at his foot answered: "He died, red sword aloft, fighting a good fight."

"Fighting for the Cross of Christ?

"Nay; fighting for a woman."

"Fighting for a woman's love who should have fallen in the Holy War? Alas! Poor son. Alas! Poor son! Alas! That we must part again forever!" And his voice, too, passed away.

Lo! An archangel advanced through the misty blackness, and the angels at head and foot stood up and saluted with their flaming spears.

"How died this child of God?" asked the figure, speaking out of the glory, a low and awful voice.

"He died by the sword," answered the angel.

"By the sword of the children of the enemy, fighting in the war of Heaven?" asked the archangel.

Then the angels were silent.

"What has Heaven to do with him, if he fought not for Heaven?" asked the voice again.

"Let him be spared," pleaded the guardians, "who was young and brave, and knew not. Send him back to earth, there to deal with his sins and be under our charge once more."

"So be it," said the voice. "Knight, live on, but live as a knight of Heaven if thou wouldst win Heaven."

"Must he then leave the woman?" asked the angels.

"It was not said," answered the voice speaking from the glory.

Suddenly, all that wild dream vanished.

Godwin awoke to hear other voices around him, voices human, well-beloved, remembered; and to see a face bending over him—a face most human, most well-beloved, most remembered—that of his cousin Rosamund. He babbled some questions, but they brought him food and told him to sleep, so he slept. Thus it went on, waking and sleeping, sleeping and waking; till at length, one morning, he woke up truly in the little room that opened out of the upper room or sitting place of the Hall of Steeple, where he and Wulf had slept since their uncle took them to his home as infants. Moreover, on the trestle bed opposite to him, his leg and arm bandaged, and a crutch by his side, sat Wulf himself. He was somewhat paler and thinner than of yore, but the same jovial, careless, yet at times fierce-faced Wulf.

"Do I still dream, my brother, or is it you, indeed?"

A happy smile spread upon the face of Wulf, for now he knew that Godwin was himself again.

"Me, sure enough," he answered. "Dream-folk don't have lame legs; they are the gifts of swords and men."

"And Rosamund? What of Rosamund? Did the gray horse swim the creek, and how came we here? Tell me quick–I faint for news!"

"She shall tell you herself." And, hobbling to the curtained door, he called, "Rosamund, my cousin Rosamund, Godwin is himself again. Hear you, Godwin is himself again, and would speak with you!"

There was a swift rustle of robes and a sound of quick feet among the rushes that strewed the floor, and then—Rosamund herself, lovely as ever, yet with all her stateliness lost in joy. She saw him, the gaunt Godwin sitting up upon the pallet, his gray eyes shining in the white and sunken face. For Godwin's eyes were gray, while Wulf's were blue, the only difference between them which a stranger would note, although in truth Wulf's lips were fuller than Godwin's, and his chin more marked; also, he was a larger man. She saw him, and with a little cry of delight ran and cast her arms about him, and kissed him on the brow.

"Be careful," said Wulf roughly, turning his head aside, "or, Rosamund, you will loose the bandages, and bring his trouble back again; he has had enough of blood-letting."

"Then I will kiss him on the hand—the hand that saved me," she said, and did so. Moments later, she pressed that poor, pale hand against her heart.

"Mine had something to do with that business also, but I don't remember that you kissed it, Rosamund. Well, I will embrace him too, and oh! God be praised, and the holy Virgin, and the holy Peter, and the holy Chad! Thanks to their aid, and the help of Rosamund here, and the prayers of the prior John and brethren at Stangate, and of Matthew, the village priest, God has given you back to us, my brother, my most beloved brother." Then he hopped to the bedside and, throwing his long, sinewy arms about Godwin, embraced him again and again.

"Be careful," said Rosamund dryly, "or, Wulf, you will disturb the bandages, and he has had enough of blood-letting."

Then before he could answer, which he seemed minded to do, there came the sound of a slow step and, swinging the curtain aside, a tall and noble-looking knight entered the little place. The man was old, but looked older than he was, for sorrow and sickness had wasted him. His snow-white hair hung upon his shoulders, his face was pale, and his features were pinched but finely chiseled and, notwithstanding the difference of their years, wonderfully like to those of the daughter Rosamund. For this was her father, the famous lord, Sir Andrew D'Arcy. Rosamund turned and bent the knee to him with a strange and Eastern grace, while Wulf bowed his head, and Godwin, since his neck was too stiff to stir, held up his hand in greeting. The old man looked at him, and there was pride in his eye.

"So you will live after all, my nephew," he said, "and for that I thank the Giver of life and death, since by God, you are a gallant man—a worthy child of the bloods of the Norman D'Arcy and of Uluin the Saxon. Yes, one of the best of them."

"Speak not so, my uncle," said Godwin; "or at least, here is a worthier," and he patted the hand of Wulf with his lean fingers. "It was Wulf who bore me through. Oh, I remember as much as that—how he lifted me onto the black horse and bade me to cling fast to mane and pommel. Ay, and I remember the charge, and his cry of 'Contre D'Arcy, contre Mort!' and the flashing of swords about us, and after that—nothing."

"Would that I had been there to help in that fight," said Sir Andrew D'Arcy, tossing his white hair. "Oh, my children, it is hard to be sick and old. A log am I—naught but a rotting log. Still, had I only known—"

"Father, Father," said Rosamund, casting her white arm about his neck. "You should not speak thus. You have done your share."

"Yes, my share; but I should like to do more. Oh, St. Andrew, ask it for me that I may die with sword aloft and my grandsire's cry upon my lips. Yes, yes; thus, not like a worn-out war-horse in his stall. There, pardon me; but in truth, my children, I am jealous of you. Why, when I found you lying in each other's arms I could have wept for rage to think that such a fray had been within a league of my own doors and I not in it."

"Do not be hard on yourself, for I know nothing of all that story," said Godwin.

"No, in truth, how can you, who have been senseless this month or more? But Rosamund knows, and she shall tell the story. Speak on, Rosamund. Lay you back, Godwin, and listen."

"The tale is yours, my cousins, and not mine," said Rosamund. "You bade me take to the water, and into it I spurred the gray horse, and we sank deep, so that the waves closed above my head. Then up we came, I floating from the saddle, but I regained it, and the horse answered to my voice and bridle, and swam out for the further shore. On it swam, somewhat slantwise with the tide, so that by turning my head I could see all that passed upon the mole. I saw them come at you, and men fall before your swords; I saw you charge them, and run back again. Lastly, after what seemed a very long while, when I was far away, I saw Wulf lift Godwin into the saddle—I knew it must be Godwin, because he set him on the black horse—and the pair of you galloped down the quay and vanished.

"By then I was near the home shore, and the gray grew very weary and sank deep in the water. But I cheered it on with my voice, and although twice its head went beneath the waves, in the end it found a footing, though a soft one. After resting awhile, it plunged forward with short rushes through the mud, and so at length came safe to land, where it stood shaking with fear and weariness. So soon as the horse got its breath again, I pressed on, for I saw them loosing the boat, and came home here as the dark closed in, to meet your uncle watching for me at the gate. Now, Father, it is your turn to take up the tale."

"There is little more to tell," said Sir Andrew. "You will remember, Nephews, that I was against this ride of Rosamund's to seek flowers, or I know not what, at St. Peter's shrine, nine miles away. Nevertheless, as the maid had set her heart on it, and there are but few pleasures here, why, I let her go with the pair of you for escort. You will mind also that you were starting without your mail, and how foolish you thought me when I called you back and made you gird it on. Well, my patron saint—or yours—put it into my head to do so, for had it not been for those same shirts of mail, you were both of you dead men today. But that morning I had been thinking of Sir Hugh Lozelle—if such a false, pirate rogue can be called a knight—and his threats after he recovered from the wound you gave him, Godwin; how that he would come back and take your cousin for all we could do to stay him. True, we heard that he had sailed for the East to war against Saladin—or with him, for he was ever a traitor; but even if this were so, men return from the East. Therefore I bade you arm, having some foresight of what was to come, for doubtless this onslaught must have been planned by him."

"I think so," said Wulf, "for, as Rosamund here knows, the tall knave, who interpreted for the foreigner whom he called his master, gave us the name of the knight Lozelle as the man who sought to carry her off."

"Was this master a Saracen?" asked Sir Andrew, anxiously.

"Nay, Uncle, how can I tell, seeing that his face was masked like the rest and he spoke through an interpreter? But I pray you go on with the story, which Godwin has not heard."

"It is short. When Rosamund told her tale of which I could make little, for the girl was crazed with grief and cold and fear, save that you had been attacked upon the old quay, and she had escaped by swimming Death Creek—which seemed a thing incredible—I got together what men I could. Then bidding her stay behind, with some of them to guard her, I set out to find you or your bodies. It was dark, but we rode hard, having lanterns with us, as we went rousing men at every stead, until we came to where the roads join at Moats. There we found a black horse—your horse, Godwin—so badly wounded that he could travel no further, and I groaned, thinking that you were dead. Still we went on, till we heard another horse whinny, and soon found the grey, also riderless, standing by the path-side with his head down.

"'A man on the ground holds him!' cried one, and I sprang from the saddle to see who it might be, to find that it was you, the pair of you, locked in each other's arms, and senseless, if not dead, as well you might be from your wounds. I bade the country folk cover you up and carry you home, and others to run to Stangate in order to fetch the monk Stephen, who is a doctor, so that he might tend you, while we pressed onwards to take vengeance if we could. We reached the quay upon the creek, but there we found nothing save some bloodstains and—this is strange—your sword, Godwin, the hilt set between two stones, and on the point a writing."

"What was the writing?" asked Godwin.

"Here it is," answered his uncle, drawing a piece of parchment from his robe. "Read it, one of you, since all of you are scholars and my eyes are dim."

Rosamund took it and read what was written, hurriedly, and in the French tongue. It ran thus: "The sword of a brave man. Bury it with him if he be dead, and give it back to him if he lives, as I hope. My master would wish me to do this honor to a gallant foe whom, in that case, he still may meet. (Signed) Hugh Lozelle, or Another."

"Another, then; not Hugh Lozelle," said Godwin, "since he cannot write, and if he could, would never pen words so knightly."

"The words may be knightly, but the writer's deeds were base enough," replied Sir Andrew; "nor, in truth, do I understand this scroll."

"The interpreter spoke of the short man as his master," suggested Wulf.

"Ay, Nephew; but him you met. This writing speaks of a master whom Godwin may meet, and who would wish the writer to pay him a certain honor."

"Perhaps he wrote thus to blind us," added Godwin.

"Perchance, perchance. The matter puzzles me. Moreover, of whom these men were I have been able to learn nothing. A boat was seen passing towards Bradwell—indeed, it seems that you saw it—and that night a boat was seen sailing southwards down St. Peter's sands towards a ship that had anchored off Foulness Point. But what that ship was, whence she came, and whither she went, none know, though the tidings of this fray have made some stir."

"Well," said Wulf, "at the least we have seen the last of her crew of women-thieves. Had they meant more mischief, they would have shown themselves again ere now."

Sir Andrew looked grave as he answered.

"So I trust, but all the tale is very strange. How came they to know that you and Rosamund were riding that day to St. Peter's-on-the-Wall, and so were able to waylay you? Surely some spy must have warned them, since that they were no common pirates is evident, for they spoke of Lozelle, and bade you two be gone unharmed, as it was Rosamund whom they needed. Also, there is the matter of the sword that fell from the hand of Godwin when he was hurt, which was returned in so strange a fashion. I have known many such deeds of chivalry done in the East by Paynim men—"

"Well, Rosamund is half an Eastern," broke in Wulf carelessly, "and perhaps that had something to do with it all."

Sir Andrew started, and the color rose to his pale face. Then in a tone in which he showed he wished to speak no more of this matter, he said:

"Enough, enough. Godwin is very weak and grows weary, and before I leave him I have a word to say. Young men, you are the sons of my blood, the nearest to it except that noble knight, my brother. I have ever loved you well, and been proud of you, but if this was so in the past, how much more is it thus today, when you have done such high service to my house? Moreover, that deed was brave and great; nothing more knightly has been told of in Essex this many a year, and those who wrought it should no longer be simple gentlemen, but very knights.

"This boon it is in my power to grant to you according to the ancient custom. Still, that none may question it, while you lay sick, but after it was believed that Godwin would live, which at first we scarcely dared to hope, I journeyed to London and sought audience of our lord the king. Having told him this tale, I prayed him that he would be pleased to grant me his command in writing that I should name you knights.

"My nephews, he was so pleased, and here I have the brief sealed with the royal signet, commanding that in his name and my own I should give you the accolade publicly in the church of the Priory at Stangate at such season as may be convenient. Therefore, Godwin, the squire, haste you to get well that you may become Sir Godwin the Knight; for you, Wulf, save for the hurt to your leg, are well enough already."

Now Godwin's white face went red with pride, and Wulf dropped his bold eyes and looked as modest as a peasant.

"Speak you," he said to his brother, "for my tongue is blunt and awkward."

"Sir," said Godwin in a weak voice, "we do not know how to thank you for so great an honor, that we never thought to win till we had done more famous deeds than the beating off of a band of robbers. Sir, we have no more to say, save that while we live we will strive to be worthy of our name and of you."

"Well spoken," said his uncle, adding as though to himself, "this man is courtly as he is brave."

Wulf looked up, a flash of merriment upon his open face.

"I, my uncle, whose speech is, I fear me, not courtly, thank you also. I will add that I think our lady cousin here should be knighted too, if such a thing were possible for a woman, seeing that to swim a horse across Death Creek was a greater deed than to fight some rascals on its quay."

"Rosamund," answered the old man in the same dreamy voice. "Her rank is high enough—too high, far too high for safety." And turning, he left the little chamber.

"Well, Cousin," said Wulf, "if you cannot be a knight, at least you can lessen all this dangerous rank of yours by becoming a knight's wife." Whereat Rosamund looked at him with indignation, mingled with a smile in her dark eyes, and murmuring that she must see to the making of Godwin's broth, followed her father from the place.

"It would have been kinder had she told us that she was glad," said Wulf when she was gone.

"Perhaps she would," answered his brother, "had it not been for your rough jests, Wulf, which might have a meaning in them."

"Nay, I had no meaning. Why should she not become a knight's wife?"

"Ay, but what knight's? Would it please either of us, Brother, if, as may well chance, he should be some stranger?"

Now Wulf swore a great oath, then flushed to the roots of his fair hair, and was silent.

"Ah!" said Godwin, "you do not think before you speak, which it is always well to do."

"She swore upon the wharf yonder," broke in Wulf.

"Forget what she swore. Words uttered in such an hour should not be remembered against a maid."

"God's truth, Brother, you are right, as ever! My tongue runs away with me, but still I can't put those words out of my mind, though which of us—"

"Wulf!" said Godwin, "can we think on other things?"

"I mean to say that we are in the path of blessing today, Godwin. Oh, our passage at arms was grand indeed! Such fighting of which I have never seen or dreamed. We won it, too! And now both of us are alive, and a knighthood for each!"

"Yes; both of us are alive, thanks to you, Wulf—nay, it is so, though you would never have done less. But as for the path we are on, it is one that has many rough turns, and perhaps before all is done we may be lead round some of them."

"You talk like a priest, not like a squire who is to be knighted at the cost of a scar on his head. For my part, I will smile while I may, even if fortune jilts me afterwards."

"Wulf," called Rosamund from without the curtain, "cease talking at the top of your voice, I pray you, and leave Godwin to sleep, for he needs it." And she entered the little chamber, bearing a bowl of broth in her hand.

Thereon, saying that ladies should not listen to what did not concern them, Wulf seized his crutch and hobbled from the place.

Chapter III
The Knighting of the Brethren

Another month had gone by, and though Godwin was still somewhat weak and suffered from headaches at times, the brethren had recovered from their wounds. On the last day of November, about two o'clock in the afternoon, a great procession might have been seen wending its way from the old Hall at Steeple. In it rode many knights fully armed, before whom were borne their banners. These went first. Then came old Sir Andrew D'Arcy, also fully armed, attended by squires and retainers. He was accompanied by his lovely daughter, the lady Rosamund, clad in beautiful apparel under her cloak of fur, who rode at his right hand on that same horse which had swum Death Creek. Next appeared the brethren, modestly arrayed as simple gentlemen, followed each of them by his squire, descendants of the noble houses of Salcote and of Dengie. After them rode yet more knights, squires, tenants of various degree, and servants, surrounded by a great number of peasantry, who walked and ran with their womenfolk and children.

Following the road through the village, the procession turned to the left at the great arch which marked the boundary of the monk's lands and headed for Stangate Abbey, some two miles away, by the path that ran between the arable land and the salt marshes, which are flooded at high tide. At length they came to the stone gate of the abbey, which gave the place its name of Stangate. Here they were met by a company of the Cluniac monks, who dwelt in this wild and lonely spot upon the water's edge, headed by their prior, John Fitz Brien. He was a venerable, white-haired man, clad in wide-sleeved, black robes, and preceded by a priest carrying a silver cross. Now the procession separated, Godwin and Wulf, with certain of the knights and their esquires, being led to the priory, or community house, while the main body of it entered the church, or stood about outside its door.

Upon entering the house, the two knights-elect were taken to a room where their hair was cut and their chins were shaved by a barber who awaited them. Then, under the guidance of two old knights named Sir Anthony de Mandeville and Sir Roger de Merci, they were conducted to baths surrounded with rich cloths. Into these pools they entered and bathed themselves, while Sir Anthony and Sir Roger spoke to them through the cloths of the high duties of their vocation. This process ended as the seasoned knights proceeded to pour water over them, while making the sign of the Cross. Next they were dressed again and, preceded by minstrels, led to the church, at the porch of which they and their esquires were given wine to drink.

Here, in the presence of all the company, they were clothed first in white tunics, to signify the purity of their hearts; next in red robes, symbolical of the blood they might be called upon to shed for Christ; and lastly, in long black cloaks, emblems of the death that must be endured by all. This done, their armor was brought in and piled before them upon the steps of the altar, and the congregation departed homeward, leaving them with their esquires and the priest to spend the long winter night "in fasting and prayers."

Long, indeed, it was, in that lonesome, holy place, lit only by a lamp that swung before the altar. Wulf prayed and prayed until he could pray no more, then fell into a half dreamful state that was haunted by the face of Rosamund, where even her face should have been forgotten. Godwin, his elbow resting against the tomb that hid his father's heart, prayed also, until even his earnestness was outworn, and he began to wonder about many things.

That dream of his, for instance, in his sickness, when he had seemed to be dead. Then he thought of what might be the true duty of man. To be brave and upright? Surely. To fight for the

Cross of Christ against the Saracen? Surely, if the chance came his way. What more? To abandon the world and to spend his life muttering prayers like those priests in the darkness behind him? Could that be needful or of service to God or man? To man, perhaps, because such folk tended the sick and fed the poor. But to God? Was he not sent into the world to bear his part in the world—to live his full life? This would mean a half-life—one into which no woman might enter, to which no child might be added, since to monks and even to certain brotherhoods, all these things, which Jesus blessed and Heaven had sanctified, were deadly sin.

It would mean, for instance, that he must think no more of Rosamund. Could he do this for the sake of some alleged spiritual benefit in some future state?

Why, at the thought of it even, in that solemn place and hour of dedication, his spirit reeled, for then and there for the first time it was borne in upon him that he loved this woman more than all the world beside—more than his life; more, perhaps, than his soul. He loved her with all his pure young heart—so much that it would be a joy to him to die for her, not only in the heat of battle, as lately had almost chanced on the Death Creek wharf, but in cold blood, of set purpose, if there came need. He loved her with body and with spirit, and, after God, here to her he consecrated his body and his spirit. But what value would she put upon the gift? What if some other man—?

By his side, his elbows resting on the altar rails, his eyes fixed upon the beaming armor that he would wear in battle, knelt Wulf, his brother—a mighty man, a knight of knights, fearless, noble, open-hearted; such a one as any woman might well love. And he also loved Rosamund. Of this Godwin was sure. And, oh! Did not Rosamund love Wulf? Bitter jealousy seized upon his vitals. Yes; even then and there, black envy got hold of Godwin, and rent him so sore that, cold as was the place, the sweat poured from his brow and body.

Should he abandon hope? Should he fly the battle for fear that he might be defeated? Nay; he would fight on in all honesty and honor and, if he were overcome, would meet his fate as a brave knight should—without bitterness, but without shame. Let destiny direct the matter. It was in the hands of destiny and, stretching out his arm, he threw it around the neck of his brother, who knelt beside him, and let it rest there, until the head of the weary Wulf sank sleepily upon his shoulder, like the head of an infant upon its mother's breast.

"Oh, Jesu," Godwin moaned in his poor heart, "give me strength to fight against this sinful passion that would lead me to hate the brother whom I love. Oh, Jesu, give me strength to bear it if he should be preferred before me. Make me a perfect knight—strong to suffer and endure, and, if need be, to rejoice even in the joy of my supplanter."

At length, the gray dawn broke and the sunlight, passing through the eastern window like a golden spear, pierced the dusk of the long church, which was built to the shape of a cross, so that only its transepts remained in shadow. Then came a sound of chanting, and at the western door entered the prior, wearing all his robes, attended by the monks and acolytes, who swung censers. In the center of the nave he halted and passed to the confessional, calling on Godwin to follow.

So he went and knelt before the priest, and there poured out all his heart. He confessed his sins, although they were more numerous than either he or the priest could know. He told him of the dream during his sickness, on which the prior pondered long; of his deep love, his hopes, his fears, and his desire to be a warrior who once, as a lad, had wished to be a monk, not that he might shed blood, but to fight for the Cross of Christ against the Paynim, ending with a cry of—

"Give me counsel, O my father. Give me counsel."

"Your own heart is your best counselor," was the priest's answer. "Go as it guides you, knowing that, through it, it is God who guides. Nor fear that you will fail. But if love and the joys of life should leave you, then come back, and we will talk again. Go on, pure knight of Christ, fearing nothing and sure of the reward, and take with you the blessing of Christ and of His Church."

"What penance must I bear, Father?" asked Godwin.

"Such souls as yours inflict their own penance. The saints forbid that I should add to it," was the gentle answer.

Then with a lightened heart Godwin returned to the altar rails, while his brother Wulf was summoned to take his place in the confessional. Of the sins that he had to tell we need not speak. They were such as are common to young men, and all of them unpardonable apart from the atoning work of Jesus Christ. Before he gave him absolution, the prior admonished him to think less of his body and more of his spirit; less of the glory of feats of arms and more of the true ends to which he should enter on them. He bade him, moreover, to take his brother Godwin as an earthly guide and example, since there lived no better or wiser man of his years, and finally dismissed him, prophesying that if he would heed these counsels, he would come to great glory on earth and in heaven.

"Father, I will do my best," answered Wulf humbly; "but there cannot be two Godwins, and, Father, sometimes I fear me that our paths will cross, since two men cannot win one woman."

"I know the trouble," answered the prior anxiously, "and with less noble-natured men it might be grave. But if it should come to this, then must the lady judge according to the wishes of her own heart, and he who loses her must be loyal in sorrow as in joy. Be sure that you take no base advantage of your brother in the hour of temptation, and bear him no bitterness should he win the bride."

"I think I can be sure of that," said Wulf; "we, who have loved each other from birth, would die before we betrayed each other."

"I think so, also," answered the prior; "but Satan is very strong."

Then Wulf also returned to the altar rails, and the full Mass was sung, and the Sacrament received by the two neophytes, and the offerings made all in their appointed order. Next they were led back to the priory to rest and eat a little after their long night's vigil in the cold church, and here they abode awhile, thinking their own thoughts, seated alone in the prior's chamber. At length Wulf, who seemed to be ill at ease, rose and laid his hand upon his brother's shoulder, saying, "I can be silent no more; it was ever thus: that which is in my mind must flow out of it. I have words to say to you."

"Speak on, Wulf," said Godwin.

Wulf sat himself down again upon his stool, and for a while stared hard at nothing, for he did not seem to find it easy to begin this talk. Now Godwin could read his brother's mind like a book, but Wulf could not always read Godwin's, although, being twins who had been together from birth, their hearts were for the most part open to each other without the need of words.

"It is of our cousin Rosamund, is it not?" asked Godwin abruptly.

"Ay. Who else?"

"And you would tell me that you love her, and that now you are a knight—almost—and hard on five-and-twenty years of age, you would ask her to become your affianced wife?"

"Yes, Godwin; it came into my heart when she rode the grey horse into the water, there upon the pier, and I thought that I should never see her any more. I tell you it came into my heart that life was not worth living nor death worth dying without her."

"Then, Wulf," answered Godwin slowly, "what more is there to say? Ask on, and prosper. Why not? We have some lands, if not many, and Rosamund will not lack for them. Nor do I think that our uncle would forbid you, if she wills it, seeing that you are the most proper man and the bravest in all this country-side."

"Except my brother Godwin, who is all these things, and good and learned to boot, which I am not," replied Wulf musingly. Then there was silence for a while, which he broke.

"Godwin, our ill-luck is that you love her also, and that you thought the same thoughts which I did yonder on the wharf-head."

Godwin flushed a little, and his long fingers tightened their grip upon his knee.

"It is so," he said quietly. "To my grief, it is so. But Rosamund knows nothing of this, and should never know it if you will keep a watch upon your tongue. Moreover, you need not be jealous of me, before marriage or after."

"What, then, would you have me do?" asked Wulf hotly. "Seek her heart, and perchance—though this I doubt—let her yield it to me, she thinking that you care naught for her?"

"Why not?" asked Godwin again, with a sigh; "it might save her some pain and you some doubt, and make my own path clearer. Marriage is more to you than to me, Wulf, who think sometimes that my sword should be my spouse and duty my only aim."

"I am little surprised that from your heart of gold, that even in such a thing as this you will not bar the path of the brother whom you love. Nay, Godwin, as I am a sinful man, and as I desire her above all things on earth, I will play no such coward's game, nor conquer one who will not lift his sword lest he should hurt me. Sooner would I bid you all farewell, and go to seek fortune or death in the wars without word spoken."

"Leaving Rosamund to pine, perchance. Oh, could we be sure that she had no mind toward either of us, that would be best—to be gone together. But, Wulf, we cannot be sure, since at times, to be honest, I have thought she loves you."

"And at times, to be honest, Godwin, I have been sure that she loves you, although I should like to try my luck and hear it from her lips, which on such terms as you have deemed I will not do."

"What, then, is your plan, Wulf?" asked Godwin.

"My plan is that if our uncle gives us leave, we should both speak to her—you first, as the elder, setting out your case as best you can, and asking her to think of it and give you your answer within a day. Then, before that day is done I also should speak, so that she may know all the story, and play her part in it with opened eyes, not deeming, as otherwise she might, that we know each other's minds, and that you ask because I have no will that way."

"It is very fair," replied Godwin; "and worthy of you, who are the most honest of men. Yet, Wulf, I am troubled. See, you my brother, have ever brethren loved each other as we do? And now must the shadow of a woman fall upon and blight that love which is so fair and precious?"

"Why so?" asked Wulf. "Come, Godwin, let us make a pact that it shall not be thus, and keep it by the help of Heaven. Let us show the world that two men can love one woman and still love each other, not knowing as yet which of them she will choose—if, indeed, she chooses either. For, Godwin, we are not the only gentlemen whose eyes have turned, or yet may turn, towards the high-born, rich, and lovely lady Rosamund. Is it your will that we should make such a pact?"

Godwin thought a little, then answered, "Yes; but if so, it must be one so strong that for her sake and for both our sakes we cannot break it and live with honor."

"So be it," said Wulf; "this is man's work, not child's make-believe."

Then Godwin rose and, going to the door, bade his squire, who watched without, to summon the prior John to come to them as they sought his counsel in a matter. So he came and, standing before him with downcast head, Godwin told him all the tale, which, indeed, he who knew so much already was quick to understand, and of their purpose as well. While both men paused, Wulf answered that it was well and truly said, nothing having been kept back. Then they asked him if it was lawful that they should take such an oath, to which he replied that he thought it not only lawful, but very good.

So in the end, kneeling together hand in hand before the Rood that stood in the chamber, they repeated this oath after him, both of them together, "We brethren, Godwin and Wulf D'Arcy, do swear by the holy Cross of Christ, and by the patron saint of this place, St. Mary Magdalene, and our own patron saints, St. Peter and St. Chad, standing in the presence of God, of our guardian angels, and of you, John, that being both of us enamored of our cousin, Rosamund D'Arcy, we will ask her to wife in the manner we have agreed, and no other. That we will abide by her decision, should she choose either of us, nor seek to alter it by tempting her from her troth, in any fashion overt or covert. That he of us whom she refuses will thenceforth be a brother to her and no more, however Satan may tempt his heart otherwise. That so far as may be possible to us, who are but sinful men, we will suffer neither bitterness nor jealousy to come between our love because of this woman, and that in war or peace we will remain faithful comrades and brethren. Thus we swear with a true heart and purpose, and in token thereof, knowing that he who breaks this oath will be a knight dishonored and a vessel fit for the wrath of God, we kiss this Rood."

This, then, these brethren said and did, and with light minds and joyful faces received the blessing of the prior, who had christened them in infancy, and went down to meet the great company that had ridden forth to lead them back to Steeple, where their knighting should be done.

So to Steeple, preceded by the squires, who rode before them bareheaded, carrying their swords by the scabbarded points, with their gold spurs hanging from the hilts, they came at last. Here the hall was set for a great feast, a space having been left between the tables and the dais, to which the brethren were conducted. Then came forward Sir Anthony de Mandeville and Sir Roger de Merci in full armor, and presented to Sir Andrew D'Arcy, their uncle, who stood upon the edge of the dais, also in his armor, their swords and spurs, of which he gave back to them two of the latter, bidding them affix these upon the candidates' right heels. This done, the prior John blessed the swords, after which Sir Andrew girded them about the waists of his nephews, saying, "Take ye back the swords that you have used so well."

Next, he drew his own silver-hilted blade that had been his father's and his grandfather's and, whilst they knelt before him, smote each of them three blows upon the right shoulder, crying with a loud voice: "In the name of God, St. Michael, and St. George, I knight ye. Be ye good knights."

Thereafter came forward Rosamund as their nearest kinswoman, and, helped by other ladies, clad upon them their hauberks, or coats of mail, their helms of steel, and their kite-shaped shields, emblazoned with a skull, the cognizance of their race. This done, with the musicians marching before them, they walked to Steeple Church—a distance of two hundred paces from the hall, where they laid their swords upon the altar and took them up again, swearing to be good servants of Christ and defenders of the Church. As they left its doors, who should meet them but the cook, carrying his chopper in his hand and crying aloud at the same time, "If either of you young knights should do aught to disgrace your honor and of the oaths that you have sworn—from which may God and his saints prevent you!—then with my chopper will I hack these spurs from off your heels."

Thus at last the long ceremony was ended, and after it came a very great feast, for at the high table were entertained many noble knights and ladies, and below, in the hall their squires, and other gentlemen, and outside all the yeomanry and villagers, whilst the children and the aged had food and drink given to them in the nave of the church itself. When the eating at length was done, the center of the hall was cleared, and while men drank, the minstrels made music. All were very merry with wine and more than a little vain talk arose among them as to which of these brethren—Sir Godwin or Sir Wulf—was the more brave, the more handsome, and the more learned and courteous.

Now a knight—it was Sir Surin de Salcote—seeing that the argument grew hot and might lead to blows, rose and declared that this should be decided by beauty alone, and that none could be more fitted to judge than the fair lady whom the two of them had saved from woman-thieves at the Death Creek wharf. They all called, "Ay, let her settle it," and it was agreed that she would give the kerchief from her neck to the bravest, a beaker of wine to the handsomest, and a Book of Hours to the most learned.

So, seeing no way to avoid the controversy, since many of the men gentle and simple alike, had begun to grow heated with wine, and were very agitated, Rosamund took the silk kerchief from her neck. Then coming to the edge of the dais, where they were seated in the sight of all, she stood before her cousins, not knowing, poor maid, to which of them she should offer it. But Godwin whispered a word to Wulf, and both of them stretching out their right hands, snatched an end of the kerchief which she held towards them, and rending it, twisted the severed halves round their sword hilts. The company laughed at their wit, and cried, "The wine for the more handsome. They cannot separate that thus."

Rosamund thought a moment; then she lifted a great silver beaker, the largest on the board and, having filled it full of wine, once more came forward and held it before them as though pondering. Thereon the brethren, as though by a single movement, bent forward and each of them touched the beaker with his lips. Again a great laugh went up, and even Rosamund smiled.

"The Book! The Book!" cried the guests. "They dare not rend the Holy Book for it contains sacred writings!"

So for the third time Rosamund advanced, bearing the missal.

"Knights," she said, "you have torn my kerchief and drunk my wine. Now I offer this hallowed writing to him who can read it best."

"Give it to Godwin," said Wulf. "I am a swordsman, not a clerk."

"Well said! Well said!" roared the company. "The sword for us—not the pen!"

But Rosamund turned on them and answered, "He who wields sword is brave, and he who wields pen is wise, but better is he who can handle both sword and pen—like my cousin Godwin, the brave and learned."

"Hear her! Hear her!" cried the revelers, knocking their horns upon the board, while in the silence that followed a woman's voice said, "Sir Godwin's luck is great, but give me Sir Wulf's strong arms."

Then the drinking began again, and Rosamund and the ladies slipped away, as well they might—for the times were crude, as even nobles struggled to discern God's ways from the foolish traditions and theological errors of their time which placed physical powers above biblical wisdom.

On the morrow, after most of the guests were gone, many of them with aching heads, Godwin and Wulf sought their uncle, Sir Andrew, in the room where he sat alone. The newly knighted duo knew Rosamund had walked to the church close by with two of the serving women to make it ready for the Friday's mass, after the feast of the peasants that had been held in the nave. Coming to his oaken chair by the open hearth, which had a chimney to it—no common thing in those days—they knelt before him.

"What is it now, my nephews?" asked the old man, smiling. "Do you wish that I should knight you afresh?"

"No, sir," answered Godwin; "we seek a greater boon."

"Then you seek in vain, for there is none."

"Another sort of boon," broke in Wulf.

Sir Andrew pulled his beard and looked at them. Perhaps the prior John had spoken a word to him, and he guessed what was coming.

"Speak," he said to Godwin. "The gift is great that I would not give to either of you if it be within my power."

"Sir," said Godwin, "we seek the leave to ask your daughter's hand in marriage."

"What! The two of you?"

"Yes, sir; the two of us."

Then Sir Andrew, who seldom laughed, laughed outright.

"Truly," he said, "of all the strange things I have known, this is the strangest—that two knights should ask one wife between them."

"It seems strange, sir; but when you have heard our tale you will understand."

So he listened while they told him all that had passed between them and of the solemn oath that they had sworn.

"Noble in this as in other things," commented Sir Andrew when they had done; "but I fear that one of you may find that vow hard to keep. By all the saints, Nephews, you were right when you said that you asked a great boon. Do you know, although I have told you nothing of it, that, not to speak of the knave Lozelle, already two of the greatest men in this land have sought my daughter Rosamund in marriage?"

"It may well be so," said Wulf.

"It is so, and now I will tell you why one or other of the pair will not be her husband, which in some ways I regret. The simple reason is that I asked her, and she had no mind to either. Her mother married when her heart was ready, so I have sworn that the daughter should do, or not at all—for better a nunnery than a loveless bridal.

"Now let us see what you have in your favor. You are of good blood—that of Uluin by your mother, and mine, as well as her own side. As squires to your sponsors of yesterday, the knights Sir Anthony de Mandeville and Sir Roger de Merci, you bore yourselves bravely in the Scottish War; indeed, your loyal king Henry remembered it, and that is why he granted my petition so readily. Since then, although you loved the position little, because I asked it of you, you have rested here at home with me, and done no feats of arms, save that great one of two months gone which made you knights, and, in truth, gives you some claim on Rosamund.

"For the rest, your father being the younger son, your lands are small, and you have no other gear. Outside the borders of this shire you are unknown men, with all your deeds to do—for I will not count those Scottish battles when you were but boys. And she whom you ask is one of the fairest and noblest and most learned ladies in this land, for I, who have some skill in such things, have taught her myself from childhood. Moreover, as I have no other heir, she will be wealthy. Well, what more have you to offer for all this?"

"Ourselves," answered Wulf boldly. "We are true knights of whom you know the best and worst, and we love her. We learned it for once and for all on Death Creek wharf, for till then she was our sister and no more."

"Ay," added Godwin, "when she swore herself to us and blessed us, then light broke on both."

"Stand up," said Sir Andrew, "and let me look at you."

So they stood side by side in the full light of the blazing fire, for little other came through those narrow windows.

"Proper men; proper men," said the old knight; "and as like to one another as two grains of wheat from the same sample. Six feet high, each of you, and broad-chested, though Wulf is larger made and the stronger of the two. One sports sandy hair and the other brown, save for that line of white where the sword hit yours, Godwin—Godwin with gray eyes that dream and Wulf with the blue eyes that shine like swords. Ah! Your grandsire had eyes like that, Wulf; and I have been told that when he leapt from the tower to the wall at the taking of Jerusalem, the Saracens did not love the light, which shone in them—nor, in faith, did I, his son, when he was angry. Proper men, the pair of you; but Sir Wulf most warrior-like, and Sir Godwin most courtly.

"Now which do you think would please a woman most?"

"That, sir, depends upon the woman," answered Godwin, and straightway his eyes began to dream.

"That, sir, we seek to learn before the day is out, if you give us leave," added Wulf; "though, if you would know, I think my chance a poor one."

"Ah, well; it is a very pretty riddle. But I do not envy her who has its answering, for it might well trouble a maid's mind, neither is it certain when all is done that she will guess best for her own peace. Would it not be wiser, then, that I should forbid them to ask this riddle?" he added, as though to himself, and fell to thinking while they trembled, seeing that he was minded to refuse their suit.

At length, he looked up again and said, "Nay, let it go as God wills, who holds the future in His hand. Nephews, because you are good knights and true, either of whom would ward her well—and she may need warding—because you are my only brother's sons, whom I have promised him to care for; and most of all because I love you both with an equal love, have your wish, and go try your fortunes at the hands of my daughter Rosamund in the fashion you have agreed. Godwin, the elder, first, as is his right; then Wulf. Nay, no thanks; but go swiftly, for I whose hours are short wish to learn the answer to this riddle."

So they bowed and went, walking side by side. At the door of the hall, Wulf stopped and said, "Rosamund is in the church. Seek her there, and—oh! I would that I could wish you good fortune; but, Godwin, I cannot. I fear me that this may be the edge of that shadow of woman's love whereof you spoke, falling cold upon my heart."

"There is no shadow; there is light, now and always, as we have sworn that it should be," answered Godwin.

CHAPTER IV
THE LETTER OF SALADIN

It was past three in the afternoon, and snow clouds were fast covering up the last gray gleam of the December day, as Godwin, wishing that his road was longer, walked to Steeple Church across the meadow. At the door of it he met the two serving women coming out with brooms in their hands, and bearing between them a great basket filled with broken meats and foul rushes. Of them he asked if the Lady Rosamund were still in the church, to which they answered, curtseying, "Yes, Sir Godwin; and she bade us desire of you that you would come to lead her to the hall when she had finished making her prayers before the altar."

"I wonder," mused Godwin, "whether I shall ever lead her from the altar to the hall, or whether—I shall bide alone by the altar?" Still, he thought it a good omen that she had bidden him thus, though some might have read it otherwise.

Godwin entered the church, walking softly on the rushes with which its nave was strewn, and by the light of the lamp that burnt there always. He saw Rosamund kneeling before a little shrine, her gracious head bowed upon her hands, praying earnestly. About what, he wondered—about what?

Still, she did not hear him; so, coming into the chancel, he stood behind her and waited patiently. At length, with a deep sigh, Rosamund rose from her knees and turned, and he noted by the light of the lamp that there were tearstains upon her face. Perhaps she, too, had spoken with the prior John, who was her confessor also. Who knows? At the least, when her eyes fell upon Godwin standing like a statue before her, she started, and there broke from her lips the words, "Oh, how swift an answer!" Then, recovering herself, added, "To my message, I mean, Cousin."

"I met the women at the door," he said.

"It is kind of you to come," Rosamund went on; "but, in truth, since that day on Death Creek I fear to walk a bow-shot's length alone or in the company of women only. With you I feel safe."

"Or with Wulf?"

"Yes; or with Wulf," she repeated; "that is, when he is not thinking of wars and adventures far away."

By now they had reached the porch of the church, to find that the snow was falling fast.

"Let us bide here a minute," he said; "it is but a passing cloud."

So they stayed there in the gloom, and for a while there was silence between them. Then he spoke.

"Rosamund, my cousin and lady, I come to put a question to you, but first—why you will understand afterwards—it is my duty to ask that you give me no answer to that question until a full day has passed."

"Surely, Godwin, that is easy to promise. But what is this wonderful question which may not be answered?"

"One short and simple. Will you give yourself to me in marriage, Rosamund?"

She leaned back against the wall of the porch.

"My father—" she began.

"Rosamund, I have his leave."

"How can I answer since you yourself forbid me?"

"Till this time tomorrow only. Meanwhile, I pray you hear me, Rosamund. I am your cousin, and we were brought up together—indeed, except when I was away at the Scottish war, we have never been apart. Therefore, we know each other well, as well as any can who are not wedded. Therefore, too, you will know that I have always loved you, first as a brother loves his sister, and now as a man loves a woman."

"Nay, Godwin, I knew it not; indeed, I thought that, as it used to be, your heart was other-where."

"Other-where? What lady—?"

"Nay, no lady; but in your dreams."

"Dreams? Dreams of what?"

"I cannot say. Perchance of things that are not here—things higher than the person of a poor maid."

"Cousin, in part you are right, for it is not only the maid whom I love, but her spirit also. Oh, in truth, you are to me a dream—a symbol of all that is noble, high and pure. In you and through you, Rosamund, I worship the heaven I hope to share with you."

"A dream? A symbol? Heaven? Are not these glittering garments to hang about a woman's shape? Why, when the truth came out you would find her but a skull in a jeweled mask, and learn to loath her for a deceit that was not her own, but yours. Godwin, such trappings as your imagination pictures could only fit an angel's face."

"They fit a face that will become an angel's."

"An angel's? How know you? I am half an Eastern; the blood runs warm in me at times. I, too, have my thoughts and dreams. I think at times that I love power and the delights of life—a different life from this. Are you sure, Godwin, that this poor face will be an angel's?"

"I wish I were as sure of other things. At least I'll risk it."

"Think of your soul, Godwin. It might be tarnished. You would not risk that for me, would you?"

He thought. Then answered, "No; since your soul is a part of mine, I would not risk yours in the venture, Rosamund."

"I like you for that answer," she said. "Yes; more than for all you have said before, because I know that it is true. Indeed, you are an honorable knight, and I am proud—very proud—that you should love me, though perhaps it would have been better otherwise." And ever so little she bent the knee to him.

"Whatever chances, in life or death those words will make me happy, Rosamund."

Suddenly she caught his arm. "Whatever chances? Ah! What is about to chance? Great things, I think, for you and Wulf and me. Remember, I am half an Eastern, and we children of the East can feel the shadow of the future before it lays its hands upon us and becomes the present. I fear it, Godwin—I tell you that I fear it."

"Fear it not, Rosamund. Why should you fear? On God's knees lies the scroll of our lives and of His purposes. The words we see and the words we guess may be terrible, but He who wrote it knows the end of the scroll and that it is good. Do not fear, therefore, but read on with an untroubled heart, taking no thought for the morrow."

She looked at him wonderingly and asked, "Are these the words of a wooer or of a saint? I know not, and do you know yourself? But you say you love me, and that you would wed me, and I believe it; also that the woman whom Godwin weds will be fortunate, since such men are rare. But I am forbidden to answer till tomorrow. Well, then I will answer as I am given grace. So till then be what you were of old, and—the snow has ceased; guide me home, my cousin Godwin."

So home they went through the darkness and the cold, speaking no word. They entered the wide hall, where a great fire built in its center roared upwards towards an opening in the roof, whence the smoke escaped, looking very pleasant and cheerful to those escaping the cold winter night and the moaning wind.

There, standing in front of the fire, also pleasant and cheerful to behold, although his brow seemed somewhat puckered, was Wulf. At the sight of him Godwin turned back through the great door, and having, as it were, stood for one moment in the light, vanished again into the darkness, closing the door behind him. But Rosamund walked on towards the fire.

"You seem cold, Cousin," said Wulf, studying her. "Godwin has kept you too long to pray with him in church. Well, it is his custom, from which I myself have suffered. Be seated on this settle and warm yourself."

She obeyed without a word and, opening her fur cloak, stretched out her hands towards the flame, which played upon her dark and lovely face. Wulf looked round him. The hall was empty. Then he looked at Rosamund.

"I am glad to find this chance of speaking with you alone, Cousin, since I have a question to ask of you; but I must pray of you to give me no answer to it until four-and-twenty hours be passed."

"Agreed," she said. "I have given one such promise; let it serve for both; now for your question."

"Ah!" replied Wulf cheerfully; "I am glad that Godwin went first, since it saves me words, at which he is better than I am."

"I do not know that, Wulf; at least, you have more of them," answered Rosamund, with a little smile.

"More perhaps, but of a different quality—that is what you mean. Well, happily here mere words are not in question."

"What, then, is in question, Wulf?"

"Hearts. Your heart and my heart—and, I suppose, Godwin's heart, if he has one—in that way."

"Why should not Godwin have a heart?"

"'Why? Well, you see just now it is my business to belittle Godwin. Therefore I declare—which you, who know more about it, can believe or not as it pleases you—that Godwin's heart is like that of the old saint in the reliquary at Stangate—a thing which may have beaten once, and will perhaps beat again in heaven, but now is somewhat dead—to this world."

Rosamund smiled, and thought to herself that this dead heart had shown signs of life not long ago. But aloud she said, "If you have no more to say to me than of Godwin's heart, I will be gone to read with my father, who waits for me."

"Nay, I have much more to say of my own." Then suddenly Wulf became very earnest—so earnest that his great frame shook, and when he strove to speak he could but stammer. At length it all came forth in a flood of burning words.

"I love you, Rosamund! I love you—all of you, as I have ever loved you—though I did not know it till the other day—that of the fight, and ever shall love you—and I seek you for my wife. I know that I am only a rough soldier-man, full of faults, not holy and learned like Godwin. Yet I swear that I would be a true knight to you all my life, and, if the saints give me grace and strength, do great deeds in your honor and watch you right well. Oh! What more is there to say?"

"Nothing, Wulf," answered Rosamund, lifting her downcast eyes. "You do not wish that I should answer you, so I will thank you—yes, from my heart, though, in truth, I am grieved that we can be no more brother and sister, as we have been in the past. I must be going now."

"Nay, Rosamund, not yet. Although you may not speak, surely you might give me some little sign, who am in torment, and thus must stay until this time tomorrow. For instance, you might let me kiss your hand—the pact said nothing about kissing."

"I know naught of this pact, Wulf," answered Rosamund sternly, although a smile crept about the corners of her mouth, "but I do know that I shall not suffer you to touch my hand."

"Then I will kiss your robe," and seizing a corner of her cloak, he pressed it to his lips.

"You are strong—I am weak, Wulf, and cannot wrench my garment from you, but I tell you that this play advantages you nothing."

He let the cloak fall.

"Your pardon. I should have remembered that Godwin would never have presumed so far."

"Godwin," she said, tapping her foot upon the ground, "if he gave a promise, would keep it in the spirit as well as in the letter."

"I suppose so. See what it is for an erring man to have a saint for a brother and a rival! Nay, be not angry with me, Rosamund, who cannot tread the path of saints."

"That I believe, but at least, Wulf, there is no need to mock those who can."

"I mock him not. I love him as well as—you do." And he watched her face.

It never changed, for in Rosamund's heart were hid the secret strength and silence of the East, which can throw a mask impenetrable over face and features.

"I am glad that you love him, Wulf. See to it that you never forget your love and duty."

"I will; yes—even if you reject me for him."

"Those are honest words, such as I looked to hear you speak," she replied in a gentle voice. "And now, dear Wulf, farewell, for I am weary—"

"Tomorrow—" he broke in.

"Ay," she answered in a heavy voice. "Tomorrow I must speak, and—you must listen."

The sun had run its course again, and once more it was near four o'clock in the afternoon. The brethren stood by the great fire in the hall looking at each other doubtfully—as, indeed, they had looked through all the long hours of the night, during which neither of them had closed an eye.

"It is time," said Wulf, and Godwin nodded.

As he spoke, a woman was seen descending from the upper room, and they knew her errand.

"Which?" asked Wulf, but Godwin shook his head.

"Sir Andrew bids me say that he would speak with you both," said the woman and went her way.

"By the saints, I believe it's neither!" exclaimed Wulf, with a little laugh.

"It may be thus," said Godwin, "and perhaps that would be best for all."

"I don't think so," answered Wulf, as he followed him up the steps to the upper room.

Now they had passed the passage and closed the door, and before them was Sir Andrew seated in his chair by the fire, but not alone, for at his side, her hand resting upon his shoulder, stood Rosamund. They noted that she was clad in her richest robes, and a bitter thought came into their minds that this might be to show them how beautiful was the woman whom both of them must lose. As they advanced they bowed first to her and then to their uncle, while, lifting her eyes from the ground, she smiled a little in greeting.

"Speak, Rosamund," said her father. "These knights are in doubt and pain."

"Now for the coup de grace," muttered Wulf.

"My cousins," began Rosamund in a low, quiet voice, as though she was saying a lesson, "as to the matter of which you spoke to me yesterday, I have taken counsel with my father and with my own heart. You did me great honor, both of you, in asking me to be the wife of such worthy knights, with whom I have been brought up and have loved since childhood as a sister loves her brothers. I will be brief as I may. Alas! I can give to neither of you the answer which you wish."

"Coup de grace, indeed," muttered Wulf, "through hauberk, gambeson, and shirt, right home to the heart."

But Godwin only turned a trifle paler and said nothing.

Now there was silence for a little space, while from beneath his bushy eyebrows the old knight watched their faces, on which the light of the tapers fell. Then Godwin spoke, "We thank you, Cousin. Come, Wulf, we have our answer; let us be going."

"Not all of it," broke in Rosamund hastily, and they seemed to breathe again.

"Listen," she said, "for if it pleases you, I am willing to make a promise which my father has approved. Come to me this time two years hence, and if we all three live, should both of you still wish for me to wife, that there may be no further space of pain or waiting, I will name the man whom I shall choose, and marry him at once."

"And if one of us is dead?" asked Godwin.

"Then," replied Rosamund, "if his name be untarnished, and he has done no deed that is not knightly, I will forthwith wed the other."

"Pardon me—" broke in Wulf.

She held up her hand and stopped him, saying, "You think this a strange saying, and so, perhaps, it is; but the matter is also strange, and for me the case is hard. Remember, all my life is at stake, and I may desire more time wherein to make my choice, that between two such men no maiden would find easy. We are all of us still young for marriage, for which, if God guards our lives, there will be time and to spare. Also in two years I may learn which of you is in truth the worthier knight, who today both seem so worthy."

"Then is neither of us more to you than the other?" asked Wulf outright.

Rosamund turned red, and her body heaved as she replied, "I will not answer that question."

"And Wulf should not have asked it," said Godwin. "Brother, I read Rosamund's saying thus: Between us she finds not much to choose, or if she does in her secret heart, out of her kindness—since she is determined not to marry for a while—she will not suffer us to see it and thereby bring grief on one of us. So she says, 'Go forth, you knights, and do deeds worthy of such a lady, and perchance he who does the highest deeds shall receive the great reward.' For my part, I find this judgment wise and just, and I am content to abide its issue. Nay, I am even glad of it, since it gives us time and opportunity to show our sweet cousin here, and all our fellows, the mettle whereof we are made, and strive to outshine each other in the achievement of great feats which, as always, we shall attempt side by side."

"Well spoken," said Sir Andrew. "And you, Wulf?"

Then Wulf, feeling that Rosamund was watching his face beneath the shadow of her long eyelashes, answered, "Before Heaven, I am content also, for whatever may be said against it, now at least there will be two years of war in which one or both of us well may fall, and for that while at least no woman can come between our brotherhood. Uncle, I crave your leave to go serve my liege in Normandy."

"And I, also," said Godwin.

"In the spring; in the spring," replied Sir Andrew hastily, "when King Henry moves his power. Meanwhile, bide you here in all good fellowship, for, who knows?—much may happen between now and then, and perhaps your strong arms will be needed as they were not long ago. Moreover, I look to all three of you to hear no more of this talk of love and marriage, which, in truth, disturbs my mind and house. For good or ill, the matter is now settled for two years to come, by which time it is likely I shall be in my grave and beyond all troubling.

"I do not say that things have gone altogether as I could have wished, but they are as Rosamund wishes, and that is enough for me. On which of you she looks with the more favor I do not know, and be you content to remain in ignorance of what a father does not think it wise to seek to learn. A maid's heart is her own, and her future lies in the hand of God and His saints, where let it bide, say I. Now we have done with all this business. Rosamund, dismiss your knights, and be you all three brothers and sister once more till this time the year after next, when those who live will find an answer to the riddle."

So Rosamund came forward, and without a word gave her right hand to Godwin and her left to Wulf, and suffered that they should press their lips upon them. So for a while, this was the end of their asking of her in marriage.

The brethren left the upper room side by side as they had come into it, but changed men in a sense, for now their lives were afire with a great purpose, which bade them dare and do and win. Yet they were lighter-hearted than when they entered there, since at least neither had been scorned, while both had hope, and all the future, which the young so seldom fear, laying before them.

As they descended the steps their eyes fell upon the figure of a tall man clad in a pilgrim's cape, hood, and low-crowned hat, of which the front was bent upwards and laced, who carried in his hand a pilgrim's staff, and about his waist the scrip and water bottle.

"What do you seek, holy palmer?" asked Godwin, coming towards him. "A night's lodging in my uncle's house?"

The man bowed, then, fixing on him a pair of beadlike brown eyes, which reminded Godwin of some he had seen, he knew not when or where, answered in the humble voice affected by his class, "Even so, most noble knight. Shelter for man and beast, for my mule is held without. Also—a word with the lord, Sir Andrew D'Arcy, for whom I have a message."

"A mule?" said Wulf. "I thought that pilgrims always went afoot?"

"True, Sir Knight; but, as it chances, I have baggage. Nay, not my own, whose earthly gear is all upon my back—but a chest, that contains I know not what, which I am charged to deliver to Sir Andrew D'Arcy, the owner of this hall, or should he be dead, then to the lady Rosamund, his daughter."

"Charged? By whom?" asked Wulf.

"That, sir," said the palmer, bowing, "I will tell to Sir Andrew, who, I understand, still lives. Have I your leave to bring in the chest, and if so, will one of your servants help me, for it is heavy?"

"We will help you," said Godwin. And they went with him into the courtyard, where by the scant light of the stars they saw a fine mule standing by one of the serving men, and bound upon its back a long-shaped package sewn over with sacking. This the pilgrim unloosed and then grabbed one end, while Wulf, after bidding the man stable the mule, took the other. They bore it into the hall, Godwin going before them to summon his uncle. Presently he came and the palmer bowed to him.

"What is your name, pilgrim, and whence is this box?" asked the old knight, looking at him keenly.

"My name, Sir Andrew, is Nicholas of Salisbury, and as to who sent me, with your leave I will whisper in your ear." And, leaning forward, he did so.

Sir Andrew heard and staggered back as though a dart had pierced him.

"What?" he said. "Are you, a holy palmer, the messenger of—" and he stopped suddenly.

"I was his prisoner," answered the man, "and he—who at least ever keeps his word—gave me my life—for I had been condemned to die—at the price that I brought this to you, and took back your answer, or hers, which I have sworn to do."

"Answer? To what?"

"Nay, I know nothing save that there is a writing in the chest. Its intent I am not told, who am but a messenger bound by oath to do certain things. Open the chest, lord, and meanwhile, if you have food, I have traveled far and fast."

Sir Andrew went to a door and called to his men-servants, whom he bade give meat to the palmer and stay with him while he ate. Then he told Godwin and Wulf to lift the box and bring it to the upper room, and with it a hammer and chisel, in case they should be needed, which they did, setting it upon the oaken table.

"Open," said Sir Andrew. So they ripped off the canvas, two folds of it, revealing within a box of dark, foreign-looking wood bound with iron bands, at which they labored long before they could break them. At length it was done, and there within was another box beautifully made of polished ebony, and sealed at the front and ends with a strange device. This box had a lock of silver, to which was tied a silver key.

"At least it has not been tampered with," said Wulf, examining the unbroken seals.

But Sir Andrew only repeated, "Open, and be swift. Here, Godwin, take the key, for my hand shakes with cold."

The lock turned easily, and the seals being broken, the lid rose upon its hinges, while, as it did so, a scent of precious odors filled the place. Beneath, covering the contents of the chest was an oblong piece of worked silk, and lying on it a parchment.

Sir Andrew broke the thread and seal, and unrolled the parchment. Within it was written over in strange characters. Also, there was a second unsealed roll, written in a clerkly hand in Norman French, and headed: "Translation of this letter, in case the knight, Sir Andrew D'Arcy, has forgotten the Arabic tongue, or that his daughter, the lady Rosamund, has not yet learned the same."

Sir Andrew glanced at both headings, then said, "Nay, I have not forgotten Arabic, who, while my lady lived, spoke little else with her, and who taught it to our daughter. But the light is bad, and, Godwin, you are scholarly; read me the French. We can compare them afterwards."

At this moment Rosamund entered the upper room from her chamber and, seeing the three of them so strangely employed, said, "Is it your will that I go, Father?"

"No, Daughter. Since you are here, stay here. I think that this matter concerns you as well as me. Read on, Godwin."

So Godwin read:

"In the Name of Allah, the Merciful and Compassionate! I, Saladin, Yusuf ibn Ayoub, Commander of the Faithful, cause these words to be written, and seal them with my own hand. My words go out to the Frankish lord, Sir Andrew D'Arcy, husband of my sister by another mother, Sitt Zobeide, the beautiful and faithless, on whom Allah has taken vengeance for her sin. Or if he be dead also, then to his daughter, who is my niece, and by blood a princess of Syria and Egypt, who among the English is named the lady Rose of the World.

"You, Sir Andrew, will remember how, many years ago, when we were friends, you, by an evil chance, became acquainted with my sister Zobeide, while you were a prisoner and sick in my father's house. How, too, Satan put it into her heart to listen to your words of love, so that she became a Cross-worshipper, and was married to you after the Frankish custom, and fled with you to England. You will remember also, although at the time we could not recapture her from your vessel, how I sent a messenger to you, saying that soon or late I would yet tear her from your arms and deal with her as we deal with faithless women. But within six years of that time sure news reached me that Allah had taken her, therefore I mourned for my sister and her fate awhile, and forgot her and you.

"Know that a certain knight named Lozelle, who dwelt in the part of England where you have your castle, has told me that Zobeide left a daughter, who is very beautiful. Now my heart, which loved her mother, goes out towards this niece whom I have never seen. Although she is your child and a Cross-worshipper, at least—save in the matter of her mother's theft—you were a brave and noble knight, of good blood, as, indeed, I remember your brother was also, he who fell in the fight at Harenc.

"Learn now that, having by the will of Allah come to great estate here at Damascus and throughout the East, I desire to lift your daughter up to be a princess of my house. Therefore I invite her to journey to Damascus, and you with her, if you live. Moreover, lest you should fear some trap, on behalf of myself, my successors, and my councilors, I promise by the word of Saladin, which never yet was broken, that although I trust that the just God may change her heart so that she enters it of her own will, I will not force her to accept the Faith or to bind herself in any marriage which she does not desire. Nor will I take vengeance upon you, Sir Andrew, for what you have done in the past, or suffer others to do so, but will rather raise you to great honor and live with you in friendship as of yore.

"But if my messenger returns and tells me that my niece refuses this, my loving offer, then I warn her that my arm is long, and I will surely take her as I can.

"Therefore, within a year of the day that I receive the answer of the lady, my niece, who is named Rose of the World, my emissaries will appear wherever she may be, married or single, to lead her to me, with honor if she be willing, but still to lead her to me if she be unwilling. Meanwhile, in token of my love, I send certain gifts of precious things, and with them my patent of her title as Princess, and Lady of the City of Baalbec, which title, with its revenue and prerogatives, are registered in the archives of my empire in favor of her and her lawful heirs, and declared to be binding upon me and my successors forever.

"The bearer of this letter and of my gifts is a certain Cross-worshipper named Nicholas, to whom let your answer be handed for delivery to me. This mission he is under oath to perform and will perform it, for he knows that if he fails therein, then he must surely die.

"Signed by Saladin, Commander of the Faithful, at Damascus, and sealed with his seal, in the spring season of the year of the Hegira 581,

"Take note also that this writing was read to me by my secretary before I set my name and seal thereunto so that I might be sure of its message. I perceive that you, Sir Andrew, or you, Lady Rose of the World, may think it strange that I should be at such pains and cost over a maid who is not of my religion and whom I never saw, and may therefore doubt my honesty in the matter. Know then the true reason. Since I heard that you, Lady Rose of the World, lived, I have thrice been visited by a dream concerning you, and in it I saw your face.

"Now this was the dream—that the oath I made as regards your mother is binding as regards you, also; therefore, it is my duty to bring you back to your homeland to atone for the fact that I strove in vain to rescue your mother."

Chapter V
The Wine Merchant

Godwin laid down the letter, and all of them stared at one another in amazement.

"Surely," said Wulf, "this is some fool's trick played off upon our uncle as an evil jest."

In place of an answer, Sir Andrew told him to lift the silk that hid the contents of the coffer to see what lay there. Wulf did so, and then threw back his head like a man whom some sudden light had blinded, as well he might, for from it came such a flare of gems as Essex had rarely seen before. Red, green, and blue they sparkled; and among them were the dull glow of gold and the white sheen of pearls.

"Oh, how beautiful! How beautiful!" said Rosamund.

"Ay," agreed Godwin; "beautiful enough to maze a woman's mind till she knows not right from wrong."

Wulf said nothing, but one by one drew its treasures from the chest—coronet, necklace of pearls, breast ornaments of rubies, girdle of sapphires, jeweled anklets, and with them veil, sandals, robes, and other garments of gold-embroidered purple silk. Moreover, among these, also sealed with the seals of Saladin, his officers of state, and secretaries, was that patent of which the letter spoke, setting out the full titles of the Princess of Baalbec; the extent and boundaries of her great estates, and the amount of her annual revenue.

"I was wrong," said Wulf. "Even the sultan of the East could not afford a jest so costly."

"Jest?" broke in Sir Andrew; "it is no jest, as I was sure from the first line of that letter. It breathes the very spirit of Saladin, who, though he be a Saracen, is no minstrel. He is in deadly earnest, as I, who was a friend of his youth, know well. Jest? Nay, no jest, but because of a vision in the night, which he believes to be the voice of God, he has been deeply stirred and led on in this wild adventure."

He paused awhile, then looked up and said, "Girl, do you know what Saladin has made of you? Why, there are queens in Europe who would be glad to own that rank and those estates in the rich lands above Damascus. I know the city and the castle of which he speaks. It is a mighty place upon the banks of Litani and Orontes, and after its military governor—for that rule he would not give a Christian—you will be first in it, beneath the seal of Saladin—the surest title in all the East. Will you go then, and leave us for the royal post of queen?"

Rosamund gazed at the gleaming gems and the writings that made her royal, and her eyes flashed as they had done by the church of St. Peter on the Essex coast. Thrice she looked while they watched her, then turned her head as from the bait of some great temptation and answered one word only —"Nay."

"Well spoken," said her father, who knew her blood and its longings. "At least, had the 'nay' been 'yea,' you must have gone alone. Give me ink and parchment, Godwin."

They were brought, and he wrote,

"To Sultan Saladin, from Andrew D'Arcy and his daughter Rosamund.

"We have received your letter, and we answer that where we are there we will bide in such state as God has given us. Nevertheless, we thank you, Sultan, since we believe you sincere, and we wish you well, except in your wars against the Cross. As for your threats, we will do our best to bring them to nothing. Knowing the customs of the East, we do not send back your gifts to you, since to do so would be to offer insult; but if you choose to ask for them, they are yours —not ours. Of your dream we say that it was but an empty vision of the night, which a wise man should forget. —Your servant and your niece."

Then he signed, and Rosamund signed after him, and the writing was done up, wrapped in silk, and sealed.

"Now," said Sir Andrew, "hide away this wealth, since were it known that we had such treasures in our possession, every thief in England would be our visitor, some of them bearing high names, I think."

So they laid the gold-embroidered robes and the priceless sets of gems back in their coffer and, having locked it, hid it away in the great iron-bound chest that stood in Sir Andrew's sleeping chamber.

When everything was finished, Sir Andrew said, "Listen now, Rosamund, and you also, my nephews. I have never told you the true tale of how the sister of Saladin, who was known as Zobeide, daughter of Ayoub, and afterwards christened into our faith by the name of Mary, came to be my wife. Yet you should learn it, if only to show how evil returns upon a man. After the great Nur-ed-din took Damascus, Ayoub was made its governor; then some three-and-twenty years ago came the capture of Harenc, in which my brother fell. Here I was wounded and taken prisoner. They bore me to Damascus, where I was lodged in the palace of Ayoub and kindly treated. Here too it was, while I lay sick, that I made friends with the young Saladin, and with his sister Zobeide, whom I met secretly in the gardens of the palace. The rest may be guessed. Although she numbered but half my years, she loved me as I loved her, and for my sake offered to change her faith and flee with me to England if opportunity could be found, which was hard.

"Now, as it chanced, I had a friend, a dark and secret man named Jebal, the young sheik of a terrible people, whose cruel rites no Christian understands. They are the subjects of one Mahomet, in Persia, and live in castles at Masyaf. This man had been in alliance with the Franks, and once in a battle I saved his life from the Saracens at the risk of my own, whereon he swore that did I summon him from the ends of the earth he would come to me if I needed help. Moreover, he gave me his signet-ring as a token, and, by virtue of it, so he said, power in his dominions equal to his own, though these I never visited. You know it," and holding up his hand, Sir Andrew showed them a heavy gold ring, in which was set a black stone, with red veins running across the stone in the exact shape of a dagger, and beneath the dagger words cut in unknown characters.

"So in my plight I bethought me of Jebal, and found means to send him a letter sealed with his ring. Nor did he forget his promise, for within twelve days Zobeide and I were galloping for Beirut on two horses so swift that all the cavalry of Ayoub could not overtake them. We reached the city, and there were married, Rosamund. There, too, your mother was baptized a Christian. Thence since it was not safe for us to stay in the East, we took ship and came safe home, bearing this ring of Jebal with us, for I would not give it up, as his servants demanded that I should do, except to him alone. But before that vessel sailed, a man disguised as a fisherman brought me a message from Ayoub and his son Saladin, swearing that they would yet recapture Zobeide, the daughter of one of them and sister of the other.

"That is the story, and you see that their oath has not been forgotten, though when in later years they learned of my wife's death, they let the matter lie. But since then Saladin, who in those days was but a youth, has become the greatest sultan that the East has ever known, and having been told of you, Rosamund, by that traitor Lozelle, he seeks to take you in your mother's place. Daughter, I tell you that I fear him."

"At least we have a year or longer in which to prepare ourselves, or to hide," said Rosamund. "The pilgrim bearing gifts must travel back to the East before my uncle Saladin can have our answer."

"Ay," said Sir Andrew; "perhaps we have a year."

"What of the attack on the wharf?" asked Godwin, who had been thinking. "The knight Lozelle was named there. Yet if Saladin had to do with it, it seems strange that the blow should have come before the word."

Sir Andrew brooded a while, then said, "Bring in this palmer. I will question him."

So the man Nicholas, who was found still eating as though his hunger would never be satisfied, was brought in by Wulf. He bowed low before the old knight and Rosamund, studying them the while with his sharp eyes, and the roof and the floor, and every other detail of the chamber. For those eyes of his seemed to miss nothing.

"You have brought me a letter from far away, Sir Palmer, who are named Nicholas," said Sir Andrew.

"I have brought you a chest from Damascus, Sir Knight, but of its contents I know nothing. At least you will bear me witness that it has not been tampered with," answered Nicholas.

"I find it strange," went on the old knight, "that one in your holy garb should be chosen as the messenger of Saladin, with whom Christian men have little to do."

"But Saladin has much to do with Christian men, Sir Andrew. Thus he takes them prisoner even in times of peace, as he did me."

"Did he, then, take the knight Lozelle prisoner?"

"The knight Lozelle?" repeated the palmer. "Was he a big, red-faced man, with a scar upon his forehead, who always wore a black cloak over his mail?

"That might be he."

"Then he was not taken prisoner, but he came to visit the Sultan at Damascus while I lay in bonds there, for I saw him twice or thrice, though what his business was I do not know. Afterwards he left, and at Jaffa I heard that he had sailed for Europe three months before I did."

Now the brethren looked at each other. So Lozelle was in England. But Sir Andrew made no comment, only he said, "Tell me your story, and be careful that you speak the truth."

"Why should I not, who have nothing to hide?" answered Nicholas. "I was captured by some Arabs as I journeyed to the Jordan upon a pilgrimage, who, when they found that I had no goods to be robbed of, would have killed me. This, indeed, they were about to do, had not some of Saladin's soldiers come by and commanded them to hold their hands and give me over to them. They did so, and the soldiers took me to Damascus. There I was imprisoned, but not close, and then it was that I saw Lozelle, or, at least, a Christian man who had some such name, and, as he seemed to be in favor with the Saracens, I begged him to intercede for me. Afterwards I was brought before the court of Saladin and, having questioned me, the Sultan himself told me that I must either worship the false prophet or die, to which you can guess my answer. So they led me away, as I presumed to my death, but none acted to do me hurt.

"Three days later Saladin sent for me again, and offered to spare my life if I would swear an oath, which oath was that I should take a certain package and deliver it to you, or to your daughter named the Lady Rosamund, here at your hall of Steeple, in Essex, and bring back the answer to Damascus. Not wishing to die, I said that I would do this, if the sultan passed his word, which he never breaks, that I should be set free afterwards."

"And now that you are safe in England, do you purpose to return to Damascus with the answer, and, if so, why?"

"For two reasons, Sir Andrew. First, because I have sworn to do so, and I do not break my word any more than does Saladin. Secondly, because I continue to wish to live, and the sultan promised me that if I failed in my mission, he would bring about my death wherever I might be, which I am sure he has the power to do by magic or otherwise. Well, the rest of the tale is short. The chest was handed over to me as you see it, and with it money sufficient for my faring to and fro and something to spare. Then I was escorted to Joppa, where I took passage on a ship bound to Italy, where I found another ship named *The Holy Mary* sailing for Calais, which we reached after being nearly cast away. Thence I came to Dover in a fishing boat, landing there eight days ago, and having bought a mule, joined some travelers to London, and so on here."

"And how will you return?"

The pilgrim shrugged his shoulders.

"As best I may, and as quickly. Is your answer ready, Sir Andrew?"

"Yes; it is here," and he handed him the roll, which Nicholas hid away in the folds of his great cloak. Then Sir Andrew added, "You say you know nothing of all the business in which you play this part?"

"Nothing; or, rather, only this—the officer who escorted me to Jaffa told me that there was a stir among the learned doctors and diviners at the court because of a certain dream which the sultan had dreamed three times. It had to do with a lady who was half of the blood of Ayoub and half English, and they said that my mission was mixed up with this matter. Now I see that the noble lady before me has eyes strangely like those of the Sultan Saladin." And he spread out his hands and ceased.

"You seem to see a good deal, friend Nicholas."

"Sir Andrew, a poor palmer who wishes to preserve his throat unslit must keep his eyes open. Now I have eaten well, and I am weary. Is there any place where I may sleep? I must be gone at daybreak, for those who do Saladin's business dare not tarry, and I have your letter."

"There is a place," answered Sir Andrew. "Wulf, take him to it, and tomorrow, before he leaves, we will speak again. Till then, farewell, holy Nicholas."

With one more searching glance the palmer bowed and went. When the door closed behind him Sir Andrew beckoned Godwin to him, and whispered, "Tomorrow, Godwin, you must take some men and follow this Nicholas to see where he goes and what he does, for I tell you I do not trust him—ay, I fear him much! These embassies to and from Saracens are strange traffic for a Christian man. Also, though he says his life hangs on it, I think that were he honest, once safe in England here he would stop, since the first priest would absolve him of an oath forced from him by the infidel."

"Were he dishonest would he not have stolen those jewels?" asked Godwin. "They are worth some risk. What do you think, Rosamund?"

"I?" she answered. "Oh, I think there is more in this than any of us dream. I think," she added in a voice of distress and with an involuntary ringing motion of the hands, "that for this house and those who dwell in it time is big with death, and that sharp-eyed palmer is its midwife. How strange is the destiny that wraps us all about! And now comes the sword of Saladin to shape it, and the hand of Saladin to drag me from my peaceful state to a dignity which I do not seek; and the dreams of Saladin, of whose kin I am, to interweave my life with the bloody policies of Syria and the unending war between Cross and Crescent." Then, with a woeful gesture, Rosamund turned and left them.

Her father watched her go and said, "The maid is right. Great business is afoot in which all of us must bear our parts. For no little thing would Saladin stir thus—he who braces himself as I know well, for the final struggle for Jerusalem and its crusader strongholds. Rosamund is right. On her brow shines the crescent diadem of the house of Ayoub, and at her heart hangs the black cross of the Christian, and round her struggle creeds and nations. What, Wulf, does the man sleep already?"

"Like a dog, for he seems outworn with travel."

"Like a dog with one eye open, perhaps. I do not wish that he should give us the slip during the night, as I want more talk with him and other things, of which I have spoken to Godwin."

"No fear of that, Uncle. I have locked the stable door, and a sainted palmer will scarcely leave us the present of such a mule."

"Not he, if I know his tribe," answered Sir Andrew. "Now let us sup and afterwards take counsel together, for we shall need it before all is done."

An hour before dawn the following morning Godwin and Wulf were up, and with them certain trusted men who had been warned that their services would be needed. Presently Wulf, bearing a lantern in his hand, came to where his brother stood by the fire in the hall.

"Where have you been?" Godwin asked. "To wake the palmer?"

"No. To place a man to watch the road to Steeple Hill, and another at the creek path; also to feed his mule, which is a very fine beast—too good for a palmer. Doubtless he will be stirring soon, as he said that he must be up early."

Godwin nodded, and they sat together on the bench beside the fire, for the weather was bitter, and dozed till the dawn began to break. Then Wulf rose and shook himself, saying, "He will not think it uncourteous if we rouse him now," and walking to the far end of the hall, he drew a curtain and called out, "Awake, holy Nicholas! Awake! It is time for you to say your prayers, and breakfast will soon be cooking."

But no Nicholas answered.

"Of a truth," grumbled Wulf, as he came back for his lantern, "that pilgrim sleeps as though Saladin had already cut his throat." Then having lit it, he returned to the guest place.

"Godwin," he called presently, "come here. The man has gone!"

"Gone?" said Godwin as he ran to the curtain. "Gone where?"

"Back to his friend Saladin, I think," answered Wulf. "Look, that is how he went." And he pointed to the shutter of the sleeping place, that stood wide open, and to an oaken stool beneath, by means of which the sainted Nicholas had climbed up to and through the narrow window slit.

"He must be without, grooming the mule which he would never have left," said Godwin.

"Honest guests do not part from their hosts thus," answered Wulf; "but let us go and see."

So they ran to the stable and found it locked and the mule safe enough within. Nor—though they looked—could they find any trace of the palmer—not even a footstep, since the ground was frost-bound. Only on examining the door of the stable they discovered that an attempt had been made to lift the lock with some sharp instrument.

"It seems that he was determined to be gone, either with or without the beast," said Wulf. "Well, perhaps we can catch him yet," and he called to the men to saddle up and ride with him to search the country.

For three hours they hunted far and wide, but nothing did they see of Nicholas.

"The knave has slipped away like a night hawk, and left as little trace," reported Wulf. "Now, my uncle, what does this mean?"

"I do not know, save that it is in keeping with the rest, and that I like it little," answered the old knight anxiously. "Here the value of the beast was of no account, that is plain. What the man held of account was that he should be gone in such a fashion that none could follow him or know whither he went. The net is about us, my nephews, and I think that Saladin draws its string."

Still less pleased would Sir Andrew have been, could he have seen the imposter Nicholas creeping round the hall while all men slept, before he girded up his long gown and ran like a hare for London. Yet he had done this by the light of the bright stars, taking note of every window slit in it, more especially of those of the upper room; of the plan of the outbuildings also, and of the path that ran to Steeple Creek some five hundred yards away.

From that day forward fear settled on the place—fear of some blow that none were able to foresee, and against which they could not guard. Sir Andrew even talked of leaving Steeple and of taking up his abode in London, where he thought that they might be safer, but such foul weather set in that it was impossible to travel the roads, and still less to sail the sea. So it was arranged that if they moved at all—and there were many things against it, not the least of which were Sir Andrew's weak health and the lack of a house to go to—it should not be till after New Year's Day.

Thus the time went on, and nothing happened to disturb them. The friends of whom the old knight took counsel laughed at his forebodings. They said that so long as they did not wander about unguarded, there was little danger of any fresh attack upon them, and if one should by chance be made, with the aid of the men they had they could hold the hall against a company until help was summoned. Moreover, at heart, none of them believed that Saladin or his emissaries would stir in this business before the spring, or more probably until another year had passed. Still, they always set guards at night, and, besides themselves, kept twenty men sleeping at the hall. Also, they arranged that on the lighting of a signal fire upon the tower of Steeple Church their neighbors would come to aid them.

So the time went on towards Christmas, before which the weather changed and became calm, with sharp frost.

It was on the shortest day that Prior John rode up to the hall and told them that he was going to Southminster to buy some wine for the Christmas feast. Sir Andrew asked what wine there was at Southminster. The prior answered that he had heard that a ship, laden amongst other things with wine of Cyprus of wonderful quality, had come into the river Crouch with her rudder broken. He added that as no shipwrights could be found in London to repair it till after Christmas, the chapman, a Cypriote, who was in charge of the wine, was selling as much as he could in Southminster and to the houses about at a cheap rate, and delivering it by means of a wagon that he had hired.

Sir Andrew replied that this seemed like a fair chance to get fine drink, which was hard to come by in Essex in those times. The end of it was that he directed Wulf, whose taste in wine was sound, to ride with the prior into Southminster, and if he liked the stuff to buy a few casks of it for them to make merry with at Christmas—although he himself, because of his ailments, now drank only water.

So Wulf went, happily enough, for in this dark season of the year when there was no fishing, it grew very dull loitering about the hall. Both Wulf and Godwin had recently spent long hours by the fire at night watching Rosamund going to and fro upon her tasks, but not speaking with her very much. For notwithstanding all their pretense of forgetfulness, some sort of veil had fallen between the brethren and Rosamund, and their contact was not so open and familiar as of old. She could not but remember that they were no more her cousins only, but her lovers also, and that she must guard herself lest she seemed to show preference to one above the other. The brethren for their part would also need to bear in mind that they were bound not to show their love, and that their cousin Rosamund was no longer a simple English lady, but also by creation, as by blood, a princess of the East, whom destiny might yet lift beyond the reach of either of them.

Moreover, as has been said, dread sat upon that manor like a croaking raven, nor could they escape from the shadow of its wing. Far away in the East a mighty monarch had turned his thoughts towards this English home and the maid of his royal blood who dwelt there, and who was mingled with his visions of conquest and of the triumph of his faith. Driven on by no dead oath, by no mere fancy or imperial desire, but by the need to atone for his past mistakes, he had determined to draw her to him, by fair means if he could; if not, by foul. Already means both foul and fair had failed, for that the attack at Death Creek wharf had to do with this matter they could no longer doubt. It was certain also that others would be tried again and again till his end was won or Rosamund was dead—for here, if even she would go back upon her word, marriage itself could not shield her.

So the house was sad, and saddest of all seemed the face of the old knight, Sir Andrew, oppressed as he was with sickness, with memories and fears. Therefore, Wulf could find pleasure even in an errand to Southminster to buy wine, which, in truth, he would normally have been glad to leave to others.

So away he rode up Steeple Hill with the prior, laughing as he used to do before Rosamund led him to gather flowers at St. Peter's-on-the-Wall.

Asking where the foreign merchant dwelt who had wine to sell, they were directed to an inn near the minster. Here in a back room they found a short, stout man, wearing a red cloth cap, who was seated on a pillow between two kegs. In front of him stood a number of folk, gentry and others, who bargained with him for his wine and the silks and embroideries that he had to sell, giving the latter to be handled and samples of the drink to all who asked for them.

"Clean cups," he said, speaking in bad French, to the drawer who stood beside him. "Clean cups, for here come a holy man and a gallant knight who wish to taste from my kegs. Nay, fellow, fill them up, for the top of Mount Trooidos in winter is not so cold as this cursed place, to say nothing of its damp, which is that of a dungeon," and he shivered, drawing his costly shawl closer round him.

"Sir Abbot, which will you taste first—the red wine or the yellow? The red is the stronger, but the yellow is the more costly and a drink for saints in Paradise and abbots upon earth. The yellow from Kyrenia? Well, you are wise. They say it was my patron St.

Helena's favorite vintage when she visited Cyprus, bringing with her Disma's cross."

"Are you a Christian, then?" asked the prior. "I took you for a Paynim."

"Were I not a Christian would I visit this foggy land of yours to trade in wine—a liquor forbidden to the Moslems?" answered the man, drawing aside the folds of his shawl and revealing a silver crucifix upon his broad breast. "I am a merchant of Famagusta in Cyprus, Georgios by name, and of the Greek Church which you Westerners hold to be heretical. But what do you think of that wine, Abbot?"

The prior smacked his lips.

"Friend Georgios, it is indeed a drink for the saints," he answered.

"Ay, and has been a drink for sinners ere now—for this is the very tipple that Cleopatra, Queen of Egypt, drank with her Roman lover Antony, of whom you, being a learned man, may have heard. And you, Sir Knight, what say you of the black stuff—'Mavro,' we call it—not the common, but that which has been twenty years in cask?"

"I have tasted worse," said Wulf, holding out his horn to be filled again.

"Ay, and will never taste better if you live as long as Methusala himself. Well, sirs, may I take your orders? If you are wise you will make them large, since no such chance is likely to come your way again, and that wine, yellow or red, will keep a century."

Then the chaffering began, and it was long and keen. Indeed, at one time they nearly left the place without purchasing, but the merchant Georgios called them back and offered to come to their terms if they would take double the quantity, so as to make up a cartload between them, which he said he would deliver before Christmas Day. To this they consented at length, and departed homewards made happy by the gifts with which the chapman clinched his bargain, after the Eastern fashion. To the prior he gave a roll of worked silk to be used as an edging to an altar cloth or banner, and to Wulf a dagger handle, quaintly carved in olive wood to the fashion of a rampant lion. Wulf thanked him, and then asked him with a somewhat shamed face if he had more embroidery for sale, whereat the prior smiled. The quick-eyed Cypriote saw the smile, and inquired if it might be needed for a lady's wear, at which some neighbors present in the room laughed outright.

"Do not laugh at me, gentlemen," said the Eastern; "for how can I, a stranger, know this young knight's affairs, and whether he has mother, or sisters, or wife, or lover? Well here are broideries fit for any of them." Then bidding his servant bring a small trunk, he opened it, and began to show his goods, which, indeed, were very beautiful. In the end Wulf purchased a veil of gauze-like silk worked with golden stars as a Christmas gift for Rosamund. Afterwards, remembering that even in such a matter he must take no advantage of his brother, he added to it a tunic broidered with gold and silver flowers such as he had never seen—for they were Eastern tulips and anemones—which Godwin could give her also if he wished.

These silks were costly, and Wulf turned to the prior to borrow money, but he had no more upon him. Georgios said, however, that it mattered nothing, as he would take a guide from the town and bring the wine in person, when he could receive payment for the broideries, of which he hoped to sell more to the ladies of the house.

He offered also to go with the prior and Wulf to where his ship lay in the river, and show them many other goods aboard of her, which, he explained to them, were the property of a company of Cyprian merchants who had embarked upon this venture jointly with himself. This they declined, however, as the darkness was not far off; but Wulf added that he would come after Christmas with his brother to see the vessel that had made so great a voyage. Georgios replied that they would be very welcome, but if possible he wished to finish the repairs to his rudder, as he was anxious to sail for London while the weather held calm, for there he looked to sell the bulk of his cargo. He added that he had expected to spend Christmas at that city, but their helm having gone wrong in the rough weather, they were driven past the mouth of the Thames, and had they not drifted into that of the Crouch, would, he thought, have foundered. So he bade them farewell for that time, but not before he had asked and received the blessing of the prior.

Thus the pair of them departed, well pleased with their purchases and the Cypriote Georgios, whom they found to be a very pleasant merchant. Prior John stopped to eat at the hall that night, when he and Wulf told of all their dealings with this man. Sir Andrew laughed at the story, showing them how they had been persuaded by the Eastern to buy a great deal more wine than they needed, so that it was he and not they who had the best of the bargain. Then he went on to tell tales of the rich island of Cyprus, where he had landed many years before and stayed awhile, and of the gorgeous court of its emperor, and of its inhabitants. These were, he said, the cunningest traders in the world—so cunning, indeed, that no Jew could overmatch them; bold sailors, also, which they had from the Phoenicians of Holy Writ, who, with the Greeks, were their forefathers, adding that what they told him of this Georgios accorded well with the character of that people.

Thus it came to pass that no suspicion of Georgios or his ship entered the mind of any one of them, which, indeed, was scarcely strange, seeing how well his tale held together, and how plain were the reasons of his presence and the purpose of his dealings in wines and silks.

Chapter VI
The Christmas Feast at Steeple

The fourth day after Wulf's visit to Southminster was Christmas morning and, the weather being bad, Sir Andrew and his household did not ride to Stangate, but attended mass in Steeple Church. Here, after service, according to his custom on this day, he gave a largesse to his tenants, and with it his good wishes and a caution that they should not become drunk at their Yuletide feast, as was the common habit of the time.

"We shall not taste of wine, even in moderation," said Wulf, as they walked to the hall, "since that merchant Georgios has not delivered the wine, of which I hoped to drink a cup tonight."

"Perhaps he has sold it at a better price to someone else; it would be like a Cypriote," answered Sir Andrew, smiling.

Then they went into the hall and, as had been agreed between them, together the brethren gave their Christmas gifts to Rosamund. She thanked them heartily enough, and then admired the beauty of the work. When they told her that it had not yet been paid for, she laughed and said that, however they were come by, she would wear both tunic and veil at their feast, which was to be held at nightfall.

About two o'clock in the afternoon a servant came into the hall to say that a wagon drawn by three horses and accompanied by two men, one of whom led the horses, was coming down the road from Steeple Village.

"Our merchant—and in time after all," said Wulf, and, followed by the others, he went out to meet him.

Georgios it was, sure enough, wrapped in a great sheepskin cloak such as Cypriotes wear in winter, and seated on the head of one of his own barrels.

"Your pardon, knights," he said as he scrambled nimbly to the ground. "The roads in this country are such that, although I have left nearly half my load at Stangate, it has taken me four long hours to come from the abbey. Most of this time was spent in mud-holes that have wearied the horses and, as I fear, strained the wheels of my wagon. Still, here we are at last, and, noble sir," he added, bowing to Sir Andrew, "here too is the wine that your son bought of me."

"My nephew," interrupted Sir Andrew.

"Once more your pardon. I thought from their likeness to you that these knights were your sons."

"Has he bought all that stuff?" asked Sir Andrew—for there were five tubs on the wagon, besides one or two smaller kegs and some packages wrapped in sheepskin.

"No, alas!" answered the Cypriote ruefully, while shrugging his shoulders. "Only two of the Mavro. The rest I took to the abbey, for I understood the prior to say he would purchase six casks, but it seems that it was but three he needed."

"He said three," put in Wulf.

"Did he, sir? Then doubtless the error was mine, who speak your tongue but ill. So I must drag the rest back again over those accursed roads," and he made another grimace. "Yet I will ask you, sir," he added to Sir Andrew, "to lighten the load a little by accepting this small keg of the old sweet vintage that grows on the slopes of Trooidos."

"I remember it well," said Sir Andrew, with a smile; "but, friend, I do not wish to take your wine for nothing."

At these words the face of Georgios beamed.

"What, noble sir," he exclaimed, "do you know my land of Cyprus? Oh, then indeed I kiss your hands, and surely you will not affront me by refusing this little present? Indeed, to be frank, I can afford to lose its price, who have done a good trade, even here in Essex."

"As you will," said Sir Andrew. "I thank you, and perhaps you have other things to sell."

"I have indeed; a few embroideries if this most gracious lady would be pleased to look at them. Some carpets also, such as the Moslems used to pray on in the name of their false prophet, Mahomet," and, turning, he spat upon the ground.

"I see that you are a Christian," said Sir Andrew. "Yet, although I fought against them, I have learned to respect the skill and dedication of the Moslem warriors even though they have been deceived by the artifice of Satan."

"Indeed, good uncle," said Godwin reflectively. "Noble servants of Christ should fight the enemies of the Cross and pray for their souls, not spit at them."

The merchant looked at them curiously, fingering the silver crucifix that hung upon his breast. "The captors of the Holy City thought otherwise," he said, "when they rode into the Mosque El Aksa up to their horses' knees in blood, and I have been taught otherwise. But the times grow liberal, and, after all, what right has a poor trader whose mind, alas! is set more on gain than on the sufferings of the blessed Son of Mary," and he crossed himself, "to form a judgment upon such high matters? Pardon me, I accept your reproof, who perhaps am bigoted."

Yet, had they but known it, this "reproof" was to save the life of many a man that night.

"May I ask help with these packages?" he went on, "as I cannot open them here, and am too weary to move the casks? Nay, the little keg I will carry myself, as I hope that you will taste of it at your Christmas feast. It must be gently handled, though I fear me that those roads of yours will not improve its quality." Then, twisting the keg from the end of the wagon onto his shoulder in such a fashion that it remained upright, he walked off lightly towards the open door of the hall.

"For one not tall that man is strangely strong," thought Wulf, who followed with a bale of carpets.

Then the other casks of wine were stowed away in the stone cellar beneath the hall.

Leaving his servant—a silent, stupid-looking, dark-eyed fellow named Petros—to bait the horses, Georgios entered the hall and began to unpack his carpets and embroideries with all the skill of one who had been trained in the bazaars of Cairo, Damascus, or Nicosia. Beautiful things they were which he had to show; broideries that dazzled the eye, and rugs of many hues, yet soft and bright as an otter's pelt. As Sir Andrew looked at them, remembering his younger days, his face softened.

"I will buy that rug," he said, "for of a truth it might be one on which I lay sick many a year ago in the house of Ayoub at Damascus. Nay, I haggle not at the price. I will buy it." Then he fell to thinking how, whilst lying on such a rug (indeed, although he knew it not, it was the same), looking through the rounded beads of the wooden lattice-work of his window, he had first seen his Eastern wife walking in the orange garden with her father Ayoub. Afterwards, still recalling his youth, he began to talk of Cyprus, and so time went on until the dark was falling.

Now Georgios said that he must be going, as he had sent back his guide to Southminster, where the man desired to eat his Christmas feast. So the reckoning was paid—it was a long one—and while the horses were harnessed to the wagon the merchant bored holes in the little cask of wine and set spigots in them, bidding them all be sure to drink of it that night. Then calling down good fortune on them for their kindness and liberality, he made his salaams in the Eastern fashion and departed, accompanied by Wulf.

Within five minutes there was a sound of shouting, and Wulf was back again saying that the wheel of the wagon had broken at the first turn, so that now it was lying upon its side in the courtyard. Sir Andrew and Godwin went out to see to the matter, and there they found Georgios wringing his hands, as only an Eastern merchant can, and cursing in some foreign tongue.

"Noble knights," he said, "what am I to do? Already it is nearly dark, and how I shall find my way up yonder steep hill I know not. As for the priceless broideries, I suppose they must stay here for the night, since that wheel cannot be mended till tomorrow—"

"As you had best do also," said Sir Andrew kindly. "Come, man, do not grieve; we are used to broken axles here in Essex, and you and your servant may as well eat your Christmas dinners at Steeple as in Southminster."

"I thank you, Sir Knight; I thank you. But why should I, who am but a merchant, thrust myself upon your noble company? Let me stop outside with my man, Petros, and dine with your people in that barn, where I see they are making ready their food."

"By no means," answered Sir Andrew. "Leave your servant with my people, who will look after him, and come you into the hall, and tell me some more of Cyprus till our food is ready, which will be soon. Do not fear for your goods; they shall be placed under cover."

"All unworthy as I am, I obey," answered Georgios in humble tones. "Petros, do you understand? This noble lord gives us hospitality for the night. His people will show you where to eat and sleep, and help you with your horses."

This man, who, he explained, was a Cypriote—a fisherman in summer and a muleteer in winter—bowed and, fixing his dark eyes upon those of his master, spoke in some foreign tongue.

"You hear what he says, the silly fellow?" said Georgios. "What? You do not understand Greek—only Arabic? Well, he asks me to give him money to pay for his dinner and his night's lodging. You must forgive him, for he is but a simple peasant, and cannot believe that anyone may be lodged and fed without payment. I will explain to him, the pig!" And explain he did in shrill, high notes, of which no one else could understand a word.

"There, Sir Knight, I do not think he will offend you so again. Ah! Look. He is walking off—he is sulky. Well, let him alone; he will be back for his dinner, the pig! Oh, the wet and the wind! A Cypriote does not mind them in his sheepskins, in which he will sleep even in the snow."

So, as Georgios continued to elaborate upon the shortcomings of his servant, they went back into the hall. Here the conversation soon turned upon other matters, such as the differences between the creeds of the Greek and Latin churches—a subject upon which he seemed to be an expert—and the fear of the

Christians in Cyprus lest Saladin should attempt to capture that island.

At length, five o'clock came, and Georgios having first been taken to the lavatory—it was but a stone trough—to wash his hands, was led to the dinner, or rather to the supper-table, which stood upon a dais in front of the entrance to the upper room. Here places were laid for six—Sir Andrew, his nephews, Rosamund, the chaplain, Matthew, who celebrated masses in the church and ate at the hall on feast-days, and the Cypriote merchant, Georgios himself. Below the dais, and between it and the fire, was another table, at which were already gathered twelve guests, being the chief tenants of Sir Andrew and the reeves of his outlying lands. On most days the servants of the house, with the huntsmen, swineherds, and others, sat at a third table beyond the fire. But as nothing would stop these from growing drunken on the good ale at a feast and, though many ladies thought little of it, there was no sin that Rosamund hated so much as this, now their lord sent them to eat and drink at their ease in the barn. This building stood in the courtyard with its back to the moat.

When all had taken their seats, the chaplain said grace, and the meal began. It was rude but very plentiful. First, borne in by the cook on a wooden platter, came a great codfish, whereof he helped portions to each in turn, laying them on their "trenchers"—that is, large slices of bread—whence they ate them with the spoons that were given to each. After the fish appeared the meats, of which there were many sorts, served on silver spits. These included fowls, partridges, duck, and, chief of all, a great swan, that the tenants greeted by knocking their horn mugs upon the table; after which came the pastries, and with them nuts and apples. For drink, ale was served at the lower table. On the dais, however, they drank some of the black wine which Wulf had bought—that is, except Sir Andrew and Rosamund, the former because he dared not, and the latter because she had always hated any drink but water.

Thus they grew merry since their guest proved himself a cheerful fellow, who told them many stories of love and war, for he seemed to know much of loves, and to have been in several wars. At these even Sir Andrew, forgetting his ailments and forebodings, laughed well, while Rosamund, looking more beautiful than ever in the gold-starred veil and the broidered tunic, which the brethren had given her, listened to them, smiling somewhat absently. At last the feast drew towards its end, when suddenly, as though struck by a sudden recollection, Georgios exclaimed, "The wine! The liquid amber from Trooidos! I had forgotten it. Noble knight, have I your leave to draw?"

"Ay, excellent merchant," answered Sir Andrew. "Certainly you can draw your own wine."

So Georgios rose, and took a large jug and a silver tankard from the sideboard where such things were displayed. With these he went to the little keg which, it will be remembered, had been stood ready upon the trestles, and, bending over it while he drew the spigots, filled the vessels to the brim. Then he beckoned to a servant sitting at the lower table to bring him a leather jack that stood upon the board. Having rinsed it out with wine, he filled that also, handing it with the jug to the servant to drink their lord's health on this Yule night. The silver vessel he bore back to the high table, and with his own hand filled the horn cups of all present, Rosamund alone excepted, for she would touch none, although he pressed her hard and looked vexed at her refusal. Indeed, it was because it seemed to pain the man that Sir Andrew, ever courteous, took a little himself, although, when his back was turned, he filled the goblet up with water. At length, when all was ready, Georgios charged, or seemed to charge, his own horn, and, lifting it, said, "Let us drink, everyone of us here, to the noble knight, Sir Andrew D'Arcy, to whom I wish, in the phrase of my own people, that he may live forever. Drink, friends, drink deep, for never will wine such as this pass your lips again."

Then, lifting his tankard, he appeared to drain it in great gulps—an example which all followed, even Sir Andrew drinking a little from his cup, which was three parts filled with water. There followed a long murmur of satisfaction.

"Wine! It is nectar!" said Wulf presumptuously.

"Ay," put in the chaplain, Matthew; "Adam might have drunk this in the Garden," while from the lower table came jovial shouts of praise for this smooth, creamlike vintage.

Certainly that wine was both rich and strong. Thus, after his cup was mostly drained, a veil as it were seemed to fall on the mind of Sir Andrew and to cloud it up. It lifted again, and lo! His brain was full of memories and foresights. Circumstances, which he had forgotten for many years came back to him altogether, like a crowd of children tumbling out to play. These passed, and he grew suddenly afraid. Yet what had he to fear that night? The gates across the moat were locked and guarded. Trusty men, a score or more of them, ate in his outbuildings within those gates; while others, still more trusted, sat in his hall; and on his right hand and on his left were those two strong and valiant knights, Sir Godwin and Sir Wulf. No, there was nothing to fear—and yet he felt afraid. Suddenly he heard a voice speak. It was Rosamund's; and she said, "Why is there such silence, Father? A while ago I heard the servants and bondsmen carousing in the barn; now they are still as death. Oh, and look! Are all here drunken? Godwin—"

But as she spoke Godwin's head fell forward on the table, while Wulf rose, half drew his sword, then threw his arm around the neck of the priest and sank with him to the ground. As it was with these, so it seemed with all, for folk rocked to and fro, then sank to sleep, every one of them, save the merchant Georgios, who rose to call another toast.

"Stranger," said Sir Andrew, in a heavy voice, "your wine is very strong."

"It would seem so, Sir Knight," he answered; "but I will wake them from their wassail." Springing from the dais lightly as a cat, he ran down the hall crying, "Air is what they need. Air!" Now coming to the door, he threw it wide open and, drawing a silver whistle from his robe, blew it long and loud. "What," he laughed, "do they still sleep? Why, then, I must give a toast that will rouse them all," and seizing a horn mug, he waved it and shouted:

"Arouse you, ye drunkards, and drink to the lady Rose of the World, princess of Baalbec, and niece to my royal master, Yusuf Saladin, who sends me to lead her to him!"

"Oh, Father," shrieked Rosamund, "the wine was drugged and we are betrayed!"

As the words passed her lips there rose a sound of running feet, and through the open door at the far end of the hall burst in a score of armed men. Then at last Sir Andrew saw and understood.

With a roar of rage like that of a wounded lion, he seized his daughter and dragged her towards the passage that led into the upper room where a fire burned and lights had been lit, ready for their retiring. The huge oak door that hung by the entryway was flung shut and bolted behind them.

"Swift!" he said, as he tore his gown from him, "there is no escape, but at least I can die fighting for you. Give me my mail."

She snatched his hauberk from the wall, and while they thundered at the door, did it on to him—ay, and his steel helm also, and gave him his long sword and his shield.

"Now," he said, "help me." And they thrust the oak table forward and overset it in front of the door, throwing the chairs and stools on either side, that men might stumble on them.

"There is a bow," he said, "and you can use it as I have taught you. Get to one side and out of reach of the sword sweeps, and shoot past me as they rush; it may stay one of them. Oh, that Godwin and Wulf were here, and we would still teach these Paynim dogs a lesson!"

Rosamund made no answer but there came into her mind a vision of the agony of Godwin and of Wulf should they ever wake again to learn what had happened to her and them. She looked round. Against the wall stood a little desk, at which Godwin often wrote, and on it lay pen and parchment. She seized them, and as the door gave slowly inwards, scrawled, "Follow me to Saladin. In that hope I live on—Rosamund."

Then, as the stout door finally crashed in, Rosamund turned what she had written face downwards on the desk and, seizing the bow, set an arrow to its string. Now it was down and on rushed the mob up the six feet of narrow passage. At the end of it, in front of the overturned table, they halted suddenly. For there before them, skull-emblazoned shield on arm, his long sword lifted, and a terrible wrath burning in his eyes, stood the old knight, like a wolf at bay, and by his side, bow in hand, the beauteous lady Rosamund, clad in all her festal broideries.

"Yield, you!" cried a voice. By way of answer the bowstring twanged, and an arrow sped home to its feathers through the throat of the speaker, so that he went down, grabbing at it, and spoke no more forever.

As he fell clattering to the floor, Sir Andrew cried in a great voice, "We yield not to pagan dogs and poisoners. A D'Arcy! A D'Arcy! Meet D'Arcy, meet Death!"

Thus for the last time did old Sir Andrew utter the war cry of his race, which he had feared would never pass his lips again. His prayer had been heard, and he was to die, as he had desired.

"Down with him; seize the princess!" said a voice. It was that of Georgios, no longer humble with a merchant's whine, but speaking in tones of cold command and in Arabic.

For a moment the swarthy mob hung back, as well they might in the face of that glittering sword. Then with a cry of "Saladin! Saladin!" on they surged, with flashing spears and scimitars. The overthrown table was in front of them, and one leapt upon its edge, but as he leapt, the old knight, all his years and sickness forgotten now, sprang forward and struck downwards, so heavy a blow that in the darkling mouth of the passage the sparks streamed out, and where the Saracen's head had been, appeared his heels. Back Sir Andrew stepped again to win space for his sword-play, while round the ends of the table broke two fierce-faced men. At one of them Rosamund shot with her bow, and the arrow pierced his thigh, but as he fell he struck with his keen scimitar and shore the end off the bow, so that it was useless.

The second man caught his foot in the bar of the oak chair which he did not see, and went down prone, while Sir Andrew, taking no heed of him, rushed with a shout at the crowd who followed and, catching their blows upon his shield, rained down others so desperate that, being hampered by their very number, they gave before him and staggered back along the passage.

"Guard your right, Father!" cried Rosamund. He sprang round, to see the Saracen who had fallen on his feet again. At him he went, nor did the man wait the onset, but turned to flee, only to meet his end, for the great sword caught him between neck and shoulders. Now a voice cried, "We make poor sport with this old lion, and lose men. Keep clear of his claws, and whelm him with spear casts."

But Rosamund, who understood their tongue, sprang in front of him, and answered in Arabic, "Ay, through my breast; and go, tell that tale to Saladin!"

Then, clear and calm, was heard the command of Georgios. "He who harms a hair of the princess dies. Take them both living if you may, but lay no hand on her. Stay, let us talk."

So they ceased from their onslaught and began to consult together.

Rosamund touched her father and pointed to the man who lay upon the floor with an arrow through his thigh. He was struggling to his knee, raising the heavy scimitar in his hand. Sir Andrew lifted his sword as a husbandman lifts a stick to kill a rat, then let it fall again, saying, "I fight not with the wounded. Drop that steel, and get you back to your own folk."

The fellow obeyed him—yes, and even touched the floor with his forehead in salaam as he crawled away, for he knew that he had been given his life, and that the deed was noble towards him who had planned a coward's stroke.

Then Georgios stepped forward, no longer the same Georgios who had sold poisoned wine and Eastern broideries, but a proud-looking, high-browed Saracen clad in the mail which he wore beneath his merchant's robe, and in place of the crucifix wearing on his breast a great star-shaped jewel, the emblem of his house and rank.

"Sir Andrew," he said, "hearken to me, I pray you. Noble was that act," and he pointed to the wounded man being dragged away by his fellows, "and noble has been your defense—well worthy of your lineage and your knighthood. It is a tale that my master," and he bowed as he said the word, "will love to hear if it pleases Allah that we return to him in safety. Also you will think that I have played a knave's trick upon you, overcoming the might of those gallant knights, Sir Godwin and Sir Wulf, not with sword blows but with drugged wine, and treating all your servants in like fashion, since not one of them can shake off its fumes before tomorrow's light. So indeed it is—a very scurvy trick, which I shall remember with shame to my life's end, and that perchance may yet fall back upon my head in blood and vengeance. Yet bethink you how we stand, and forgive us. We are but a little company of men in your great country, hidden, as it were, in a den of lions, who, if they saw us, would slay us without mercy. That, indeed, is a small thing, for what are our lives, of which your sword has taken tithe, and not only yours, but those of the twin brethren on the wharf by the water?"

"I thought it," broke in Sir Andrew contemptuously. "Indeed, that deed was worthy of you—twenty or more men against two."

Georgios held up his hand.

"Judge us not harshly," he said, speaking slowly, who, for his own ends wished to gain time, "you who have read the letter of our lord. See you, these were my commands: To secure the lady Rose of the World as best I might, but if possible without bloodshed. Now I was reconnoitering the country with a troop of the sailors from my ship who are but poor fighters, and a few of my own people, when my spies brought me word that she had ridden out attended by only two men, and surely I thought that already she was in my hands. But the knights foiled me by strategy and strength, and you know the end of it. So afterwards my messenger presented the letter, which, indeed, should have been done at first. The letter failed also, for neither you, nor the princess"—and he bowed to Rosamund— "could be bought. More, the whole country was awakened; you were surrounded with armed men; the knightly brethren kept watch and ward over you, and you were about to fly to London, where it would have been hard to snare you. Therefore, I who am a prince and an emir, who also, although you remember it not, have crossed swords with you in my youth; yes, at Harenc—became a dealer in drugged wine.

"Now hearken. Yield you, Sir Andrew, who have done enough to make your name a song for generations, and accept the love of Saladin, whose word you have, the word that, as you know well, cannot be broken, which I, the lord El-Hassan will uphold.

Yield you, and save your life, and live on in honor, clinging to your own faith, till Azrael takes you from the pleasant fields of Baalbec to the waters of Paradise—if such there be for infidels, however gallant.

"For know, this deed must be done. Did we return without the princess Rose of the World, we should die, every one of us, and did we offer her harm or insult, then more horribly than I can tell you. This is no fancy of a great king that drives him on to the stealing of a woman, although she be of his own high blood. The voice of Allah has spoken to Saladin by the mouth of his angel Sleep. Thrice has Allah spoken in dreams, telling him who is merciful that through your daughter and her nobleness alone can he gain the victory. Therefore, sooner than she should escape him, he would lose even the half of all his empire. Outwit us, defeat us now, capture us, cause us to be tortured and destroyed, and other messengers would come to do his bidding—indeed, they are already on the way. Moreover, it is useless to shed more blood, seeing that this lady, Rose of the World, must return to the East where she was begot, there to fulfill her destiny."

"Then, Emir El-Hassan, I shall return as a spirit," said Rosamund proudly.

"Not so, Princess," he answered, bowing, "for Allah alone has power over your life, and it is otherwise decreed. Sir Andrew, the time grows short, and I must fulfill my mission. Will you take the peace of Saladin, or force his servants to take your life?"

The old knight listened, resting on his reddened sword; then he lifted his head and spoke, "I am aged and near my death, wine-seller Georgios, or Prince El-Hassan, whichever you may be. In my youth I swore to make no pact with Paynims, and even now I will not break that vow. While I can lift sword I will defend my daughter, even against the might of Saladin. Get to your coward's work again, and let things go as God has willed them."

"Then, Princess," answered El-Hassan, "bear me witness throughout the East that I am innocent of your father's blood. On his own head be it, and on yours," and for the second time he blew upon the whistle that hung around his neck.

Chapter VII
The Banner of Saladin

As the echoes of Hassan's whistle died away there was a crash amongst the wooden shutters of the window behind them, and down into the room leaped a long, dark figure, holding an axe aloft. Before Sir Andrew could turn, that axe dealt him a fearful blow between the shoulders which, although the ringed mail remained unshorn, shattered his spine beneath. Down he fell, rolled onto his back, and lay there, still able to speak and without pain, but helpless as a child. The lion-hearted knight was paralyzed, and never more would move hand or foot or head.

In the silence that followed he spoke in a heavy voice, letting his eyes rest upon the man who had struck him down.

"A knightly blow, it was not; but one worthy of a Judas who does murder for Paynim pay! Traitor to God and man, who have eaten my bread and now slaughter me like an ox on my hearth-stone, may your own end be even worse, and at the hands of those you serve."

The palmer Nicholas, for it was he, although he no longer wore the palmer's robe, slunk away muttering, and was lost among the crowd in the passage. Then, with a sudden and a bitter cry, Rosamund swooped forward, as a bird swoops, snatched up the sword her sire would never lift again and, setting its hilt upon the floor, cast herself forward. But its point never touched her breast, for the emir sprang swiftly and struck the steel aside; then, as she fell, caught her in his arms.

"Lady," he said, loosing her very gently. "Allah does not need you yet. I have told you that it is not fated. Now will you give me your word—for being of the blood of Saladin and D'Arcy, you, too, cannot lie—that neither now nor afterwards will you attempt to harm yourself? If not, I must bind you, which I am loath to do—it is a sacrilege to which I pray you will not force me."

"Promise, Rosamund," said the hollow voice of her father, "and go to fulfill your fate. Self-murder is a crime, and the man is right; it is decreed. I bid you promise."

"I obey and promise," said Rosamund. "It is your hour, my lord Hassan."

He bowed deeply and answered, "I am satisfied, and henceforth we are your servants. Princess, the night air is bitter; you cannot travel thus. In which chamber are your garments?"

She pointed with her finger. A man took a torch, and, accompanied by two others, entered the place, to return presently with their arms full of all the apparel they could find. Indeed, they even brought her missal and the silver crucifix that hung above her bed, and with it her leathern case of trinkets.

H & S Lt

H. R. MILLAR. 1903

"Keep out the warmest cloak," said Hassan, "and tie the rest up in those carpets."

So the rugs that Sir Andrew had bought that day from the merchant Georgios were made to serve as traveling bags to hold his daughter's gear. Thus even in this hour of haste and danger thought was taken for her comfort.

"Princess," said Hassan, bowing, "my master, your uncle, sent you certain jewels of no mean value. Is it your wish that they should accompany you?"

Without lifting her eyes from her dying father's face, Rosamund answered heavily, "Where they are, there let them bide. What have I to do with jewels?"

"Your will is my law," he said; "and others will be found for you. Princess, all is ready; we wait your pleasure."

"My pleasure? Oh, God, my pleasure?" exclaimed Rosamund in the same drear voice, still staring at her father, who lay before her on the ground.

"I could not help it," said Hassan, answering the question in her eyes, and there was intensity in his tone. "He would not come, he brought it on himself; though in truth I wish that accursed Frank had not struck so shrewdly. If you ask it, we will bear him with you; but, lady, it is idle to hide the truth—he is close to death. I have studied medicine, and I know."

"Nay," said Sir Andrew from the floor; "leave me here. Daughter, we must part awhile. As I stole his child from Ayoub, so Ayoub's son steals my child from me. Daughter, cling to the faith—that we may meet again."

"To the death," she answered.

"Be comforted," said Hassan. "Has not Saladin passed his word that except her own will or that of Allah should change her heart, a Cross-worshipper she may live and die? Lady, for your own sake as well as ours, let this sad farewell be brief. Be gone, my servants, taking these dead and wounded with you. There are things it is not fitting that common eyes should see."

They obeyed, and the three of them remained alone together. Then Rosamund knelt down beside her father, and they whispered into each other's ears. Hassan turned his back upon them and threw the corner of his cloak over his head and eyes that he might neither see nor hear their voices in this dread and holy hour of parting.

It would seem that they found some kind of hope and consolation in it—at least when Rosamund kissed him for the last time, Sir Andrew smiled and said, "Yes, yes; it may all be for the best. God will guard you, and His will be done. But I forgot. Tell me, Daughter, which?"

Again she whispered into his ear, and when he had thought a moment, he answered, "Maybe you are right. I think that is wisest for all. And now on the three of you—aye, and on your children's children's children—let my blessing rest, as rest it shall. Come hither, Emir."

Hassan heard him through his cloak, and, uncovering, came.

"Say to Saladin, your master, that he has been too strong for me and paid me back in my own coin. Well, had it been otherwise, my daughter and I must soon have parted, for death drew near to me. At least it is the decree of God, to which I bow my head, trusting there may be justice in the end. But to Saladin say also that whatever his false faith may teach, for Christian and for Paynim there is the judgement seat of Christ beyond the grave. Say that if aught of wrong or insult is done towards this maiden, I swear by the God who made us both that there I will hold him to account. Now, since it must be so, take her and go your way, knowing that my spirit follows after you and her; yes, and that even in this world she will find avengers."

"I hear your words, and I will deliver them," answered Hassan. "Therefore, Sir Andrew D'Arcy, forgive us, who are but the instruments of Allah, and die in peace."

"I, who have so much to be forgiven, forgive you," answered the old knight slowly.

Then his eyes fixed themselves upon his daughter's face with one long, searching look, and closed.

"I think that he is dead," said Hassan. "He has fought his last battle and now he rests." And taking a white garment from the wall, he flung it over him, adding, "Lady, come."

Thrice Rosamund looked at the shrouded figure on the floor; once she wrung her hands and seemed about to fall. Then, as though a thought struck her, she lifted her father's sword from where it lay, and gathering her strength, drew herself up and passed like a queen down the blood-stained passage. In the hall beneath waited the band of Hassan, who bowed as she came—a vision of despairing loveliness that held aloft a red and naked sword. There, too, lay the drugged men fallen this way and that, and among them Wulf across the table, and Godwin on the dais. Rosamund spoke.

"Are these dead or sleeping?"

"Have no fear," answered Hassan. "By my hope of Paradise, they do but sleep, and will awake before morning."

Rosamund pointed to the renegade Nicholas—he that had struck down her father from behind—who had an evil look upon his face and stood apart from the Saracens, holding in his hand a lighted torch.

"What does this man with the torch?" she asked.

"If you would know, lady," Nicholas answered with a sneer, "I wait till you are out of it to fire the hall."

"Prince Hassan," said Rosamund, "is this a deed that the mighty Saladin would wish, to burn drugged men beneath their own roof? Now, as you shall answer to him, in the name of Saladin I, a daughter of his household, command you, strike the fire from that man's hand, and in my hearing give your order that none should even think of such an act of shame."

"What?" broke in Nicholas; "and leave knights like these, whose quality you know"—and he pointed to the brethren—"to follow in our path, and take our lives in vengeance? Why, it is madness!"

"Are you master here, traitor, or am I?" asked Hassan in cold contempt. "Let them follow if they will, and I for one shall rejoice to meet foes so brave in open battle, and there, give them their revenge. Ali," he added, addressing the man who had been disguised as a merchant's underling, and who had drugged the men in the barn as his master had drugged those in the hall, and opened the moat gate to the band, "Ali, stamp upon the torch and guard that Frank till we reach the boat lest the fool should alert the country around us with his fires. Now, Princess, are you satisfied?"

"Ay, having your word," she answered. "One moment, I pray you. I would leave a token to my knights."

Then, while they watched her with wondering eyes, she unfastened the gold cross and chain that hung around her neck and, slipping the cross from the chain, went to where Godwin lay, and placed it on his breast. Next, with a swift movement, she wound the chain about the silver hilt of Sir Andrew's sword, and passing to Wulf, with one strong thrust, drove the point between the oak boards of the table. It stood before him—at once a cross, a call to battle, and a lady's token.

"His grandsire bore it," she said in Arabic, "when he leapt onto the walls of Jerusalem. It is my last gift to him." But the Saracens muttered and turned pale at these words of evil omen.

Then taking the hand of Hassan, who stood searching her white, inscrutable face, with never a word or a backward look, she swept down the length of the long hall and out into the night beyond.

"It would have been well to take my counsel and fire the place, or at least to cut the throats of all within it," said the man Nicholas to his guard Ali as they followed with the rest. "If I know aught of these brethren, cross and sword will soon be hard upon our track, and men's lives must pay the price of such soft folly." And he shivered as though in fear.

"It may be so, spy," answered the Saracen, looking at him with sombre, contemptuous eyes. "It may be that your life will pay the price."

Wulf was dreaming, dreaming that he stood on his head upon a wooden plank, as once he had seen a juggler do, which turned round one way while he turned round the other, till at length someone shouted at him, and he tumbled off the board and hurt himself. Then he awoke to hear a voice shouting surely enough—the voice of Matthew, the chaplain of Steeple Church.

"Awake!" said the voice. "In God's name, I beg you, awake!"

"What is it?" he said, lifting his head sleepily and becoming conscious of a dull pain across his forehead.

"It is that death and the devil have been here, Sir Wulf."

"Well, they are often near together. But I thirst. Give me water."

A serving woman, pallid, disheveled, heavy-eyed, who was stumbling to and fro, lighting torches and tapers, for it was still dark, brought it to him in a leathern jack, from which he drank deeply.

"That is better," he said. Then his eye fell upon the bloody sword set point downwards in the wooden table before him, and he exclaimed, "Mother of God! What is that? My uncle's silver-hilted sword, red with blood, and Rosamund's gold chain upon the hilt! Priest, where is the lady Rosamund?"

"Gone," answered the chaplain in a voice that sounded like a groan. "The women woke and found her gone, and Sir Andrew lies dead or dying in the upper room—and oh! We have all been drugged. Look at them!" and he waved his hand towards the recumbent forms. "I say that the devil has been here."

Wulf sprang to his feet with an oath.

"The devil? Ah! I have it now. You mean the Cyprian chapman Georgios. He who sold wine."

"He who sold drugged wine," echoed the chaplain, and has stolen away the lady Rosamund."

Then Wulf seemed to go mad with rage, and then shouted:

"Stolen Rosamund over our sleeping carcasses! Stolen Rosamund with never a blow struck by us to save her! O, Christ, that I should live to hear it!" And he, the mighty man, the knight of skill and strength, broke down and wept like a very child. But not for long, for soon he shouted in a voice of thunder, "Awake, ye drunkards! Awake, and learn what has happened to us. Your lady Rosamund has been stolen away while we were lost in sleep!"

At the sound of that great voice a tall form arose from the floor and staggered towards him, holding a gold cross in its hand.

"What awful words are those, my brother?" asked Godwin, who, pale and dull-eyed, rocked to and fro before him. Then he, too, saw the red sword and stared, first at it and next at the gold cross in his hand. "My uncle's sword, Rosamund's chain, Rosamund's cross! Where, then, is Rosamund?"

"Gone! Gone! Gone!" cried Wulf. "Tell him, priest."

So the chaplain told him all he knew.

"Thus have we kept our oaths," went on Wulf. "Oh, what can we do now, save die of very shame?"

"Nay," answered Godwin, dreamingly; "we can live on to save her. See, these are her tokens—the cross for me, the blood-stained sword for you, and about its hilt the chain, a symbol of her slavery. Now both of us must bear the cross; both of us must wield the sword—, and both of us must cut the chain, or if we fail, then die."

"You rave," said Wulf; "and little wonder. Here, drink water. Would that we had never touched aught else, as she did, and desired that we should do. What said you of my uncle, priest? Dead, or only dying? Nay, answer not, let us see. Come, Brother."

Now together they ran, or rather reeled, torch in hand, along the passage.

Wulf saw the bloodstains on the floor and laughed savagely.

"The old man made a good fight," he said, "while, like drunken brutes, we slept."

They arrived at the upper room and before them, beneath the white, shroud-like cloak, lay Sir Andrew, the steel helm on his head, and his face beneath it even whiter than the cloak. At the sound of their footsteps he opened his eyes.

"Who has come?" he whispered. "Oh, how many hours have I waited for you? Nay, be silent, for I do not know how long my strength will last, but listen—kneel down and listen."

So they knelt on either side of him; and in quick, fierce words he told them all—of the drugging, of the fight, of the long parley carried on to give the palmer knave time to climb to the window; of his cowardly blow, and of what happened afterwards. Then his strength seemed to fail him, but they poured drink down his throat, and it came back again.

"Take horse swiftly," he gasped, pausing now and again to rest, "and rouse the countryside. There is still a chance. Nay, seven hours have gone by; there is no chance. Their plans were too well laid; by now they will be at sea. So hear me. Go to Palestine. There is money for your faring in my chest, but go alone, with no company, for in time of peace these would betray you. Godwin, draw off this ring from my finger and, with it as a token, find out Jebal, the black sheik of the Mountain Tribe at Masyaf on Lebanon. Bid him remember the vow he made to Andrew D'Arcy, the English knight. If any can aid you, it will be Jebal, who hates the houses of Nur-ed-din and of Ayoub. So, I charge you, let nothing—I say nothing—turn you aside from seeking him.

"Afterwards, act as God shall guide you. If they still live, kill that traitor Nicholas and Hugh Lozelle, but, save in open war, spare Emir Hassan, who did but do his duty as an Eastern reads it. He alone has shown some mercy, for he could have slain or burnt us all. This riddle has been hard for me; yet now, in my dying hour, I seem to see its answer. I think that Saladin did not dream in vain. Keep brave hearts, for at Masyaf you will find friends, and eventually things will yet go well, and our sorrows bear good fruit.

"What is that you said? She left you my father's sword, Wulf? Then wield it bravely, winning honor for our name. She left you the cross, Godwin? Wear it worthily, winning glory for the Lord and salvation to your soul. Remember what you have sworn. Whate'er befall, bear no bitterness to one another. Be true to one another, and to her, your lady, so that when at the last you make your report to me before high Heaven, I may have no cause to be ashamed of you, my nephews, Godwin and Wulf."

For a moment the dying man was silent, until his face lit up as with a great gladness, and he cried in a loud, clear voice, "Beloved wife, I hear you! O, God, I come!"

Then though his eyes stayed open, and the smile still rested on his face, his jaw fell.

Thus died Sir Andrew D'Arcy.

Still kneeling on either side of him, the brethren watched the end, and, as his spirit passed, bowed their heads in prayer.

"We have seen a great death," said Godwin quietly. "Let us learn a lesson from it, that when our time comes we may die like him."

"Ay," answered Wulf, springing to his feet; "but first let us take vengeance for it. Why, what is this? Rosamund's writing! Read it, Godwin."

Godwin took the parchment and read:

"Follow me to Saladin. In that hope I live on."

"Surely we will follow you, Rosamund," he cried aloud, "follow you through life to death or victory."

Then he threw down the paper and, calling for the chaplain to come to watch the body, they ran into the hall. By this time about half of the folk were awake from their drugged sleep, whilst others who had been doctored by the man Ali in the barn staggered into the hall—wild-eyed, white-faced, and holding their hands to their heads and hearts. They were so sick and bewildered, indeed, that it was difficult to make them understand what had happened, and when they learned the truth, most of them could only groan. Still, a few were found strong enough in wit and body to grope their way through the darkness and the falling snow to Stangate Abbey, to Southminster, and to the houses of their neighbors. They sought to rouse every true man to arms and to ride with them in the hunt. Wulf, meanwhile, called the priest Matthew from his prayers by their dead uncle, and charged him to climb the church tower as swiftly as he could, and set light to the beacon that was laid ready there.

Away he went, taking flint, steel, and tinder with him, and ten minutes later the blaze was flaring furiously above the roof of Steeple Church, warning all men of the need for help. Then they armed, saddled such horses as they had, amongst them the three that had been left there by the merchant Georgios, and gathered all of them who were not too sick to ride in the courtyard of the hall. But as yet their haste availed them little, for the moon was down. Snow fell also, and the night was still black as death—so black that a man could scarcely see the hand he held before his face. So they must wait, and wait they did, eating their hearts out with grief and rage, while they bathed their aching brows in icy water.

At length the dawn began to break, and by its first gray light they saw men mounted and afoot feeling their way through the snow, shouting to each other as they came to know what dreadful thing had happened at Steeple. Quickly the tidings spread among them that Sir Andrew was slain, and the lady Rosamund snatched away by Paynims, while all who feasted in the place had been drugged with poisoned wine by a man whom they believed to be a merchant. So soon as a band was got together—perhaps thirty men in all—and there was light to stir by, they set out and began to search, though where to look they knew not, for the snow had covered up all traces of their foes.

"One thing is certain," said Godwin, "they must have come by water."

"Ay," answered Wulf; "and landed nearby, since, had they far to go, they would have taken the horses, and must run the risk also of losing their path in the darkness. To the staithe! Let us try Steeple Staithe."

So on they went across the meadow to the creek. It lay but three bow-shots distant. At first they could see nothing, for the snow covered the stones of the little pier, but presently a man cried out that the lock of the water house, in which the brethren kept their fishing boat, was broken, and next minute, that the boat was gone.

"She was small; she would hold but six men," cried a voice. "So great a company could never have crowded into her."

"Fool!" one answered, "there may have been other boats."

So they looked again and, beneath the thin coating of ice, found a mark in the mud by the staithe, made by the prow of a large boat, and not far from it a hole in the earth into which a peg had been driven to make her fast. Now the thing seemed clear enough, but it was to be made yet clearer, for moments later, even through the driving snow, the quick eye of Wulf caught sight of some glittering thing which hung to the edge of a clump of dead reeds. A man with a lance lifted it out at his command and gave it to him.

"I thought so," he said in a heavy voice; "it is a fragment of that star-wrought veil which was my Christmas gift to Rosamund, and she has torn it off and left it here to show us her road. To St. Peter's-on-the-Wall! To St. Peter's, I say, for there the boats or ship must pass, and maybe that in the darkness they have not yet won out to sea."

So they turned their horses' heads, and those of them that were mounted rode for St. Peter's by the inland path that runs through Steeple, St. Lawrence, and Bradwell town, while those who were not started to search along the saltings and the river bank. On they galloped through the falling snow, Godwin and Wulf leading the way. Meanwhile, behind them thundered an ever gathering train of knights, squires and yeomen, who had seen the beacon flare on Steeple tower, or learned the tale from messengers from Southminster.

Hard they rode, but the lanes were heavy with fallen snow and mud beneath, and the way was far, so that an hour had gone by before Bradwell was left behind, and the shrine of St. Chad lay but half a mile in front. The snow abruptly ceased, and a strong northerly wind springing up drove the thick mist before it and left the sky hard and blue behind. Still riding in this mist, they pressed on to where the old tower loomed in front of them, then drew rein and waited.

"What is that?" said Godwin alertly, pointing to a great, dim thing upon the vapor-hidden sea.

As he spoke, a strong gust of wind tore away the last veils of mist, revealing the red face of the risen sun, and not a hundred yards away from them—for the tide was high—the tall masts of a galley creeping out to sea beneath her banks of oars. As they stared, the wind caught her, and on the main mast rose her bellying sail, while a shout of laughter told them that they themselves were seen. They shook their swords in the madness of their rage, knowing well who was aboard that galley; while to the fore peak ran up the yellow flag of Saladin, streaming there like gold in the golden sunlight.

Nor was this all, for on the high poop appeared the tall shape of Rosamund herself, and on one side of her, clad now in coat of mail and turban, Emir Hassan, whom they had known as the merchant Georgios, and on the other a stout man, also clad in mail, who at that distance looked like a Christian knight. Rosamund stretched out her arms towards them. Then suddenly she sprang forward as though she would throw herself into the sea, had not Hassan caught her by the arm and held her back, whilst the other man who was watching slipped between her and the bulwark.

In his fury and despair Wulf drove his horse into the water till the waves broke about his middle, and there, since he could go no further, sat shaking his sword and shouting, "Fear not! We follow! We follow!" in such a voice of thunder, that even through the wind and across the ever widening space of foam his words may have reached the ship. At least Rosamund seemed to hear them, for she tossed up her arms as though in token.

But Hassan, one hand pressed upon his heart and the other on his forehead, only bowed thrice in courteous farewell.

Then the great sail filled, the oars were drawn in, and the vessel swept away swiftly across the dancing waves, till at length she vanished, and they could only see the sunlight playing on the golden banner of Saladin which floated from her stern.

Chapter VIII
The Widow Masouda

Many months had gone by since the brethren sat upon their horses that winter morning, and from the shrine of St. Peter's-on-the-Wall, at the mouth of the Blackwater in Essex, watched with anguished hearts the galley of Saladin sailing southwards; their love and cousin, Rosamund, standing a prisoner on the deck. Having no ship in which to follow her—and this, indeed, it would have been too late to do—they thanked those who had come to aid them and returned home to Steeple, where they had matters to arrange. As they went they gathered from this man and that tidings which made the whole tale clear to them.

They learned, for instance, then and afterwards, that the galley which had been thought to be a merchantman put into the river Crouch by design, feigning an injury to her rudder, and that on Christmas eve she had moved up with the tide, and anchored in the Blackwater about three miles from its mouth. In a smaller boat, which she towed behind her, and which was afterwards found abandoned, the party rowed in the dusk to the mouth of Steeple Creek, which they quietly entered at dark, making fast to the staithe, unseen of any. Her crew of thirty men or more, guided by the false palmer Nicholas, then hid themselves in a grove of trees about fifty yards from the house, where traces of them were found afterwards. At this spot they waited for the signal and, if it were necessary, were ready to attack and burn the hall while all men feasted there. But it was not necessary, since the cunning scheme of the drugged wine succeeded. So it happened that the one man they had to meet in arms was an old knight, of which doubtless they were glad, as their numbers being few, they wished to avoid a desperate battle, wherein many must fall, and, if help came, they might all be destroyed.

When it was over they led Rosamund to the boat, felt their way down the creek, towing behind them the little skiff which they had taken from the water house—laden with their dead and wounded. This, indeed, proved the most perilous part of their adventures, since it was very dark, and the snow came hard; also, twice they grounded upon mud banks. Still guided by Nicholas, who had studied the river, they reached the galley before dawn, and with the first light weighed anchor, and very cautiously rowed out to sea. The rest is known.

Two days later, since there was no time to spare, Sir Andrew was buried with great pomp at Stangate Abbey, in the same tomb where lay the heart of his brother, the father of the brethren, who had fallen in the Eastern wars. After he had been laid to rest amidst much lamentation and in the presence of a great concourse of people, for the fame of these strange happenings had traveled far and wide, his will was opened. Then it was found that with the exception of certain sums of money left to his nephews, a legacy to Stangate Abbey, and another to be devoted to masses for the repose of his soul, with some gifts to his servants and the poor, all his estate was devised to his daughter Rosamund. The brethren, or the survivor of them, however, held it in trust on her behalf, with the charge that they should keep watch and ward over her and manage her lands till she took a husband.

These lands, together with their own, the brethren placed in the hands of Prior John of Stangate, in the presence of witnesses, to administer for them subject to the provisions of the will, taking a tithe of the rents and profits for his efforts. The priceless jewels also that had been sent by Saladin were given into his keeping, and a receipt with a list of the same signed in duplicate, deposited with a clerk at Southminster. This, indeed, was necessary, seeing that none save the brethren and the prior knew of these jewels, of which, being of so great a value, it was not safe to speak. Their affairs arranged, having first made their wills in favor of each other, they also included a provision for their heirs-at-law, since it was scarcely to be hoped that both of them would return alive from such a quest. Later that day, they received Communion, and with it a blessing from the hands of Prior John. Then early one morning, before any were awake, they rode quietly away to London.

On the top of Steeple Hill, sending forward the servant who led the mule laden with their baggage—that same mule which had been left by the spy Nicholas—the brethren turned their horses' heads to look in farewell on their home. There to the north of them lay the Blackwater, and to the west the parish of Mayland, towards which the laden barges crept along the stream of Steeple Creek. Below was the wide, flat plain outlined with trees, and in it, marked by the plantation where the Saracens had hid, the hall and church of Steeple, the home in which they had grown from childhood to youth, and from youth to manhood. It was during these years that they became the companion to the fair, lost Rosamund, who was the love of both, and whom both went forth to seek. That past was all behind them, and in front a dark and challenging future, of which they could not read the mystery nor guess the end.

Would they ever look on Steeple Hall again? Were they who stood there about to match their strength and courage against all the might of Saladin, doomed to fail or gloriously to succeed?

Through the darkness that shrouded their forward path shone one bright star of love— but for which of them did that star shine, or was it perchance for neither? They knew not. How could they know anything except that the venture seemed very desperate. Indeed, the few to whom they had spoken of it thought they were insane. Yet they remembered the last words of Sir Andrew, bidding them to keep a brave heart, since he believed that things would yet go well. It seemed to them, in truth, that they were not quite alone—as though his brave spirit accompanied them on their search, guiding their feet with ghostly counsel, which they could not hear.

They remembered also their oaths to him, to one another, and to Rosamund; and in silent token that they would keep them to the death, pressed each other's hands. Then, turning their horses southwards, they rode forward with light hearts, not caring what befell, if only at the last, living or dead, Rosamund and her father should, in his own words, find no cause to be ashamed of them.

Through the hot haze of a July morning a dromon, as certain merchant vessels of that time were called, might have been seen drifting before a light breeze into St. George's Bay at Beirut, on the coast of Syria. Cyprus, whence she had sailed last, was not a hundred miles away, yet she had taken six days to do the journey, not on account of storms—of which there were none at this time of year—but through lack of wind to move her. Still, her captain and the motley crowd of passengers—for the most part Eastern merchants and their servants, together with a number of pilgrims of all nations—thanked God for so prosperous a voyage—for in those times he who crossed the seas without shipwreck was very blessed.

Among these passengers were Godwin and Wulf, traveling, as their uncle had bidden them, unattended by squires or by servants. Upon the ship they passed themselves off as brothers named Peter and John of Lincoln, a town of which they knew something, having stayed there on their way to the Scottish wars; simple gentlemen of small estate, making a pilgrimage to the Holy Land in penitence for their sins and for the repose of the souls of their father and mother. At this tale their fellow passengers, with whom they had sailed from Genoa, to which place they traveled overland, shrugged their shoulders. For these brethren looked like what they were, knights of high degree; and considering their great stature, long swords, and the coats of mail they wore beneath their cloaks, few believed them to be plain gentlefolk bent on a pious errand. Indeed, they nicknamed them Sir Peter and Sir John, and as such they were known throughout the voyage.

The brethren were seated together in the bow of the ship and engaged, Godwin in reading from an Arabic translation of the Gospels made by some Egyptian monk, and Wulf in following it with little ease in the Latin version. Of the former tongue, indeed, they had acquired much in their youth, since they learned it from Sir Andrew with Rosamund, although they could not talk it as she did, who had been taught to lisp it as an infant by her mother. Knowing, too, that much might hang upon knowledge of this tongue, they occupied their long journey in studying it from such books as they could get; also in speaking it with a priest, who had spent many years in the East, and instructed them for a fee, and with certain Syrian merchants and sailors.

"Shut the book, Brother," said Wulf; "there is Lebanon at last," and he pointed to the great line of mountains revealing themselves dimly through their wrappings of mist. "Glad I am to see them, who have had enough of these crooked scrolls and learnings."

"Ay," said Godwin, "it is the Promised Land."

"And the Land of Promise for us," answered his brother. "Well, thank God that the time has come to act, though how we are to set about it is more than I can say."

"Doubtless time will show. As our uncle advised, we will seek out this Sheik Jebal—"

"Hush!" said Wulf, for just then some merchants, and with them a number of pilgrims, crowded forward to the bow to obtain their first view of the Holy Land, and there burst into prayers and songs of thanksgiving. Indeed, one of these men— a trader known as Thomas of Ipswich— was, they found, standing close to them, and seemed as though he listened to their talk.

The brethren mingled with them while this same Thomas of Ipswich, who had visited the place before, or so it seemed, pointed out the beauties of the city, of the fertile country by which it was surrounded, and of the distant cedar-clad mountains where, as he said, Hiram, King of Tyre, had cut the timber for Solomon's Temple.

"Have you been on them?" asked Wulf.

"Ay, following my business," he answered, "but no further." And he showed them a great snow-capped peak to the north. "Few ever go further."

"Why not?" asked Godwin.

"Because there begins the territory of the Sheik Al-Jebal"— and he looked at them meaningly—"whom," he added, "neither

Christian nor Saracen visit without an invitation, which is seldom given."

Again they inquired why not.

"Because," answered the trader, still watching them, "most men love their lives, and that man is the lord of death and magic. Strange things are to be seen in his castle, and about it lie wonderful gardens inhabited by lovely women that are evil spirits, who bring the souls of men to ruin. Also, this Old Man of the Mountain is a great murderer, of whom even all the princes of the East are terrified. When he speaks a word to his fedais—or servants—who are initiated, and they go forth and bring to death any whom he hates. Young men, I like you well, and I say to you, be warned. In this Syria there are many wonders to be seen; leave those of Masyaf and its fearful lord alone if you desire to look again upon the towers of Lincoln."

"Fear not; we will," answered Godwin, "who come to seek holy places—not haunts of devils."

"Of course we will," added Wulf. "Still, that country must be worth traveling in."

Then boats came out to greet them from the shore—for at that time Beirut was in the hands of the Franks—and in the shouting and confusion which followed they saw no more of this merchant Thomas. Nor did they seek him out again, since they thought it unwise to show themselves too curious about the Sheik Al-Jebal. Indeed, it would have been useless, since that trader was ashore two full hours before they were permitted to leave the ship, from which he departed alone in a private boat.

At length they stood with the motley Eastern crowd upon the wharf, wondering where they could find an inn that was quiet and inexpensive, since they did not wish to be considered persons of wealth or importance. As they lingered here, somewhat bewildered, a tall, veiled woman whom they had noted watching them, drew near, accompanied by a porter, who led a donkey. This man, without more ado, seized their baggage, and helped by other porters began to fasten it upon the back of the donkey with great rapidity, and when they would have forbidden him, pointed to the veiled woman.

"Your pardon," said Godwin to her at length and speaking in French; "but this man—"

"Loads up your baggage to take it to my inn. It is cheap, quiet and comfortable—things which I heard you say you required just now, did I not?" she answered in a sweet voice, also speaking in good French.

Godwin looked at Wulf, and Wulf at Godwin, and they began to discuss together what they should do. When they had agreed that it seemed not wise to trust themselves to the care of strange women in this fashion, they looked up to see the donkey laden with their trunks being led away by the porter.

"Too late to say no, I fear," said the woman with a laugh, "so you must be my guests awhile if you would not lose your baggage. Come, after so long a journey you need to wash and eat. Follow me, sirs, I pray you."

Then she walked through the crowd, which, they noted, parted for her as she went, to a post where a fine mule was tied. Loosing it, she leaped to the saddle without help and began to ride away, looking back from time to time to see that they were following her, as, indeed, they must.

"Whither go we, I wonder," said Godwin, as they trudged through the sands of Beirut, with the hot sun striking on their heads.

"Who can tell when a strange woman leads?" replied Wulf, with a laugh.

At last the woman on the mule turned through a doorway in a wall of unburnt brick, and they found themselves before the porch of a white, rambling house. This dwelling stood next to a large garden planted with mulberries, oranges, and other fruit trees that were strange to them, and was situated on the borders of the city.

Here the woman dismounted and gave the mule to a Nubian who was waiting. Then, with a quick movement she unveiled herself and turned towards them as though to show her beauty. Beautiful she was, of that there could be no doubt, with her graceful posture, and her dark and liquid eyes, her rounded features and strangely impassive countenance. She was young also—perhaps twenty-five, no more— and very fair-skinned for an Eastern.

"My poor house is for pilgrims and merchants, not for famous knights; yet, sirs, I welcome you to it," she said slyly, scanning them out of the corners of her eyes.

"We are but squires in our own country, who make the pilgrimage," replied Godwin. "For what sum each day will you give us board and a good room to sleep in?"

"These strangers," she said in Arabic to the porter, "do not speak the truth."

"What is that to you?" he answered, as he busied himself in loosening the baggage. "They will pay their debts, and all sorts of knights come to this country, pretending to be what they are not. Also you sought them—why, I know not—not they you."

"Mad or sane, they are proper men," said the inquisitive woman, as though to herself, then added in French, "Sirs, I repeat, this is but a humble place, scarce fit for knights like you, but if you will honor it, the charge is—so much."

"We are satisfied," said Godwin, "especially," he added, with a bow and removing the cap from his head, "as, having brought us here without permission, we are sure that you will treat us who are strangers kindly."

"As kindly as possible in our humble way," said the woman. "Now, I will settle with the porter; he would surely cheat you."

Then followed a wrangle five minutes long between this strange woman and the porter, who, after the Eastern fashion, lashed himself into a frenzy over the sum she offered, and at length began to call her by ill names.

She stood looking at him quite unmoved, although Godwin, who understood all, but pretended to understand nothing, wondered at her patience. Moments later, however, in a perfect foam of passion the porter said, or rather spat out, "No wonder, Masouda the Spy, that after hiring me to do your evil work, you take the part of these Christian dogs against a true believer, you child of Al-Jebal!"

Instantly, the woman seemed to stiffen like a snake about to strike.

"Who is he?" she said coldly. "Do you mean the lord—who kills?" And she looked at him with fire in her black eyes.

At that glance all the anger seemed to go out of the man.

"Your pardon, widow Masouda," he said. "I forgot that you are a Christian, and naturally side with Christians. The money will not pay for the wear of my ass's hoofs, but give it me, and let me go to pilgrims who will reward me better."

She gave him the sum, adding in her quiet voice, "Go; and if you love life, keep better watch over your words."

Then the porter went, and now so humble was his posture that in his dirty turban and long, tattered robe he looked, Wulf thought, more like a bundle of rags than a man mounted on the donkey's back. Also, it came into his mind that their strange hostess had powers not possessed by innkeepers in England. When she had watched him through the gate, Masouda turned to them and said in French, "Forgive me, but here in Beirut these Saracen porters are greedy, especially towards us Christians. He was deceived by your appearance. He thought that you were knights, not

simple pilgrims as you avow yourselves, who happen to be dressed and armed like knights beneath your cloaks; and," she added, fixing her eyes upon the crude scar beneath Godwin's hairline where the sword had struck him in the struggle on Death Creek Wharf, "show the wounds of knights, though it is true that a man might come by such in any brawl in a tavern. Well, pay me a good price, and you shall have my best room while it pleases you to honor me with your company. Ah! Your baggage. You do not wish to leave it. Slave, come here."

With startling suddenness the Nubian who had led away the mule appeared and took up some of the packages. Then she led them down a passage into a large, sparsely-furnished room with high windows, in which were two beds laid on a stone floor. She then asked them if it pleased them.

They said, "Yes; it will serve."

Reading what passed in their minds, she added: "Have no fear for your baggage. Were you as rich as you say you are poor, and as noble as you say you are humble, both it and you are safe in the inn of the widow Masouda. O my guests—how are you named?"

"Peter and John," responded the knights awkwardly.

"O, my guests, Peter and John, who have come to visit the land of Peter and John and other holy founders of our faith—"

"And have been so fortunate as to be captured on its shore by the widow Masouda," answered Godwin, bowing again.

"Wait to speak of the fortune until you have done with her, Sir—is it Peter, or John?" she replied, with something like a smile upon her face.

"Peter," answered Godwin. "Remember the pilgrim with the thin white scar is Peter."

"You need it to distinguish you apart, who, I suppose, are twins. Let me see—Peter has a beautiful scar and gray eyes. John has blue eyes. John also is the greater warrior, if a pilgrim can be a warrior—look at his muscles; but Peter thinks the more. It would be hard for a woman to choose between Peter and John, who must both of them be hungry, so I go to prepare their food."

"A strange hostess," said Wulf, laughing, when she had left the room; "but I like her, though she knows very well our background. I wonder why? What is more, Brother Godwin, she likes you, which is as well, since she may be useful. But, friend Peter, do not let it go too far, since, like that porter, I think also that she may be dangerous. Remember, he called her a spy, and probably she is one."

Godwin turned to reprove him, when the voice of the widow Masouda was heard without saying, "Brothers Peter and John, I forgot to caution you to speak low in this house, as there is latticework over the doors to let in the air. Do not be afraid. I only heard the voice of John, not what he said."

"I hope not," muttered Wulf, and this time he spoke very low indeed.

Then they undid their baggage and, having taken from it clean garments, washed themselves after their long journey with the water that had been placed ready for them in great jars. This, indeed, they needed, for on that crowded dromon there was little chance to wash. By the time they had clothed themselves afresh, putting on their shirts of mail beneath their tunics, the Nubian came and led them to another room, large and lighted with high-set lattices, where cushions were piled upon the floor round a rug that laid in its center. Motioning them to be seated on the cushions, he went away, to return again accompanied by Masouda bearing dishes upon brass platters. These she placed before them, bidding them eat. What that food was they did not know, because of the sauces with which it had been covered, until she told them that it was fish. After the fish came flesh, and after the flesh fowls, and after the fowls cakes and sweetmeats and fruits. At this point, ravenous as they were, who for days had fed upon salted pork and biscuits full of worms washed down with bad water, they were forced to beg her to bring no more.

"Drink another cup of wine at least," she said, smiling and filling their mugs with the sweet vintage of Lebanon—for it seemed to please her to see them eat so heartily of her fare.

Forgetting the troubles associated with their last drink of wine, they obeyed, mixing the wine with water. While they drank she asked them suddenly what were their plans, and how long they wished to stay in Beirut. They answered that for the next few days they had none, as they needed to rest, to see the town and its neighborhood, and to buy good horses—a matter in which perhaps she could help them. Masouda nodded again, and asked where they wished to ride on horses.

"Out yonder," said Wulf, waving his hand towards the mountains. "We desire to look upon the cedars of Lebanon and its great hills before we go on towards Jerusalem."

"Cedars of Lebanon?" she replied. "That is scarcely safe for two men alone, for in those mountains are many wild beasts and wilder people who rob and kill. Moreover, the lord of those mountains has just now a quarrel with the Christians, and would take any whom he found prisoners."

"How is that lord named?" asked Godwin.

"Sinan," she answered, and they noted that she looked round quickly as she spoke the word.

"Oh," he said, "we thought the name was Jebal."

Now she stared at him with wide, wondering eyes, and replied, "He is so called, also; but, Sir Pilgrims, what know you of the dread lord Al-Jebal?"

"Only that he lives at a place called Masyaf, which we wish to visit."

Again she stared intently at the two men.

"Are you that eager to die?" she queried, then checked herself, and clapped her hands for the slave to remove the dishes.

While this was being done they said they would like to take a walk.

"Good," answered Masouda; "the man shall accompany you—nay, it is best that you do not go alone, as you might lose your way. Also, the place is not always safe for strangers, however humble they may seem," she added with meaning. "Would you wish to visit the governor at the castle, where there are a few English knights, also some priests who give advice to pilgrims?"

"We think not," answered Godwin; "we are not worthy of such high company. But, lady, why do you look at us so strangely?"

"I am wondering, Sir Peter and Sir John, why you think it worthwhile to tell lies to a poor widow? Say, in your own country did you ever hear of certain twin brethren named—oh, how are they named?—Sir Godwin and Sir Wulf, of the house of D'Arcy, which has been told of in this land?"

Now Godwin's jaw dropped, but Wulf laughed out loud, and seeing that they were alone in the room, for the slave had departed, asked in his turn, "Surely those twins would be pleased to find themselves so famous. But how did you chance to hear of them, O widowed hostess of a Syrian inn?"

"I? Oh, from a man on the dromon who called here while I made ready your food and told me a strange story that he had learned in England of a band sent by Saladin—may his name be accursed!—to capture a certain lady. Of how the brethren named Godwin and Wulf fought and held them off—a very knightly deed he said it was—while the lady escaped; and of how afterwards they were taken in a snare, as those are apt to be who deal with the sultan, and this time the lady was snatched away."

"A wild tale, truly," said Godwin. "But did this man tell you further whether that lady has chanced to come to Palestine?"

She shook her head.

"Of that he told me nothing, and I have heard nothing. Now listen, my guests. You think it strange that I should know so much, but it is not strange, since here in Syria, knowledge is the business of some of us. Did you then believe, O foolish children, that two knights like you, who have played a part in a very great story, whereof already whispers run throughout the East, could travel by land and sea and not be known? Did you then think that none were left behind to watch your movements and to make report of them to that mighty one who sent out the ship of war, charged with a certain mission? Well, what he knows I know. Have I not said it is my business to know? Now, why do I tell you this? Well, perhaps because I like such knights as you are, and I like that tale of two men who stood side by side upon a pier while a woman swam the stream behind them, and afterwards, sore wounded, charged their way through a host of foes. In the East we love such deeds of chivalry. Perhaps also because I would warn you not to throw away lives so gallant by attempting to win through the guarded gates of Damascus by wild quests.

"What, you still stare at me and doubt? Good, I have been telling you lies. I was not awaiting you upon the wharf, and that porter with whom I seemed to quarrel was not charged to seize your baggage and bring it to my house. No spies watched your movements from England to Beirut. Only since you have been at dinner I visited your room and read some writings which, foolishly, you have left among your baggage, and opened some books in which other names than Peter and John were written, and drew a great sword from its scabbard on which was engraved a motto: 'Meet D'Arcy, meet Death!' and heard Peter call John Wulf, and John call Peter Godwin, and so forth."

"It seems," said Wulf in English, "that we are flies in a web, and that the spider is called the widow Masouda, though of what use we are to her I know not. Now, Brother, what is to be done since we are over matched? Make friends with the spider?"

"An ill ally," answered Godwin. Then, looking her straight in the face, he asked: "Hostess, who know so much, tell me why, amongst other names, did that donkey driver call you 'daughter of Al-Jebal'?"

She started, and answered, "So you understand Arabic? I thought it. Why do you ask? What does it matter to you?"

"Not much, except that, as we are going to visit Al-Jebal, of course we think ourselves fortunate to have met his daughter."

"Going to visit Al-Jebal? Yes, you hinted as much upon the ship, did you not? Perhaps that is why I came to meet you. Well, your throats will be cut before ever you reach the first of his castles."

"I think not," said Godwin, and, putting his hand into his breast, he drew thence a ring, with which he began to play carelessly.

"Where did you get that ring?" she said, with fear and wonder in her eyes. "It is—" and she ceased.

"From one to whom it was given and who has charged us with a message. Now, hostess, let us be plain with one another. You know a great deal about us, but although it has suited us to call ourselves the pilgrims Peter and John, in all this there is nothing of which we need be ashamed, especially as you say that our secret is no secret, which I can well believe. Now, this secret being out, I propose that we remove ourselves from your roof and go to stay with our own people at the castle, where, I doubt not, we shall be welcome, telling them that we would bide no longer with one who is called a spy, whom we have discovered also to be a 'daughter of Al-Jebal.' After which, perhaps, you will bide no longer in Beirut, where, as we gather, spies and the 'daughters of Al-Jebal' are not welcome."

She listened with a calm face and answered, "Doubtless you have heard that one of us who was so named was burned here recently as a witch?"

"Yes," broke in Wulf, who now learned this fact for the first time; "we heard that."

"And think to bring a like fate upon me. Why, foolish men, I can lay you both dead before ever those words pass your lips."

"You think you can," said Godwin; "but for my part I am sure that this is not fated, and am sure also that you do not wish to harm us any more than we wish to harm you. To be plain, then, it is necessary for us to visit Al-Jebal. As chance has brought us together—if it be chance—will you aid us in this, as I think you can, or must we seek other help?"

"I do not know. I will tell you after four days. If you are not satisfied with that, go, denounce me, do your worst, and I will do mine, for which we both will be sorry."

"Where is the security that you will not do it if we are satisfied?" asked Wulf bluntly.

"You must take the word of a 'daughter of Al-Jebal.' I have none other to offer," she replied.

"That may mean death," said Wulf.

"You said just now that was not fated, and although I have sought your company for my own reasons, I have no quarrel with you—as yet. Choose your own path. Still, I tell you that if you go, who, chancing to know Arabic, have learned my secret, you die, and that if you stay you are safe—at least while you are in this house. I swear it on the token of Al-Jebal," and bending forward she touched the ring in Godwin's hand; "but remember that for the future I cannot answer."

Godwin and Wulf looked at each other. Then Godwin replied, "I think that we will trust you, and stay," words at which she smiled a little as though she were pleased, then said, "Now, if you wish to walk abroad, guests Peter and John, I will summon the slave to guide you, and in four days we will talk more of this matter of your journey, which, until then, had best be forgotten."

So the man came, armed with a sword, and led them out, clad in their pilgrims' robes, through the streets of this Eastern town, where everything was so strange that for awhile they forgot their troubles in studying the new life about them. They noted, moreover, that though they went into quarters where no Franks were to be seen, and where fierce-looking servants of the Prophet stared at them sourly, the presence of this slave of Masouda seemed to be sufficient to protect them from affront, since on seeing him even the turbaned Saracens nudged each other and turned aside. In due course, they came to the inn again, having met no one whom they knew, except two pilgrims who had been their fellow passengers on the dromon. These men were astonished when they said that they had been through the Saracen quarter of the city, where, although this town was in the hands of the Christians, it was scarcely thought safe for Franks to venture without a strong guard.

When the brethren were back in their chamber, seated at the far end of it, and speaking very low, lest they should be overheard, they consulted together long and earnestly as to what they should do. This was clear—they and something of their mission were known, and doubtless notice of their coming would soon be given to the Sultan Saladin. From the king and great Christian lords in Jerusalem they could expect little help, since to give it might be to bring about an open rupture with Saladin, such as the Franks dreaded, and for which they were ill prepared. Indeed, if they went to them, it seemed likely that they would be prevented from engaging in this dangerous search for a woman who was the niece of Saladin, and for all they knew thrown into prison, or shipped back to Europe. True, they might try to find their way to Damascus alone, but if the sultan was warned of their coming, would he not cause them to be killed upon the road, or cast into some dungeon where they would languish out their lives? The more they spoke of these matters the more they were perplexed, till at length Godwin said, "Brother, our uncle bade us earnestly to seek out this Al-Jebal, and though it seems that to do so is very dangerous, I think that we had best obey him who may have been given foresight at the last. When all paths are full of thorns what matter which you tread?"

"A good saying," answered Wulf. "I am weary of doubts and troubling. Let us follow our uncle's will, and visit this Old Man of the Mountains. In this regard, I think the widow Masouda is the woman to help us. If we die on that journey, well, at least we shall have done our best."

Chapter IX
The Horses Flame and Smoke

On the following morning, when they came into the eating-room of the inn, Godwin and Wulf found they were no longer alone in the house, for several other guests sat there partaking of their morning meal. Among them were a grave merchant of Damascus, another from Alexandria in Egypt, a man who seemed to be an Arab chief, a Jew of Jerusalem, and none other than the English trader Thomas of Ipswich, their fellow passenger, who greeted them warmly.

They truly looked like a strange and mismatched set of men, as the young and stately widow Masouda moved from one to the other, talking to each in turn while she attended to their wants. It came into Godwin's mind that they might be spies meeting there to gain or exchange information, or even to make report to their hostess, in whose pay perhaps they were. Still, if so, of this they showed no sign. Indeed, for the most part they spoke in French, which all of them understood, on general matters, such as the heat of the weather, the price of transport animals or merchandise, and the cities where they purposed to travel.

The trader Thomas, it appeared, had intended to start for Jerusalem that morning with his goods. But the riding mule he had bought proved to be lame from a prick in the hoof, nor had all his hired camels arrived from the mountains, so that he must wait a few days, or so he said. Under these circumstances, he offered the brethren his company in their ramblings about the town. This they thought it wise not to refuse, although they felt little confidence in the man, believing that it was he who had found out their story and true names and revealed them to Masouda, either through talkativeness or with a purpose.

However these things might be, this Thomas proved of service to them, since, although he had just landed, he seemed to know all that had passed in Syria since he left it, and all that was passing then. Thus he told them how Guy of Lusignan had just made himself king in Jerusalem on the death of the child Baldwin, and how Raymond of Tripoli refused to acknowledge him and was about to be besieged in Tiberias. Thomas also told how Saladin was gathering a great host at Damascus to make war upon the Christians, and many other things, false and true.

In his company, then, and sometimes in that of the other guests—none of whom showed any curiosity concerning them, though whether this was from good manners or for other reasons they could not be sure—the brethren passed the hours profitably enough.

It was on the third morning of their stay that their hostess Masouda, with whom as yet they had no further private talk, asked them if they still wished to buy horses. On their answering "Yes," she added that she had told a certain man to bring two for them to look at, which were now in the stable beyond the garden.

To this stable they went, accompanied by Masouda, where they found a somber Arab, wrapped in a garment of camel's hair and carrying a spear in his hand. He stood at the door of the cave, which served the purpose of a stable, as is common in the East where the heat is so great. As they advanced towards him, Masouda said, "If you like the horses, leave me to bargain, and seem to understand nothing of my talk."

The Arab, who took no notice of them, saluted Masouda, and said to her in Arabic, "Is it then for Franks that I have been ordered to bring the two priceless ones?"

"What is that to you, my uncle, Son of the Sand?" she asked. "Let them be led forth that I may know whether they are those for which I sent."

The man turned and called into the door of the cave, "Flame, come out!" As he spoke, there was a sound of hoofs, and through the low archway leapt the most beautiful horse that ever their eyes had seen. It was gray in color, with flowing mane and tail, and on its forehead was a black star; not over tall, but with a barrel-like shape of great strength, small-headed, large-eyed; wide-nostriled, big-boned, but fine beneath the knee, and round-hoofed. Out it sprang snorting; then seeing its master, the Arab, checked itself and stood still by him as though it had been turned to stone.

"Come here, Smoke," called the Arab again, and another horse appeared and ranged itself by the first. In size and shape it was the same, but the color was coal-black and the star upon its forehead white. Also, the eye was more fiery.

"These are the horses," said the Arab, Masouda translating. "They are twins, seven years old and never backed until they were nearly six, cast at a birth by the swiftest mare in Syria, and of a pedigree that can be counted for a hundred years."

"Horses, indeed!" said Wulf. "Horses, indeed! But what is the price of them?"

Masouda repeated the question in Arabic, whereon the man replied in the same tongue with a slight shrug of the shoulders.

"Be not foolish. You know this is no question of price, for they are beyond price. Say what you will."

"He says," said Masouda, "that it is a hundred gold pieces for the pair. Can you pay as much?"

The brethren looked at each other. The sum was large.

"Such horses have saved men's lives in times past," added Masouda, "and I do not think that I can ask him to take less, seeing that, did he but know it, in Jerusalem they could be sold for twice as much. But if you wish, I could lend you money, since doubtless you have jewels or other articles of value you could give as security—that ring in your breast, for instance, Peter."

"We have the gold itself," answered Wulf, who would have paid to his last piece for those horses.

"They buy," said Masouda.

"They buy, but can they ride?" asked the Arab. "These horses are not for children or pilgrims. Unless they can ride well they shall not have them—no, not even if you ask it of me."

Godwin said that he thought so—at least, they would try. Then the Arab, leaving the horses standing there, went into the stable and, with the help of two of the inn servants, brought out bridles and saddles unlike any they had seen. They were but thickly-quilted pads stretching far back upon the horses' loins, with strong hide girths strapped with wool and chased stirrups fashioned like half hoofs. The bits also were only snaffles without curbs.

When all was ready and the stirrups had been let down to the length they desired, the Arab motioned to them to mount. As they prepared to do so, however, he spoke some word, and suddenly those meek, quiet horses were turned into two devils. They reared up on their hind legs and threatened them with their teeth and their front hoofs that were shod with thin plates of iron. Godwin stood wondering, but Wulf, who was angry at the trick, got behind the horses and, watching for his chance, put his hands upon the flanks of the stallion named Smoke, and with one spring leapt into the saddle. Masouda smiled, and even the Arab muttered, "Good," while Smoke, feeling himself backed, came to the ground again and became quiet as a sheep. Then the Arab spoke to the horse Flame, and Godwin was allowed to vault into the saddle also.

"Where shall we go?" he asked.

Masouda said they would show them, and, accompanied by her and the Arab, they walked the horses until they were quite clear of the town. The company soon found themselves on a road that had the sea to the left, and to the right a stretch of flat land, some of it cultivated, above which rose the steep and stony sides of hills. Here on this road the brethren trotted and cantered the horses to and fro, till they began to be at home in their strange saddles who from childhood had ridden bare-backed in the Essex marshes, and to learn what pressure on the bit was needed to check or turn them. When they came back to where the pair stood, Masouda said that if they were not afraid the seller wished to show them that the horses were both strong and swift.

"We fear no ride that he dares to take himself," answered Wulf angrily, whereon the Arab smiled grimly and said something in a low voice to Masouda. Then, placing his hand upon Smoke's flank, he leapt up behind Wulf, the horse never stirring.

"Say, Peter, are you minded to take a companion for this ride?" asked Masouda; and as she spoke a strange look came into her eyes, a wild look that was new to the brethren.

"Surely," answered Godwin, "but where is the companion?"

Her reply was to do as the Arab had done and, seating herself straddle-legged behind Godwin, to clasp him around the middle.

"Truly you look a pretty pilgrim now, Brother," said Wulf, laughing aloud, while even the grave Arab smiled. Godwin was much less amused, and nearly blurted out a proverb about impulsive women, before he finally resigned himself to his task. But aloud he said, "I am indeed honored; yet, friend Masouda, if harm should come of this, do not blame me."

"No harm will come—to you, friend Peter; and as I have been so long cooped in an inn that I, who am desert-born, wish for a gallop on the mountains with a good horse beneath me and a brave knight in front. Listen, you brethren; you say you do not fear; then leave your bridles loose, and where'er we go and whate'er we meet seek not to check or turn the horses Flame and Smoke. Now, Son of the Sand, we will test these nags of which you sing so loud a song. Away, and let the ride be fast and far!"

"On your head be it then, Daughter," answered the old Arab. "Pray Allah that these Franks can sit a horse!"

Then his somber eyes seemed to take fire and, gripping the encircling saddle girth, he uttered some word of command, at which the stallions threw up their heads and began to move at a long, swinging gallop towards the mountains a mile away. At first they went over cultivated land off which the crops had been already cut, taking two or three ditches and a low wall in their stride so smoothly that the brethren felt as though they were seated upon swallows. Then came a space of sandy ground, half a mile or more, where their pace quickened, after which they began to crest the long slope of a hill, picking their way amongst its stones like cats.

Ever steeper it grew, till in places it was so sheer that Godwin must clutch the mane of Flame, and Masouda must cling close to Godwin's middle to save themselves from slipping off behind. Yet, notwithstanding the double weights they bore, those gallant steeds never seemed to falter or to tire. At one spot they plunged through a mountain stream. Godwin noted that not fifty yards to their right this stream fell over a little precipice cutting its way between cliffs which were full eighteen feet from bank to bank, and thought to himself that had they struck it lower down, that ride must have ended. Beyond the stream lay a hundred yards or so of level ground, and above it still steeper country, up which they pushed their way through bushes, till at length they came to the top of the mountain and saw the plain they had left lying two miles or more below them.

"These horses climb hills like goats," Wulf said, "but one thing is certain: we must lead them down."

Now on the top of the mountain was a stretch of land almost flat and without stones, over which they cantered forward, gathering speed as the horses recovered their wind till the pace grew fast. Suddenly, the stallions threw themselves onto their haunches and stopped, as well they might, for they were on the verge of a chasm, at whose far end a river brawled in foam. For a moment they stood; then, at some word from the Arab, wheeled round, and, bearing to the left, began to gallop back across the tableland, until they approached the edge of the mountainside, where the brethren thought that they would stop. But Masouda cried to the Arab, and the Arab cried to the horses, and Wulf cried to Godwin in the English tongue, "Show no fear, Brother. Where they go, we can go."

"Pray God that the girths may hold," answered Godwin, leaning back against Masouda behind him. As he spoke they began to descend the hill, slowly at first, afterwards faster and yet faster, till they rushed downwards like a whirlwind.

How did those horses keep their footing? They never knew, and certainly none that were bred in England could have done so. Yet never falling, never stumbling even, on they sped, taking great rocks in their stride, till at length they reached the level piece of land above the stream. Godwin saw and turned cold. Were these folk mad that they would put double-laden horses at such a jump? If they hung back, if they missed their stride, if they caught hoof or fell short, swift death was their portion.

But the old Arab seated behind Wulf only shouted aloud, and Masouda only tightened her round arms about Godwin's middle and laughed in his ear. The horses heard the shout and, seeming to see what was before them, stretched out their long necks and rushed forward over the flat ground.

Now they were on the edge of the terrible place and, like a man in a dream, Godwin noted the sharp, sheer lips of the cliff, the gulf between them, and the white foam of the stream nearly twenty yards beneath. Then he felt the brave horse Flame gather itself together and next instant fly into the air like a bird. Also—and was this dream indeed, or even as they sped over that horrible pit did he feel a woman's lips pressed upon his cheek? He was not sure. Who could have been at such a time, with death beneath them? Perchance it was the wind that kissed him, or a lock of her loose hair, which struck across his face. Indeed, at the moment he thought of other things than women's lips—those of the black and yawning gulf, for instance.

They swooped through the air, the white foam vanished, and they were safe. How tight those arms clung about him. How close that face was pressed against his own. Lo! it was over. They were speeding down the hill, and alongside of the gray horse Flame raced the black horse Smoke. Wulf on its back, with eyes that seemed to be starting from his head, was shouting, "A D'Arcy! A D'Arcy!" and behind him, turban gone, and white burnoose floating like a banner on the air, the grim-visaged Arab, who also shouted.

Swifter and yet swifter. Did ever horses gallop so fast? Swifter and yet swifter, till the air sang past them and the ground seemed to fly away beneath. The slope was done. They were on the flat; the flat was past, they were in the fields; the fields were left behind; and, behold! side by side, with hanging heads and panting flanks, the horses Smoke and Flame stood still upon the road, their sweating hides dyed red in the light of the sinking sun.

The grip loosened from about Godwin's middle. It had been close; on Masouda's round and naked arms were the prints of the steel shirt beneath his tunic, for she slipped to the ground and stood looking at them. Then she smiled one of her slow, thrilling smiles, gasped and said, "You ride well, pilgrim Peter, and pilgrim John rides well also, and these are good horses; and, oh! That ride was worth the riding, even though death had been its end. Son of the Sand, my uncle, what say you?"

"That I grow old for such gallops—two on one horse, with nothing to win."

"Nothing to win?" said Masouda. "I am not so sure!" and she looked at Godwin. "Well, you have sold your horses to pilgrims who can ride, and they have proved them; and I have had a change from my cooking in the inn, to which I must now get me back again."

Wulf wiped the sweat from his brow, shook his head, and remarked, "I always heard the East was full of madmen and devils; now I know that it is true."

But Godwin said nothing.

They led the horses back to the inn, where the brethren groomed them down under the direction of the Arab, that the gallant beasts might get used to them, which, after carrying them upon that fearful ride, they did readily enough. Then they fed them with chopped barley, ear and straw together, and gave them water to drink that had stood in the sun all day to warm, in which the Arab mixed flour and some white wine.

The next morning at dawn they rose to see how Flame and Smoke fared after that journey. Entering the stable, they heard the sound of a man weeping, and hidden in the shadow, saw by the low light of the morning that it was the old Arab, who stood with his back to them, an arm around the neck of each horse, which he kissed from time to time. Moreover, he talked aloud in his own tongue to them, calling them his children, and saying that rather would he sell his wife and his sister to the Franks.

"But," he added, "she has spoken—why, I know not—and I must obey. Well, at least they are gallant men and worthy of such steeds. Half I hoped that you and the three of us and my niece Masouda, the woman with the secret face and eyes that have looked on fear, might perish in the cleft of the stream; but it was not willed of Allah. So farewell, Flame, and farewell, Smoke, children of the desert, who are swifter than arrows, for never more shall I ride you in battle. Well, at least I have others of your matchless blood."

Then Godwin touched Wulf on the shoulder, and they crept away from the stable without the Arab knowing that they had been there, for it seemed shameful to pry upon his grief. When they reached their room again Godwin asked Wulf, "Why does this man sell us those noble steeds?"

"Because his niece Masouda has bid him so to do," he answered.

"And why has she bidden him?"

"Ah!" replied Wulf. "He called her 'the woman with the secret face and eyes that have looked on fear,' didn't he? Well, for reasons that have to do with his family perhaps, or with her secrets, or us, with whom she plays some game of which we know neither the beginning nor the end. But, Brother Godwin, you are wiser than I. Why do you ask me these riddles? For my part, I do not wish to trouble my head about them. All I know is that the game is a worthy one, and I mean to go through with it, especially as I believe that this playing will lead us to Rosamund."

"May it lead us nowhere worse," answered Godwin with something like a groan, for he remembered the hazards of the journey that he had just completed with Masouda and her uncle.

When the sun was fully up they prepared to go out again, taking with them the gold to pay the Arab; but on opening the door of their room they met Masouda, apparently about to knock upon it.

"Whither go you, friends Peter and John, and so early?" she asked, looking at them with a smile upon her beautiful face that was as thrilling as it was mysterious. Godwin thought to himself that it was like another smile, that on the face of the woman-headed, stone sphinx that they had seen set up in the marketplace of Beirut.

"To visit our horses and pay your uncle, the Arab, his money," answered Wulf.

"Indeed! I thought I saw you do the first an hour ago, and as for the second, it is useless; Son of the Sand has gone."

"Gone! With the horses?"

"Nay, he has left them behind."

"Did you pay him, then, lady?" asked Godwin.

It was easy to see that Masouda was pleased at this courteous word, for her voice, which in general seemed a little hard, softened as she answered, for the first time giving him his own title.

"Why do you call me 'lady,' Sir Godwin D'Arcy, who am but an innkeeper, for whom sometimes men find hard names? Well, perhaps I was a lady once before I became an innkeeper; but now I am the widow Masouda, as you are the pilgrim Peter. Still, I thank you for this bad guess of yours." Then stepping back a foot or two towards the door, which she had closed behind her, she made him a curtsey so full of dignity and grace that any who saw it must be sure that, wherever she might dwell, Masouda was not bred in inns.

Godwin returned the bow, removing his cap. Their eyes met, and in hers he learned that he had no treachery to fear from this woman, whatever else he might have to fear. Indeed, from that moment, however black and doubtful seemed the road, he would have trusted his life to her; for this was the message written there, a message which she meant that he should read. Yet at his heart he felt terribly afraid of where this relationship would end.

Wulf, who saw something of all this and guessed more, also was afraid. He wondered what Rosamund would have thought of it, if she had seen that strange and turbulent look in the eyes of this woman who had been a lady and was an innkeeper; of one whom men called "spy," and daughter of Satan, and child of Al-Jebal. To his mind that look was like a flash of lightning upon a dark night, which for a second illumines some mysterious landscape, after which comes the night again, blacker than before.

Now the widow Masouda was saying in her somewhat stern voice, "No; I did not pay him. At the last he would take no money; but, having passed it, neither would he break his word to knights who ride so well and boldly. So I made a bargain with him on behalf of both of you, which I expect that you will keep, since my good faith is pledged, and this Arab is a chief and my kinsman. It is this, that if you and these horses should live, and the time comes when you have no more need of them, you will cause it to be cried in the marketplace of whatever town is nearest to you, by the voice of the public crier, that for six days they stand to be returned to him who lent them. Then if he comes not they can be sold, which must not be sold or given away to anyone without this proclamation. Do you consent?"

"Aye," answered both of them, but Wulf added, "Only we would like to know why the Arab, Son of the Sand, who is your kinsman, trusts his glorious horses to us in this fashion."

"Your breakfast is served, my guests," answered Masouda in tones that rang like the clash of metal, so steely were they. Whereon Wulf shook his head and followed her into the eating room, which was now empty again as it had been on the afternoon of their arrival.

Most of that day they spent with their horses. In the evening, this time unaccompanied by Masouda, they rode out for a little way, though rather doubtfully, since they were not sure that these beasts, which seemed to be almost human, would not take the bits between their teeth and rush with them back to the desert whence they came. But although from time to time they looked around them for their master, the Arab, whinnying as they looked, they did not seek to run wild. In fact, these magnificent horses could not have been quieter. It was as though they knew that these knights were their new lords and wished to make friends of them. An hour later, the brethren returned Smoke and Flame to their dwelling place.

The next day was a Sunday, and, attended by Masouda's slave, without whom she would not permit them to walk in the town, the brethren went to mass in the big church, which once had been a mosque, wearing pilgrims' robes over their mail.

"Do you not accompany us, who are of the faith?" asked Wulf.

"No," answered Masouda, "I am in no mood to make confession. This day I count my beads at home."

So they went alone and, mingling with a crowd of humble persons at the back of the church, which was large and dim, watched the knights and priests of various nations struggling for precedence of place beneath the dome. Also, they heard the bishop of the town preach a sermon from which they learnt much. He spoke at length of the great coming war with Saladin, whom he named Anti-Christ. Moreover, he prayed them all to compose their differences and prepare for that awful struggle, lest in the end the Cross of their Master should be trampled under foot of the Saracen, His soldiers slain, and His people slaughtered or driven into the sea—words of warning that were received in heavy silence. The bishop closed his message by reminding the worshippers that the Pope had declared that all those who fought and died to defend Jerusalem and the Church of the Holy Sepulcher would receive "Remission of all sins, past and present."

"Four full days have gone by. Let us ask our hostess if she has any news for us," said Wulf as they walked back to the inn.

"Aye, we will ask her," answered Godwin.

As it chanced, there was no need, for when they entered their chamber they found Masouda standing in the center of it, apparently lost in thought.

"I have come to speak with you," she said, looking up. "Do you still wish to visit the Sheik Al-Jebal?"

They answered, "Yes."

"Good. I have leave for you to go; but I counsel you not to go, since it is dangerous. Let us be open with one another. I know your object. I knew it an hour before you ever set foot upon this shore, and that is why you were brought to my house. You would seek the help of the lord Sinan against Saladin, from whom you hope to rescue a certain great lady of his blood who is your kinswoman and whom both of you desire in marriage. You see, I have learned that also. Well, this land is full of spies, who travel to and from Europe and make report of all things to those who pay them enough. For instance—I can say it, as you will not see him again—the trader Thomas, with whom you stayed in this house, is such a spy. To him your story has been passed on by other spies in England, and he passed it on to me."

"Are then you a spy, also, as the porter called you?" asked Wulf outright.

"I am what I am," she answered coldly. Perhaps I also have sworn oaths and serve as you serve. Who my master is or why I do so is naught to you. But I like you well, and we have ridden together—a wild ride. Therefore I warn you, though perhaps I should not say so much, that the lord Al-Jebal is one who takes payment for what he gives, and—that this business may cost you your lives."

"You warned us against Saladin, also," said Godwin, "so what is left to us if we may dare a visit to neither?"

She shrugged her shoulders. "To take service under one of the great Frankish lords and wait a chance that will never come. Or, better still, to sew some cockle shells into your hats, go home as holy men who have made the pilgrimage, marry the richest wives that you can find, and forget Masouda the widow, and Al-Jebal and Saladin and the lady about whom he has dreamed a dream. Only then," she added in a changed voice, "remember, you must leave the horses Flame and Smoke behind you."

"We wish to ride those horses," said Wulf lightly, while Godwin turned on her with anger in his eyes.

"You seem to know our story," he said, "and the mission to which we are sworn. What sort of knights do you think us, then, that you offer us counsel that is fitter for those spies from whom you learn your tidings? You talk of our lives. Well, we hold our lives in trust, and when they are asked of us we will yield them up, having done all that we may do."

"Well spoken," answered Masouda. "I would have thought less of you had you said otherwise. But why must you go to Al-Jebal?"

"Because our uncle at his death bade us so to do without fail, and having no other counsel we will take what comes our way."

"Well spoken, again! Then to Al-Jebal you shall go, and let come what may—to all three of us!"

"To all three of us?" said Wulf. "What, then, is your part in this matter?"

"I do not know, but perhaps more than you think. At least, I must be your guide."

"Do you mean to betray us?" asked Wulf bluntly.

She drew herself up and looked him in the eyes till he grew red, then said, "Ask your brother if he thinks that I mean to betray you. No, I mean to save you, if I can, and it comes into my mind that before all is done you will need saving, who speak so roughly to those who would befriend you. No, answer not; it is not strange that you should doubt.

"Pilgrims to the fearful shrine of Al-Jebal, if it pleases you, we will ride at nightfall. Do not trouble about food and such matters. I will make preparation, but we go alone and secretly. Take only your arms and what garments you may need; the rest I will store, and for it give you my receipt. Now I go to make things ready. See, I pray of you, that the horses Flame and Smoke are saddled by sunset."

At sundown, accordingly, the brethren stood waiting in their room. They were fully armed beneath their rough pilgrims' robes, even to the bucklers that had been hidden in their baggage. Also the saddle-bags of carpet that Masouda had given them were packed with such things as they must take, the rest having been handed over to her keeping.

Presently, the door opened, and a young man stood before them clothed in a simple hooded cloak, or burnoose, which is common in the East.

"What do you want?" asked Godwin.

"I want you, brothers Peter and John," was the reply, and they saw that the slim young man was Masouda. "What! You English innocents, do you not know a woman through a camel-hair cloak?" she added as she led the way to the stable. "Well, so much the better, for it shows that my disguise is good. Henceforth be pleased to forget the widow Masouda and, until we reach the land of Al-Jebal, to remember that I am your servant, a half-breed from Jaffa named David, of no religion—or of all."

In the stable the horses stood saddled, and near to them another—a good Arab—and two laden Cyprian mules, but no attendant was to be seen. They brought them out and mounted, Masouda riding like a man and leading the mules, of which the head of one was tied to the tail of the other. Five minutes later they were clear of Beirut, and through the solemn twilight hush, followed the road whereon they had tested the horses, towards the Dog River, three leagues away, which Masouda said they would reach by moonrise.

Soon it grew very dark, and she rode alongside of them to show them the path, but they did not talk much. Wulf asked her who would take care of the inn while she was absent, to which she answered sharply that the inn would take care of itself, and no more. Picking their way along the stony road at a slow amble, they crossed the bed of two streams then almost dry, till at length they heard running water from the slow wash of the sea to their left, where Masouda told them to halt. So they waited until the moon rose in a clear sky, revealing a wide river in front, the pale ocean a hundred feet beneath them to the left, and to the right great mountains, along the face of which their path was cut. So bright was it that Godwin could see strange shapes carved on the sheer face of the rock, and beneath them writing which he could not read.

"What are these?" he asked Masouda.

"The tablets of kings," she answered, "whose names are written in your Holy Book, who ruled Syria and Egypt thousands of years ago. They were great in their day when they took this land, greater even than Saladin, and now these images which they set upon this rock are all that is left of them."

Godwin and Wulf stared at the weather-worn sculptures, and in the silence of that moonlit place there arose in their minds a vision of the mighty armies of different tongues and peoples who had stood in their pride on this road and looked upon yonder river and the great stone wolf that guarded it, which wolf, so said the legend, howled at the approach of foes. But now he howled no more, for he lay headless beneath the waters, and there he lies to this day. Well, they were dead, every one of them, and even their deeds were forgotten, and oh! How small the thought of it made them feel, these two young men bent upon a desperate quest in a strange and dangerous land. Masouda read what was passing in their hearts and, as they came to the brink of the river, pointed to the bubbles that chased each other towards the sea, bursting and forming again before their eyes.

"Such are we," she said briefly; "but the ocean is always yonder, and the river is always here, and of fresh bubbles there will always be a plenty. So dance on life's water while you may, in the sunlight, in the moonlight, beneath the storm, beneath the stars, for ocean calls and bubbles burst. Now follow me, for I know the ford, and at this season the stream is not deep. Pilgrim Peter, ride you at my side in case I should be washed from the saddle; and pilgrim John, come you behind, and if they hang back, prick the mules with your sword point."

Thus, then, they entered the river, which many might have feared to do at night, and, although once or twice the water rose to their saddles and the mules were stubborn in the swift stream, in the end gained the further bank in safety. In this manner they pursued their path through the mountains till at length the sun rose and they found themselves in a lonely land where no one was to be seen. Here they halted in a grove of oaks, dismounted their animals, tethered and fed them with barley that they had brought upon a mule, and ate of the food that Masouda had provided. Then, having secured the beasts, they lay down to sleep, all three of them, since Masouda said that there was nothing to fear at this spot. They were all weary, and slept on till the heat of noon was past, when once more they fed the horses and mules, and having dined themselves, set forward upon their way.

Now their road—if road it could be called, for they could see none—ran ever upwards through rough, mountainous country, where seemed to dwell neither man nor beast. At sunset they halted again, and at moonrise went forward till the night turned towards morning, when they came to a place where was a little cave. Before they reached this spot, the silence of those lonely hills was broken by a sound of roaring, not very near to them, but so loud and so long that it echoed and re-echoed from the cliff. At it the horses Flame and Smoke pricked their ears and trembled, while the mules strove to break away and run back.

"What is that?" asked Wulf, who had never heard its like.

"Lions," answered Masouda. "We draw near the country where there are many of them, and therefore shall do well to halt presently, since it is best to pass through that land in daylight."

So when they came to the cave, having heard no more of the lion, or lions, they unsaddled there, purposing to put the horses into it, where they would be safe from the attack of any such ravening beast. But when they tried to do this, Smoke and Flame spread out their nostrils and, setting their feet firm before them, refused to enter the place, about which there was an evil smell.

"Perhaps jackals have been here," said Masouda. "Let us tether them all in the open."

This then they did, building a fire in front of them with dry wood that lay about in plenty, for here grew somber cedar trees. The brethren sat by this fire; but, the night being hot, Masouda laid herself down about fifteen paces away under a cedar tree, which grew almost in front of the mouth of the cave, and slept, being tired after her long ride. Wulf slept also, since Godwin had agreed to keep watch for the first part of the night.

For an hour or more he sat close by the horses and noted that they fed uneasily and would not lie down. Soon, however, he was lost in his own thoughts, and, as he heard no more of the lions, fell to wondering over the strangeness of their journey and of what the end of it might be. He wondered also about Masouda, who she was, how she came to know so much, why she befriended them if she really was a friend, and other things—for instance, of that leap over the sunken stream; and whether—no, surely he had been mistaken; her eyes had never looked at him like that. Why, he was sleeping at his post, and the eyes in the darkness yonder were not those of a woman. Women's eyes were not green and gold; they did not grow large, then lessen and vanish away.

Godwin sprang to his feet. In a moment, after he roused himself, he saw no more eyes. He had dreamed; that was all. So he took cedar boughs and threw them onto the fire, where soon they flared gloriously. After this was done he sat down again close to Wulf, who was lost in heavy slumber.

The night was very still and the silence so deep that it pressed upon him like a weight. He could bear it no longer and, rising, began to walk up and down in front of the cave, drawing his sword and holding it in his hand as sentries do. Masouda lay upon the ground, with her head pillowed on a saddle-bag, and the moonlight fell through the cedar boughs upon her face. Godwin stopped to look at it, and wondered that he had never noted before how beautiful she was. Perhaps it was but the soft and silvery light that clothed those delicate features with so much mystery and charm. She might be dead, not sleeping; but even as he thought this, life came into her face, color stole up beneath the pale, olive-hued skin, the red lips opened, seeming to mutter some words, and she stretched out her rounded arms as though to clasp a vision of her dream.

Godwin turned aside; it seemed not right to watch her thus, although in truth he had only come to know that she was safe. He went back to the fire and, lifting a cedar bough, which blazed like a torch in his left hand, was about to lay it down again on the center of the flame, when suddenly he heard the sharp and terrible cry of a woman in an agony of pain or fear, and at the same moment the horses and mules began to plunge and snort. In an instant, the blazing bough still in his hand, he was back by the cave, and lo! There before him, the form of Masouda hanging from its jaws, stood a great yellow beast, which, although he had never seen its like, he knew must be a lioness. It was heading for the cave then, catching sight of him, turned and bounded away in the direction of the fire, purposing to re-enter the wood beyond.

But the woman in its mouth slowed it and, running swiftly, Godwin came face to face with the brute just opposite the fire.

He hurled the burning bough at it, whereon it dropped Masouda and, rearing itself straight upon its hind legs, stretched out its claws and seemed about to fall on him. For this Godwin did not wait. He was afraid, indeed, who had never before fought lions, but he knew that he must do or die. Therefore, he charged straight at it, and with all the strength of his strong arm drove his long sword into the yellow breast, till it seemed to him that the steel vanished and he could see nothing but the hilt.

Then a shock, a sound of furious snarling, and down he went to earth beneath a soft and heavy weight, and there his senses left him.

When they came back again something soft was still upon his face; but this proved to be only the hand of Masouda, who bathed his brow with a cloth dipped in water, while Wulf rubbed his hands. Godwin sat up and, in the light of the new risen sun, saw a dead lioness lying before him, its breast still transfixed with his own sword.

"So I saved you," he said faintly.

"Yes, you saved me," answered Masouda, and kneeling down she kissed his feet; then rising again, with her long, soft hair wiped away the blood that was running from a wound in his arm.

Chapter X
On Board the Galley

Rosamund was led from the hall of Steeple, through the meadow, down to the quay where a great boat waited—the very boat of which the brethren had found an impression in the mud. In this the raiders embarked, placing their dead and wounded, with one or two to tend them, in the fishing skiff that had belonged to her father. Once this skiff was secured to the stern of the boat, they pushed off, and in utter silence rowed down the creek till they reached the tidal stream of the Blackwater, where they turned their bow seawards. Through the thick night and the falling snow slowly they felt their way along, sometimes rowing, sometimes drifting, while the false palmer Nicholas steered them. The journey proved dangerous, for they could scarcely see the shore, although they kept as close to it as they dared.

The end of it was that they grounded on a mud bank, and, do what they would, could not thrust themselves free. Now hope rose in the heart of Rosamund, who sat still as a statue in the middle of the boat, the prince Hassan at her side and the armed men—twenty or thirty of them—all around her. Perhaps, she thought, they would remain stuck there till daybreak, and be seen and rescued when the brethren woke from their drugged sleep. But Hassan read her mind, and said to her gently enough, "Be not deceived, lady, for I must tell you that if the worst comes to the worst, we shall place you in the little skiff and go on, leaving the rest to take their chance."

As it happened, at the full tide they floated off the bank and drifted with the ebb down towards the sea. At the first break of dawn she looked up, and there, looming large in the mist, laid a galley, anchored in the mouth of the river. Giving thanks to Allah for their safe arrival, the band brought her aboard and led her towards the cabin. On the poop stood a tall man, who was commanding the sailors that they should get up the anchor. As she came he advanced to her, bowing and saying, "Lady Rosamund, thus you find me once more, who doubtless you never thought to see again."

She looked at him in the faint light, and her blood went cold. It was the knight Lozelle.

"You here, Sir Hugh?" she gasped.

"Where you are, there I am," he answered, with a sneer upon his coarse, handsome face. "Did I not swear that it should be so, beauteous Rosamund, after your saintly cousin worsted me in the fray?"

"You here?" she repeated, "you, a Christian knight, and in the pay of Saladin!"

"In the pay of anyone who leads me to you, Rosamund." Then, seeing the emir Hassan approach, he turned to give some orders to the sailors, and she passed on to the cabin and in her agony fell upon her knees.

When Rosamund sat up, she felt that the ship was moving, and, desiring to look one last time on Essex land, went out again upon the poop, where Hassan and Sir Hugh placed themselves, one upon either side of her. Then it was that she saw the tower of St. Peter's on the Wall and her cousins seated on horseback in front of it, the light of the risen sun shining upon their mail. Also, she saw Wulf spur his horse into the sea, and faintly heard his great cry of "Fear not! We follow, we follow!"

A thought came to her, and she sprang towards the bulwark; but they were watching and held her, so that all that she could do was to throw up her arms in token.

Now the wind caught the sail, and the ship went forward swiftly, so that soon she lost sight of them. Then in her grief and rage Rosamund turned upon Sir Hugh Lozelle and beat him with bitter words till he shrank before her.

"Coward and traitor!" she said. "So it was you who planned this, knowing every secret of our home, where often you were a guest! You who for Paynim gold have murdered my father, not daring to show your face before his sword, but hanging like a thief upon the coast, ready to receive what braver men had stolen. Oh! May God avenge his blood and me on you, false knight—false to Him and me and faith and honor—as avenge He will! Heard you not what my kinsman called to me? 'We follow. We follow!' Yes, they follow, and their swords—those swords you feared to look on—shall yet pierce your heart and give up your soul to your master Satan," and she paused, trembling with her righteous wrath. Hassan was sitting nearby and stared at her and declared, "By Allah, a princess indeed! So have I seen Saladin look in his rage. Yes, and she has his very eyes."

But Sir Hugh answered in a thick voice, "Let them follow—one or both. I fear them not, and out there my foot will not slip in the snow."

"Then I say that it shall slip in the sand or on a rock," she answered and, turning, fled to the cabin and cast herself down and wept till she thought that her heart would break.

Well might Rosamund weep whose beloved sire was slain, who was torn from her home to find herself in the power of a man she hated. Yet there was hope for her. Hassan, Eastern trickster as he might be, was her friend; and her uncle, Saladin, at least, would never wish that she should be shamed. But Saladin was far away, and her home lay behind her, and her cousins and lovers were eating out their hearts upon that fading shore. And she—one woman alone—was on this ship with the evil man Lozelle, and there were none except pagans to protect her, none save them—and God, who had permitted that such things should be.

The ship swayed, then she grew sick and faint. Hassan brought her food with his own hands, but she loathed it who only desired to die. The day turned to night, the night turned to day again, and always Hassan brought her food and strove to comfort her, till at length she remembered no more.

Then came a long, long sleep, and in the sleep dreams of her father standing with his face to the foe and sweeping them down with his long sword as a sickle sweeps corn—of her father felled by the pilgrim knave, dying upon the floor of his own house, and saying "God will guard you. His will be done." Dreams of Godwin and Wulf also fighting to save her, and between the dreams blackness.

Rosamund awoke to feel the sun streaming warmly through the shutter of her cabin, and to see a woman who held a cup in her hand, watching her—a stout woman of middle age with a kind face. She looked around her and remembered all. So she was still in the ship.

"Where did you come from?" she asked the woman.

"From France, lady. This ship put in at Marseilles, and there I was hired to nurse one who lay sick, which suited me very well, as I wished to go to Jerusalem to seek my husband, and good money was offered me. Still, had I known that they were all Saracens on this ship, I am not sure that I would have come—that is, except the captain, Sir Hugh, and the palmer Nicholas; though what they, or you either, are doing in such company I cannot guess."

"What is your name?" asked Rosamund as she stretched out her arms.

"Marie—Marie Bouchet. My husband is a fishmonger, or was, until one of those crusading priests got hold of him and took him off to kill Paynims and save his soul, much against my will. Well, I promised him that if he did not return in five years I would come to look for him. So here I am, but where he may be is another matter."

"It is brave of you to go," said Rosamund, and then added by an afterthought, "How long is it since we left Marseilles?"

Marie counted on her fat fingers, and answered:

"Five—nearly six weeks. You have been wandering in your mind all that time, talking of many strange things, and we have called at three ports. I forget their names, but the last one was an island with a beautiful harbor. Now, in about twenty days, if all goes well, we will reach another island called Cyprus. But you must not talk so much; you must sleep. The Saracen called Hassan, who is a clever doctor, told me so."

So Rosamund slept, and from that time forward, floating on the calm Mediterranean Sea, her strength began to come back again rapidly, who was young and strong in body and constitution. Three days later she was helped to the deck, where the first man she saw was Hassan, who came forward to greet her with many Eastern salutations and joy written on his dark, wrinkled face.

"I give thanks to Allah for your sake and my own," he said. "For yours that you still live whom I thought would die, and for myself that had you died your life would have been required at my hands by Saladin, my master."

"If so, he should have blamed Azrael, not you," answered Rosamund, smiling; then suddenly turned cold, for before her was Sir Hugh Lozelle, who also thanked Heaven that she had recovered. She listened to him coldly, and then he went away, but soon was at her side again. Indeed, she could never be free from him, for whenever she appeared on deck he was there, nor could he be repelled, since neither silence nor rebuff would stir him. Always he sat near, talking in his false, hateful voice, and devouring her with his greedy eyes, which she could feel fixed upon her face. With him often was his jackal, the false palmer Nicholas, who crawled about her like a snake and strove to flatter her, but to this man she would never speak a word.

At last she could bear it no longer, and when her health had returned to her, summoned Hassan to her cabin.

"Tell me, Prince," she said, "who rules upon this vessel?"

"Three people," he answered, bowing. "The knight, Sir Hugh Lozelle, who, as a skilled navigator, is the captain and rules the sailors; I, who rule the fighting men; and you, Princess, who rule us all."

"Then I command that the rogue named Nicholas shall not be allowed to approach me. Is it to be borne that I must associate with my father's murderer?"

"I fear that in that business we all had a hand; nevertheless, your order shall be obeyed. To tell you the truth, lady, I hate the fellow, who is but a common spy."

"I desire, also," went on Rosamund, "to speak no more with Sir Hugh Lozelle."

"That is more difficult," said Hassan, "since he is the captain whom my master ordered me to obey in all things that have to do with the ship."

"I have nothing to do with the ship," answered Rosamund; "and surely the princess of Baalbec, if so I am, may choose her own companions. I wish to see more of you and less of Sir Hugh Lozelle."

"I am honored," replied Hassan, "and will do my best."

For some days after this, although he was always watching her, Lozelle approached Rosamund but seldom, and whenever he did so he found Hassan at her side, or rather standing behind her like a guard.

At length, as it happened, the prince was taken with a sickness from drinking bad water, which held him to his bed for some days, and then Lozelle found his opportunity. Rosamund strove to keep her cabin to avoid him, but the heat of the summer sun in the Mediterranean drove her out of it to a place beneath an awning on the poop, where she sat with the woman Marie. Here Lozelle approached her, pretending to bring her food or to inquire after her comfort, but she would answer him nothing. At length, since Marie could understand what he said in French, he addressed her in Arabic, which he spoke well, but she feigned not to understand him. Then he used the English tongue as it was used among the common people in Essex, and said, "Lady, how sorely you misjudge me. What is my crime against you? I am an Essex man of good lineage, who met you in Essex and learnt to love you there. Is that a crime, in one who is not poor, who, moreover, was knighted for his deeds by no mean hand? Your father said me nay, and you said me nay, and, stung by my disappointment and his words—for he called me sea-thief and I talked as I should not have done, swearing that I would wed you yet in spite of all. For this I was called to account with justice, when your cousin, the young knight Godwin, who was then a squire, struck me in the face. Well, he worsted and wounded me, fortune favoring him, and I departed with my vessel to the East, for that is my business, to trade between Syria and England.

"Now, as it chanced, there being peace at the time between the sultan and the Christians, I visited Damascus to buy merchandise. Whilst I was there Saladin sent for me and asked if it were true that I belonged to a part of England called Essex. When I answered yes, he asked if I knew Sir Andrew D'Arcy and his daughter. Again I said yes, whereon he told me that strange tale of your kinship to him, of which I had heard already; also a still stranger tale of some dream that he had dreamed concerning you, which made it necessary that you should be brought to his court, where he was minded to raise you to great honor. In the end, he offered to hire my finest ship for a large sum, if I would sail it to England to fetch you; but he did not tell me that any force was to be used, and I, on my part, said that I would lift no hand against you or your father, nor indeed have I done so."

"Who remembered the swords of Godwin and Wulf," broke in Rosamund scornfully, "and preferred that braver men should face them."

"Lady," answered Lozelle, coloring, "hitherto none have accused me of a lack of courage. Of your courtesy, listen, I pray you. I did wrong to enter on this business; but lady, it was love for you that drove me to it, for the thought of this long voyage in your company was a bait I could not withstand."

"Paynim gold was the bait you could not withstand—that is what you mean. Be brief, I pray you. I weary of this talk."

"Lady, you are harsh and misjudge me, as I will show," and he looked about him cautiously. "Within a week from now, if all goes well, we cast anchor at Limazol in Cyprus, to take in food and water before we run to a secret port near Antioch, whence you are to be taken overland to Damascus, avoiding all cities of the Franks. Now, the emperor Isaac of Cyprus is my friend, and over him Saladin has no power. Once in his court, you would be safe until such time as you found opportunity to return to England. This, then, is my plan—that you should escape from the ship at night as I can arrange."

"And what is your payment," she asked, "Who are a merchant knight?"

"My payment, lady, is—yourself. In Cyprus we will be wed—oh! Think before you answer. At Damascus many dangers await you; with me you will find safety and a Christian husband who loves you well—so well that for your sake he is willing to lose his ship and, what is more, to break faith with Saladin, whose arm is long."

"Have done," she said coldly. "Sooner will I trust myself to an honest Saracen than to you, Sir Hugh. Yes, sooner would I take death than you, who for your own base ends devised the plot that brought about my father's murder and me to slavery. Have done, I say, and never dare again to speak of love to me," and rising, she walked past him to her cabin.

But Lozelle, looking after her, commented to himself, "Nay, fair lady, I have but begun; nor will I forget your bitter words, for which you shall pay the merchant knight in kisses."

From her cabin Rosamund sent a message to Hassan, saying that she desired to speak with him.

He came, still pale with illness, and asked her will. She proceeded to tell him what had passed between Lozelle and herself, demanding his protection against this man. Hassan's eyes flashed.

"Yonder he stands," he said, "alone. Will you come and speak to him?"

She bowed her head and, giving her his hand, he led her to the poop.

"Sir Captain," he began, addressing Lozelle, "the princess here tells me a strange story—that you have dared to offer your love to her, by Allah! To her, a niece of Saladin."

"What of it, Sir Saracen?" answered Lozelle, insolently. "Is not a Christian knight a fit mate for the blood of an Eastern chief? Had I offered her less than marriage, you might have spoken."

"You!" answered Hassan, with rage in his low voice, "you, huckstering thief and renegade, who swear by Mahomet in Damascus and by your prophet Jesus in England—ay, deny it not, I have heard you, as I have heard that rogue, Nicholas, your servant. You, her fit mate? Why, were it not that you must guide this ship, and that my master bade me not to quarrel with you till your task was done, I would behead you now and cut from your throat the tongue that dared to speak such words," and as he spoke he gripped the handle of his scimitar.

Lozelle quailed before his fierce eyes, for well he knew Hassan, and knew also that if it came to fighting his sailors were no match for the emir and his picked Saracens.

"When our duty is done you shall answer for those words," he said, trying to look brave.

"By Allah! I hold you to the promise," replied Hassan. "Before Saladin I will answer for them when and where you will, as you shall answer to him for your treachery."

"Of what, then, am I accused?" asked Lozelle. "Of loving the lady Rosamund, as do all men—perhaps yourself, old and withered as you are, among them?"

"Ay, and for that crime I will repay you, old and withered as I am, Sir Renegade. But with Saladin, you have another score to settle—that by promising her escape you tried to seduce her from this ship, where you were sworn to guard her, saying that you would find her refuge among the Greeks of Cyprus."

"Were this true," replied Lozelle, "the sultan might have cause of complaint against me. But it is not true. Hearken, since speak I must. The lady Rosamund prayed me to do this deed, and I told her that for my honor's sake it is not possible, although it was true that I loved her now as always and would dare much for her. Then she said that if I did but save her from you Saracens, I should not go without my reward, since she would wed me. Again, although it cost me sore, I answered that it might not be, but when once I had brought my ship to land, I was her true knight, and being freed of my oath, would do my best to save her."

"Princess, you hear," said Hassan, turning to Rosamund. "What say you?"

"I say," she answered coldly, "that this man lies to save himself. I say, moreover, that I answered to him that sooner would I die than that he should lay a finger on me."

"I hold also that he lies," said Hassan. "Nay; unclasp that dagger if you would live to see another sun. Here, I will not fight with you, but Saladin shall learn all this case when we reach his court, and judge between the word of the princess of Baalbec and of his hired servant, the false Frank and pirate, Sir Hugh Lozelle."

"Let him learn it—when we reach his court," answered Lozelle, with meaning; then added, "Have you aught else to say to me, Prince Hassan? Because if not, I must be attending to the business of my ship, which you suppose that I was about to abandon to win a lady's smile."

"Only this, that the ship is the sultan's and not yours, for he bought it from you, and that henceforth this lady will be guarded day and night, and doubly guarded when we come to the shores of Cyprus, where it seems that you have friends. Understand and remember."

"I understand, and certainly I will remember," replied Lozelle, and so they parted.

"I think," said Rosamund, when he had gone, "that we shall be fortunate if we land safe in Syria."

"That was in my mind, also, lady. I think, too, that I have forgot my wisdom, but my heart rose against this man and, being still weak from sickness, I lost my judgment and spoke what was in my heart, who would have done better to wait. Now, perhaps, it will be best to kill him, if it were not that he alone has the skill to navigate the ship, which is a trade that he has followed from his youth. Nay, let it go as Allah wills. He is just, and will bring the matter to judgment in due time."

"Yes, but to what judgment?" asked Rosamund.

"I hope to that of the sword," answered Hassan, as he bowed and left her.

From that time forward armed men watched all the night through before Rosamund's cabin, and when she walked the deck armed men walked after her. Nor was she troubled by Lozelle, who sought to speak with her no more, or to Hassan either. Only with the man Nicholas he spoke much.

Several days later, upon one golden evening—for Lozelle was a skillful pilot, one of the best, indeed, who sailed those seas—they came to the shores of Cyprus and cast anchor. Before them, stretched along the beach, lay the white town of Limazol, with palm trees standing up amidst its gardens, while beyond the fertile plain rose the mighty mountain range of Trooidos. Sick and weary of the endless ocean, Rosamund gazed with rapture at this green and beauteous shore, the home of so much history, and sighed to think that on it she might set no foot. Lozelle saw her look and heard her sigh and, as he climbed into the boat which had come out to row him into the harbor, mocked her, saying, "Will you not change your mind, lady, and come with me to visit my friend, the emperor Isaac? I swear that his court is a festive place, not packed full of sour Saracens or pilgrims thinking of their souls. In Cyprus they only make pilgrimages to Paphos yonder, where Venus was born from out of the foam and has reigned since the beginning of the world—ay, and will reign until its end."

Rosamund made no answer and Lozelle, descending into the boat, was rowed toward shore through the breakers by the dark-skinned, Cyprian oarsmen, who wore flowers in their hair and sang as they labored at the oars.

For ten whole days they rolled off Limazol, although the weather was fair and the wind blew straight for Syria. When Rosamund asked why they waited there so long, Hassan stamped his foot and said it was because the emperor refused to supply them with more food or water than was sufficient for their daily need, unless he, Hassan, would land and travel to an inland town called Nicosia, where his court lay, and there do homage to him. This, scenting a trap, he feared to do, nor could they put out to sea without provisions.

"Cannot Sir Hugh Lozelle see to it?" asked Rosamund.

"Doubtless, if he will," answered Hassan, grinding his teeth; "but he swears that he is powerless."

So there they bode day after day, baked by the sweltering summer sun and rocked to and fro on the long ocean rollers till their hearts grew sick within them, and their bodies also, for some of them were seized with a fever common to the shores of Cyprus, of which two died. Now and again some officer would come off from the shore with Lozelle and a little food and water, and bargain with them, saying that before their wants were supplied the prince Hassan must visit the emperor and bring with him the fair lady who was his passenger, whom he desired to see.

Hassan would answer no, and double the guard about Rosamund, for at night boats appeared that cruised round them. In the daytime also bands of men, fantastically dressed in silks, and with them women, could be seen riding to and fro upon the shore and staring at them, as though they were striving to make up their minds to attack the ship.

Then Hassan armed his grim Saracens and ordered them to stand in line upon the bulwarks, drawn scimitar in hand, a sight that seemed to frighten the Cypriotes—at least they always rode away towards the great square tower of Colossi.

At length, Hassan could bear it no more. One morning, Lozelle came off from Limazol, where he slept at night, bringing with him three Cyprian lords, who visited the ship—not to bargain as they pretended, but to obtain sight of the beauteous princess Rosamund. Thereon the common talk began of homage that must be paid before food was granted, failing which the emperor would bid his seamen capture the ship. Hassan listened a while, then suddenly issued an order that the lords should be seized.

"Now," he said to Lozelle, "bid your sailors haul up the anchor, and let us be gone for Syria."

"But," answered the knight; "we have neither food nor water for more than one day."

"I care not," answered Hassan, "we may as well die of thirst and starvation at sea as rot here with fever. What we can bear these Cyprian gallants can bear, also. Bid the sailors lift the anchor and hoist the sail, or I loose my scimitars among them."

Now Lozelle stamped and foamed, but without avail, so he turned to the three lords, who were pale with fear, and said, "Which will you do: find food and water for this ship, or put to sea without them, which is but to die?"

They answered that they would go ashore and supply all that was needful.

"Nay," said Hassan, "you remain here until it comes."

In the end, then, this happened, for one of the lords happened to be a nephew of the emperor, who, when he learned that he was captive, sent supplies in plenty. Thus it came about that, the Cyprian lords having been sent back with the last empty boat, within two days they were at sea again.

Rosamund soon noticed that the spy, Nicholas, was missing, and told Hassan, who made inquiry of Captain Lozelle. He said that he went ashore and vanished there on the first day of their landing in Cyprus, though whether he had been killed in some brawl, or fallen sick, or hidden himself away, he did not know. Hassan shrugged his shoulders, and Rosamund was glad enough to be rid of him, but in her heart she wondered for what evil purpose Nicholas had left the ship.

When the galley was one day out from Cyprus, steering for the coast of Syria, they fell into a calm such as is common in those seas in summer. This calm lasted eight whole days, during which they made but little progress. At length, when all were weary of staring at the glass-like sea, a wind sprang up that grew gradually to a gale blowing towards Syria, and before it they flew along swiftly. Worse and stronger grew that gale, till on the evening of the second day, when they seemed in danger of being capsized, they saw a great mountain far away, at the sight of which Lozelle thanked God aloud.

"Are those the mountains near Antioch?" asked Hassan.

"Nay," he answered, "they are more than fifty miles south of them, between Ladikiya and Jebela. There, by the mercy of Heaven, is a good haven, for I have visited it, where we can lie till this storm is past."

"But we are steering for Darbesak, not for a haven near Jebela, which is a Frankish port," answered Hassan, angrily.

"Then put the ship about and steer there yourself," said Lozelle, "and I promise you this, that within two hours every one of you will be dead at the bottom of the sea."

Hassan considered. It was true, for then the waves would strike them broadside, and they would fill and sink.

"On your head be it," he answered shortly.

The darkness fell, and by the light of the great lantern at their prow they saw the white seas hiss past as they drove towards shore beneath bare masts, for they dared hoist no sail.

All that night they pitched and rolled, till the stoutest of them fell sick. Some prayed to God and others to Allah that they might have light by which to enter the harbor. At length, they saw the top of the loftiest mountain grow luminous with the coming dawn, although the land itself was still lost in shadow, and saw also that it seemed to be towering almost over them.

"Take courage," cried Lozelle, "I think that we are saved," and he hoisted a second lantern at his masthead—why, they did not know.

After this the sea began to fall, only to grow rough again for a while as they crossed some bar, to find themselves in calm water, and on either side of them what appeared in the dim, uncertain light to be the bush-clad banks of a river. For a while they ran on, till Lozelle called in a loud voice to the sailors to let the anchor go and sent a messenger to say that all might rest now, as they were safe. So they all laid down and tried to sleep.

But Rosamund could not sleep. Several minutes later she rose and, throwing on her cloak, went to the door of the cabin and looked at the beauty of the mountains, rosy with the newborn light, and at the misty surface of the harbor. It was a lonely place—at least, she could see no town or house, although they were lying not fifty yards from the tree-hidden shore. As she stood in this place, she heard the sound of boats being rowed through the mist, and noticed that three or four of these were quietly approaching the ship. She also perceived that Lozelle, who stood alone upon the deck, was watching their approach. Now the first boat was secured and a man in the prow rose up and began to speak to Lozelle in a low voice. As he did so the hood fell back from his head, and Rosamund saw the face. It was that of the spy Nicholas! For a moment she stood amazed, for they had left this man in Cyprus; then understanding came to her, and she cried aloud, "Treachery! Prince Hassan, there is treachery!"

As the words left her lips, fierce, wild-looking men began to scramble aboard at the low end of the galley, to which boat after boat was secured. The Saracens also tumbled from the benches where they slept and ran aft to the deck where Rosamund was, all except one of them, who was cut off in the prow of the ship. Prince Hassan appeared, too, scimitar in hand, clad in his jeweled turban and coat of mail, but without his cloak, shouting orders as he came, while the hired crew of the ship flung themselves upon their knees and begged for mercy. To him Rosamund cried out that they were

betrayed and by Nicholas, whom she had seen. Then a huge man, wearing a white burnoose and holding a naked sword in his hand, stepped forward and said in Arabic, "Yield you now, for you are outnumbered and your captain is captured," and he pointed to Lozelle, who was being held by two men while his arms were bound behind him.

"In whose flame do you bid me yield?" asked the prince, glaring about him like a lion in a trap.

"In the dread name of Sinan, in the name of the lord Al-Jebal, O servant of Saladin."

At these words a groan of fear went up even from the brave Saracens, for now they realized that they had to fight with the chief of the dreaded Assassins.

"Is there then war between the sultan and Sinan?" asked Hassan.

"Aye, there is always war. Moreover, you have one with you," and he pointed to Rosamund, "who is dear to Saladin, whom, therefore, my master desires as a hostage."

"How knew you that?" said Hassan, to gain time while his men formed up.

"How does the lord Sinan know all things?" was the answer. "Come, yield, and perhaps he will show you mercy."

"Through spies," hissed Hassan, "such spies as Nicholas, who has come from Cyprus before us, and that Frankish dog who is called a knight," and he pointed to Lozelle. "Nay, we yield not, and here, Assassins, you have to do not with poisons and the knife, but with bare swords and brave men. Ay, and I warn you—and your lord—that Saladin will take vengeance for this deed."

"Let him try it if he wishes to die, who until now has been spared," answered the tall man quietly. Then he said to his followers, "Cut them down, all except the women," for the Frenchwoman, Marie, was now clinging to the arm of Rosamund—"and Emir Hassan, whom I am commanded to bring living to Masyaf."

"Back to your cabin, lady," said Hassan, "and remember that whatever befalls, we have done our best to save you. Ay, and tell it to my lord, that my honor may be clean in his eyes. Now, soldiers of Saladin, fight and die as he has taught you how. The gates of Paradise stand open, and no coward will enter there."

They answered with a fierce, guttural cry. Then, as Rosamund fled to the cabin, the fight began, a hideous combat. On came the Assassins with sword and dagger, striving to storm the deck. Again and again they were beaten back, till the deck seemed full of their corpses. Man by man they fell beneath the curved scimitars, and again and again they charged these men who, when their master ordered, knew neither fear nor pity. But more boatloads came from the shore, and the Saracens were but few, worn also with storm and sickness, so at last Rosamund, peeping beneath her hand, saw that the poop was gained.

Here and there a man fought on until he fell beneath the cruel knives in the midst of the circle of the dead, among them the warrior-prince Hassan. Watching him with fascinated eyes as he strove alone against a host, Rosamund was put in mind of another scene, when her father, also alone, had striven thus against that emir and his soldiers, and even then she thought of the justice of God.

See! His foot slipped on the blood-stained deck. He was down, and ere he could rise again they had thrown cloaks over him, these fierce, silent men who, even with their lives at stake, remembered the command of their captain, to take him living. So living they took him, with not a wound upon his skin, who when he struck them down had never struck back at him lest the command of Sinan should be broken.

Rosamund noted it, and remembering that his command was also that she should be brought to him unharmed, knew that she had no violence to fear at the hands of these cruel murderers. From this thought, and because Hassan still lived, she took such comfort as she might.

"It is finished," said the tall man, in his cold voice. "Cast these dogs into the sea who have dared to disobey the command of Al-Jebal."

So they took them up, dead and living together, and threw them into the water, where they sank, nor did one of the wounded Saracens ask them for mercy. Then they served their own dead likewise, but those that were only wounded they took ashore. This done, the tall man advanced to the cabin and said, "Lady, come, we are ready to start upon our journey."

Having no choice, Rosamund obeyed him. As she went she remembered how from a scene of battle and bloodshed she had been brought aboard that ship to be carried she knew not where, while now she likewise left in a scene of battle and bloodshed to be carried to a place she knew not.

"Oh!" she cried aloud, pointing to the corpses they were hurling into the deep, "ill has it gone with these who stole me, and ill may it go with you also, servant of Al-Jebal."

But the tall man answered nothing as, followed by the weeping Marie and the prince Hassan, he led her to the boat.

Soon they reached the shore, and here they tore Marie from her, nor did Rosamund ever learn what became of her, or whether or not this poor woman found her husband whom she had risked so much to seek.

Chapter XI
The City of Al-Jebal

"Please do not trouble yourself," said Godwin, "it is but a scratch from the beast's claws. I am ashamed that you should put your hair to such vile uses. Give me a little water."

He asked it of Wulf, but Masouda rose without a word and fetched the water, in which she mingled wine. Godwin drank of it and his faintness left him, so that he was able to stand up and move his arms and legs.

"Why," he said, "it is nothing; I was only shaken. That lioness did not hurt me at all."

"But you hurt the lioness," said Wulf, with a laugh. "By St. Chad, a good thrust!" and he pointed to the long sword driven up to the hilt in the brute's breast. "Why, I swear I could not have made a better myself."

"I think it was the lion that thrust," answered Godwin. "I only held the sword straight. Drag it out, Brother, I am still too weak."

So Wulf set his foot upon the breast of the lion and tugged and tugged until he loosened the sword, saying as he strained at it, "Oh! What an Essex hog am I, who slept through it all, never waking until Masouda seized me by the hair, and I opened my eyes to see you upon the ground with this yellow beast crouched on the top of you like a hen on a nest egg. I thought that it was alive and smote it with my sword, which, had I been fully awake, I doubt if I should have found the courage to do. Look," and he pushed the lioness's head with his foot, whereon it twisted round in such a fashion that they perceived for the first time that it only hung to the shoulders by a thread of skin.

"I am glad you did not strike a little harder," said Godwin, "or I would now be in two pieces and drowned in my own blood, instead of in that of this dead brute," and he looked ruefully at his burnoose and hauberk, that were soaked with gore.

"Yes," said Wulf, "I never thought of that. Who would, in such a hurry?"

"Lady Masouda," asked Godwin, "when last I saw you, you were hanging from those jaws. Say, are you hurt?"

"Nay," she answered, "for I wear mail like you, and the teeth glanced on it so that she held me by the cloak only. Come, let us skin the beast, and take its pelt as a present to the lord Al-Jebal."

"Good," said Godwin, "and I shall give you the claws for a necklace."

"Be sure that I will wear them," she answered, and helped Wulf to flay the lioness while he sat by resting. When it was done Wulf went to the little cave and walked into it, to come out again with a bound.

"Why!" he said, "there are more of them in there. I saw their eyes and heard them snarl. Now, give me a burning branch and I will show you, Brother, that you are not the only one who can fight a lion."

"Let be, you foolish man," broke in Masouda. "Doubtless those are her cubs, and if you kill them her mate will follow us for miles; but if they are left safe he will stay to feed them. Come, let us leave this place as swiftly as we can."

So, having shown them the skin of the lion, that they might know it was but a dead thing, at the sight of which they snorted and trembled, they packed it upon one of the mules and rode off slowly into a valley some five miles away. Here, since Godwin needed rest, they stopped all that day and the night which followed, seeing no more of lions, though they watched for them sharply enough. The next morning, having slept well, he was himself again, and they started forward through a desolate country towards a deep cleft, on either side of which stood a tall mountain.

"This is Al-Jebal's gateway," said Masouda, "and tonight we will sleep in the gate, then one day's ride brings us to his city."

So on they rode till, at length, perched upon the sides of the cleft, they saw a castle, a massive building, with high walls, to which they came at sunset. It seemed that they were expected in this place, for men hastened to meet them, who greeted Masouda and eyed the brethren curiously, especially after they had heard of the adventure with the lion. These took them, not into the castle, but to a kind of inn at its back, where they were furnished with food and slept the night.

Next morning they went on again to a hilly country with beautiful and fertile valleys. Through this they rode for two hours, passing on their way several villages, where somber-eyed people were laboring in the fields. From each village, as they drew near to it, horsemen would gallop out and challenge them, whereon Masouda rode forward and spoke with the leader alone. Then he would touch his forehead with his hand and bow his head, and they rode on unmolested.

"See," she said, after they had been stopped for the fourth time, "what chance you had of winning through to Masyaf unguarded. Why, I tell you, brethren, that you would have been dead before ever you passed the gates of the first castle."

Now they rode up a long slope, and at its crest paused to look upon a marvelous scene. Below them stretched a vast plain, full of villages, cornfields, olive groves, and vineyards. In the center of this plain, some fifteen miles away, rose a great mountain, which seemed to be walled all about. Within the wall was a city filled with white, flat-roofed houses that climbed the slopes of the mountain, and on its crest a level space of land covered with trees and a great, many-towered castle surrounded by more houses.

"Behold the home of Al-Jebal, Lord of the Mountain," said Masouda, "where we must sleep tonight. Now, brethren, listen to me. Few strangers who enter that castle come out alive. There is still time; I can take you back as I brought you here. Will you go on?"

"We will go on," they answered with one breath.

"Why? What have you to gain? You seek a certain maiden. Why seek her here whom you say has been taken to Saladin?

Because the Al-Jebal in bygone days swore to befriend one of your blood. But that Al-Jebal is dead, and another of his line rules who took no such oath. How do you know that he will befriend you—how that he will not enslave or kill you? I have power in this land, why or how does not matter, and I can protect you against all that dwell in it as I swear I will, for did not one of you save my life?" and she glanced at Godwin—"all except my lord Sinan, against whom I have no power, for I am his slave."

"He is the enemy of Saladin, and may help us for his hate's sake."

"Yes, he is the enemy of Saladin now more than ever. He may help you or he may not. Also," she added with meaning, "you may not wish the help he offers. Oh!" and there was a note of urgency in her voice, "think, think! For the last time, I pray you think!"

"We have thought," answered Godwin solemnly; "and, whatever chances, we will obey the command of the dead."

She heard and bowed her head in assent, then said, looking up again, "So be it. You are not easily turned from your purpose, and I like that spirit well. But hear my counsel. While you are in this city speak no Arabic and pretend to understand none. Also drink nothing but water, which is good here, for the lord Sinan sets strange wines before his guests, that, if they pass the lips, produce visions and a kind of waking madness in which you might do deeds whereof you were afterwards ashamed. Or you might swear oaths that would sit heavy on your souls, and yet could not be broken except at the cost of life."

"Fear not," answered Wulf. "Water shall be our drink, who have had enough of drugged wines," for he remembered the Christmas feast in the hall at Steeple.

"You, Sir Godwin," went on Masouda, "have about your neck a certain ring which you were foolish enough to show to me, a stranger—a ring with writing on it which none can read save the great men that in this land are called the dais. Well, as it chances, the secret is safe with me; but be wise; say nothing of that ring and let no eye see it."

"Why not?" asked Godwin. "It is the token of our dead uncle to the Al-Jebal."

She looked round her cautiously and replied, "Because it is, or was once, the great Signet, and a day may come when it will save your lives. Doubtless when the lord who is dead thought it gone forever he caused another to be fashioned, so like that I who have had both in my hand could not tell the two apart. To him who holds that ring all gates are open; but to let it be known that you have its double means death. Do you understand?"

They nodded, and Masouda continued, "Lastly—though you may think that this seems much to ask—trust me always, even if I seem to play you false, who for your sakes," and she sighed, "have broken oaths and spoken words for which the punishment is to die by torment. Nay, thank me not, for I do only what I must who am a slave—a slave."

"A slave to whom?" asked Godwin, staring at her.

"To the Lord of all the Mountains," she answered, with a smile that was sweet yet very sad, and without another word spurred on her horse.

"What does she mean," asked Godwin of Wulf, when she was out of hearing, "seeing that if she speaks truth, for our sakes, in warning us against him, Masouda is breaking her fealty to this lord?"

"I do not know, Brother, and I do not seek to know. All her talk may be a part of a plot to blind us, or it may not. Let well enough alone and trust in fortune, say I."

"A good counsel," answered Godwin, and they rode forward in silence.

They crossed the plain, and towards evening came to the wall of the outer city, halting in front of its great gateway. Here, as at the first castle, a band of solemn-looking mounted men came out to meet them, and, having spoken a few words with Masouda, led them over the drawbridge that spanned the first rock-cut moat and through triple gates of iron into the city. Then they passed up a street very steep and narrow, from the roofs and windows of the houses on either side of which hundreds of people—many of whom seemed to be engaged at their evening prayer—watched them go by. At the head of this street they reached another fortified gateway, on the turrets of which, so motionless that at first they took them to be statues cut in stone, stood guards wrapped in long white robes. After discussion, this also was opened to them, and again they rode through triple doors.

Then they saw all the wonder of that place, for between the outer city where they stood and the castle, with its inner town, which was built around and beneath it, yawned a vast gulf over ninety feet in depth. Across this gulf, built of blocks of stone, quite unrailed, and not more than three paces wide, ran a causeway some two hundred yards in length. The causeway was supported upon arches reared up at intervals from the bottom of the gulf.

"Ride on and have no fear," said Masouda. "Your horses are trained to heights, and the mules and mine will follow."

So Godwin, showing nothing in his face of the doubt that he felt in his heart, patted Flame upon the neck, and, after hanging back a little, the horse started lifting its hoofs high and glancing from side to side at the terrible gulf beneath. Where Flame went Smoke knew that he could go, and came on bravely, but snorting a little, while the mules, that did not fear heights so long as the ground was firm beneath their feet, followed. Only Masouda's horse was terrified, backed, and strove to wheel round, till she drove the spur into it. This act caused the beast to regain its focus and it came over at a gallop.

One minute later they were across, and, passing under another gateway, which had broad terraces on either side of it, rode up the long street beyond and entered a great courtyard, around which stood the castle, a vast and frowning fortress. Here a white-robed officer came forward, greeting them with a low bow, and with him servants who assisted them to dismount. These men took the horses to a range of stables on one side of the courtyard, where the brethren followed to see their beasts groomed and fed. Then the officer, who had stood patiently by their side, conducted them through doorways and down passages to the guest chambers; large, stone-roofed rooms, where they found their baggage ready for them. Here Masouda said that she would see them again on the following morning and departed in company with the officer.

Wulf looked round the great vaulted chamber, which, now that the dark had fallen, was lit by flickering lamps set in iron brackets upon the wall, and said, "Well, for my part, I had rather pass the night in a desert among the lions than in this dismal place."

Scarcely were the words out of his lips when curtains swung aside and beautiful women entered, clad in gauzy veils and bearing dishes of food. These they placed upon the ground before them, inviting them to eat with nods and smiles, while others brought basins of scented water, which they poured over their hands. Then they sat down and ate the food that was strange to them, but very pleasant to the taste; and while they ate, women whom they could not see sang sweet songs and played upon harps and lutes. Wine was offered to them also; but of this, remembering Masouda's words, they would not drink, asking by signs for water, which was brought after a little pause.

When their meal was done, the beautiful women bore away the dishes, and black slaves appeared. These men led them to baths such as they had never seen, where they washed first in hot water, then in cold. Afterwards, they were rubbed with spicy-smelling oils and, having been wrapped in white robes, conducted back to their chamber, where they found beds spread for them. On these, being very weary, they lay down, when the strange, sweet music broke out afresh, and to the sound of it they fell asleep.

When they awoke, it was to see the light streaming through the high, latticed windows.

"Did you sleep well, Godwin?" asked Wulf.

"Well enough," answered his brother, "only I dreamed that throughout the night people came and looked at me."

"I dreamed that, also," said Wulf; "moreover, I think that it was not all a dream, since there is a blanket on my bed which was not there when I went to sleep."

Godwin looked at his own, where also was another blanket added, doubtless as the night grew colder in that high place.

"I have heard of enchanted castles," he said; "now I think that we have found one."

"Aye," replied Wulf, "and it is well enough while it lasts."

They rose and dressed themselves, putting on clean garments and their best cloaks that they had brought with them on the mules, after which the veiled women entered the room with breakfast, and they ate. When this was finished, having nothing else to do, they made signs to one of the women that they wished for cloths wherewith to clean their armor, for, as they had been bidden, they pretended to understand no word of Arabic. She nodded and soon returned with a companion carrying leathers and paste in a jar. Nor did they leave them, but, sitting upon the ground, took the shirts of mail and rubbed them till they shone like silver, while Godwin and Wulf polished their helms, spurs, and bucklers, cleansing their swords and daggers also, and sharpening them with a stone which they carried for that purpose.

Now as these women worked, they began to talk to each other in a low voice, and some of their talk, though not all, the brethren understood.

"A handsome pair, truly," said the first. "We should be fortunate if we had such men for husbands, although they are Franks and infidels."

"Aye," answered the other; "and from their likeness they must be twins. Now which of them would you choose?"

Then for a long while they discussed them, comparing them feature by feature and limb by limb, until the brethren felt their faces grow red beneath the sunburn and scrubbed furiously at their armor to show a reason for it. A few minutes later one of the women said, "It was cruel of the lady Masouda to bring these birds into the Master's net. She might have warned them."

"Masouda was ever cruel," answered the other, "who hates all men, which is unnatural. Yet I think if she loved a man she would love him well, and perhaps that might be worse for him than her hate."

"Are these knights spies?" asked the first.

"I suppose so," was the answer, "silly fellows who think that they can spy upon a nation of spies. They would have done better to keep to fighting, at which, doubtless, they are good enough. What will happen to them?"

"What always happens, I suppose—a pleasant time at first; then, if they can be put to no other use, a choice between the faith and the cup. Or, perhaps, as they seem men of rank, they may be imprisoned in the dungeon tower and held to ransom. Yes, yes; it was cruel of Masouda to trick them so, who may be but travelers after all, desiring to see our city."

Just then the curtain was drawn, and through it entered Masouda herself. She was dressed in a white robe that had a dagger worked in red over the left breast, and her long black hair fell upon her shoulders, although it was half hid by the veil, open in front, which hung from her head. Never had they seen her look so beautiful.

"'Greetings, brothers Peter and John. Is this fit work for pilgrims?" she said in French, pointing to the long swords, which they were sharpening.

"Aye," answered Wulf, as they rose and bowed to her, "for pilgrims to this—holy city."

The women who were cleaning the mail bowed also, for it seemed that here Masouda was a person of importance. She took the hauberks from their hands.

"Poorly cleaned," she said sharply. "I think that you girls talk better than you work. Well, they will have to suffice. Help these lords to don them. Fools, that is the shirt of the gray-eyed knight. Give it me; I will be his squire," and she snatched the hauberk from their hands. A moment later, when her back was turned, they glanced at one another.

"Now," she said, when they were fully armed and had donned their mantles, "you brethren look as pilgrims should. Listen, I have a message for you. The Master"—and she bowed her head, as did the women, guessing of whom she spoke— "will receive you in an hour's time, till when, if it please you, we can walk in the gardens, which are worth your seeing."

So they went out with her, and as they passed towards the curtain she whispered: "For your lives' sake, remember all that I have told you—above everything, about the wine and the ring, for if you dream the drink-dream you will be searched. Speak no word to me save of common matters."

In the passage beyond the curtain white-robed guards were standing, armed with spears, who turned and followed them without a word. First they went to the stables to visit Flame and Smoke, which whinnied as they drew near. These they found well-fed and tended—indeed, a company of grooms were gathered round them, discussing their points and beauty, who saluted as the owners of such steeds approached. Leaving the stable, they passed through an archway into the famous gardens, which were said to be the most beautiful in all the East. Beautiful they were indeed, planted with trees, shrubs, and flowers such as are seldom seen, while between fern-clad rocks flowed rills which fell over deep cliffs in waterfalls of foam. In places, the shade of cedars lay so dense that the brightness of day was changed to twilight, but in others the ground was open and carpeted with flowers, which filled the air with perfume. Everywhere grew roses, myrtles, and trees laden with rich fruits, while from all sides came the sound of cooing doves and the voices of many bright-winged birds which flashed from palm to palm.

On they walked, down the sand-strewn paths for a mile or more, accompanied by Masouda and the guard. At length, passing through a brake of whispering, reed-like plants, they suddenly came to a low wall, and saw, yawning black and wide at their very feet, that vast cleft which they had crossed before they entered the castle.

"It encircles the inner city, the fortress, and its grounds," said Masouda; "and who lives today that could throw a bridge across it? Now come back."

So, following the gulf round, they returned to the castle by another path, and were ushered into an anteroom, where stood a watch of twelve men. Here Masouda left them in the midst of the men, who stared at them with stony eyes. She returned quickly and beckoned to them to follow her. Walking down a long passage they came to curtains, in front of which were two sentries, who drew these curtains as they approached. Then, side by side, they entered a great hall, long as Stangate Abbey Church, and passed through a number of people, all crouched upon the ground. Beyond these the hall narrowed.

Here sat and stood more people, fierce-eyed, turbaned men, who wore great knives in their girdles. These, as they learned afterwards, were called the fedai, the sworn assassins, who lived but to do the command of their lord the great Assassin. At the end of this chancel were more curtains, beyond which was a guarded door. It opened, and on its further side they found themselves in full sunlight on an unwalled terrace, surrounded by the mighty gulf into which it projected. On the right and left edges of this terrace sat old and bearded men, twelve in number, their heads bowed humbly and their eyes fixed upon the ground. These were the dais, or councilors.

At the head of the terrace, under an open and beautifully carved pavilion of wood, stood two gigantic soldiers, having the red dagger blazoned on their white robes. Between them was a black cushion, and on the cushion a black heap. At first, staring out of the bright sunlight at this heap in the shadow, the brethren wondered what it might be. Then they caught sight of the glitter of eyes, and knew that the heap was a man who wore a black turban on his head and a black, bell-shaped robe clasped at the breast with a red jewel. The weight of the man had sunk him down deep into the soft cushion, so that there was nothing of him to be seen save the folds of the bell-shaped cloak, the red jewel, and the head. He looked like a coiled-up snake; the dark and glittering eyes also were those of a snake. Of his features, in the deep shade of the canopy and of the wide black turban, they could see nothing.

The aspect of this figure was so terrible and inhuman that the brethren trembled at the sight of him. They were men and he was a man, but between that huddled, beady-eyed heap and those two tall Western warriors, clad in their gleaming mail and colored cloaks, there existed a contrast that was as clear as life and death.

Chapter XII
The Lord of Death

Masouda ran forward and prostrated herself at full length, but Godwin and Wulf stared at the heap, and the heap stared at them. Then, at some motion of his chin, Masouda arose and said, "Strangers, you stand in the presence of the Master, Sinan, Lord of Death. Kneel, and do homage to the Master."

But the brethren stiffened their backs and would not kneel. They lifted their hands to their brows in salute, but no more.

Then from between the black turban and the black cloak came a hollow voice, speaking in Arabic, and saying,

"Are these the men who brought me the lion's skin? Well, what seek ye, Franks?"

They stood silent.

"Dread lord," said Masouda, "these knights are but now come from England over sea, and do not understand our tongue."

"Set out their story and their request," said Al-Jebal, "that we may judge of them."

"Dread lord," answered Masouda, "as I sent you word, they say that they are the kin of a certain knight who in battle saved the life of him who ruled before you, but is now an inhabitant of Paradise."

"I have heard that there was such a knight," said the voice. "He was named D'Arcy, and he bore the same cognizance on his shield—the sign of a skull."

"Lord, these brethren are also named D'Arcy, and now they come to ask your help against Saladin."

At that name the heap stirred as a snake stirs when it hears danger, and the head erected itself a little beneath the great turban.

"What help, and why?" asked the voice.

"Lord, Saladin has stolen a woman of their house who is his niece, and these knights, her brothers, ask you to aid them to recover her."

The beady eyes instantly became interested.

"Report has been made to me of that story," said the voice; "but what sign do these Franks show? He who went before me gave a ring, and with it certain rights in this land, to the knight D'Arcy who befriended him in danger. Where is that sacred ring, with which he parted in his foolishness?"

Masouda translated and, seeing the warning in her eyes and remembering her words, the brethren shook their heads, while Wulf answered, "Our uncle, the knight Sir Andrew, was cut down by the soldiers of Saladin, and as he died bade us seek you out. What time had he to tell us of any ring?"

The sultan hung his head slowly.

"I hoped," said Sinan to Masouda, "that they had the ring, and it was for this reason, woman, that I allowed you to lead these knights hither, after you had reported of them and their quest to me from Beirut. It is not well that there should be two holy Signets in the world, and he who went before me, when he lay dying, charged me to recover his if that were possible. Let them go back to their own land and return to me with the ancient ring, and I will help them."

Masouda translated the last sentence only, and again the brethren shook their heads. This time it was Godwin who spoke.

"Our land is far away, O lord, and where shall we find this long-lost ring? Let not our journey be in vain. O Mighty One, give us justice against Saladin."

"All my years have I sought justice on Saladin," answered Sinan, "and yet he prevails against me. Now I make you an offer. Go, Franks, and bring me his head, or at least put him to death as I shall show you how, and we will talk again."

When they heard this saying Wulf said to Godwin, in English, "I think that we had best go; I do not like this company." But Godwin made no answer.

As they stood silent thus, not knowing what to say, a man entered through the door, and, throwing himself on his hands and knees, crawled towards the cushion through the double line of councilors or dais.

"Your report?" said Sinan in Arabic.

"Lord," answered the man, "I acquaint you that your will has been done in the matter of the vessel." Then he went on speaking in a low voice, so rapidly that the brethren could scarcely hear much less understand him.

Sinan listened, then said, "Let the fedai enter and make his own report, bringing with him his prisoners."

Now one of the dais, he who sat nearest the canopy, rose and, pointing towards the brethren, said, "Touching these Franks, what is your will?"

The beady eyes, which seemed to search out their souls, fixed themselves upon them, and for a long while Sinan considered. They trembled, knowing that he was passing some judgment concerning them in his heart, and that on his next words much might hang—even their lives.

"Let them stay here," he said at, length. "I may have questions to ask them."

For a time there was silence. Sinan, Lord of Death, seemed to be lost in thought under the black shade of his canopy; the double line of dais stared at nothingness across the passage way; the giant guards stood still as statues; Masouda watched the brethren from beneath her long eyelashes, while the brethren watched the sharp edge of the shadow of the canopy on the marble floor. They strove to seem unconcerned, but their hearts were beating fast within them, who felt that great things were about to happen, though what these might be they knew not.

So intense was the silence, so dreadful seemed that inhuman, snake-like man, so strange his aged, passionless councilors, and the place of council surrounded by a dizzy gulf, that fear took hold of them like the fear of an evil dream. Godwin wondered if Sinan could see the ring upon his breast, and what would happen to him if he did see it; while Wulf longed to shout aloud, to do anything that would break this deathly, sunlit quiet. To them those minutes seemed like hours; indeed, for all they knew, they might have been hours.

At length, there was a stir behind the brethren, and at a word from Masouda they separated, falling apart a pace or two, and stood opposite each other and sideways to Sinan. Standing thus, they saw the curtains drawn. Through them came four men, carrying a stretcher covered with a cloth, beneath which they could see the outline of a form that lay there motionless. The four men brought the stretcher to the front of the canopy, set it on the ground, prostrated themselves, and retired, walking backwards down the length of the terrace.

Again there was silence, while the brethren wondered whose corpse it was that lay beneath the cloth, for a corpse it must surely be; though neither the Lord of the Mountain nor his dais and guards seemed to concern themselves in the matter. Again the curtains parted, and a procession advanced up the terrace. First came a great man clad in a white robe blazoned with the bleeding dagger, after whom walked a tall woman shrouded in a long veil, who was followed by a thick-set knight clad in Frankish armor and wearing a cape of which the cowl covered his head as though to keep the rays of the sun from beating on his helm. Lastly entered four guards. Up the long place they marched, through the double line of dais, while with a strange stirring in their breasts the brethren watched the shape and movements of the veiled woman who stepped forward rapidly. The woman did not see them, for she turned her head neither to the right nor left. The leader of the little band reached the space before the canopy, and, prostrating himself by the side of the stretcher, lay still. She who walked behind him stopped also, and, seeing the black heap upon the cushion, shuddered.

"Woman, unveil," commanded the voice of Sinan.

She hesitated, then swiftly undid some fastening, so that her drapery fell from her head. The brethren stared, rubbed their eyes, and stared again.

Before them stood Rosamund!

Yes, it was Rosamund, worn with sickness, terrors, and travel, yet Rosamund herself beyond all doubt. At the sight of her pale, queenly beauty the heap on the cushion stirred beneath his black cloak, and the beady eyes were filled with an evil, eager light. Even the dais seemed to wake from their contemplation, and Masouda bit her red lip, turned pale beneath her olive skin, and watched with devouring eyes, waiting to read this woman's heart.

"Rosamund!" cried the brethren with one voice.

She heard. As they sprang towards her she glanced wildly from face to face, then with a low cry flung an arm about the neck of each and would have fallen in the ecstasy of her joy had they not held her. Indeed, her knees touched the ground. As they stooped to lift her it flashed into Godwin's mind that Masouda had told Sinan that they were her brethren. The thought was followed by another. If this were so, they might be left with her, whereas otherwise that black-robed devil—

"Listen," he whispered in English; "we are not your cousins we are your brothers, your half-brothers, and we know no Arabic."

She heard and Wulf heard, but the watchers thought that they were but welcoming each other, for Wulf began to talk also, random words in French, such as "Greeting, Sister!" "Well found, Sister!" and kissed her on the forehead.

Rosamund opened her eyes, which had closed, and, gaining her feet, gave one hand to each of the brethren. Then the voice of Masouda was heard interpreting the words of Sinan.

"It seems, lady, that you know these knights."

"I do—well. They are my brothers, from whom I was stolen when they were drugged and our father was killed."

"How is that, lady, seeing that you are said to be the niece of Saladin? Are these knights, then, the nephews of that man of blood?"

"Nay," answered Rosamund, "they are my father's sons, but of another wife."

The answer appeared to satisfy Sinan, who fixed his eyes upon the pale beauty of Rosamund and asked no more questions. While he remained thus thinking, a noise arose at the end of the terrace, and the brethren, turning their heads, saw that the thick-set knight was striving to thrust his way through the guards who stood by the curtains and barred his path with the shafts of their spears. Then it came into Godwin's mind that just before Rosamund unveiled he had seen this knight suddenly turn and walk down the terrace.

The lord Sinan looked up at the sound and made a sign. Thereon two of the dais sprang to their feet and ran towards the curtain, where they spoke with the knight, who turned and came back with them, though slowly, as one who is unwilling. Now his hood had fallen from his head, and Godwin and Wulf stared at him as he advanced, for surely they knew those great shoulders, those round black eyes, those thick lips, and that heavy jowl.

"Lozelle! It is Lozelle!" said Godwin.

"Aye," echoed Rosamund, "it is Lozelle, the double traitor, who betrayed me first to the soldiers of Saladin, and, because I would have none of his love, next to this lord Sinan."

Wulf heard, and, as Lozelle drew near to them, sprang forward with an oath and struck him across the face with his mailed hand. Instantly guards thrust themselves between them, and Sinan asked through Masouda:

"Why do you dare to strike this Frank in my presence?"

"Because, lord," answered Wulf, "he is a rogue who has brought all these troubles on our house. I challenge him to meet me in battle to the death."

"And I, also," said Godwin.

"I am ready," shouted Lozelle, stung to fury by the blow.

"Then, dog, why did you try to run away when you saw our faces?" asked Wulf.

Masouda held up her hand and began to interpret, addressing Lozelle, and speaking in the first person as the "mouth" of Sinan.

"I thank you for your service who have served me before. Your messenger came, a Frank whom I knew in old days. As you had arranged it should be, I sent one of my fedais with soldiers to kill the men of Saladin on the ship and capture this lady who is his niece, all of which it seems has been done. The bargain that your messenger made was that the lady should be given over to you—"

Here Godwin and Wulf ground their teeth and glared at him.

"But these knights say that you stole her, their kinswoman, from them, and one of them has struck you and challenged you to single combat, which challenge you have accepted. I sanction the combat gladly, who have long desired to see two knights of the Franks fight in tourney according to their custom. I will set the course, and you shall be given the best horse in my kingdom; this knight shall ride his own. These are the conditions—the course shall be on the bridge between the inner and outer gates of the castle city, and the fight, which must be to the death, shall take place on the night of the full moon—that is, three days from now. If you are victor, we will talk of the matter of the lady for whom you bargained as a wife."

"My lord, my lord," answered Lozelle, "who can lay a lance on that terrible place in moonlight? Is it thus that you keep faith with me?"

"I can and will!" cried Wulf. "Dog, I would fight you in the gates of hell, with my soul on the hazard."

"Keep faith with yourself," said Sinan, "who said that you accepted the challenge of this knight and made no conditions, and when you have proved upon his body that his quarrel is not just, then speak of my faith with you. Nay, no more words; when this fight is done we will speak again, and not before. Let him be led to the outer castle and there given of our best. Let my great black horse be brought to him that he may gallop it to and fro upon the bridge, or where he will within the circuit of the walls, by day or by night; but see that he has no speech with this lady whom he has betrayed into my power, or with these knights his foes, nor suffer him to come into my presence. I will not talk with a man who has been struck in the face until he has washed away the blow in blood."

As Masouda finished translating, and before Lozelle could answer, the lord Sinan moved his head, whereon guards sprang forward and conducted Lozelle from the terrace.

"Farewell, Sir Thief," cried Wulf after him, "till we meet again upon the narrow bridge and there settle our account. You have fought Godwin, perhaps you will have better luck with Wulf."

Lozelle glared back at him, and, finding no answer, went on his way.

"Your report," said Sinan, addressing the tall fedai who all this while had lain upon his face before him, still as the form that was stretched upon the bier. "There should have been another prisoner, the great emir Hassan. Also, where is the Frankish spy?"

The fedai rose and spoke.

"Lord," he said, "I did your bidding. The knight who has gone steered the ship into the bay, as had been arranged. I attacked with the daylight. The soldiers of Saladin fought bravely, for the lady here saw us, and gave them time to gather, and we lost many men. We overcame and killed them all, except the prince Hassan, whom we took prisoner. I left some men to watch the ship. The crew we spared, as they were the servants of the Frank Lozelle, setting them loose upon the beach, together with a Frankish woman, who was the servant of the lady here, to find their way to the nearest city. This woman I would have killed, but the lady your captive begged for her life, saying she had come from the land of the Franks to seek her husband; so, having no orders, I let her go. Yesterday morning we started for Masyaf, the prince Hassan riding in a litter together with that Frankish spy who was here a while ago and told you of the coming of the ship. At night they slept in the same tent; I left the prince bound and set a guard, but in the morning when we looked we found him gone—how, I know not—and lying in the tent the Frankish spy, dead, with a knife wound through his heart. Behold!" and withdrawing the cloth from the stretcher he revealed the stiff form of the spy Nicholas, who lay there dead, a look of terror frozen on his face.

"At least this one has come to an end he deserved," muttered Wulf to Godwin.

"So, having searched without avail, I came on here with the lady your prisoner and the Frank Lozelle. I have spoken."

Now when he had heard this report, forgetting his calm, Sinan arose from the cushion and stepped forward two paces. There he halted, with fury in his glittering eyes, looking like a man clothed in a black bell. For a moment he stroked his beard, and the brethren noted that on the first finger of his right hand was a ring so similar to that which hung about the neck of Godwin that none could have told them apart.

"Man," Sinan said in a low voice, "what have you done? You have left the emir Hassan go, who is the most trusted friend and general of the sultan of Damascus. By now he is there, or near it, and within six days we shall see the army of Saladin riding across the plain. Also, you have not killed the crew and the Frankish woman, and they too will make report of the taking of the ship and the capture of this lady, who is of the house of Saladin and whom he seeks as earnestly as all the kingdom of the Franks. What have you to say?"

"Lord," answered the tall fedai, and his hand trembled as he spoke, "most mighty lord, I had no orders as to the killing of the crew from your lips, and the Frank Lozelle told me that he had agreed with you that they should be spared."

"Then, slave, he lied. He agreed with me through that dead spy that they should be slain, and do you not know that if I give no orders in such a case I mean death, not life? But what of the prince Hassan?"

"Lord, I have nothing to say. I think he must have bribed the spy named Nicholas"—and he pointed to the corpse—"to cut his bonds, and afterwards killed the man for vengeance sake, for by the body we found a heavy purse of gold. That he hated him as he hated yonder Lozelle I know, for he called them dogs and traitors in the boat; and since he could not strike them, his hands being bound, he spat in their faces, cursing them in the name of Allah. That is why, Lozelle being afraid to be near him, I set the spy Nicholas, who was a bold fellow, as a watch over him, and two soldiers outside the tent, while Lozelle and I watched the lady."

"Let those soldiers be brought," said Sinan, "and tell their story."

They were brought and stood by their captain, but they had no story to tell. They swore that they had not slept on guard, nor heard a sound, yet when morning came the prince was gone. Again the Lord of Death stroked his black beard. Then he held up the Signet before the eyes of the three men, saying, "You see the token. Go."

"Lord," said the fedai, "I have served you well for many years."

"Your service is ended. Go!" was the stern answer.

The fedai bowed his head in salute, stood for a moment as though lost in thought, then, turning suddenly, walked with a steady step to the edge of the abyss and leapt. For an instant the sunlight shone on his white and fluttering robe, then from the depths of that darksome place floated up the sound of a heavy fall, and all was still.

"Follow your captain to Paradise," said Sinan to the two soldiers, whereon one of them drew a knife to stab himself, but a dai sprang up, saying, "Beast, would you shed blood before your lord? Do you not know the custom? Be gone!"

So the poor men went, the first with a steady step, and the second, who was not so brave, reeling over the edge of the precipice as one might who is drunken.

"It is finished," said the dais, clapping their hands gently. "Dread lord, we thank thee for thy justice."

But Rosamund turned sick and faint, and even the brethren paled. This man was terrible indeed—if he were a man and not a devil. How long would it be, they wondered, before they also were bidden to walk that gulf? Only Wulf swore in his heart that if he went down this road Sinan would go with him.

Then the corpse of the false palmer was borne away to be thrown to the eagles which always hovered over that house of death, and Sinan, having reseated himself upon the cushion, began to talk again through his "mouth" Masouda, in a low, quiet voice, as though nothing had happened to anger him.

"Lady," he said to Rosamund, "your story is known to me. Saladin seeks you, nor is it wonderful"—here his eyes glittered with a new and horrible light—"that he should desire to see such loveliness at his court, although the Frank Lozelle swore through yonder dead spy that you are precious in his eyes because of some vision that has come to him. Well, this heretic sultan is my enemy whom Satan protects, for even my fedais have failed to kill him, and perhaps there will be war on account of you. But have no fear, for the price at which you shall be delivered to him is higher than Saladin himself would care to pay, even for you. So, since this castle is impregnable, here you may dwell at peace, nor shall any desire be denied you. Speak, and your wishes are fulfilled."

"I desire," said Rosamund in a low, steady voice, "protection against Sir Hugh Lozelle and all men."

"It is yours. The Lord of the Mountain covers you with his own mantle."

"I desire," she went on, "that my brothers here may lodge with me, that I may not feel alone among strange people."

He thought awhile, and answered, "Your brethren shall lodge near you in the guest castle. Why not, since from them you cannot need protection? They shall meet you at the feast and in the garden. But, lady, do you know it? They came here upon faith of some old tale of a promise made by him who went before me to ask my help to recover you from Saladin, not knowing that I was your host, not Saladin. That they should meet you thus is a chance which makes even my wisdom wonder, for in it I see omens. Now, she whom they wished to rescue from Saladin, these tall brethren of yours might wish to rescue you from Al-Jebal. Understand then, all of you, that from the Lord of Death there is but one escape. Yonder runs its path," and he pointed to the dizzy place whence his three servants had leapt to their doom.

"Knights," he went on, addressing Godwin and Wulf, "lead your sister hence. This evening I bid her, and you, to my banquet. Till then, farewell. Woman," he added to Masouda, "accompany them. You know your duties; this lady is in your charge. See that no strange man comes near her—above all, the Frank Lozelle. Dais, take notice and let it be proclaimed—to these three is given the protection of the Signet in all things, save that they must not leave my walls except under sanction of the Signet—nay, in its very presence."

The dais rose, bowed, and seated themselves again. Then, guided by Masouda and preceded and followed by guards, the brethren and Rosamund walked down the terrace through the curtains into the chancel-like place where men crouched upon the ground; through the great hall were more men crouched upon the ground; through the antechamber where, at a word from Masouda, the guards saluted; through passages to that place where they had slept. Here Masouda halted and said, "Lady Rose of the World, who are fitly so named, I go to prepare your chamber. Doubtless you will wish to speak awhile with these your—brothers. Speak on and fear not, for it shall be my care that you are left alone, if only for a little while. Yet walls have ears, so I counsel you use that English tongue which none of us understand in the land of Al-Jebal, not even I."

Then she bowed and went.

Chapter XIII
The Embassy

The brethren and Rosamund looked at each other, for having so much to say it seemed that they could not speak at all. Then with a low cry Rosamund said, "Oh! Let us thank God, who, after all these black months of travel and of danger, has thus brought us together again," and, kneeling down there together in the guest hall of the Lord of Death, they gave earnest thanks.

Then, moving to the center of the chamber where they thought that none would hear them, they began to speak in low voices and in English.

"Tell you your tale first, Rosamund," said Godwin.

She told it as shortly as she could, as they listened without a word.

Then Godwin spoke and told her theirs. Rosamund heard it, and asked a question almost in a whisper.

"Why does that beautiful dark-eyed woman befriend you?"

"I do not know," answered Godwin, "unless it is because of the incident when I saved her from the lion."

Rosamund looked at him and smiled a little, and Wulf smiled, also. Then she said, "Blessings be on that lion and all its tribe! I pray that she may not soon forget the deed, for it seems that our lives hang upon her favor. How strange is this story, and how desperate our case! How strange also that you should have traveled here against her counsel, which looks to have been wise."

"We were led," answered Godwin. "Your father had wisdom at his death, and saw what we could not see."

"Aye," added Wulf, "but I would that it had been into some other place, for I fear this lord Al-Jebal at whose nod men hurl themselves to death."

"He is hateful," answered Rosamund, with a shudder. "The Sultan is even worse than the knight Lozelle; and when he fixes his eyes on me, my heart grows sick. Oh! That we could escape this place!"

"An eel in a steel trap has more chance of freedom," said Wulf gloomily. "Let us at least be thankful that we are caged together—for how long, I wonder?"

As he spoke, Masouda appeared, attended by waiting women, and, bowing to Rosamund, said, "It is the will of the Master, lady, that I lead you to the chambers that have been made ready for you, there to rest until the hour of the feast. Fear not; you shall meet your brethren then. You knights have leave, if it so pleases you, to exercise your horses in the gardens. They stand saddled in the courtyard, to which this woman will bring you," and she pointed to one of those two maids who had cleaned the armor, "and with them are guides and an escort."

"She means that we must go," stated Godwin, adding aloud, "farewell, Sister, until tonight."

So they parted, unwillingly enough. In the courtyard they found the horses, Flame and Smoke, as they had been told, also a mounted escort of four fierce-looking fedais and an officer. When they were in the saddle, this man, motioning to them to follow him, passed by an archway out of the courtyard into the gardens. Hence ran a broad road strewn with sand, along which he began to gallop. This road followed the gulf which encircled the citadel and inner town of Masyaf, that was, as it were, an island on a mountaintop with a circumference of over three miles.

As they went, the gulf always on their right hand, holding in their horses to prevent their passing that of their guide, swift as it was, they saw another troop approaching them. This was also preceded by an officer of the Assassins, as these servants of Al-Jebal were called by the Franks, and behind him, mounted on a splendid coal-black steed and followed by guards, rode a mail-clad Frankish knight.

"It is Lozelle," said Wulf, "upon the horse that Sinan promised him."

At the sight of the man a fury took hold of Godwin. With a shout of warning, he drew his sword. Lozelle saw, and out leapt his blade in answer. Then, sweeping past the officers who were with them and reining up their steeds, in a second they were face to face. Lozelle struck first and Godwin caught the stroke upon his buckler, but before he could return it the fedais of either party rushed between them and pushed them aside.

"A pity," said Godwin, as they dragged his horse away. "Had they left us alone I think, Brother, I might have saved you a moonlight duel."

"That I do not want to miss, but the chance at his head was good if those fellows would have let you take it," answered Wulf reflectively.

Then the horses began to gallop again, and they saw no more of Lozelle. Now, skirting the edge of the town, they came to the narrow, wall-less bridge that spanned the gulf between it and the outer gate and city. Here the officer wheeled his horse, and, beckoning to them to follow, charged it at full gallop. After him went the brethren—Godwin first, then Wulf. In the deep gateway on the farther side they reined up. The captain turned and began to gallop back faster than he had come—as fast, indeed, as his good beast would travel.

"Pass him!" cried Godwin, and shaking the reins loose upon the neck of Flame he called to him aloud.

Forward he sprang, with Smoke at his heels. Now they had overtaken the captain, and now even on that narrow way they had swept past him. Not an inch was there to spare between them and the abyss, and the man, brave as he was, expecting to be thrust to death, clung to his horse's mane with terror in his eyes. On the city side the brethren pulled up laughing among the astonished fedais who had waited for them there.

"By the Signet," cried the officer, thinking that the knights could not understand, "these are not men; they are devils, and their horses are goats of the mountains. I thought to frighten them, but it is I who was frightened, for they swept past me like eagles of the air."

"Gallant riders and swift, well-trained steeds," answered one of the fedais, with admiration in his voice. "The fight at the full moon will be worth our seeing."

Then once more they took the sand-strewn road and galloped on. Three times they passed round the city thus, the last time by themselves, for the captain and the fedais were far outstripped. Indeed, it was not until they had unsaddled Flame and Smoke in their stalls that these appeared, spurring their foaming horses. Taking no heed of them, the brethren thrust aside the grooms, dressed their steeds down, fed and watered them.

Then, having seen them eat, there being no more to do, they walked back to the guest house, hoping to find Rosamund. But they found no Rosamund, so sat down together and talked of the wonderful things that had befallen them, and of what might befall them in the future; of the mercy of Heaven also which had brought them all three together safe and sound, although it was in this house of hell. So the time passed on, till about the hour of sunset, when servants came and led them to the bathing area. The two men washed themselves and put on fresh clothing.

When they came out the sun was down, and the women, bearing torches in their hands, conducted them to a great and gorgeous hall, which they had not seen before, built of fretted stone and having a carved and painted roof. Along one side of this hall, that was lit with cressets, were a number of round-headed open arches supported by elegant white columns, and beyond these a marble terrace with flights of steps which led to the gardens beneath. On the floor of this hall, each seated upon his cushion beside low tables inlaid with pearl sat the guests, a hundred or more, all dressed in white robes on which the red dagger was blazoned, and all as silent as though they were asleep.

When the brethren reached the place, the women left them, and servants with gold chains round their necks escorted them to a dais in the middle of the hall where were many cushions, as yet unoccupied, arranged in a semicircle, of which the center was slightly higher and more gorgeous than the rest.

Here places were pointed out to them opposite the divan, and they took their stand by them. They had not long to wait, for soon there was the sound of music, and, heralded by troops of singing women, the lord Sinan approached, walking slowly down the length of the great hall. It was a strange procession, for after the women came the aged, white-robed dais, then the lord Al-Jebal himself, clad now in his blood-red, festal robe, and wearing jewels on his turban.

Around him marched four slaves, black as ebony, each of whom held a flaming torch on high, while behind followed the two gigantic guards who had stood sentry over him when he sat under the canopy of justice. As he advanced down the hall every man in it rose and prostrated himself, and so remained until their lord was seated, save only the two brethren, who stood erect like the survivors among the slain of a battle. Settling himself among the cushions at one end of the divan, he waved his hand, whereon the feasters, and with them Godwin and Wulf, sat themselves down.

Now there was a pause, while Sinan glanced along the hall impatiently. Soon the brethren saw why, since at the end opposite to that by which he had entered appeared more singing women, and after them, also escorted by four black torchbearers, only these were women, walked Rosamund and, behind her, Masouda.

Rosamund it was without doubt, but Rosamund transformed, for now she had the look of an Eastern queen. Round her head was a coronet of gems from which hung a veil, but not so as to hide her face. Jeweled, too, were her heavy plaits of hair, jeweled the rose-silk garments that she wore, the girdle at her waist, her naked, ivory arms and even the slippers on her feet. As she approached in her royal-looking beauty all the guests at that strange feast stared first at her and next at each other. Then, as though by a single impulse, they rose and bowed.

"What can this mean?" muttered Wulf to Godwin as they did likewise. But Godwin made no answer.

On came Rosamund, and now, behold! the lord Al-Jebal rose also and, giving her his hand, seated her by him on the royal couch or divan.

"Show no surprise, Wulf," insisted Godwin, who had caught a warning look in the eyes of Masouda as she took up her position behind Rosamund.

Now the feast began. Slaves, running to and fro, set dish after dish filled with strange and savory meats upon the little inlaid tables, those that were served to Sinan and his guests fashioned, all of them, of silver or of gold.

Godwin and Wulf ate, though not for hunger's sake, but of what they ate they remembered nothing, who were watching Sinan and straining their ears to catch all he said without seeming to take note or listen. Although she strove to hide it and to appear indifferent, it was plain to them that Rosamund was very afraid. Again and again Sinan presented to her choice morsels of food, sometimes on the dishes and sometimes with his fingers, and these she was obliged to take. All the while, also, he devoured her with his fierce eyes so that she shrank away from him to the furthest limit of the divan.

Then wine, perfumed and spiced, was brought in golden cups, of which, having drunk, he offered to Rosamund. But she shook her head and asked Masouda for water, saying that she touched nothing stronger, and it was given her, cooled with snow. The brethren asked for water also, whereon Sinan looked at them suspiciously and demanded the reason. Godwin replied through Masouda that they were under an oath to touch no wine till they returned to their own country, having fulfilled their mission. To this he answered sincerely that it was good and right to keep oaths, but he feared that theirs would make them water-drinkers for the rest of their lives.

Now the wine that he had drunk took hold of Sinan, and he began to talk who without it was so silent.

"You met the Frank Lozelle today," he said to Godwin, through Masouda, "when riding in my gardens, and drew your sword on him. Why did you not kill him? Is he the better man?"

"It seems not, as once before I worsted him and I sit here unhurt, lord," answered Godwin. "Your servants thrust between and separated us."

"Aye," replied Sinan, "I remember; they had orders. Still, I wish that you had killed him, the unbelieving dog, who has dared to lift his eyes to this Rose of Roses, your sister. Fear not," he went on, addressing Rosamund, "he shall offer you no more insult, who are henceforth under the protection of the Signet," and stretching out his thin, cruel-looking hand, on which gleamed the ring of power, he patted her on the arm.

All of these things Masouda translated, while Rosamund dropped her head to hide her face, though on it were not the blushes that he thought, but loathing and alarm.

Wulf glared at Sultan Al-Jebal, whose head was turned away, and so fierce was the rage swelling in his heart that a mist seemed to gather before his eyes, and through it this devilish chief of murderers, clothed in his robe of flaming red, looked like a man steeped in blood. The thought came to him suddenly that he would make an end of him, and his hand passed to his sword-hilt. But Godwin saw the terror in Masouda's eyes, saw Wulf's hand also, and guessed what was about to happen. With a swift movement of his arm he struck a golden dish from the table to the marble floor, then said, in a clear voice in French, "Brother, be not so awkward; pick up that dish and answer the lord Sinan as is your right—I mean, touching the matter of Lozelle."

Wulf stooped to obey, and his mind cleared which had been so near to madness.

"I wish it not, lord," he said, "who, if I can, have your good leave to slay this fellow on the third night from now. If I fail, then let my brother take my place, but not before."

"Yes, I forgot," said Sinan. "So I decreed, and that will be a fight I wish to see. If he kills you then your brother shall meet him. And if he kills you both, then perhaps I, Sinan, will meet him—in my own fashion. Sweet lady, knowing where the course is laid, say, do you fear to see this contest?"

Rosamund's face paled, but she answered proudly, "Why should I fear what my brethren do not fear? They are brave knights, bred to arms, and God, in whose hand are all our destinies—even yours, O Lord of Death—He will guard the right."

When this speech was translated to him Sinan quailed a little. Then he answered, "Lady, know that I am the voice and the prophet of Allah—aye, and his sword to punish evil-doers and those who do not believe. Well, if what I hear is true, your brethren are skilled horsemen who even dared to pass my servant on the narrow bridge, so victory may rest with them. Tell me which of them do you love the least, for he shall first face the sword of Lozelle."

Now as Rosamund prepared herself to answer Masouda scanned her face through her half-closed eyes. But, whatever she may have felt within, it remained calm and cold as though it were cut in stone.

"To me they are as one man," she said. "When one speaks, both speak. I love them equally."

"Then, guest of my heart, it shall go as I have said. Brother Blue-eyes shall fight first, and if he falls then Brother Gray-eyes. The feast is ended, and it is my hour for prayer. Slaves, bid the people fill their cups. Lady, I pray of you, stand forward on the dais."

She obeyed, and at a sign the black slave-women gathered behind her with their flaming torches. Then Sinan rose also, and cried with a loud voice, "Servants of Al-Jebal, pledge, I command you, to this flower of flowers, the high-born princess of Baalbec, the niece of the sultan, Saladin, whom men call the Great." Then Sinan added, "though he be not so great as I, this queen of maids who soon—" Then, checking himself, he drank of his wine, and with a low bow presented the empty, jeweled cup to Rosamund.

All the company drank also, and shouted till the hall rang, for her loveliness as she stood thus in the fierce light of the torches, aflame as these men were with the vision-breeding wine of Al-Jebal, moved them to madness.

"Queen! Queen!" they shouted. "Queen of our Master and of us all!"

Sinan heard and smiled. Then, motioning for silence, he took the hand of Rosamund, kissed it and, turning, passed from the hall preceded by his singing women and surrounded by the dais and guards.

Godwin and Wulf stepped forward to speak with Rosamund, but Masouda interposed herself between them, saying in a cold, clear voice, "It is not permitted. Go, knights, and cool your brows in yonder garden, where sweet water runs. Your sister is my charge. Fear not, for she is guarded."

"Come," said Godwin to Wulf; "we had best obey."

So together they walked through the crowd of those feasters that remained, for most of them had already left the hall, who made way, not without reverence for the brethren of this new star of beauty, onto the terrace, and from the terrace into the gardens. Here they stood awhile in the sweet freshness of the night, which was very welcome after the heated, perfume-laden air of the banquet; then began to wander up and down among the scented trees and flowers. The moon, floating in a cloudless sky, was almost at its full, and by her light they saw a wondrous scene. Under many of the trees and in tents set about here and there, rugs were spread, and to them came men who had drunk of the wine of the feast, and cast themselves down to sleep.

"Are they drunk?" asked Wulf.

"It would seem so," answered Godwin.

Yet these men appeared to be hypnotized rather than drunk, for they walked steadily enough, but with wide-set, dreamy eyes; nor did they seem to sleep upon the rugs, but lay there staring at the sky and muttering with their lips, their faces steeped in a strange, unholy rapture. Sometimes they would rise and walk a few paces with outstretched arms, till the arms closed as though they clasped something invisible, to which they bent their heads to babble awhile. Then they walked back to their rugs again, where they remained silent.

As they lay thus, white-veiled women appeared, who crouched by the heads of these sleepers, whispering into their ears, and when from time to time they sat up, gave them to drink from cups they carried, after partaking of which they lay down again and became quite senseless.

Only the women would move on to others and serve them likewise. Some of them approached the brethren with a slow, gliding motion, and offered them the cup; but they walked forward, taking no notice, whereupon the girls left them, laughing softly, and saying such things as "Tomorrow we shall meet," or "Soon you will be glad to drink and enter into Paradise."

"When the time comes doubtless we shall be glad, who have dwelt here," answered Godwin gravely, but as he spoke in French they did not understand him.

"Step out, Brother," said Wulf, "for at the very sight of those rugs I grow sleepy, and the wine in the cups sparkles as bright as their bearers' eyes."

So they walked on towards the sound of a waterfall, and, when they came to it, drank, and bathed their faces and heads.

"'This is better than their wine," said Wulf. Then, catching sight of more women flitting round them, looking like shadows amid the moonlit glades, they pressed forward till they reached an open area where there were no rugs, no sleepers, and no cup-bearers. "Now," said Wulf, halting, "tell me what does all this mean?"

"Are you deaf and blind?" asked Godwin. "Cannot you see that yonder fiend is in love with Rosamund, and means to take her, as he well may do?"

Wulf groaned aloud, and then answered, "I swear that first I will send his soul to hell, even though my own may keep it company."

"Aye," answered Godwin, "I saw; you came close to the next life earlier tonight. But remember, if you make a hasty decision it is the end for all of us. Let us wait then to strike until we must—to save her from worse things."

"Who knows if we may find another chance? Meanwhile, Rosamund—" and again he groaned.

"As they spoke they had moved towards the edge of the glade, and halting there stood silent, till presently from under the shadow of a cedar tree appeared a solitary, white-robed woman.

"Let us be going," said Wulf; "here is another of them with her accursed cup."

But before they could turn the woman glided up to them and suddenly unveiled. It was Masouda.

"Follow me, brothers Peter and John," she said in a laughing whisper. "I have words to say to you. What! You will not drink? Well, it is wisest." And emptying the cup upon the ground, she moved ahead of them.

Silently she went, now appearing in the open spaces, now vanishing beneath the dense gloom of cedar boughs, till she reached a naked, lonely rock which stood almost upon the edge of the gulf. Opposite to this rock was a great mound such as ancient peoples reared over the bodies of their dead, and in the mound, cunningly hidden by growing shrubs, a massive door. Masouda took a key from her girdle, and, having looked around to see that they were alone, unlocked it.

"Enter," she said, pushing them before her.

They obeyed, and through the darkness within heard her close the door.

"Now we are safe awhile," she said with a sigh, "or, at least, so I think. But I will lead you to where there is more light."

Then, taking each of them by the hand, she went forward along a smooth incline, till they saw the moonlight, and by it discovered that they stood at the mouth of a cave, which was fringed with bushes. Running up from the depths of the gulf below to this opening was a ridge or shoulder of rock, very steep and narrow.

"See the only road that leads from the citadel of Masyaf with the exception of the one across the bridge," said Masouda.

"A bad one," answered Wulf, staring downward.

"Aye, yet horses trained to rocks can follow it. At its foot is the bottom of the gulf, and a mile or more away to the left a deep cleft which leads to the top of the mountain and to freedom. Will you not take it now? By tomorrow's dawn you might be far away."

"And where would the lady Rosamund be?" asked Wulf.

"In the harem of the lord Sinan—that is, very soon," she answered, coolly.

"Oh, say it not!" he exclaimed, clasping her arm, while Godwin leaned back against the wall of the cave.

"Why should I hide the truth? Have you no eyes to see that he is enamored of her loveliness—like others?

"Listen; a while ago my master Sinan chanced to lose his queen—how, we need not ask, but it is said that she wearied him. Now, as he must by law, he mourns for her a month, from full moon to full moon. But on the day after the full moon—that is, the third morning from now—he may wed again, and I think there will be a marriage. Till then, however, your sister is as safe as though she yet sat at home in England before Saladin dreamed his dream."

"Therefore," said Godwin, "within that time she must escape."

"There is a third way," answered Masouda, shrugging her shoulders. "She might stay and become the wife of Sinan."

Wulf uttered something between his teeth, then stepped towards her threateningly, saying, "Rescue her, or—"

"Stand back, pilgrim John," she said, with a laugh. "If I rescue her, which indeed would be hard, it will not be for fear of your great sword."

"What, then, will avail, Masouda?" asked Godwin in a sad voice. "To promise you money would be useless, even if we could."

"I am glad that you spared me that insult," she replied with flashing eyes, "for then there had been an end. Yet," she added more humbly, "seeing my home and business, and what I appear to be," and she glanced at her dress and the empty cup in her hand, "it would not have been strange. Now hear me, and forget no word. At present you are in favor with Sinan, who believes you to be the brothers of the lady Rosamund, not her lovers; but from the moment he learns the truth your doom is sealed. Now what the Frank Lozelle knows, that the Al-Jebal may know at any time—and will know, if these should meet.

"Meanwhile, you are free; so tomorrow, while you ride about the garden, as you will do, take note of the tall rock that stands without, and how to reach it from any point, even in the dark. Tomorrow, also, when the moon is up, they will lead you to the narrow bridge, to ride your horses to and fro there, that they may learn not to fear it in that light. When you have stabled them go into the gardens and come hither unobserved, as the place being so far away you can do. The guards will let you pass, thinking only that you desire to drink a cup of wine with some fair friend, as is the custom of our guests. Enter this cave—here is the key," and she handed it to Wulf, "and if I be not there, await me. Then I will tell you my plan, if I have any, but until then I must scheme and think. Now it grows late—go."

"And you, Masouda," said Godwin, doubtfully; "how will you escape this place?"

"By a road you do not know of, for I am mistress of the secrets of this city. Still, I thank you for your thought of me. Go, I say, and lock the door behind you."

So they went in silence, doing as she told them, and walked back through the gardens, that now seemed empty enough, to the stable entrance of the guest house, where the guards admitted them without question.

That night, the brethren slept together in one bed, fearing that if they lay separate they might be searched in their sleep and not awake. Indeed, it seemed to them that, as before, they heard footsteps and voices in the darkness.

Next morning, after they had breakfast, the two knights sought to locate either Masouda or Rosamund; but they could not find Rosamund, and Masouda did not come. A few minutes later, however, an officer appeared, and beckoned to them to follow him. So they followed, and were led through the halls and passages to the terrace of justice, where Sinan, clad in his black robe, sat as before beneath a canopy in the midst of the sunlit marble floor. There, too, beside him, also beneath the canopy and gorgeously apparelled, sat Rosamund. They strove to advance and speak with her, but guards came between them, pointing out a place where they must stand a few yards away. Only Wulf said in a loud voice, in English, "Tell us, Rosamund, is it well with you?" Lifting her pale face, she smiled and nodded.

Then, at the bidding of Sinan, Masouda commanded them to be silent, saying that it was not lawful for them to speak to the Lord of the Mountain, or his companion, unless they were first bidden so to do. So, having learnt what they wished to know, they were silent.

Moments later, some of the dais drew near the canopy, and consulted with their master on what seemed to be a great matter, for their faces were troubled. Presently he gave an order, whereon they resumed their seats and messengers left the terrace. When they appeared again, in their company were three noble-looking Saracens, accompanied by a retinue of servants who wore green turbans, showing that they were descendants of the Prophet. These men, who seemed weary with long travel, marched up the terrace with a dignified air, not looking at the dais or anyone until they saw the brethren standing side by side, at whom they stared a little. Next they caught sight of Rosamund sitting in the shadow of the canopy, and bowed to her, but of the Al-Jebal they took no notice.

"Who are you, and what is your pleasure?" asked Sinan, after he had eyed them awhile. "I am the ruler of this country. These are my ministers," and he pointed to the dais, "and here is my scepter," and he touched the blood-red dagger broidered on his robe of black.

Now that Sinan had declared himself, the embassy bowed to him, courteously enough. Then their spokesman answered him.

"That scepter we know; it has been seen afar. Twice already we have cut down its bearers even in the tent of our master. Lord of Murder, we acknowledge the emblem of murder, and we bow to you whose title is the Great Murderer. As for our mission, it is this. We are the ambassadors of Saladin, Commander of the Faithful, Sultan of the East; in these papers signed with his signet are our credentials, if you would read them."

"So," answered Sinan, "I have heard of that chief. What is his will with me?"

"This, Al-Jebal. A Frank in your pay, and a traitor, has betrayed to you a certain lady niece of Saladin, the princess of Baalbec, whose mother was married to a Frankish noble named D'Arcy, and who herself is named Rose of the World. The sultan, Saladin, having been informed of this matter by his servant, the prince Hassan, who escaped from your soldiers, demands that this lady, his niece, be delivered to him forthwith, and with her the head of the Frank Lozelle."

"The head of the Frank Lozelle he may have if he will after tomorrow night. The lady I keep," snarled Sinan. "What more have you, then?"

"Then, Al-Jebal, in the name of Saladin, we declare war on you—war till this high place of yours is pulled stone from stone; war till your tribe be dead, till the last man, woman, and child be slain, until your carcass is tossed to the crows to feed on."

Now Sinan rose in fury and pulled at his beard.

"Go back," he said, "and tell that dog you name a sultan, that low as he is, the humble-born son of Ayoub, I, Al-Jebal, do him an honor that he does not observe. My queen is dead, and two days from now, when my month of mourning is expired, I shall take to wife his niece, the princess of Baalbec, who sits here beside me, my bride-elect."

At these words Rosamund, who had been listening intently, started like one who has been stung by a snake, put her hands before her face and groaned.

"Princess," said the ambassador, who was watching her, "You seem to understand our language; is this your will, to mate your noble blood with that of the heretic chief of the Assassins?"

"Nay, nay!" she cried. "It is no will of mine, who am a helpless prisoner and by faith a Christian. If my uncle Saladin is indeed as great as I have heard, then let him show his power and deliver me, and with me these my brethren, the knights Sir Godwin and Sir Wulf."

"So you speak Arabic," said Sinan. "Good; our loving converse will be easier, and for the rest—well, the whims of women change. Now, you messengers of Saladin, be gone, lest I send you on a longer journey, and tell your master that if he dares to lift his standards against my walls my fedais shall speak with him. By day and by night, not for one moment shall he be safe. Poison shall lurk in his cup and a dagger in his bed. Let him kill a hundred of them, and another hundred shall appear. His most trusted guards shall be his executioners. The women in his harem shall bring him to his doom—ay, death shall be in the very air he breathes. If he would escape it, therefore, let him hide himself within the walls of his city of Damascus, or amuse himself with wars against the mad Cross-worshippers, and leave me to live in peace with this lady whom I have chosen."

"Great words, worthy of the Great Assassin," said the ambassador.

"Great words in truth, which shall be followed by great deeds. What chance has this lord of yours against a nation sworn to obey to the death? You smile? Then come hither you—and you." And he summoned two of his dais by name.

They rose and bowed before him.

"Now, my worthy servants," he said, "show these heretic dogs how you obey, that their master may learn the power of your master. You are old and weary of life. Be gone, and await me in Paradise."

The old men bowed again, trembling a little. Then, straightening themselves, without a word they ran side by side and leapt into the abyss.

"Has Saladin servants such as these?" asked Sinan in the silence that followed. "Well, what they have done, all would do, if I bid them. Back, now; and, if you will, take these Franks with you, who are my guests, that they may bear witness of what you have seen, and of the state in which you left their sister. Translate to the knights, woman."

So Masouda translated. Then Godwin answered through her.

"We understand little of this matter, who are ignorant of your tongue, but, O Al-Jebal, ere we leave your sheltering roof we have a quarrel to settle with the man Lozelle. After that, with your permission, we will go, but not before."

Now Rosamund sighed as if in relief, and Sinan answered, "As you will; so be it," adding, "Give these envoys food and drink before they go."

But their spokesman answered, "We partake not of the bread and salt of murderers, lest we should become of their fellowship. Al-Jebal, we depart, but within a week we appear again in the company of ten thousand spears, and on one of them shall your head be set. Your safe-conduct guards us till the sunset. After that, do your worst, as we will do ours."

Then, bowing to the princess of Baalbec one by one, they turned and marched down the terrace, followed by their servants.

As the men departed, Sinan waved his hand and the court broke up. Rosamund was the first to leave, accompanied by Masouda and escorted by guards, after which the brethren were commanded to depart as well.

So they went, talking earnestly of all these things, but finding no hope at all—except in God.

Chapter XIV
The Combat on the Bridge

"Saladin will come," said Wulf the hopeful, and from the high place where they stood he pointed to the plain beneath, across which a band of horsemen moved at full gallop. "Look; yonder goes his embassy."

"Aye," answered Godwin, "he will come, but I fear me, too late."

"Yes, Brother, unless we go to meet him. Masouda has promised."

"Masouda," sighed Godwin. "Ah! To think that so much should hang upon the faithfulness of one woman."

"It does not hang on her," said Wulf; "it hangs on the will of Heaven. Come, let us ride."

So, followed by their escort, they rode in the gardens, taking note, without seeming to do so, of the position of the tall rock, and of how it could be approached from every side. Then they went in again and waited for some sign or word from Rosamund, but in vain. That night there was no feast, and their meal was brought to them in the guest house. While they sat at it Masouda appeared for a moment to tell them that they had leave to ride the bridge in the moonlight, and that their escort would await them at a certain hour.

The brethren asked if their sister Rosamund was not coming to dine with them. Masouda answered that as the queen-elect of the Al-Jebal it was not lawful that she should eat with any other men, even her brothers. Then as she turned to leave, stumbling as though by accident, she brushed against Godwin, and whispered, "Remember, tonight," and was gone.

When the moon had been up an hour the officer of their escort appeared and led them to their horses, which were waiting, and they rode away to the castle bridge. As they approached it they saw Lozelle departing on his great black stallion, which was in a lather of foam. Lozelle had apparently already ridden the perilous bridge path, for the people, of whom there were many gathered there, clapped their hands and shouted, "Well ridden, Frank! Well ridden!"

Moments later, the brethren faced the bridge and walked their horses over it. Flame and Smoke followed without hesitation, although they snorted a little at the black gulf on either side. Next they returned at a trot, then over again, and yet again at a canter and a gallop, sometimes together and sometimes singly. Lastly, Wulf made Godwin halt in the middle of the bridge and galloped down upon him at speed, till within a lance's length. Then suddenly he checked his horse, and while his audience shouted, wheeled it around on its hind legs, its fore hoofs beating the air, and galloped back again, followed by Godwin.

"All went well," Wulf said as they rode to the castle, "and nobler or more gentle horses were never crossed by men. I have good hopes for tomorrow night."

"Aye, Brother, but I had no sword in my hand. Be not over confident, for Lozelle is desperate and a skilled fighter, as I know who have stood face to face with him. Moreover, his black stallion is well trained, and has more weight than ours. Also, yonder is a fearsome place on which to ride a course, and one of which none but that devil Sinan would have thought."

"I shall do my best," answered Wulf, "and if I fall, why, then, act upon your own counsel. At least, let him not kill both of us."

Having stabled their horses, the brethren wandered into the garden, and, avoiding the cup-bearing women with their drugged drink, drew by a roundabout road to the tall rock. Then, finding themselves alone, they unlocked the door and, slipping through it, locked it again on the further side and groped their way to the moonlit mouth of the cave. Here they stood awhile studying the descent of the gulf as best they could in that light, till suddenly

Godwin, feeling a hand upon his shoulder, started round to find himself face to face with Masouda.

"How did you come?" he asked.

"By a road in which is your only hope," she answered. "Now, Sir Godwin, waste no words, for my time is short, but if you think that you can trust me—and this is for you to judge—give me the Signet which hangs about your neck. If not, go back to the castle and do your best to save the lady Rosamund and yourselves."

Thrusting down his hand between his mail shirt and his breast, Godwin drew out the ancient ring, carved with the mysterious signs and veined with the emblem of the dagger, and handed it to Masouda.

"You trust, indeed," she said with a little laugh, as, after scanning it closely by the light of the moon and touching her forehead with it, she hid it in her bosom.

"Yes, lady," he answered, "I trust you, though why you should risk so much for us I do not know."

"Why? Well, perhaps for hate's sake, for Sinan does not rule by love; perhaps because, being of a wild blood, I am willing to set my life at hazard, who care not if I win or die; perhaps because you saved me from the lioness. What is it to you, Sir Godwin, why a certain woman-spy of the Assassins, whom in your own land you would spit on, chooses to do this or that?"

She ceased and stood before him with heaving breast and flashing eyes, a mysterious white figure in the moonlight, most beautiful to see.

Godwin felt his heart stir and the blood flow to his brow, but before he could speak Wulf broke in, saying, "You bade us spare words, lady Masouda, so tell us what we must do."

"This," she answered, becoming calm again. "Tomorrow night about this hour you fight Lozelle upon the narrow way. That is certain, for all the city talks of it, and, whatever happens Al-Jebal will not deprive them of the spectacle of this fight to the death. Well, you may fall, though that man at heart is a coward, for here courage alone will avail little but rather skill and horsemanship and trick of war. If so, then Sir Godwin fights him, and of this business none can tell the end. Should both of you go down, then I will do my best to save your lady and take her to Saladin, with whom she will be safe."

"You swear that?" said Wulf.

"I have said it; it is enough," she answered impatiently.

"Then I face the bridge and the knave Lozelle with a light heart," said Wulf again.

Masouda went on, "Now if you conquer, Sir Wulf, or if you fall and your brother conquers, both of you—or one of you, as it may happen—must gallop back at full speed toward the stable gate that lies more than a mile from the castle bridge. Mounted as you are, no horse can keep pace with you, nor must you stop at the gate, but ride on, ride like the wind till you reach this place. The gardens will be empty of feasters and of cupbearers, who with every soul within the city will have gathered on the walls and on the housetops to see the combat. There is but one fear—by then a guard may be set before this mound, seeing that Saladin has declared war upon Al-Jebal, and though yonder road is known to few, it is a road, and sentries may watch here. If so, you must cut them down or be cut down, and bring your story to an end. Sir Godwin, here is another key that you may use if you are alone. Take it."

He did so, and she continued; "Now if both of you, or one of you, win through to this cave, enter with your horses, lock the door, bar it, and wait. It may be I will join you here with the princess. But if I do not come by the dawn and you are not discovered and overwhelmed—which should not be, seeing that one man can hold that door against many—then know that the worst has happened, and fly to Saladin and tell him of this road, by which he may take vengeance upon his foe Sinan. Only then, I pray you, doubt not that I have done my best, who if I fail must die most horribly. Now, farewell, until we meet again or—do not meet again. Go; you know the road."

They turned to obey, but when they had gone a few paces Godwin looked round and saw Masouda watching them. The moonlight shone full upon her face, and by it he saw also that tears were running from her dark and tender eyes. Back he came again, and with him Wulf, for that sight drew them. Down he bent before her till his knee touched the ground, and, taking her hand, he kissed it, and said in his gentle voice, "Henceforth through life, through death, we serve two ladies," and what he did Wulf did also.

"Perhaps," she answered sadly; "two ladies—but one love."

Then they went, and, creeping through the bushes to the path, wandered about awhile among the revelers and came to the guest house safely.

Once more it was night, and high above the mountain fortress of Masyaf shone the full summer moon, lighting crag and tower as with some vast silver lamp. Forth from the guest house gate rode the brethren, side by side upon their splendid steeds, and the moon-rays sparkled on their coats of mail, their polished bucklers, blazoned with the cognizance of a grinning skull, their close-fitting helms, and the points of the long, tough lances that had been given them. Round them rode their escort, while in front and behind went a mob of people.

The nation of the Assassins had thrown off its gloom this night. For the sake of the contest it was no longer oppressed even by the fear of attack from Saladin, its mighty foe. To death it was accustomed; death was its watchword; death in many dreadful forms its daily bread.

From the walls of Masyaf, day by day, fedais went out to murder this great one, or that great one, at the bidding of their lord Sinan. For the most part they came not back again; they waited week by week, month by month, year by year, till the moment was ripe, then gave the poisoned cup or drove home the dagger, and escaped or were slain. Death waited them abroad, and if they failed, death waited them at home. Their dreadful sultan was himself a sword of death. At his will they hurled themselves from towers or from precipices; to satisfy his policy they sacrificed their wives and children. And their reward—in life, the drugged cup and voluptuous dreams; after it, as they believed, a still more voluptuous Paradise.

All forms of human agony and doom were known to this people; but now they were promised an unfamiliar sight, that of Frankish knights slaying each other in single combat beneath the silent moon, tilting at full gallop upon a narrow place where many might hesitate to walk, and—oh, joy!—falling perchance, horse and rider together, into the depths below. So they were happy, for to them this was a night of festival, to be followed by a morrow of still greater festival, when their sultan and their god took to himself this stranger beauty as a wife. Doubtless, too, he would soon weary of her, and they would be called together to see her cast from some topmost tower and hear her frail bones break on the cruel rocks below, or—as had happened to the last queen—to watch her writhe out her life in the pangs of poison upon a charge of sorcery. It was indeed a night of festival, a night filled full of promise of rich joys for those who loved death.

On rode the brethren, with stern, impassive faces, but wondering in their hearts whether they would live to see another dawn. The shouting crowd surged round them, breaking through the circle of their guards. A hand was thrust up to Godwin; in it was a letter, which he took and read by the bright moonlight. It was written in English, and brief, "I cannot speak with you. God be with you both, my brothers, God and the spirit of my father. Strike home, Wulf, strike home, Godwin, and fear not for me who will guard myself. Conquer or die, and in life or death, await me. Tomorrow, in the flesh, or in the spirit, we will talk—Rosamund."

Godwin handed the paper to Wulf, and, as he did so, saw that the guards had caught its bearer, a withered, gray-haired woman. They asked her some questions, but she shook her head. Then they cast her down, trampled the life out of her beneath their horses' hoofs, and went on laughing. The mob laughed, also.

"Tear that paper up," said Godwin. Wulf did so, saying, "Our Rosamund has a brave heart. Well, we are of the same blood, and will not fail her."

Now they were come to the open space in front of the narrow bridge, where, tier on tier, the multitude were situated, kept back from its center by lines of guards. On the flat-roofed houses also they were crowded thick as swarming bees, on the circling walls, and on the battlements that protected the far end of the bridge. Before the stone bridge was a low gateway, and upon its roof sat the Al-Jebal, clad in his scarlet robe of festival and by his side, the moonlight gleaming on her jewels, Rosamund. In front, draped in a rich garment, a dagger of gems in her dark hair, stood the interpreter or "mouth" Masouda, and behind her were the dais and guards.

The brethren rode to the space before the arch and halted, saluting with their pennoned spears. Then from the further side advanced another procession, which, opening, revealed the knight Lozelle riding on his great black horse. He had the look of a huge man and fierce he seemed in his armor.

"What!" he shouted, glowering at them. "Am I to fight one against two? Is this your chivalry?"

"Nay, nay, Sir Traitor," answered Wulf. "Nay, nay, betrayer of Christian maids to the power of the heathen dog; you have fought Godwin; now it is the turn of Wulf. Kill Wulf and Godwin remains. Kill Godwin and God remains. Knave, you look your last upon the moon."

Lozelle heard, and seemed to go mad with rage, or fear, or both.

"Lord Sinan," he shouted in Arabic, "this is murder. Am I, who have done you so much service, to be butchered for your pleasure by the lovers of that woman, whom you would honor with the name of wife?"

Sinan heard, and stared at him with dull, angry eyes.

"Aye, you may stare," went on the maddened Lozelle, "but it is true—they are her lovers, not her brothers. Would men take so much pain for a sister's sake, think you? Would they swim into this net of yours for a sister's sake?"

Sinan held up his hand for silence.

"Let the lots be cast," he said, "for whatever these men are, this fight must go on, and it shall be fair."

So a steward, standing by himself, cast lots upon the ground, and having read them, announced that Lozelle must run the first course from the further side of the bridge. Then one took his bridle to lead him across. As he passed the brethren, he grinned in their faces and said, "At least this is sure, you also look your last upon the moon. I am avenged already. The bait that hooked me is a meat for yonder pike, and he will kill you both before her eyes to whet his appetite."

But the brethren answered nothing.

The black horse of Lozelle grew dim in the distance of the moonlit bridge and vanished beneath the farther archway that led to the outer city. Then a herald cried, Masouda translating his words, which another herald echoed from beyond the gulf.

"Thrice will the trumpets blow. At the third blast of the trumpets the knights shall charge and meet in the center of the bridge. Thenceforward they may fight as it pleases them, on horseback or afoot, with lance, with sword, or with dagger, but to the vanquished no mercy will be shown. If he be brought living from the bridge, living he shall be cast into the gulf. Hear the decree of the Al-Jebal!"

Then Wulf's horse was led forward to the entrance of the bridge, and from the further side was led forward the horse of Lozelle.

"Good luck, Brother," said Godwin, as he passed him. "Would that I rode this course instead of you."

"Your turn may come, Brother," answered the grim Wulf, as he set his lance in rest.

Now from some neighboring tower peeled out the first long blast of trumpets, and dead silence fell on all the multitude. Grooms came forward to look to girth and bridle and stirrup strap, but Wulf waved them back.

"I mind my own harness," he said.

The second blast blew, and he loosened the great sword in its scabbard, that sword which had flamed in his forbear's hand upon the turrets of Jerusalem.

"Your gift," he cried back to Rosamund.

And her answer came clear and sweet, "Bear it like your fathers, Wulf. Bear it as it was last borne in the hall at Steeple."

Then there was another silence—a silence, long and deep. Wulf looked at the white and narrow ribbon of the bridge, looked at the black gulf on either side, looked at the gray sky above, in which floated the great globe of the golden moon. Then he leant forward and patted Smoke upon the neck.

For the third time the trumpets blew, and from either end of that bridge, two hundred paces long, the knights flashed towards each other like living bolts of steel. The multitude rose to watch; even Sinan rose. Only Rosamund sat still, gripping the cushions with her hands. Hollow rang the hoofs of the horses upon the stonework, swifter and swifter they flew; lower and lower bent the knights upon their saddles. Soon they were near, and then they met. The spears seemed to shiver, the horses to hustle together on the narrow way and overhang its edge, then on came the black horse towards the inner city, and on sped Smoke towards the farther gate.

"They have passed! They have passed!" roared the multitude.

Look! Lozelle approached, reeling in his saddle, as well he might, for the helm was torn from his head and blood ran from his skull where the lance had grazed it.

"Too high, Wulf; too high," said Godwin sadly. "But oh! If those laces had but held!"

A few moments later, soldiers caught the horse and turned it.

"Another helm!" cried Lozelle.

"Nay," answered Sinan; "yonder knight has lost his shield. New lances—that is all."

So they gave him a fresh lance, and, presently, at the blast of the trumpets again the horses were seen speeding together over the narrow way. They met, and lo! Lozelle, torn from his saddle, but still clinging to the reins, was flung backwards, far backwards, to fall on the stonework of the bridge. Down, too, beneath the mighty shock went his black horse, a huddled heap, and lay there struggling.

"Wulf will fall over him!" cried Rosamund. But Smoke did not fall; the stallion gathered itself together—the moonlight shone so clear that every watcher saw it—and since stop it could not, leapt straight over the fallen black horse—ay, and over the rider beyond—and sped on in its stride. Then the black found its feet again and galloped forward to the further gate. Lozelle also found his feet and turned to run.

"Stand! Stand, coward!" yelled ten thousand voices, and, hearing them, he drew his sword and stood.

Within three great strides Wulf dragged his charger to its haunches, then wheeled it round.

"Charge him!" shouted the multitude; but Wulf remained seated, as though unwilling to attack a horseless man. Next he sprang from his saddle, and accompanied by the horse Smoke, which followed him as a dog follows its master, walked slowly towards Lozelle. As Wulf walked, he cast away his lance and drew his great, cross-hilted sword.

Again the silence fell, and through it rang the cry of Godwin, "A D'Arcy! A D'Arcy !"

"A D'Arcy! A D'Arcy!" came back Wulf's answer from the bridge, and his voice echoed thin and hollow in the spaces of the gulf. Yet they rejoiced to hear it, for it told them that he was sound and strong.

Wulf had no shield and Lozelle had no helm—the fight was even. They crouched opposite each other, the swords flashed aloft in the moonlight; from far away came the distant clank of steel, a soft, continual clamor of iron on iron. A glancing blow fell on Wulf's mail, who had no shield wherewith to guard himself, and he staggered back. Another blow, another, and another, and back, still back he reeled—back to the edge of the bridge, back till he struck against the horse that stood behind him, and, resting there a moment, as it seemed, regained his balance.

Then there was a change of tactics. Wulf rushed forward, wielding the great blade in both hands. The stroke fell upon Lozelle's shield and seemed to shear it in two, for in that stillness all could hear the clang of its upper half as it fell upon the stones. Beneath the weight of it he staggered, sank to his knee, gained his feet again, and in his turn gave back. Yes, now it was Lozelle who rocked and reeled. The wayward knight lunged forward but soon fell beneath a mighty blow, which missed his head but fell squarely upon his shoulder. He lay there like a log, till presently the moonlight shone upon his mailed hand stretched upward in a prayer for mercy.

From housetop and terrace wall, from soaring gates and battlements, the multitude of the people of the Assassins gathered on either side of the gulf broke into a roar that beat up the mountain sides like a voice of thunder. And the roar shaped itself to these words, "Kill him! Kill him! Kill him!"

Sinan held up his hand, and a sudden silence fell. Then he, too, screamed in his thin voice, "Kill him! He is conquered!"

But the great Wulf only leaned upon the cross-handle of his brand, and looked at the fallen foe. Several seconds later, he seemed to speak with him; then Lozelle lifted the blade that lay beside him and gave it to him in token of surrender. Wulf handled it awhile, shook it on high in triumph, and whirled it about his head till it shone in the moonlight. Next, with a shout he cast it from him far into the gulf, where it was seen for a moment, an arc of gleaming light, and then was gone.

Now, taking no more heed of the conquered knight, Wulf turned and began to walk towards his horse.

Scarcely was his back towards him when Lozelle was on his feet again, a dagger in his hand.

"Look behind you!" yelled Godwin; but the spectators, pleased that the fight was not yet done, broke into a roar of cheers. Wulf heard and swung round. As he faced Lozelle the dagger struck him on the breast, and well must it have been for him that his mail was good. To use his sword he had neither space nor time, but before the next stroke could fall Wulf's arms were around Lozelle, and the fight for life begun.

To and fro they reeled and staggered, whirling round and round, till none could tell which of them was Wulf or which his foe. Now they were on the edge of the abyss, and, in that last dread strain for mastery, seemed to stand there still as stone. Then one man began to bend down. See! His head hung over. Further and further he bent, but his arms could not be loosened.

"They will both go!" cried the multitude in their joy.

Look! A dagger flashed. Once, twice, thrice it gleamed, and those wrestlers fell apart, while from deep down in the gulf came the thud of a fallen body.

"Which—oh, which?" cried Rosamundfrom her battlement.

"Sir Hugh Lozelle," answered Godwin in a solemn voice.

Then the head of Rosamund fell forward on her breast, and for a while she seemed to sleep.

Wulf went to his horse, turned it about on the bridge and, throwing his arm around its neck, rested for a space. Then he mounted and walked slowly towards the inner gate. Pushing through the guard and officers, Godwin rode out to meet him.

"Bravely done, Brother," he said, when they came face to face. "Say, are you hurt?"

"Bruised and shaken—no more," answered Wulf.

"A good beginning, truly. Now for the rest," said Godwin. Then he glanced over his shoulder, and added, "See, they are leading Rosamund away, but Sinan remains, to speak with you doubtless, for Masouda beckons."

"What shall we do?" asked Wulf. "Make a plan, Brother, for my head swims."

"Hear what he has to say. Then, as your horse is not wounded either, ride for it when I give the signal as Masouda bade us. There is no other way. Pretend that you are wounded."

So, Godwin leading, while the multitude roared a welcome to the conquering Wulf who had borne himself so bravely for their pleasure, they rode to the mouth of the bridge and halted in the little space before the archway. There Al-Jebal spoke by Masouda.

"A noble fight," he said. "I did not think that Franks could fight so well. Say, Sir Knight, will you feast with me in my palace?"

"I thank you, lord," answered Wulf, "but I must rest while my brother tends my hurts," and he pointed to blood upon his mail. "Tomorrow, if it pleases you."

Sinan stared at them and stroked his beard, while they trembled, waiting for the word of life or death.

It came.

"Good. So be it. Tomorrow I wed the lady Rose of Roses, and you two—her brothers—shall give her to me, as is fitting," and he sneered. "Then also you shall receive the reward of valor—a great reward, I promise you."

While he spoke, Godwin, staring upward, had noted a little wandering cloud floating across the moon. Slowly it covered it, and the place grew dim.

"Now," he whispered, and bowing to the Al-Jebal, they pushed their horses through the open gate where the mob closed in on them, thus for a little while holding back the escort from following on their heels. They spoke to Flame and Smoke, and the good horses plunged onward side by side, separating the crowd as the prows of boats separate the water. In ten paces it grew thin, in thirty it was behind them, for all folk were gathered about the archway where they could see, and none beyond. Forward they cantered, till the broad road turned to the left, and in that faint light they were hidden.

"Away!" said Godwin, shaking his reins.

Forward leapt the horses at speed. Again Godwin turned, taking that road which ran round the city wall and through the gardens, soon passing the guest castle to the left. The escort that followed assumed they had taken the road, which passed along the main street of the inner town, thinking that they were ahead of them. Three minutes more and the brothers were in the lonely gardens, in which that night no women wandered and no neophytes dreamed in the pavilions.

"Wulf," said Godwin, as they swept forward, skimming the turf like swallows, "draw your sword and be ready. Remember the secret cave may be guarded, and, if so, we must kill or be killed."

Wulf nodded, and next instant two long blades flashed in the moonlight, for the little cloud had passed away. Within a hundred paces of them rose the tall rock, but between it and the mound were two mounted guards. These heard the beating of horses' hoofs and, wheeling about, stared to see two armed knights sweeping down upon them like a whirlwind. They called to them to stop, hesitating, then rode forward a few paces, as though wondering whether this were not a vision.

In a moment the brethren were on them. The soldiers lifted their lances, but before they could thrust, the sword of Godwin caught one between neck and shoulder and sunk to his breast bone, while the sword of Wulf, used as a spear, had pierced the other through and through, so that those men fell dead by the door of the mound, never knowing who had slain them.

The brethren pulled upon their bridles and spoke to Flame and Smoke, halting them within a dozen yards. Then they wheeled round and sprang from their saddles. One of the dead guards still held his horse's reins, and the other beast stood by snorting. Godwin caught it before it stirred, then, holding all four of them, threw the key to Wulf and urged him to unlock the door. Soon it was done, although he staggered at the task; then he held the horses, while one by one Godwin led them in, and that without trouble, for the beasts thought that this was but a cave-hewn stable of a kind to which they were accustomed.

"What of the dead men?" said Wulf.

"They had best keep us company," answered Godwin; and, running out, he carried in first one and then the other.

"Swift!" he said, as he threw down the second corpse. "Shut the door. I caught sight of horsemen riding through the trees. Nay, they saw nothing."

So they locked the massive door and barred it, and with beating hearts waited in the dark, expecting every moment to hear soldiers battering at its timbers. But no sound came; the searchers, if such they were, had passed on to other locations.

Now while Wulf made the effort to fasten up the horses near the mouth of the cave, Godwin gathered stones as large as he could lift and piled them up against the door.

It would take many men an hour or more to break through this door, for it was banded with iron and set fast in the living rock.

Chapter XV
The Flight to Emesa

The brethren found it difficult, as men of action inevitably do, to wait patiently in the dreary confines of their rock cavern. Water trickled down from the walls of this cave, and Wulf, who was parched with thirst, gathered it in his hands and drank till he was satisfied. Godwin placed a damp cool cloth upon his brother's aching head and cleaned as many of his brother's wounds as possible.

When this was done, and he had looked to the saddles and trappings of the horses, Wulf told of all that had passed between him and Lozelle on the bridge.

"Never," concluded Wulf, "shall I forget the look of that man's eyes as he fell backwards, or the whistling scream which came from his pierced throat."

"At least there is one less rogue in the world, although he was a brave one in his own knavish fashion," answered Godwin. "Moreover, my brother," he added, placing his arm around Wulf's neck, "I am glad it fell to you to fight him, for at the last grip your might overcame, where I, who am not so strong, should have failed. Further, I think you did well to show mercy, as a good knight should; that thereby you have gained great honor, and that if his spirit can see through the darkness, our dead uncle is proud of you now, as I am, my brother."

"I thank you," replied Wulf simply; "but, in this hour of torment, who can think of such things as honor gained or lost?"

Then, lest he should grow stiff, who was sorely bruised beneath his mail, they began to walk up and down the cave from where the horses stood to where the two dead Assassins lay by the door, the faint light gleaming upon their stern, dark features. Ill company they seemed in that silent, lonely place.

The time crept on; the moon sank towards the mountains.

"What if they do not come?" asked Wulf.

"Let us wait to think of it till dawn," answered Godwin.

Again they walked the length of the cave and back.

"How can they come, the door being barred?" asked Wulf.

"How did Masouda come and go?" answered Godwin. Oh, question me no more; it is in the hand of God."

"Look," said Wulf, in a whisper. "Who stands yonder at the end of the cave—there by the dead men?"

"Their spirits, perchance," answered Godwin, drawing his sword and leaning forward. Then he looked, and true enough there stood two figures faintly outlined in the gloom. They glided towards them, and now the level moonlight shone upon their white robes and gleamed in the gems they wore.

"I cannot see them," said a voice. "Oh, those dead soldiers, what do they portend?"

"At least yonder stand their horses," answered another voice.

Now the brethren guessed the truth, and, like men in a dream, stepped forward from the shadow of the wall.

"Rosamund!" they said.

"Oh, Godwin! Oh, Wulf!" she cried in answer. "Oh, Jesu, I thank Thee, I thank Thee—Thee, and this brave woman!" and, casting her arms about Masouda, she kissed her on the cheek.

Masouda pushed her back, and said, in a voice that was almost harsh, "It is not fitting, Princess, that your pure lips should touch the cheek of a woman of the Assassins."

But Rosamund would not be repulsed.

"It is most fitting," she sobbed, "that I should give you thanks who but for you must also have become 'a woman of the Assassins,' or an inhabitant of the House of Death."

Then Masouda kissed her back, and, thrusting her away into the arms of Wulf, said roughly, "So, pilgrims Peter and John, your patron saints have brought you through so far; and, John, you fight right well. Nay, do not stop for our story, if you wish us to live to tell it. What! You have the soldiers' horses with your own? Well done! I did not credit you with so much wit. Now, Sir Wulf, can you walk? Yes; so much the better; it will save you a rough ride, for this place is steep, though not so steep as one you know of. Now set the princess upon Flame, for no cat is surer-footed than that horse, as you may remember. Peter, I who know the path will lead it. John, take you the other two; Peter, do you follow last of all with Smoke, and, if they hang back, prick them with your sword. Come, Flame, be not afraid, Flame. Where I go, you can come," and Masouda thrust her way through the bushes and over the edge of the cliff, talking to the snorting horse and patting its neck.

A minute more, and they were scrambling down a mountain ridge so steep that it seemed as though they must fall and be dashed to pieces at the bottom. Yet they fell not, for, made as it had been to meet such hours of need, this road was safer than it appeared, with ridges cut in the rock at the worst places.

Down they went, and down, till at length, panting, but safe, they stood at the bottom of the darksome gulf where only the starlight shone, for here the rays of the low moon could not reach.

"Mount," said Masouda. "Princess, stay you on Flame; he is the surest and the swiftest. Sir Wulf, keep your own horse Smoke; your brother and I will ride those of the soldiers. Though not very swift, doubtless they are good beasts, and accustomed to such roads." Then she leapt to the saddle as a woman born in the desert can, and pushed her horse in front.

For a mile or more Masouda led them along the rocky bottom of the gulf, where because of the stones they could only travel at a foot pace, till they came to a deep cleft on the left hand, up which they began to ride. By now the moon was quite behind the mountains, and such faint light as came from the stars began to be obscured with drifting clouds. Still, they stumbled on till they reached a little glade where water ran and grass grew.

"Halt," said Masouda. "Here we must wait till dawn, for in this darkness the horses cannot keep their footing on the stones. Moreover, all about us lie precipices, over one of which we might fall."

"But they will pursue us," pleaded Rosamund.

"Not until they have light to see by," answered Masouda, "or at least we must take the risk, for to go forward would be madness. Sit down and rest a while, and let the horses drink a little and eat a mouthful of grass, holding their reins in our hands, for they and we may need all our strength before tomorrow's sun is set. Sir Wulf, say, are you much hurt?"

"But very little," he answered in a cheerful voice; "a few bruises beneath my mail—that is all, for Lozelle's sword was heavy. Tell us, I pray you, what happened, after we rode away from the castle bridge."

"This, knights. The princess here, being overcome, was escorted by the slaves back to her chambers, but Sinan told me to stay with him awhile that he might speak to you through me. Do you know what was in his mind? To have you killed at once, both of you, whom Lozelle had told him were this lady's lovers, and not her brothers. Only he feared that there might be trouble with the people, who were pleased with the fighting, so held his hand. Then he bade you to the supper, whence you would not have returned; but when Sir Wulf said that he was hurt, I whispered to him that what he wished to do could best be done on the morrow at the wedding feast when he was in his own halls, surrounded by his guards.

"'Aye,' he answered, 'these brethren shall fight with them until they are driven into the gulf. It will be a goodly sight for me and my queen to see.'"

"Oh! Horrible, horrible," said Rosamund.

Godwin muttered, "I swear that I would have fought, not with his guards, but with Sinan only."

"So he permitted you to go, and I left him, also. Before I went he spoke to me, bidding me bring the princess to him privately within two hours after we had supped, as he wished to speak to her alone about the ceremony of her marriage on the morrow, and to make her gifts. I answered aloud that his commands should be obeyed, and hurried to the guest castle. There I found your lady recovered from her faintness, but mad with fear, and forced her to eat and drink.

"The rest is short. Before the two hours were gone a messenger came, saying that Al-Jebal required me to do what he had commanded.

"'Return,' I answered; 'the princess adorns herself. We follow promptly and alone, as it is commanded.'

"Then I threw this cloak around her and told her to be brave, and, if we failed, to choose whether she would take Sinan or death for lord. Next, I took the ring you had, the Signet of the dead Al-Jebal, who gave it to your kinsman, and held it before the slaves, who bowed and let me pass. We came to the guards, and to them again I showed the ring. They bowed also, but when they saw that we turned down the passage to the left and not to the right, as we should have done to come to the doors of the inner palace, they tried to stop us.

"'Acknowledge the Signet,' I answered. 'Dogs, what is it to you which road the Signet takes?' Then they also let us pass.

"Now, following the passage, we were out of the guest house and in the gardens, and I led her to what is called the prison tower, where runs the secret way. Here were more guards whom I ordered to open in the name of Sinan. They said, 'We obey not. This place is shut save to the Signet itself.'

"'Behold it!' I answered.

"The officer looked and said: 'It is the very Signet, sure enough, and there is no other.' Yet he paused, studying the black stone veined with the red dagger and the ancient writing on it.

"'Are you then weary of life?' I asked. 'Fool, the Al-Jebal will not be kept waiting. He enters secretly from the palace. Woe to you if he does not find his lady there!'

"'It is the Signet that he must have sent, sure enough,' the captain said again, 'to disobey its sign is death.'

"'Yes, open, open,' whispered his companions.

"So they opened, though doubtfully, and we entered, and I barred the door behind us. Then, to be short, through the darkness of the tower basement, guiding ourselves by the wall, we crept to the entrance of that way of which I know the secret. Aye, and along all its length and through the rock door of escape at the end which I set so that none can turn it, save skilled masons with their tools, and into the cave where we found you. It was no great matter, having the Signet, although without the Signet it had not been possible tonight, when every gate is guarded."

"No great matter!" gasped Rosamund. "Oh, Godwin and Wulf! If you could know how she thought of and made ready everything; if you could have seen how all those cruel men glared at us, searching out our very souls! If you could have heard how boldly she answered them, waving that ring before their eyes and bidding them to obey its presence, or to die!"

"Which they surely have done by now," broke in Masouda quietly, "though I do not pity them, who were wicked. No; thank me not; I have done what I promised to do, neither less nor more, and—I love danger and a high stake. Tell us your story, Sir Godwin."

So, seated there on the grass in the darkness, he told them of their mad ride and of the slaying of the guards. Rosamund listened and raised her hands and thanked Heaven for its mercies in bringing them beyond those accursed walls.

"You may be within them again before sunset," said Masouda grimly.

"Yes," answered Wulf, "but not alive. Now what plan have you? To ride for the coast towns?"

"No," replied Masouda; "at least not straight, since to do so we must pass through the country of the Assassins, who by this day's light will be warned to watch for us. We must ride through the desert mountain lands to Emesa, many miles away, and cross the Orontes there, then down into Baalbec, and so back to Beirut."

"Emesa?" said Godwin. "Why, Saladin holds that place, and of Baalbec the lady Rosamund is princess."

"Which is best?" asked Masouda shortly. "That she should fall into the hands of Saladin, or back into those of the master of the Assassins? Choose which you wish."

"I choose Saladin," broke in Rosamund, "for at least he is my uncle, and will do me no wrong." Nor, knowing the case, did the others disagree with her.

As time moved on, the summer day began to break, and while it was still too dark to travel, Godwin and Rosamund let the horses graze, holding them by their bridles. Masouda, also, taking off the hauberk of Wulf, doctored his bruises as best she could with the crushed leaves of a bush that grew by the stream, having first washed them with water, and though the time was short, helped him much. Then, so soon as the dawn was gray, having drunk their fill and, as they had nothing else, eaten some watercress that grew in the stream, they tightened their saddle girths and started. Scarcely had they gone a hundred yards when, from the gulf beneath, that was hidden in gray mists, they heard the sound of horses' hoofs and men's voices.

"Push on," said Masouda, "Al-Jebal is on our tracks."

Upwards they climbed through the gathering light, skirting the edge of dreadful precipices which in the gloom it would have been impossible to pass, till at length they reached a great plateau, that ran to the foot of some mountains a dozen miles or more away. Among those mountains soared two peaks, set close together. To these Masouda pointed, saying that their road ran between them, and that beyond lay the valley of the Orontes. While she spoke, far behind them they heard the sound of men shouting, although they could see nothing because of the dense mist.

"Push on," said Masouda; "there is no time to spare," and they went forward, but only at a steady gallop, for the ground was still rough and the light uncertain.

When they had covered some six miles of the distance between them and the mountain pass, the sun rose suddenly and sucked up the mist. This was what they saw. Before them lay a flat, sandy plain; behind, the stony ground that they had traversed, and riding over it, two miles from them, some twenty men of the Assassins.

"They cannot catch us," said Wulf; but Masouda pointed to the right, where the mist still hung, and said, "I suggest you look at those spears."

As the mist cleared, a mile away they saw hundreds of mounted soldiers.

"Look," she said; "they have come round during the night, as I feared they would. Now we must cross the path before them or be taken," and she struck her horse fiercely with a stick she had cut from the stream. Half a mile further, a shout from the great body of men to their right, which was answered by another shout from those behind, told them that they had been seen.

"On!" said Masouda. "The race will be close." So they began to gallop their best.

Two miles were done, but although the group behind was far off, the great cloud of dust to their right grew ever nearer till it seemed as though it must reach the mouth of the mountain pass before them. Then Godwin spoke, "Wulf and Rosamund, ride on. Your horses are swift and can outpace them. At the crest of the mountain pass wait a while to breathe the beasts, and see if we come. If not, ride on again, and God be with you."

"Hurry," said Masouda, "ride and head for the Emesa Bridge—it can be seen from far—and there yield yourselves to the officers of Saladin."

They hung back, but in a stern voice Godwin repeated, "Ride, I command you both."

"For Rosamund's sake, so be it," answered Wulf. Then he called to Smoke and Flame, and they stretched themselves out upon the sand and moved on swifter than swallows. Soon Godwin and Masouda, toiling behind, saw them enter the mouth of the pass.

"Good," she said. "Except those of their own breed, there are no horses in Syria that can catch those two. They will come to Emesa, have no fear."

"Who was the man who brought them to us?" asked Godwin, as they galloped side by side, their eyes fixed upon the ever-approaching cloud of dust, in which the spear points sparkled.

"My father's brother—my uncle, as I called him," she answered. "He is a sheik of the desert, who owns the ancient breed that cannot be bought for gold."

"Then you are not of the Assassins, Masouda?"

"No; I may tell you, now that the end seems near. My father was an Arab, my mother a noble Frank, a Frenchwoman, whom he found starving in the desert after a fight, and took to his tent and made his wife. The Assassins fell upon us and killed him and her, and captured me as a child of twelve. Afterwards, when I grew older, being beautiful in those days, I was taken to the harem of Sinan, and, although in secret I had been bred up a Christian by my mother, they swore me to his accursed faith. Now you will understand why I hate him so sorely who murdered my father and my mother, and made me what I am; why I hold myself so vile also. Yes, I have been forced to serve as his spy or be killed, who, although he believed me his faithful slave, desired first to be avenged upon him."

"I do not hold you vile," panted Godwin, as he spurred his laboring steed. "I hold you most noble."

"I rejoice to hear it before we die," she answered, looking him in the eyes in such a fashion that he dropped his head before her burning gaze, "who hold you dear, Sir Godwin, for whose sake I have dared these things, although I am nothing to you. Do not try to answer, the lady Rosamund has told me all that story—except its answer."

Two minutes later, they were off the sand over which they had been racing side by side, and began to crest the mountain slope, nor was Godwin sorry that the clatter of their horses' hoofs upon the stones prevented further speech between them. So far they had outpaced the Assassins, who had a longer and a rougher road to travel; but the great cloud of dust was not five hundred yards away, and in front of it, shaking their spears, rode some of their best soldiers.

"These horses still have strength; they are better than I thought them," cried Masouda. "They will not gain on us across the mountains, but afterwards—"

For the next mile they spoke no more, for they needed to keep their horses from falling as they toiled up the steep path. At length, they reached the crest, and there, on the very top of it, saw Wulf and Rosamund standing by Flame and Smoke.

"They rest," Godwin said, then he shouted, "Mount! Mount! The foe is close."

So they climbed to their saddles again, and, all four of them began to descend the long slope that stretched to the plain two leagues beneath. Far off across this plain ran a broad silver streak, beyond which from that height they could see the walls of a city.

"The Orontes!" cried Masouda. "Cross that, and we are safe." But Godwin looked first at his horse, then at Masouda, and shook his head.

Well might he do so, for, stout-hearted as they were, the beasts were much distressed that had galloped so far without drawing rein. Down the steep road they plunged, panting; indeed, at times it was hard to keep them on their feet.

"They will reach the plain—no more," said Godwin, and Masouda nodded.

The descent was almost done, and not a mile behind them the white-robed Assassins streamed endlessly. Godwin plied his spurs and Masouda her whip, though with little hope, for they knew that the end was near. Down the last slope they rushed, till suddenly, as they reached its foot, Masouda's horse reeled, stopped, and sank to the ground, while Godwin's pulled up beside it.

"Ride on!" he cried to Rosamund and Wulf in front; but they would not. He stormed at them, but they replied, "Nay, we will die together."

Masouda looked at the horses Flame and Smoke, which seemed but little troubled.

"So be it," she said; "they have carried double before, and must again. Mount in front of the lady, Sir Godwin; and, Sir Wulf, give me your hand, and you will learn what this breed can do."

So they mounted. Forward started Flame and Smoke with a long, swinging gallop, while from the Assassins above, who thought that they held them, went up a shout of rage and wonder.

"Their horses are also tired, and we may beat them yet," called the dauntless Masouda. But Godwin and Wulf looked sadly at the six miles of plain between them and the riverbank.

On they went, and on. A quarter of it was done. Half of it was done, but now the first of the fedai hung upon their flanks not two hundred yards behind. Little by little this distance lessened, until they were scarcely fifty yards away, and one of them flung a spear. In her terror, Rosamund sobbed aloud.

"Spur the horses, knights!" cried Masouda, and for the first time they spurred them.

At the sting of the steel Flame and Smoke sprang forward as though they had but just left their stable door, and the gap between pursuers and pursued widened. Two more miles were done, and scarce seven furlongs from them they saw the broad mouth of the bridge, while the towers of Emesa beyond seemed so close that in this clear air they could discern the watchmen outlined against the sky. Then they descended a little valley, and lost sight of bridge and town.

At the rise of the opposing slope the strength of Flame and Smoke at last began to fail beneath their double burdens. They panted and trembled, and, save in short rushes, no longer answered to the spur. The Assassins saw, and came on with wild shouts. Nearer and nearer they drew, and the sound of their horses' hoofs beating on the sand was like the sound of thunder. Now once more they were fifty yards away, and now but thirty, and again the spears began to flash, though none struck them.

Masouda screamed to the horses in Arabic, and gallantly did they struggle, plunging up the hill with slow, convulsive bounds. Godwin and Wulf looked at each other, then, at a signal, checked their speed, leapt to earth, and, turning, drew their swords.

"On!" they cried and, lightened of their weight, once more the reeling horses plunged forward.

The Assassins were upon them. Wulf struck a mighty blow and emptied the saddle of the first, then was swept to earth. As he fell, from behind him he heard a scream of joy, and struggling to his knees, looked round. Lo! From over the crest of the rise rushed squadron upon squadron of turbaned cavalry, who, as they came, set their lances, and shouted, "Saladin! Saladin!"

The Assassins saw also, and turned to fly—too late!

"A horse! A horse!" screamed Godwin in Arabic; and after several minutes—how he never knew—found himself mounted and charging with the Saracens.

To Wulf, too, a horse was brought, but he could not struggle to its saddle. Thrice he strove, then fell backwards and lay upon the sand, waving his sword and shouting where he lay, while Masouda stood by him, a dagger in her hand, and with her Rosamund upon her knees.

Now the pursuers were the pursued, and dreadful was the reckoning that they must pay. Their horses were worn out and could no longer run swiftly. Some of the fedai were cut down upon them. Some dismounted and, gathering themselves in little groups, fought bravely till they were slain, while a few were taken prisoners. Of all that great troop of men not a dozen made it back alive to Masyaf to make report to their master of how the chase of his lost bride had ended.

A while later and Wulf from his seat upon the ground saw Godwin riding back towards him, his red sword in his hand. With him rode a sturdy, bright-eyed man gorgeously appareled, at the sight of whom Rosamund sprang to her feet; then, as he dismounted, ran forward and with a little cry cast her arms around him.

"Hassan! Prince Hassan! Is it indeed you? Oh, God be praised!" she gasped, then, had not Masouda caught her, would have fallen.

The emir looked at her, her long hair loose, her face stained, her veil torn, but still clad in the silk and gleaming gems with which she had been decked as the bride-elect of Al-Jebal. Then low to the earth he bent his knee, while the sober Saracens watched, and taking the hem of her garment, he kissed it.

"Allah be praised, indeed!" he said. "I, his unworthy servant, thank him from my heart, who never thought to see you among the living. Soldiers, salute. Before you stands the lady Rose of the World, princess of Baalbec and niece of our lord, Saladin, Commander of the Faithful."

Then, in stately salutation to this disheveled, but still queenly woman, uprose hand, and spear, and scimitar, while Wulf cried from where he lay, "Why, it is our merchant of the drugged wine—none other! Oh! Sir Saracen, does not the memory of that chapman's trick shame you now?"

The emir Hassan heard, and his face grew red. Speaking softly he pleaded, "Like you, Sir Wulf, I am the slave of Fate, and must obey. Be not bitter against me till you know all."

"I am not bitter," answered Wulf, "but I always pay for my drink, and we will settle that score yet, as I have sworn."

"Hush!" broke in Rosamund. "Although he stole me, he is also my deliverer and friend through many a peril, and, had it not been for him, by now—" and she shuddered.

"I do not know all the story, but, Princess, it seems that you should thank not me, but these goodly cousins of yours and those splendid horses," and Hassan pointed to Smoke and Flame, which stood by quivering, with hollow flanks and drooping heads.

"There is another whom I must thank also, this noble woman, as you will call her also when you hear the story," said Rosamund, flinging her arm about the neck of Masouda.

"My master will reward her," said Hassan. "But, oh! lady, what must you think of me who seemed to desert you so basely? Yet I reasoned well. In the castle of that son of Satan, Sinan," and he spat upon the ground, "I could not have aided you, for there he would only have butchered me. But by escaping I thought that I might help, so I bribed the Frankish knave with the priceless Star of my House," and he touched the great jewel that he wore in his turban, "and with what money I had, to loose my bonds, and while he pouched the gold I stabbed him with his own knife and fled. But this morning I reached yonder city in command of ten thousand men, charged to rescue you if I could; if not, to avenge you, for the ambassadors of Saladin informed me of your plight. An hour ago, the watchmen on the towers reported that they saw two horses galloping across the plain beneath a double burden, pursued by soldiers whom from their robes they took to be Assassins. So, as I have a quarrel with the Assassins, I crossed the bridge, formed up five hundred men in a hollow, and waited, never guessing that it was you who fled. You know the rest—and the Assassins know it also, for," he added grimly, "you have been well avenged."

"Follow it up," said Wulf, "and the vengeance shall be better, for I will show you the secret way into Masyaf—or, if I cannot, Godwin will—and there you may hurl Sinan from his own towers."

Hassan shook his head and answered, "I should like it well, for with this magician my master also has an ancient quarrel. But he has other feuds upon his hands," and he looked meaningly at Wulf and Godwin, "and my orders were to rescue the princess and no more. Well, she has been rescued, and some hundreds of heads have paid the price of all that she has suffered. Also, that secret way of yours will be safe enough by now. So there I let the matter bide, glad enough that it has ended thus. Only I warn you all—and myself, also—to walk warily, since, if I know aught of him, Sinan's fedais will henceforth dog the steps of every one of us, striving to bring us to our ends by murder. Now here come litters; enter them, all of you, and be borne to the city, who have ridden far enough today. Fear not for your horses; they shall be led in gently and saved alive, if skill and care can save them. I go to count the slain, and will join you presently in the citadel."

So the bearers came and lifted up Wulf, and helped Godwin from his horse—for now that the struggle was over he could scarcely stand—and with him Rosamund and Masouda. Placing them in the litters, they carried them, escorted by cavalry, across the bridge of the Orontes into the city of Emesa, where they lodged them in the citadel.

Here also, after giving them a drink of barley gruel, and rubbing their backs and legs with ointment, they led the horses Smoke and Flame, slowly and with great trouble, for these could hardly stir, and laid them down on thick beds of straw, tempting them with food, which after awhile they ate. The four—Rosamund, Masouda, Godwin, and Wulf—ate also of some soup, and after the wounds of Wulf had been tended by a skilled doctor, went to their beds, from where they did not rise again for nearly two days.

Chapter XVI
The Sultan Saladin

On the third morning Godwin awoke to see rays of sunlight streaming through the latticed window. The sunlight also fell upon another bed nearby where Wulf still lay sleeping. He now wore bandages on his head where he had been hurt in the last charge against the Assassins, and other bandages around his arms and body, which were much bruised during the fight upon the dreadful bridge.

Wondrous was it to Godwin to watch him lying there sleeping soundly, notwithstanding his injuries, and to think of what they had gone through together with so little harm; to think, also, of how they had rescued Rosamund out of the very mouth of that earthly hell of which he could see the peaks through the open window-place—out of the very hands of that fiend, its ruler. Reckoning the tale day by day, he reflected on their adventures since they landed at Beirut, and began to recognize how Heaven had guided their every step.

In spite of the warnings that were given them, to visit the Al-Jebal in his stronghold had seemed madness. Yet there, where none could have thought that she would be, they had found Rosamund. There they had been avenged upon the false knight Sir Hugh Lozelle, who had betrayed her, first to Saladin, then to Sinan, and sent him down to death and judgment. Then they managed to escape and to rescue Rosamund.

Oh, how wise they had been to obey the dying words of their uncle, Sir Andrew, who doubtless was given foresight at the end! God and His saints had helped them, who could not have helped themselves, and His minister had been Masouda. If it had not been for Masouda, Rosamund would by now be lost or dead, and they, if their lives were still left to them, would be wanderers in the great land of Syria, seeking for one who never could be found.

Why had Masouda done these things, again and again putting her own life in danger to save theirs and the honor of another woman? As he asked himself the question Godwin felt the red blood rise to his face. Because she hated Sinan, who had murdered her parents and degraded her, she said; and doubtless that had to do with the matter. But it was no longer possible to hide the truth. She loved him, and had loved him from the first hour when they met. He had always suspected it—in that wild journey with the horses upon the mountain side, when she sat with her arms around him and her face pressed against his face; when she kissed his feet after he had saved her from the lion, and in many smaller ways.

But as they followed Wulf and Rosamund up the mountain pass while the host of the Assassins thundered at their heels, and in broken gasps she had told him of her sad history, then it was that he grew sure. Then, too, he had said that he held her not vile, but noble, as indeed he did; and, thinking that death was near, she had answered that she held him dear, and looked on him as a woman looks upon her only love—a message in her eyes that no man could fail to read. Yet if this were so, why had Masouda saved Rosamund, the lady to whom she knew well that he was sworn? Reared among those cruel folk who could wade to their desire through blood and think it honor, would she not have left her rival to her doom, seeing that oaths do not hold beyond the grave?

An answer came into the heart of Godwin, at the very thought of which he turned pale and trembled. His brother was also sworn to Rosamund, and she in her soul must be sworn to one of them. Was it not to Wulf—Wulf who was handsomer and stronger than he, to Wulf, the conqueror of Lozelle? Had Rosamund told Masouda this? No, surely not.

Yet women can read each other's hearts, piercing veils through which no man may see, and perchance Masouda had read the heart of Rosamund. She stood behind her during the dreadful duel at the gate, and watched her face when Wulf's death seemed sure; she might have heard words that broke in agony from her lips in those moments of torment.

Oh, without doubt it was so, and Masouda had protected Rosamund because she knew that her love was for Wulf and not for him. The thought was very bitter, and in its pain Godwin groaned aloud, while a fierce jealousy of the brave and handsome knight who slept at his side, dreaming, doubtless, of the fame that he had won and the reward by which it would be crowned. Such thoughts gripped at his vitals like the icy hand of death. Then Godwin remembered the oath that they two had sworn far away in the priory at Stangate, and the love passing the love of woman which he bore towards this brother. He well knew the duty of a Christian warrior whereto he was vowed, and hiding his face in his pillow he prayed for strength.

It would seem that it came to him—at least, when he lifted his head again the jealousy was gone, and only the great grief remained. Fear remained also—for what of Masouda? How should he deal with her? He was certain that this was no trivial feeling which would pass—until her life passed with it, and, beautiful as she was, and noble as she was, he did not wish her love. He could find no answer to these questions, save this—that things must go on as they were decreed. For himself, he, Godwin, would strive to do his duty, to keep his hands clean, and await the end, whatever that might be, while endevouring not to unduly encourage Masouda.

Wulf woke up, stretched his arms, then complained because that action hurt him. He proceeded to grumble at the brightness of the light upon his eyes, and said that he was very hungry. Then he arose, and with the help of Godwin, dressed himself, but not in his armor. Neither Wulf nor Godwin needed their mail for the yellow-coated soldiers of Saladin, grave-faced and watchful, were pacing before their door—for night and day they were closely guarded lest Assassins should move against them. In the fortress of Masyaf, indeed, where they were also guarded, it had been otherwise. Wulf heard the step of the sentries on the stone pavement outside and shook his great shoulders as though he shivered.

"That sound makes my backbone cold," he said. "For a moment, as my eyes opened, I thought that we were back again in the guest chambers of Al-Jebal, where folk crept round us as we slept and murderers marched to and fro outside the curtains, fingering their knife points. Well, whatever there is to come, thank the Saints, that is done with. I tell you, Brother, I have had enough of mountains, and narrow bridges, and Assassins. Henceforth, I desire to live upon a land with never a hill in sight, amidst honest folk as stupid as their own sheep, who go to church on Sundays and delight not in the shedding of blood. Give me the fields of Essex with the east winds blowing over them, and the primroses abloom upon the bank, and the lanes filled with laughing children, and for your share you may take all the scented gardens of Sinan and the cups and jewels of his ladies, with the adventures of the golden East thrown in."

"I never sought these things, and we are a long way from Essex," answered Godwin shortly.

"No," said Wulf, "but they seem to seek you. What news of Masouda? Have you seen her while I slept?"

"I have seen no one except the apothecary who tended you, the slaves who brought us food, and last evening the prince Hassan, who came to see how we fared. He told me that, like yourself, Rosamund and Masouda slept."

"I am glad to hear it," answered Wulf, "for certainly their rest was earned. By St. Chad! What a woman is this Masouda! A heart of fire and nerves of steel! Beautiful, too—most beautiful; and the best horsewoman that ever sat a steed. Had it not been for her—by Heaven! When I think of it I feel as though I loved her—don't you?"

"No," said Godwin, still more shortly.

"Ah, well, I dare say she can love enough for two who does nothing by halves, and, all things considered," he added, with one of his great laughs, "I am glad it is I of whom she thinks so little—yes, I who adore her as though she were my patron saint. Hark! The guards challenge," and, forgetting where he was, he snatched at his sword.

Then the door opened, and through it appeared the emir Hassan, who saluted them in the name of Allah, searching them with his quiet eyes.

"Few would judge, to look at you, Sir Knights," he said with a smile, "that you have been the guests of the Old Man of the Mountain, and left his house so hastily by the back door. Three days more and you will be as hardy as when we met beyond the seas upon the wharf by a certain creek. Oh, you are brave men, both of you, though you be infidels, from which error may the Prophet guide you; brave men, the flower of knighthood. Aye, I, Hassan, who have known many Frankish knights, say it from my heart," and, placing his hand to his turban, he bowed before them in admiration that was not feigned.

"We thank you, Prince, for your praise," said Godwin gravely, but Wulf stepped forward, took his hand, and shook it.

"That was an ill trick, Prince, which you played us yonder in England," he said, "and one that brought as good a warrior as ever drew a sword—our uncle Sir Andrew D'Arcy—to an end sad as it was glorious. Still, you obeyed your master, and because of all that has happened since, I forgive you, and call you friend, although should we ever meet in battle I still hope to pay you for that drugged wine."

Here Hassan bowed and said softly, "I admit that the debt is owing; also, that none sorrow more for the death of the noble lord D'Arcy than I, your servant, who, by the will of God, brought it upon him. When we meet, Sir Wulf, in war—and that, I think, will be an ill hour for me—strike, and strike home; I shall not complain. Meanwhile, we are friends, and in very truth all that I have is yours. But now I come to tell you that the princess Rose of the World—Allah bless her footsteps!—is recovered from her fatigues, and desires that you should breakfast with her in an hour's time. Also, the doctor waits to tend your bruises, and servants to lead you to the bath. Please, leave your hauberk; here the protection of Saladin and of his servants is your best armor."

"Still, I think that we will take them," said Godwin, "for faith in guardians is a poor defense against the daggers of these Assassins, who dwell not so far away."

"True," answered Hassan; "I had forgotten." So thus they departed.

An hour later they were led to the hall, where Rosamund soon appeared, and with her Masouda and Hassan. She was dressed in the rich robes of an Eastern lady, but the gems with which she had been adorned as the bride-elect of Al-Jebal were gone. When she lifted her veil the brethren saw that though her face was still somewhat pallid, her strength had come back to her, and the terror had left her eyes. She greeted them with sweet and gentle words, thanking first Godwin and then Wulf for all that they had done and, turning to Masouda, who stood by, stately, and watchful, thanked her also. Then they sat down and ate with light hearts and a good appetite.

Before their meal was finished, the guard at the door announced that messengers had arrived from the sultan. They entered, gray-haired men clad in the robes of secretaries, whom Hassan hastened to greet. When they were seated and had spoken with him awhile, one of them drew forth a letter, which Hassan, touching his forehead with it in token of respect, gave to Rosamund. She broke its seal, and, seeing that it was in Arabic, handed it to her cousin, saying, "Do you read it, Godwin, who are more learned than I."

So he read aloud, translating the letter sentence by sentence. This was its message:

"Saladin, Commander of the Faithful, the Strong-to-aid, to his niece beloved, Rose of the World, princess of Baalbec:—

"Our servant, the emir Hassan, has sent us tidings of your rescue from the power of the accursed Lord of the Mountain, Sinan, and that you are now safe in our city of Emesa, guarded by many thousands of our soldiers. You also have a woman with you named Masouda, and your kinsmen, the two Frankish knights, by whose skill in arms and courage you were saved. Now this is to command you to come to our court at Damascus so soon as you may be fit to travel, knowing that here you will be received with love and honor. Also, I invite your kinsmen to accompany you, since I knew their father, and would welcome knights who have done such great deeds, and the woman

Masouda with them. Or, if they prefer it, all three of them may return to their own lands and peoples.

"Hasten, my niece, lady Rose of the World, hasten, for my spirit seeks you, and my eyes desire to look upon you. In the name of Allah, greeting."

"You have heard," said Rosamund, as Godwin finished reading the scroll. "Now, my cousins, what will you do?"

"What else but go with you, whom we have come so far to seek?" answered Wulf, and Godwin nodded his head in assent.

"And you, Masouda?"

"I, lady? Oh, I go also, since were I to return to my former place," and she nodded towards the mountains, "my greeting would be one that I do not wish."

"Do you note their words, Prince Hassan?" asked Rosamund.

"I expected no other," he answered with a bow. "Only, knights, you must give me a promise, for even in the midst of my army such is needful from men who can fly like birds out of the fortress of Masyaf and from the knives of the Assassins—who are mounted, moreover, on the swiftest horses in Syria that have been trained to carry a double burden," and he looked at them meaningly. "It is that upon this journey you will not attempt to escape with the princess, whom you have followed from her home to rescue her out of the hand of Saladin."

Godwin drew from his tunic the cross, which Rosamund had left him in the hall at Steeple, and said: "I swear upon this holy symbol that during our journey to Damascus I will attempt no escape with or without my cousin Rosamund." He then kissed the cross.

"And I swear the same upon my sword," added Wulf, laying his hand upon the silver hilt of the great blade which had been his forefather's.

"A security that I like better," said Hassan with a smile, "but in truth, knights, your word is enough for me." Then he looked at Masouda and went on, still smiling: "It is useless to ask women of such passion for oaths, for they have little meaning. Lady, we must be content to watch you, since my lord has bidden you to his city, which, fair and brave as you are, to be plain, I would not have done."

Then he turned to speak to the secretaries, and Godwin, who was noting all, saw Masouda's dark eyes follow him, and in them a very strange light.

"Good," they seemed to say; "as you have written, so shall you read."

That same afternoon they started for Damascus with a great army of horsemen. In its midst, guarded by a thousand spears, Rosamund was borne in a litter. In front of her rode Hassan, with his yellow-robed bodyguard; at her side, Masouda; and behind—for, notwithstanding his hurts, Wulf would not be carried, the brethren, mounted upon ambling palfreys. After them, led by slaves, came the chargers, Flame and Smoke, recovered now, but still walking somewhat stiffly, and then rank upon rank of turbaned Saracens. Through the open curtains of her litter Rosamund beckoned to the brethren, who pushed alongside of her.

"Look," she said, pointing with her hand.

They looked, and there, bathed in the glory of the sinking sun, saw the mountains crowned far, far away with the impregnable city and fortress of Masyaf, and below it the slopes down which they had ridden for their lives. Nearer to them flashed the river bordered by the town of Emesa, with the golden banner of Saladin fluttering in the evening wind. Still, as she could not forget all that she had undergone in that fearful home of devil-worshippers, and the fate from which she had been snatched, Rosamund shuddered.

"It burns like a city in hell," she said, staring at Masyaf, environed by that lurid evening light and canopied with black, smoke-like clouds. "Oh! Such I think will be its doom."

"I trust so," answered Wulf fervently. "At least, in this world and the next we have done with it."

"Yes," added Godwin in his thoughtful voice; "still, out of that evil place we won good, for there we found Rosamund, and there, my brother, you conquered in such a fray as you can never hope to fight again, gaining great glory, and perhaps much more."

Then, reining in his horse, Godwin fell back behind the litter, while Wulf wondered, and Rosamund watched him with thoughtful eyes.

That evening they camped in the desert, and next morning, surrounded by wandering tribes of Bedouins mounted on their camels, marched on again, sleeping that night in the ancient fortress of Baalbec. As they approached, the garrison and people, having been warned by runners of the rank and titles of Rosamund, came out to do her homage as their lady.

Hearing of it, she left her litter and, mounting a splendid horse which they had sent her as a present, rode to meet them, the brethren, in full armor and once more bestriding Flame and Smoke, beside her, and a guard of Saladin's own Mamelukes behind. Solemn, turbaned men, who had been commanded so to do by messengers from the sultan, brought her the keys of the gates on a cushion. Minstrels and soldiers marched before her, while crowding the walls and running alongside came the citizens in their thousands.

Thus she went on, through the open gates, past the towering columns of ruined temples, once a home of the worship of heathen gods, through courts and vaults to the citadel surrounded by its gardens that in past ages had been the Acropolis of forgotten Roman emperors.

Here in the portico Rosamund turned her horse and received the salutations of the multitude as though she also were one of the world's rulers. Indeed, it seemed to the brethren watching her as she sat upon the great white horse and surveyed the shouting, bending crowd with flashing eyes, splendid in her bearing and beautiful to see, a prince at her stirrup and an army at her back, that none of those who had trod that path before her could have seemed greater or more glorious than did this English girl. Truly by blood and nature she was fitted to be a queen. Yet as Rosamund sat thus the pride passed from her face, and her eyes fell.

"Of what are you thinking?" asked Godwin at her side.

"That I would we were back among the summer fields at Steeple," she answered, "for those who are lifted high fall low.

Prince Hassan, give the captains and people my thanks and bid them be gone. I would rest."

Thus, for the first and last time did Rosamund behold the ancient palace of Baalbec, which her grandsire, the great Ayoub, had ruled before her.

That night there was feasting in the mighty, immemorial halls, and singing and minstrelsy and the dancing of fair women and the giving of gifts. For Baalbec, where birth and beauty were ever welcome, did honor to its lady, the favored niece of the mighty Saladin. Yet there were some who murmured that she would bring no good fortune to the sultan or his city, who was not all of the blood of Ayoub, but half a Frank, and a Cross-worshipper. Even these people, however, praised her beauty and her royal bearing. The brethren they praised also, although these were unbelievers, for the tale of how Wulf had fought the traitor knight upon the Narrow Way, and of how they had led their kinswoman from the haunted fortress of Masyaf, was passed from mouth to mouth.

At dawn the next day, on orders received from the sultan, they left Baalbec, escorted by the army and many of the notables of the town. That afternoon, they drew rein upon the heights that overlook the city of Damascus, Bride of the Earth, set amidst its seven streams and ringed about with gardens. Many considered it one of the most beautiful, and perhaps the most ancient city in the world. Then they rode down to the bounteous plain and, as night fell, having passed the encircling gardens, were escorted through the gates of Damascus, outside of which most of the army halted and encamped.

Along the narrow streets, bordered by yellow, flat-roofed houses, they rode slowly, looking first at the motley, many colored crowds, who watched them with grave interest, and then at the stately buildings, domed mosques and towering minarets, which everywhere stood out against the deep blue of the evening sky. They eventually came to an open space planted like a garden, beyond which was seen a huge and fantastic castle that Hassan told them was the palace of Saladin. In its courtyard they were parted, Rosamund being led away by officers of state, while the brethren were taken to chambers that had been prepared for them. After they had bathed, they were served with food.

Scarcely had they eaten it when Hassan appeared and summoned them to follow him. Passing down various passages and across a court they came to some guarded doors, where the soldiers demanded that they give up their swords and daggers.

"It is not needful," said Hassan, and they let them go by. Next came more passages and a curtain, beyond which they found themselves in a small, domed room, lit by hanging silver lamps and paved in ornate marbles. The place was strewn with rich rugs and furnished with cushioned couches.

At a sign from Hassan, the brethren stood still in the center of this room and looked around them wondering. The place was empty and very silent; they felt afraid—of what they knew not. Moments later, curtains upon its further side opened and through them came a man, turbaned and wrapped in a dark robe, who stood awhile in the shadow, gazing at them beneath the lamps.

The man was not very tall, and slight in build, yet he carried himself with authority, although his garb was such as the humblest might have worn. He came forward, lifting his head, and they saw that his features were small and finely cut; that he was bearded, and beneath his broad brow shone thoughtful yet at times piercing eyes which were brown in hue. Immediately, Prince Hassan sank to his knees and touched the marble with his forehead, and, guessing that they were in the presence of the mighty monarch Saladin, the brethren saluted in their Western fashion. Presently, the sultan spoke in a low, even voice to Hassan, to whom he motioned that he should rise, saying, "I can see that you trust these knights, Emir," and he pointed to their great swords.

"Sire," was the answer, "I trust them as I trust myself. They are brave and honorable men, although they be infidels."

The sultan stroked his beard.

"Aye," he said, "infidels. It is a pity, yet doubtless they will comprehend the might and justice of Allah in time. Noble to look on, also, like their father, whom I remember well, and, if all

I hear is true, brave indeed. Sir Knights, do you understand my language?"

"Sufficiently to speak it, Sultan," answered Godwin, "who have learned it since childhood, yet ill enough."

"Good. Then tell me, as soldiers to a soldier, what do you seek from Saladin?"

"Our cousin, the lady Rosamund, who, by your command, lord, was stolen from our home in England."

"Knights, she is your cousin, that I know, as surely as I know that she is my niece. Tell me now, why should she mean more to you?" and he searched them with those piercing eyes.

Godwin looked at Wulf, who said in English, "Speak the whole truth, Brother. From that man nothing can be hid."

Then Godwin answered, "Sire, we love her, and are betrothed to her."

The sultan stared at them in surprise.

"What! Both of you?" he asked.

"Yes, both."

"And does she love you both?"

"Yes," replied Godwin, "both, or so she says."

Saladin stroked his beard and considered them, while Hassan smiled a little.

"Then, knights," he inquired, "tell me, which of you does she love best?"

"That, sire, is known to her alone. When the time comes, she will say, and not before."

"I perceive," said Saladin, "that behind this riddle hides a story. If it is your good pleasure, be seated, and set it out to me."

So they sat down on the divan and obeyed, keeping nothing back from the beginning to the end, nor, although the tale was long, did the sultan weary of listening.

"A great story, truly," he said, when they had finished, "and one in which I seem to see the hand of Allah. Sir Knights, you will think that I have wronged you—aye, and your uncle, Sir Andrew, who was once my friend, although an older man than I, and who, by stealing away my sister, laid the foundations for this tale of woe between us.

"Now, listen. The tale that those two Frankish knaves, the priest and the false knight Lozelle, told to you was true. As I wrote to your uncle in my letter, I dreamed a dream. Thrice I dreamed it; that this niece of mine lived, and that if I could bring her here to dwell at my side she would bring me both happiness and success. Therefore, I stretched out my arm and took her from far away. And now, through you—yes, through you—she has been snatched from the power of the great Assassin, and is safe in my court, and therefore henceforth I am your friend."

"Sire, have you seen her?" asked Godwin.

"Knights, I have seen her, and the face is the face of my dreams, and therefore I know full well that my dream was not false. Listen, Sir Godwin and Sir Wulf," Saladin went on in a changed voice—a stern, commanding voice. "Ask of me what you will, and, Franks though you are, it shall be given you for your service's sake—wealth, lands, titles, all that men desire and I can grant—but ask not of me my niece, Rose of the World, princess of Baalbec, whom Allah has brought to me for his own purposes. Know, moreover, that if you strive to steal her away you shall certainly die; and that if she escapes from me and I recapture her, then she shall die. These things I have told her already, and I swear them in the name of Allah. Here she is, and in my house she must abide until the vision be fulfilled."

Now in their dismay the brethren looked at each other, for they seemed further from their desire than they had been even in the castle of Sinan. Then a light broke upon the face of Godwin, and he stood up and answered, "Dread lord of all the East, we hear you and we know our risk. You have given us your friendship; we accept it, and are thankful, and seek no more. God, you say, has brought our lady Rosamund to you for His own purposes, of which you have no doubt since her face is the very face of your dreams. Then let His purposes be accomplished according to His will, which may be in some way that we little guess. We abide His judgment who has guided us in the past, and will guide us in the future."

"Well spoken," replied Saladin. "I have warned you, my guests; therefore, blame me not if I keep my word; but I ask no promise from you who would not tempt noble knights to lie. Yes, Allah has set this strange riddle; by Allah let it be answered in his season."

Then he waved his hand to show that the audience was ended.

Chapter XVII
The Brethren Depart from Damascus

At the court of Saladin Godwin and Wulf were treated with much honor. A house was given them to dwell in, and a company of servants to minister to their comfort and to guard them. Mounted on their swift horses, Flame and Smoke, they were taken out into the desert to hunt, and, had they so willed, it would have been easy for them to out-distance their guard and companions and ride away to the nearest crusader stronghold or Christian town. Indeed, no hand would have been lifted to stop them who were free to come or go. But where were they to go without Rosamund?

Saladin they saw often, for it pleased him to tell them tales of those days when their father and uncle were in the East, or to talk with them of England and the Franks, and even now and again to reason with Godwin on matters of religion. Moreover, to show his faith in them, he gave them the rank of officers of his own bodyguard, and when, wearying of idleness, they asked it of him, allowed them to take their share of duty in the guarding of his palace. This, at a time when peace still reigned between Frank and Saracen, the brethren were not ashamed to do, who received no payment for their services.

Peace reigned indeed, but Godwin and Wulf could guess that it would not reign for long. Damascus and the plain around it were one great camp, and every day thousands of new wild tribesmen poured in and took up the quarters that had been prepared for them. They asked Masouda, who knew everything, what it meant. She answered, "It means the Jihad, the Holy War, which is being preached in every mosque throughout the East. It means that the next great struggle between Cross and Crescent is at hand, and then, pilgrims Peter and John, you will have to choose your standard."

"There can be little doubt about that," said Wulf.

"None," replied Masouda, with one of her smiles, "only it may pain you to have to make war upon the princess of Baalbec and her uncle, the Commander of the Faithful." Then she went, still smiling.

The words of Masouda were troubling to the two English knights, for there was no mistaking the fact that their cousin and their love had in truth become the princess of Baalbec. She lived in great state and freedom, at least compared to the vast majority of common women in the Muslim community. No attempt was made to force her to convert to the Muslim religion, though such was common enough in those days. No suitor was thrust upon her. But she was in a land where women were not permitted to consort with men, especially if they be high-placed. As a princess of the empire of Saladin, she must obey its rules, even to veiling herself when she went abroad, and exchanging no private words with men. Godwin and Wulf asked Saladin if they might be allowed to speak with her from time to time, but he only answered shortly, "Sir Knights, our customs are our customs. Moreover, the less you see of the princess of Baalbec the better I think it will be for her, for you, whose blood I do not wish to have upon my hands, and for myself, who await the fulfillment of that dream which the angel brought."

Then the brethren left his presence sore at heart, for although they saw her from time to time at feasts and festivals, Rosamund was as far apart from them as though she sat in Steeple Hall—aye, and further. Also, they came to see that of rescuing her from Damascus there was no hope at all. She dwelt in her own palace, whereof the walls were guarded night and day by a company of the sultan's Mamelukes, who knew that they were answerable for her with their lives. Within its walls, again, lived trusted eunuchs, under the command of a cunning fellow named Mesrour, and her retinue of women, all of them spies and watchful. How could two men hope to snatch her from the heart of such a host and to spirit her out of Damascus and through its encircling armies?

One comfort, however, was left to them. When she reached the court Rosamund had requested of the sultan that Masouda should not be separated from her, and this, because of the part she had played in his niece's rescue from the power of Sinan, he had granted, though reluctantly. Moreover, Masouda, being a person of no account except for her beauty, and a heretic, was allowed to go where she would and to speak with whom she wished. So, as she wished to speak often with Godwin, they did not lack for news of Rosamund.

From her they learned that in a fashion the princess was happy enough—who would not be that had just escaped from Al-Jebal? —Yet weary of the strange Eastern life, of the restraints upon her, and of her aimless days; vexed also that she might not mix with the brethren. Day by day she sent them her greetings, and with them warnings to attempt nothing—not even to see her—since there was no hope that they would succeed. So much afraid of them was the sultan, Rosamund said, that both she and they were watched day and night, and of any folly their lives would pay the price. When they heard all this the brethren began to despair, and their spirits sank so low that they no longer cared what would happen to them.

Then it was that a situation came to them of which the issue was to make them still more admired by Saladin and to lift Masouda to honor. One hot morning, they were seated in the courtyard of their house beside the fountain, staring at the passers-by through the bars of the bronze gates and at the sentries who marched to and fro before them. This house was in one of the principal thoroughfares of Damascus, and in front of it flowed continually an unending, many-colored stream of people.

There were white-robed Arabs of the desert, mounted on their grumbling camels; caravans of merchandise from Egypt or elsewhere; asses laden with firewood or the gray, prickly growth of the wild thyme for the bakers' ovens; water sellers with their goatskin bags and chinking brazen cups; vendors of birds or sweetmeats; women going to the bath in closed and curtained litters, escorted by the eunuchs of their households; great lords riding on their Arabian horses and preceded by their runners, who thrust the crowd asunder and beat the poor with rods; beggars, halt, maimed, and blind, beseeching alms; lepers, from whom all shrank away, who wailed their woes aloud; stately companies of soldiers, some mounted and some afoot; holy men, who gave blessings and received alms; and so forth, without number and without end.

Godwin and Wulf, seated in the shade of the painted house, watched them gloomily. They were weary of this ever-changing sameness, weary of the eternal glare and glitter of this unfamiliar life, weary of the insistent cries of the mullahs on the minarets, of the flash of the swords that would soon be red with the blood of their own people. They were weary, too, of the hopeless task to which they were sworn. Rosamund was one of this multitude; she was the princess of Baalbec, half an Eastern by her blood, and growing more Eastern day by day—or so they thought in their bitterness. As well might two Saracens hope to snatch the queen of England from her palace at Westminster, as they to drag the princess of Baalbec out of the power of a monarch more absolute than any king of England.

So they sat silent since they had nothing to say, and stared first at the passing crowd, and then at the thin stream of water falling continually into the marble basin near the city gate.

They soon heard voices at the gate, and, looking up, saw a woman wrapped in a long cloak, talking with the guard, who with a laugh thrust out his arm, as though to place it round her. Then a knife flashed, and the soldier stepped back, still laughing, and opened the wicket. The woman came in. It was Masouda. They rose and bowed to her, but she passed before them into the house. Soon they followed, while the soldier at the gate laughed again, and at the sound of his mockery Godwin's cheek grew red. Even in the cool, darkened room she noticed it, and said, bitterly enough, "What does it matter? Such insults are my daily bread whom they believe—" and she stopped.

"They had best say nothing of what they believe to me," murmured Godwin.

"I thank you," Masouda answered, with a sweet, swift smile, and, throwing off her cloak, stood before them unveiled, clad in the white robes that complemented her tall and graceful form so well, and were blazoned on the front with the cognizance of Baalbec. "Well for you," she went on, "that they hold me to be what I am not, since otherwise I should win no entry to this house."

"What of our lady Rosamund?" broke in Wulf awkwardly, for, like Godwin, he was grieved in spirit.

Masouda laid her hand upon her heart as though to still its heaving, then answered, "The princess of Baalbec, my mistress, is well and as ever, beautiful, though somewhat weary of the pomp in which she finds no joy. She sent her greetings, but did not say to which of you they should be delivered, so, pilgrims, you must share them."

Godwin winced, but Wulf asked if there were any hope of seeing her, to which Masouda answered, "None," adding, in a low voice, "I come upon another business. Do you brethren wish to do Saladin a service?"

"I don't know. What is it?" asked Godwin gloomily.

"Only to save his life—for which he may be grateful, or may not, according to his mood."

"Speak on," said Godwin, "and tell us how we two Franks can save the life of the sultan of the East."

"Do you still remember Sinan and his fedais? Yes—they are not easily forgotten, are they? Well, tonight he has plotted to murder Saladin, and afterwards to murder you if he can, and to carry away your lady Rosamund, or, failing that, to murder her, also. Oh! The tale is true enough. I have it from one of them under the Signet—surely that ring has served us well—who believes, poor fool, that I am in the plot. Now, you are the officers of the bodyguard who watch in the antechamber tonight, are you not? Well, when the guard is changed at midnight, the eight men who should replace them at the doors of the room of Saladin will not arrive; they will be decoyed away by a false order. In their stead will come eight murderers, disguised in the robes and arms of Mamelukes. They look to deceive and cut you down, kill Saladin, and escape by the further door. Can you hold your own awhile against eight men?"

"We have done so before and will try," answered Wulf. But how shall we know that they are not Mamelukes?"

"In this way—they will wish to pass the door, and you will say, 'Stop, sons of Sinan,' whereon they will spring on you to kill you. Then be ready and shout aloud."

"And if they overcome us," asked Godwin, "then the sultan would be slain?"

"This will not happen if you lock the door of the chamber of Saladin and hide away the key. The sound of the fighting will arouse the outer guard before harm can come to him. Or," she added, after thinking awhile, "perhaps it will be best to reveal the plot to the sultan at once."

"No, no," answered Wulf; "let us take the chance. I weary of doing nothing here. Hassan guards the outer gate. He will come swiftly at the sound of blows."

"Good," said Masouda; "I will see that he is there and awake. Now farewell, and pray that we may meet again. I say nothing of this story to the princess Rosamund until it is finished." Then, throwing her cloak around her shoulders, she turned and went.

"Can this be true, think you?" asked Wulf of Godwin.

"We have never found Masouda to be a liar," was his answer. "Come; let us see to our armor, for the knives of those fedai are sharp."

It was near midnight, and the brethren stood in the small, domed antechamber, from which a door opened into the sleeping rooms of Saladin. The guard of eight Mamelukes had left them, to be met by their relief in the courtyard, according to custom, but no relief had as yet appeared in the antechamber.

"It would seem that Masouda's tale is true," said Godwin, and going to the door he locked it, and hid the key beneath a cushion.

Then they took their stand in front of the locked door, before which hung curtains, standing in the shadow with the light from the hanging silver lamps pouring down in front of them. Here they waited awhile in silence, till at length they heard the tramp of men, and eight Mamelukes, clad in yellow above their mail, marched in and saluted.

"Stand!" said Godwin, and they stood a minute, then began to edge forward.

"Stand!" said both the brethren again, but still they edged forward.

"Stand, sons of Sinan!" they said a third time, drawing their swords.

Then with a hiss of disappointed rage the fedai came at them.

"A D'Arcy! A D'Arcy! Help for the sultan!" shouted the brethren, and the fight began.

Six of the men attacked them, and while they were engaged with these the other two slipped round and tried the door, only to find it locked. Then they also turned upon the brethren, thinking to take the key from off their bodies. At the first rush two of the fedai went down beneath the sweep of the long swords, but after that the murderers would not come close, and while some engaged them in front, others strove to pass and stab them from behind. Indeed, a blow from one of their long knives fell upon Godwin's shoulder, but the good mail turned it.

"Give way," he cried to Wulf, "or they will best us."

So suddenly they gave way before them till their backs were against the door, and there they stood, shouting for help and sweeping round them with their swords into reach of which the fedai dare not come. Now from without the chamber rose a cry and tumult, and the sound of heavy blows falling upon the gates that the murderers had barred behind them. Meanwhile, upon the further side of the door, which he could not open, was heard the voice of the sultan demanding to know what was going on.

The fedai heard these sounds also, and read in them their doom. Forgetting caution in their despair and rage, they hurled themselves upon the brethren, for they thought that if they could get them down they might still break through the door and slay Saladin before they themselves were slain. But for awhile the brethren stopped their rush with point and buckler, wounding two of them severely; and when at length they closed in upon them, the gates were burst, and Hassan and the outer guard were at hand.

A minute later and, but little hurt, Godwin and Wulf were leaning on their swords, and the fedai, some of them dead or wounded and some of them captive, lay before them on the marble floor. Moreover, the door had been opened, and through it came the sultan in his night gear.

"What has happened here?" he asked, looking at them doubtfully.

"Only this, lord," answered Godwin; "these men came to kill you and we held them off till help arrived."

"Kill me! My own guard kill me?"

"They are not your guard; they are fedai, disguised as your guard, and sent by Al-Jebal, as he promised."

Now Saladin turned pale, for he who feared nothing else was all his life afraid of the Assassins and their lord, who had attempted to murder him on three previous occasions.

"Strip the armor from those men," went on Godwin, "and I think that you will find truth in my words, or, if not, question such of them as still live."

They obeyed, and there upon the breast of one of them, burnt into his skin, was the symbol of the blood-red dagger. Now Saladin saw, and called the brethren aside.

"How knew you of this?" he asked, searching them with his piercing eyes.

"Masouda, the lady Rosamund's waiting woman, warned us that you, lord, and we, were to be murdered tonight by eight men, so we made ready."

"Why, then, did you not tell me?"

"Because," answered Wulf, "we were not sure that the news was true, and did not wish to bring false tidings and be made foolish. Because, also, my brother and I thought that we could hold our own awhile against eight of Sinan's rats disguised as soldiers of Saladin."

"You have done it well, though yours was a mad counsel," answered the sultan. Then he gave his hand first to one and then to the other, and said, simply, "Sir Knights, Saladin owes his life to you. Should it ever come about that you owe your lives to Saladin, he will remember this."

Thus this business ended. On the following day, those of the fedai who remained alive were questioned, and confessing freely that they had been sent to murder Saladin who had robbed their master of his bride, the two Franks who had carried her off, and the woman Masouda who had guided them. They were put to death cruelly enough. Also, many others in the city were seized and killed on suspicion, so that for a while there was no more fear from the Assassins.

Now from that day forward Saladin held the brethren in great favor and pressed gifts upon them and offered them honors. But they refused them all, saying that they needed but one thing of him, and he knew what it was—an option at which his face sank.

One morning he sent for them, and, except for the presence of Prince Hassan, the most favorite of his emirs, and a famous imam, or priest of his religion, received them alone.

"Listen," he said briefly, addressing Godwin. "I understand that my niece, the princess of Baalbec, is beloved by you. Good. Accept the Koran, and I give her to you in marriage, for thus also she may be led to the true faith, whom I have sworn not to persuade by force. If you will do this I gain a great warrior and Paradise for a brave soul. The imam here will instruct you in the truth."

Godwin only stared at him with eyes set wide in wonderment, and answered, "Sire, I thank you, but I cannot change my faith to win a woman, no matter how dearly I may love her."

"So I thought," said Saladin with a sigh, "though, indeed, it is sad that superstition should thus blind so brave and good a man. Now, Sir Wulf, it is your turn. What say you to my offer? Will you take the princess and her dominions with my love thrown in as a marriage portion?"

Wulf thought a moment, and as he thought there arose in his mind a vision of an autumn afternoon that seemed years and years ago, when they two and Rosamund had stood by the shrine of St. Chad on the shores of Essex, and jested of this very matter of a change of faith. Then he answered, with one of his great laughs, "Aye, sire, but on my own terms, not on yours, for if I took these I think that my marriage would lack blessings. Nor, indeed, would Rosamund wish to wed a servant of your Prophet, who if it pleased him might take other wives."

Saladin leaned his head upon his hand and looked at them with disappointed eyes, yet not without respect.

"The knight Lozelle was a Cross-worshipper," he said, "but you two are very different from the knight Lozelle, who accepted the Faith when it was offered to him—"

"To win your trade," said Godwin bitterly.

"I know not," answered Saladin, "though it is true the man seems to have been a Christian among the Franks, who here was a follower of the Prophet. Now I have one more thing to say to you. That Frank, Prince Arnat of Karak, whom you call Reginald de Chatillon—accursed be his name!—" and he spat upon the ground, "has once more broken the peace between me and the king of Jerusalem, slaughtering my merchants, and stealing my goods. I will permit this shame no more, and very shortly I unfurl my standards, which shall not be folded up again until they float upon the mosque of Omar and from every tower top in Palestine. Your people, and especially your Templars, are doomed. I, Yusuf Saladin," and he rose as he said the words, his very beard bristling with wrath, "declare the Holy War, and will sweep them to the sea. Choose now, you brethren. Do you fight for me or against me? Or will you give up your swords and remain here as my prisoners?"

"We are the servants of the Cross," answered Godwin, "and cannot lift steel against it and thereby lose our souls." Then he spoke with Wulf and added, "As to your second question, whether we would stay here in chains. It is one that our lady Rosamund must answer, for we are sworn to her service. We demand to see the princess of Baalbec."

"Send for her, Emir," said Saladin to the prince Hassan, who bowed and dcparted.

A while later Rosamund came, looking beautiful but, as they saw when she threw back her veil, very white and weary. She bowed to Saladin, and the brethren, who were not allowed to touch her hand, bowed to her, devouring her face with eager eyes.

"Greeting, my uncle," she said to the sultan, "and to you, my cousins, greeting also. What is your pleasure with me?"

Saladin motioned to her to be seated and told Godwin to set out the case, which he did very clearly, ending, "Is it your wish, Rosamund, that we stay in this court as prisoners, or go forth to fight with the Franks in the Great War that will soon come?"

Rosamund looked at them awhile, then answered, "To whom were you first sworn? Was it to the service of our Lord, or to the service of a woman? I have spoken."

"Such words as we expected from you, being what you are," exclaimed Godwin.

Wulf, meanwhile, nodded his head in assent, and added, "Sultan, we ask your safe conduct to Jerusalem, and leave this lady in your charge, relying on your pledge to do no violence to her faith and to protect her person."

"My safe conduct you have," replied Saladin, "and my understanding, also. Nor, indeed, would I have thought well of you had you decided otherwise. Now, henceforth we are enemies in the eyes of all men, and I shall strive to slay you, as you will strive to slay me. But as regards this lady, have no fear. What I have promised shall be fulfilled. Bid her farewell, whom you will see no more."

"Who taught your lips to say such words, O Sultan?" asked Godwin. "Is it given to you to read the future and the decrees of God?"

"I should have said," answered Saladin, "'Whom you will see no more if I am able to keep you apart.' Can you complain who, both of you, have refused to take her as a wife?"

Here Rosamund looked up wondering, and Wulf broke in, "Tell her the price. Tell her that she was asked to wed either of us who would bow the knee to Mohammed, and I think that she will not blame us."

"Never would I have spoken again to him who answered otherwise," exclaimed Rosamund, and Saladin frowned at the words. "Oh! My uncle," she went on, "you have been kind to me and raised me high, but I do not seek this greatness, nor are your ways my ways, who am of a faith that you call accursed. Let me go, I beseech you, in the care of these my kinsmen."

"And your lovers," said Saladin bitterly. "Niece, it cannot be. I love you well, but did I know even that your life must pay the price of your sojourn here, here you still should stay, since, as my dream told me, you are one key to my success, and I believe that dream. What, then, is your life, or the lives of these knights, or even my life, compared to the glory of winning Jihad for Allah? Oh! Everything that my empire can give is at your feet, but here you stay until the dream be accomplished, and," he added, looking at the brethren, "death shall be the portion of any who would steal you from my hand."

"Until the dream be accomplished?" said Rosamund, clinging to these words. "Then, when it is accomplished, shall I be free?"

"Yes," answered the sultan; "free to come or to go, unless you attempt escape, for then you will know your certain doom."

"It is a decree. Take note, my cousins, it is a decree. And you, Prince Hassan, remember it also. Oh! I pray, with all my soul I pray, my uncle, that your Holy War would come quickly to an end with little bloodshed, and with it your dream. Now go, my cousins; but, if you will, leave me Masouda, who has no other friends. Go, and take my love and blessing with you—aye, and the blessing of Jesu and His saints which shall protect you in the hour of battle and bring us together again."

So spoke Rosamund and threw her veil before her face that she might hide her tears.

Then Godwin and Wulf stepped to where she stood by the throne of Saladin, bent the knee before her, and, taking her hand, kissed it in farewell, nor did the sultan try to stop them. But when she was gone and the brethren were gone, he turned to the emir Hassan and to the great imam who had sat silent all this while, and said, "Now tell me, you who are old and wise, which of those men does the lady love? Speak, Hassan, you who know her well."

But Hassan shook his head. "One or the other. Both or neither—I know not," he answered. "Her counsel is too close for me."

Then Saladin turned to the imam—a cunning, silent man.

"When both the infidels are about to die before her face, as I still hope to see them do, we may learn the answer. But unless she wills it, never before," he replied, and the sultan noted his saying.

The next morning, having been informed that they would pass close by her dwelling, Rosamund, watching through the lattice of one of her palace windows, saw the brethren go by. They were fully armed and, mounted on their splendid chargers Flame and Smoke, looked glorious as they rode proudly side by side, the sunlight glinting on their mail. Opposite to her house they halted awhile, and, knowing that Rosamund watched, although they could not see her, drew their swords and lifted them in salute. Then, sheathing them again, they rode forward in silence, and soon were lost to sight.

Little did Rosamund guess how different they would appear when they three met again. Indeed, she scarcely dared to hope that they would ever meet, for she knew well that even if the war went in favor of the Christians she would be hurried away to some place where they would never find her. She knew well also that from Damascus her rescue was impossible, and that although Saladin respected them, as he respected all who were honest and brave, he would receive them no more as friends. Moreover, the struggle between Cross and Crescent would be fierce and to the death, and she was sure that wherever there was the closest fighting there in the midst of it would be found Godwin and Wulf. Well might it be God's will, therefore, that her eyes had looked their last upon them.

They were gone—they were gone! Even the sound of their horses' hoofs had died away, and she was desolate as a child lost in a city full of strangers. Oh! And her heart was filled with fears for them, and most of all for one of them. If he should not come back, what would her life be?

Rosamund bowed her head and wept; then, hearing a sound behind her, turned to see that Masouda was weeping, also.

"Why do you weep?" she asked.

"The maid should copy her mistress," answered Masouda with a hard laugh; "but, lady, why do you weep? At least you are beloved, and, come what may, nothing can take that from you. You will never carry my burden, for I must keep a veil upon my heart while my love burns within for a man who can never love me."

A thought rose in Rosamund's mind—a new and terrible thought. The eyes of the two women met, and those of Rosamund asked, "Which?" anxiously, as once in the moonlight she had asked it with her voice from the gate above the Narrow Way. Between them stood a table inlaid with ivory and pearl, whereon the dust from the street had gathered through the open lattice. Masouda leaned over, and with her forefinger wrote a single Arabic letter in the dust upon the table, then passed her hand across it.

Rosamund's heart beat quickly and then became steady. Then she asked, "Why did you fail to leave who are free to go with him?"

"Because he pleaded for me to stay here and watch over the lady whom he loved. So to the death—I watch."

Slowly Masouda spoke, and the heavy words seemed like blood dropping from a death wound. Then she sank forward into the arms of Rosamund.

Chapter XVIII
Wulf Pays for the Drugged Wine

Many a day had gone by since the brethren said farewell to Rosamund at Damascus. During their journeying they visited several crusader strongholds and sought counsel from a number of friars and monks. Now, one burning July night, they sat upon their horses, the moonlight gleaming on their mail. Still as statues they sat, looking out from a rocky mountaintop across the gray plain that stretches from near Nazareth to the lip of the hills at whose foot lies Tiberias on the Sea of Galilee. Beneath them, camped around the fountain of Seffurieh, were spread the hosts of the Franks, which they intended to join. This band consisted of thirteen hundred knights, twenty thousand infantrymen, and hordes of Turcopoles—that is, natives of the country, armed after the fashion of the Saracens.

Two miles away to the southeast glimmered the white houses of Nazareth, set in the lap of the mountains—Nazareth, the holy city, where for thirty years lived and toiled the Savior of the world. Doubtless, thought Godwin, His feet had often trod that mountain whereon they stood, and in the watered vales below His hands had pushed the plow or reaped the corn. Long, long had His spoken words been silent, yet to Godwin's ears it still seemed to speak in the murmur of the vast camp, and to echo from the slopes of the Galilean hills. The words that came to his mind were: "I bring not peace, but a sword" (Matthew 10:34).

On the following day, they were to advance, so rumor said, across the desert plain and give battle to Saladin, who lay with all his power by Hattin, above Tiberias. Godwin and his brother thought that it was madness; for they had seen the might of the Saracens and ridden across that thirsty plain beneath the summer sun. But who were they, two wandering, unattended knights, that they should dare to lift up their voices against those of the lords of the land, skilled from their birth in desert warfare? Yet Godwin's heart was troubled and fear took hold of him, not for himself, but for all the countless crusaders that lay asleep yonder, and for the cause of Christendom, which staked much upon this battle.

"I go to watch yonder; bide you here," he said to Wulf, and, turning the head of Flame, rode some sixty yards over a shoulder of the rock to the further edge of the mountain which looked towards the north. Here he could see neither the camp, nor Wulf, nor any living thing. He was utterly alone. Dismounting, and bidding the horse to stand still, which it would do like a dog, he walked forward a few steps to where there was a rock, and, kneeling down, began to pray with all the strength of his simple, warrior heart.

"O Lord," he prayed, "Who once wast man and a dweller in these mountains, and knowest what is in man, hear me. I am afraid for all the thousands who sleep round Nazareth; not for myself, who care nothing for my life, but for all those, Thy servants and my brethren. Yes, and for the Cross upon which Thou didst hang, and for the faith itself throughout the East. Oh! Give me light! Oh! Let me know how best to warn them, unless my fears are vain!"

So he continued to petition Heaven above and beat his hands against his chest, praying, ever praying, as he had never prayed before, that wisdom and understanding might be given to his soul.

It seemed to Godwin that a sleep fell on him—at least, his mind grew tired and cloudy. Then he began to recall a conversation that he recently had with a pious churchman from Constantinople. This stranger spoke about the teachings of Christ regarding how the Kingdom of God was ordained to grow.

He said: "Dear brother, I know, as one who lives by the sword, that you may have forgotten that God has determined to grow His Kingdom in the hearts of men through the work of the Spirit of God and not by way of bloodshed. It is the good Seed of the Gospel, sown patiently and peacefully in the hearts of men, that God will use to overcome the world and the strongholds of Satan. Consider the words of our Lord, as He gave us this parable in the Gospel of Saint Matthew; '... The kingdom of heaven is likened unto a man which sowed good seed in his field: But while men slept, his enemy came and sowed tares among the wheat, and went his way. But when the blade was sprung up, and brought forth fruit, then appeared the tares also. So the servants of the householder came and said unto him, Sir, didst not thou sow good seed in thy field? from whence then hath it tares? He said unto them, An enemy hath done this. The servants said unto him, Wilt thou then that we go and gather them up? But he said, Nay; lest while ye gather up the tares, ye root up also the wheat with them. Let both grow together until the harvest: and in the time of harvest I will say to the reapers, Gather ye together first the tares, and bind them in bundles to burn them: but gather the wheat into my barn' (Matthew 13:24–30). Now, my brave knight, can you not see that the growth of Christendom comes not by the might of armies trying to destroy all those who are outside of Christ, but by the Spirit of God converting the hearts of sinners through the Gospel?"

Godwin awoke from his dream trembling, mounted his horse, and rode back to Wulf. Beneath, as before, lay the sleeping camp, and beyond stretched the brown desert, and there sat Wulf watching both.

"Tell me," asked Godwin, "how long has it been since I left you?"

"Some few minutes—ten perhaps," answered his brother.

"A short while to have learned so much," replied Godwin.

Then Wulf looked at him curiously and asked, "What have you learned?"

"If I told you, Wulf, you would not believe."

"Tell me, and I will say."

So Godwin told him all, and at the end remarked, "Wolf, I am more convinced than ever that it is not God's will that we try to destroy the forces of Saladin. The armies of Christendom should be back defending Jerusalem and working with its leaders to promote peace and justice in the Holy Land. Give me your thoughts, Brother."

Wulf considered awhile and answered, "Well, Brother, you have touched no wine today, so you are not drunk, and you have done nothing foolish, so you have not lost your mind. Therefore, it would seem that there is some good reason why you have been given this dream just now, but what that reason may be is beyond my understanding. Our watch is ended, for I hear the horses of the knights who come to relieve us. Listen; this is my counsel. In the camp yonder is our friend with whom we traveled from Jerusalem, Egbert, the bishop of Nazareth, who marches with the host. Let us go to him and lay this matter before him, for he is a holy man and learned; no false, self-seeking priest."

Godwin nodded in assent, and when the other knights had come and they had made their report to them, the brethren rode off together to the tent of Egbert, and, leaving their horses in charge of a servant, entered.

Egbert was an Englishman who had spent more than thirty years of his life in the East. During this time, the sun had tanned his wrinkled face to the hue of bronze, that seemed the darker in contrast with his blue eyes and snow-white hair and beard. Entering the tent, they found him at his prayers. A short time later, he rose and, greeting them with a blessing, asked them what they needed.

"Your counsel, holy father," answered Wulf. "Godwin, set out your tale."

So, having seen that the tent flap was closed and that none lingered near, Godwin told him his dream.

The old man listened patiently, nor did he seem surprised at this strange story, since in those days men often spoke of the significance of their dreams, which were often accepted by the Church as true.

When he had finished, Godwin asked of him as he had asked of Wulf: "What think you, holy father? Is this a mere dream, or is it an urgent message? And if so, from whom comes the message?"

"This is difficult to say, my son," responded the bishop. "The one speaking in the opening of your dreams is certainly suspect, for on occasion, I believe, the devil himself is behind the messages we receive in our dreams. Yet, the Scripture that was placed before your mind, and the soundness of its interpretation, can scarcely be doubted. It well may be that this simple dream has been given, that through you those who rule us may be warned, and all Christendom saved from great sorrow and disgrace. Come; let us go to the king, and tell this story, for he still sits in council yonder."

So they went out together and rode to the royal tent. Here the bishop was admitted, leaving them without. Presently, he returned and beckoned to them, and as they passed, the guards whispered to them, "A strange council, sirs, and a most unwelcome!"

Already it was near midnight, but still the great pavilion was crowded with barons and chief captains who sat in groups, or sat round a narrow table made of boards placed upon trestles. At the head of that table sat the king, Guy of Lusignan, a weak-faced man, clad in splendid armor. On his right was the white-haired Count Raymond of Tripoli, and on his left the black-bearded, frowning master of the Templars, clad in his white mantle on the left breast of which the red cross was blazoned. Words had been running high, their faces showed it, but just then a silence reigned as though the disputants were weary. At this moment, the king leaned back in his chair and passed his hand to and fro across his forehead. He then looked up and, seeing the bishop, asked peevishly, "What is it now? Oh! I remember, some tale from those tall twin knights. Well, bring them forward and speak it out, for we have no time to lose."

So the three of them came forward and at Godwin's request the bishop Egbert told of the dream that had come to him not more than an hour ago while he kept watch upon the mountaintop. At first one or two of the barons seemed disposed to laugh, but when they looked at Godwin's noble and sincere face, their laughter died away, for it did not seem outrageous to them that such a man should dream dreams. Indeed, as the parable from Christ was retold, along with its interpretation, they grew white with fear, and the whitest of them all was the king, Guy of Lusignan.

"Is all this true, Sir Godwin?" he asked, when the bishop had finished.

"It is true, my lord King," answered Godwin. "I believe that our Lord would have us to know that this is the wrong battle, at the wrong time, and for the wrong reason."

"His word is not enough," broke in the master of the Templars. "Let him explain now, if he is able, how he can know for certain that this dream has any bearing on the battle that is before us with the infidel Saladin."

And the council responded, "Aye, let him explain."

"Now," broke in the voice of the master of the Templars, "It is madness to think of withdrawing our armies on the very eve of battle, on the strength of one dream. For all we know, yonder knight is merely having a nightmare, induced perhaps by a lack of courage!"

An immediate cry of outrage filled the assembly, as Godwin began to unsheath his sword.

"Put back your sword, Sir Knight," said the king. "We need every man alive to face the foe; and offenses must be settled at a later time. It would seem that a message has been sent to us from Heaven. Dare we disobey this word?"

The Grand Templar lifted his rugged, frowning face.

"A message from Heaven, said you, King? To me it seems more like a message from Saladin. Tell us, Sir Godwin, were not you and your brother once the sultan's guests at Damascus?"

"That is so, my lord Templar. We left before the war was declared."

"And," went on the master, "were you not officers of the sultan's bodyguard?"

Now all looked intently at Godwin, who hesitated a little, foreseeing how his answer would be read, whereon Wulf spoke in his loud voice, "Aye, we acted as such for awhile, and—doubtless you have heard the story—saved Saladin's life when he was attacked by the Assassins."

"Oh!" said the Templar with bitter sarcasm, "you saved Saladin's life, did you? I can well believe it. You, being Christians, who above everything should desire the death of Saladin, saved his life! Now, Sir Knights, answer me one more question—"

"Sir Templar, with my tongue or with my sword?" broke in Wulf, but the king held up his hand and signaled him to be silent.

"A truce to your tavern ruffling, young sir, and now answer this question," went on the Templar. "Sir Godwin, is your cousin, Rosamund, the daughter of Sir Andrew D'Arcy, a niece of Saladin, and has she been created by him princess of Baalbec, and is she at this moment in his city of Damascus?"

"She is his niece," answered Godwin quietly; "she is the princess of Baalbec, but at this moment is likely with Saladin himself."

"How do you know that, Sir Godwin?"

"I only know that Saladin now trusts no body of men to protect his niece. He will, I believe, keep her close to his side prior to battle."

"How much longer must we endure this frightened dreamer?" asked the master.

"You do not receive my counsel and warning," said Godwin, "nor will you believe me when I say that while I was on guard on yonder hilltop I saw the forces of Saladin grow larger and more formidable. I say again, withdraw from your indefensible position to the city of Jerusalem while you still can."

Once again, the council stared while a general gloom hung over the silent leaders.

But Godwin only shrugged his shoulders and said nothing, as the master of the Templars went on, taking no heed.

"King, we await your word, and it must be spoken soon, for in four hours it will be dawn. Do we march against Saladin like bold, Christian men, or do we run like cowards?"

Then Count Raymond of Tripoli rose and said, "Before you answer, King, hear me, if it be for the last time, who am old in war and know the Saracens. My town of Tiberias is sacked; my vassals have been put to the sword by thousands; my wife is imprisoned in her citadel, and soon must yield, if she be not rescued. Yet I say to you, and to the barons here assembled, better so than that you should advance across the desert to attack Saladin. Leave Tiberias to its fate and my wife with it, and save your army, which is the last hope of the Christians of the East. Christ has no more soldiers in these lands. Jerusalem has no other shield. The army of the sultan is larger than yours; his cavalry are more skilled. Turn his flank—or, better still, bide here and await his attack, and victory will be to the soldiers of the Cross. Advance, and the warning of that knight at whom you scoff will come true, and the cause of Christendom be lost in Syria. I have spoken, and for the last time."

"Like his friend, the knight of visions," sneered the grand master, "the count Raymond is an old ally of Saladin. Will you take such cowardly counsel? On—on! And smite these heathen dogs, or be forever shamed. On, in the name of the Cross! The Cross is with us! God wills it!"

"Aye," answered Raymond, "for the last time."

Then there arose a tumult through which every man shouted to his fellow, some saying one thing and some another, while the king sat at the head of the table, his face hidden in his hands. One minute later, he lifted it and said, "I command that we march at dawn. If the count Raymond and these brethren think the words unwise, let them leave us and remain here under guard until the issue be known."

A great silence then followed, for all there

knew that the words were fateful, in the midst of which Count Raymond said, "Nay, I go with you."

And Godwin echoed, "And we go also to show whether or not we are the spies of Saladin."

Of these speeches none of them seemed to take heed, for all were lost in their own thoughts. One by one they rose, bowed to the king, and left the tent to give their commands and rest awhile before it was time to ride. Godwin and Wulf went also, and with them the bishop of Nazareth, who wrung his hands and seemed ill at ease. But Wulf comforted him, saying, "Grieve no more, Father; let us think of the joy of battle, not of the sorrow by which it may be followed."

"I find no joy in battles," answered the holy Egbert.

When they had slept awhile, Godwin and Wulf rose and fed their horses. After they had washed and groomed them, they tested and did on their armor, then took them down to the spring to drink their fill, as their masters did. Also, Wulf, who was cunning in war, brought with him four large wineskins which he had purchased for this hour and, filling them with pure water, fastened two of them with thongs behind the saddle of Godwin and two behind his own. Further, he filled the water bottles at their saddle-bows, saying, "At least we will be among the last to die of thirst."

Then they went back and watched the host break its camp, which it did with no light heart, for many of them knew of the danger in which they stood; moreover, the tale of Godwin's dream had been spread abroad. Not knowing where to go, they and Egbert, the bishop of Nazareth—who was unarmed and rode upon a mule, for stay behind he would not—joined themselves to the great body of knights who followed the king. As they did so, the Templars, five hundred strong, came up, a fierce and gallant band, and the master, who was at their head, saw the brethren and called out, pointing to the wineskins which were hung behind their saddles, "What do these water-carriers here among brave knights who trust in God alone?"

Wulf would have answered, but Godwin asked him to be silent, saying, "Fall back; we will find less ill-omened company."

So they stood on one side and bowed themselves as the Cross went by, guarded by the mailed bishop of Acre. Then came Reginald of Chatillon, Saladin's enemy, the cause of all this woe, who saw them and cried, "Sir Knights, whatever they may say, I know you for brave men, for I have heard the tale of your doings among the Assassins. There is room for you among my suite—follow me."

"As well him as another," said Godwin. "Let us go where we are led." So they followed him.

By the time that the army reached Kenna, where once the water was made wine, the July sun was already hot, and the spring was so soon drunk dry that many men could get no water. On they pushed into the desert lands below, which lay between them and Tiberias. These lands were bordered on the right and left by hills. Now clouds of dust were seen moving across the plains, and in the heart of them bodies of Saracen horsemen, which continually attacked the vanguard under Count Raymond, and as continually retreated before they could be crushed, slaying many with their spears and arrows. Also, these came round behind them and charged the rearguard, where marched the Templars and the light-armed troops named Turcopoles, and the band of Reginald de Chatillon, with which rode the brethren.

From noon till near sundown the long, harassed line, broken now into fragments, struggled forward across the rough, stony plain, the burning heat beating upon their armor till the air danced about it as it does before a fire. Towards evening, men and horses became exhausted, and the soldiers cried to their captains to lead them to water. But in that place there was no water.

The rearguard fell behind, worn out with constant attacks that must be repelled in the burning heat, so that there was a great gap between it and the king who marched in the center. Messages reached them to push on, but they could not, and at length camp was pitched in the desert near a place called Marescalcia, and upon this camp Raymond and his vanguard were forced back. As Godwin and Wulf rode up, they saw him come in bringing his wounded with him, and noted that he petitioned the king to push on and at all hazards to cut his way through to the lake, where they might drink. A message came back from the king saying that he could not, since the soldiers would march no more that day. Then Raymond wrung his hands in despair and rode back to his men, crying aloud, "Alas! alas! Oh! Lord God, alas! We are dead, and Thy kingdom is lost."

That night none slept, for all were thirsty, and who can sleep with a burning throat? By this time Godwin and Wulf were no longer laughed at because of the water-skins they carried on their horses. Rather did great nobles come to them, and almost on their knees crave for the blessing of a single cup. Having watered their horses sparingly from a bowl, they gave what they could, till at length only two skins remained. A short time later, one of these was spilt by a thief, who crept up and slashed it with his knife that he might drink while the water ran to waste. After this the brethren drew their swords and watched, swearing that they would kill any man who so much as touched the skin which was left.

All that long night through there arose a confused clamor from the camp, of which the burden seemed to be, "Water! Give us water!" while from without came the shouts of the Saracens calling upon Allah. Here, too, the hot ground was covered with scrub dried to tinder by the summer drought, and to this the Saracens set fire so that the smoke rolled down on the Christian host and choked them, and the place became a hell.

Day dawned at last, and the army was formed up in order of battle, its two wings being thrown forward. Thus they struggled on, those of them that were not too weak to stir. Nor as yet did the Saracens attack them, since they knew that the sun was stronger than all their spears. On they labored towards the northern wells, till about mid-day the battle began with a flight of arrows so thick that it momentarily hid the heavens.

After this came charge and counter-charge, attack and repulse, and always above the noise of war that dreadful cry for water. What truly happened Godwin and Wulf never knew, for the smoke and dust blinded them so that they could see but a little way. Toward the end there was a last furious charge, and the knights with whom they were riding broke through the dense mass of Saracens like a serpent of steel, leaving a broad trail of dead behind them. When they pulled rein and wiped the sweat from their eyes it was to find themselves with thousands of others upon the top of a steep hill, of which the sides were thick with dry grass and bush that already was being fired.

"The Rood! The Rood! Rally round the Rood!" said a voice, and looking behind them they saw the black and jeweled fragment of the true Cross set upon a rock, and by it the bishop of Acre. Then the smoke of the burning grass rose up and hid the sacred relic from their sight.

Now began one of the most hideous fights that is told of in the history of the world. Again and again the Saracens attacked in thousands, and again and again they were driven back by the desperate valor of the Franks, who fought on, their jaws agape with thirst. A black-bearded man stumbled up to the brethren, his tongue protruding from his lips, and they knew him for the master of the Templars.

"For the love of Christ, give me to drink," he said, recognizing them as the knights at whom he had mocked as water-carriers.

They gave him of the little they had left, and while they and their horses drank the rest themselves, saw him rush down the hill refreshed, shaking his red sword. Then came a pause, and they heard the voice of the bishop of Nazareth, who had clung to them all this while, saying, as though to himself, "And here it was that the Savior preached the Sermon on the Mount. Yes, He preached the words of peace upon this very spot. Oh! it cannot be that He will desert us—it cannot be."

While the Saracens held off, the soldiers began to put up the king's pavilion, and with it other tents, around the rock on which stood the Cross.

"Do they mean to camp here?" asked Wulf bitterly.

"Peace," answered Godwin; "they hope to make a wall about the Rood. But it is of no avail, for this battle was lost before ere it began."

Wulf shrugged his shoulders.

"At least, let us die well," he said.

Then the last attack began. Up the hillside rose dense volumes of smoke, and with the smoke came the Saracens. Three times they were driven back; yet they came on. At the fourth onset few of the Franks could fight more, for thirst had conquered them on this waterless hill of Hattin. They lay down upon the dry grass with gaping jaws and protruding tongues, and let themselves be slain or taken prisoners. A great company of Saracen horsemen broke through the ring and rushed at the scarlet tent. It rocked to and fro, then down it fell in a red heap, entangling the king in its folds.

At the foot of the Cross, Rufinus, the bishop of Acre, still fought on bravely. Suddenly an arrow struck him in the throat and, throwing his arms wide, he fell to earth. Then the Saracens hurled themselves upon the Rood, tore it from its place, and with mockery and spittings bore it down the hill towards their camp, as ants may be seen carrying a little stick into their nest. Meanwhile, all who were left alive of the Christian army stared upwards, as though they awaited some miracle from Heaven. But no angels appeared in the brazen sky, and knowing that God had permitted them to reap what they sowed, they groaned aloud in their shame and wretchedness.

"Come," said Godwin to Wulf in a strange, quiet voice. "We have seen enough. It is time to die. Look! Yonder below us are the Mamelukes, our old regiment, and amongst them Saladin, for I see his banner. Having had water, our horses and we are still fresh and strong. Now, let us make an end of which they will tell in Essex yonder. Charge for the flag of Saladin!"

Wulf nodded, and side by side they sped down the hill. Scimitars flashed at them, arrows struck upon their mail and the shields blazoned with the Death's-head D'Arcy crest. Through it all they went unscathed, and while the army of the Saracens stared, at the foot of the Horn of Hattin turned their horses' heads straight for the royal standard of Saladin. On they struggled, felling or riding down a foe at every stride. On, still on, although Flame and Smoke bled from a score of wounds.

They were among the Mamelukes, where their line was thin; by Heaven! They were through them, and rode straight at the well known figure of the sultan, mounted on his white horse with his young son and his emir, the prince Hassan, at his side.

"Saladin for you, Hassan for me," shouted Wulf.

Then they met, and all the host of Islam cried out in dismay as they saw the Commander of the Faithful and his horse borne to the earth before the last despairing charge of these zealous Christian knights. Another instant, and the sultan was on his feet again, and a score of scimitars were striking at Godwin. His horse Flame sank down dying, but he sprang from the saddle, swinging his long sword. Now Saladin recognized the crest upon his buckler, and cried out, "Yield, you, Sir Godwin! You have done well—yield, you!"

But Godwin, who would not yield, answered, "When I am dead—not before."

Thereupon Saladin spoke a word, and while certain of his Mamelukes engaged Godwin in front, keeping out of reach of that red and terrible sword, others crept up behind and, springing on him, seized his arms and dragged him to the ground, where they tied him securely.

Meanwhile, Wulf had other business, for his horse Smoke, already stabbed in the vitals, proceeded to fall near Prince Hassan. The young knight arose but little hurt, and cried out, "Thus, Hassan, old foe and friend, we meet at last in war. Come, I would pay the debt I owe you for that drugged wine, man to man and sword to sword."

"Indeed, it is due, Sir Wulf," answered the prince, laughing. "Guards, touch not this brave knight who has dared so much to reach me. Sultan, I ask a favor. Between Sir Wulf and me there is an ancient quarrel that can only be washed away in blood. Let it be decided here and now, and let this be your decree that if I fall in fair fight, none shall set upon my conqueror, and no vengeance shall be taken for my blood."

"So be it," said Saladin. "Then Sir Wulf shall be my prisoner and no more, as his brother is already. I owe it to the men who saved my life when we were friends. Give the Frank to drink that the fight may be fair."

So they gave Wulf a cup, from which he drank. When he finished it, he handed the cup to Godwin.

Hassan sprang to the ground, saying, "Your horse is dead, Sir Wulf, so we must fight afoot."

"Generous as ever," laughed Wulf. "Even the poisoned wine was a gift!"

"If so, for the last time, I fear me," answered Hassan with a smile.

Then they faced each other, and oh! The scene was strange. Up on the slopes of Hattin the fight still raged. There amidst the smoke and fires of the burning grass little companies of soldiers stood back to back while the Saracens wheeled round them, thrusting and cutting at them till they fell. Here and there knights charged singly or in groups, and so came to death or capture. About the plain hundreds of foot soldiers were being slaughtered, while their officers were taken prisoners. Towards the camp of Saladin a company advanced with sounds of triumph, carrying aloft a black stump which was the holy Rood. Meanwhile, others drove or led mobs of prisoners, among them the king and his chosen knights.

The wilderness was red with blood; the air was rent with shouts of victory and cries of agony or despair. And there, in the midst of it all, ringed round with grave Saracens, stood the emir, clad above his mail in his white robe and jeweled turban, facing the great Christian knight, with harness hacked and reddened. Wulf's face had the light of battle shining in his fierce eyes, and a smile upon his stained features.

For those who watched, the battle was forgotten—or, rather, its interest was centered on this point.

"It will be a good fight," said one of them to Godwin, whom they had permitted to rise, "for though your brother is the younger and the heavier man, he is hurt and weary, whereas the emir is fresh and unwounded. Ah! They are at it!"

Hassan had struck first and the blow went home. Falling upon the point of Wulf's steel helm, the heavy, razor-edged scimitar glanced from it and shore away the links from the flap, which hung upon his shoulder, causing the Frank to stagger. Again he struck, this time upon the shield, and so heavily that Wulf came to his knees.

"Your brother is finished," said the Saracen captain to Godwin.

But Godwin only answered, "Wait."

As he spoke, Wulf twisted his body out of reach of a third blow, and while Hassan staggered forward with the weight of the missed stroke, placed his hand upon the ground and, springing to his feet, ran backwards six or eight paces.

"He flies!" cried the Saracens.

But again Godwin said, "Wait." Nor was there long to wait.

For now, throwing aside his buckler and grasping the great sword in both his hands, with a shout of, "A D'Arcy! A D'Arcy!" Wulf leapt at Hassan as a wounded lion leaps. The sword wheeled and fell, and lo! The shield of the Saracen was severed in two. Again it fell, and his turbaned helm was cloven. A third time, and the right arm and shoulder with the scimitar that grasped it seemed to fall away from his body. Hassan soon sank dying to the ground.

Wulf stood and looked at him, while a murmur of grief went up from those who watched, for they loved this emir. Hassan beckoned to the victor with his left hand and, throwing down his sword to show that he feared no treachery, Wulf came to him and knelt beside him.

"A good stroke," Hassan said faintly, "that could shear the double links of Damascus steel as though it were silk. Well, as I told you long ago, I knew that the hour of our meeting in war would be an ill hour for me, and my debt is paid. Farewell, brave knight. Would I could hope that we should meet in Paradise! Take that star-jewel, the badge of my house, from my turban and wear it in memory of me. Long, long and happy be your days!"

Then, while Wulf held him in his arms, Saladin came up and spoke to him, till he fell back and was dead.

Thus died Hassan, and thus ended the battle of Hattin, which caused the Christians to eventually lose control over Jerusalem and much of the East.

Chapter XIX
Before the Walls of Ascalon

When Hassan was dead, at a sign from Saladin a captain of the Mamelukes named Abdullah unfastened the jewel from the emir's turban and handed it to Wulf. It was a glorious star-shaped thing, made of great emeralds set round with diamonds. The captain Abdullah, who like all Easterners loved such ornaments, looked at it greedily, and lamented, "Alas! That an unbeliever should wear the enchanted Star, the ancient Luck of the House of Hassan!" a saying that Wulf remembered.

He took the jewel, then turned to Saladin and said, pointing to the dead body of Hassan, "Have I your peace, Sultan, after such a deed?"

"Did I not give you and your brother to drink?" asked Saladin with meaning. "Whoever dies, you are safe. There is but one sin, for which I will not pardon—you know what it is," and he looked at them. "As for Hassan, he was my beloved friend and servant, but you slew him in fair fight, and his soul is now in Paradise. None in my army will raise a blood feud against you on that score."

Then, dismissing the matter with a wave of his hand, he turned to receive a great body of Christian prisoners that, panting and stumbling like over-driven sheep, were being thrust on towards the camp with curses, blows, and mockery by the victorious Saracens.

Among them, the brethren rejoiced to see Egbert, the gentle and holy bishop of Nazareth, whom they had thought dead. Also, wounded in many places, his hacked harness hanging about him like a beggar's rags, there was the black-browed master of the Templars, who even now could be fierce and insolent.

"So I was right," he mocked in a husky voice, "and here you are, safe with your friends the Saracens, Sir Dreamer and knight of the water-skins—"

"From which you were glad enough to drink just now," said Godwin. "Also," he added sadly, "you had best look to your men's needs, for this day is not done." And turning, he looked towards a blazoned tent, where the sultan's great pavilion was being pitched by the Arab camp-setters. The master saw and trembled, for he knew this to be the judgment seat of Saladin.

"Is it there that you mean to murder me, traitor and wizard?" he asked.

Then rage took hold of Godwin and he answered him, "Were it not for your plight, here and now I would thrust those words down your throat, as, should we both live, I yet shall hope to do. You call us traitors. Is it the work of traitors to have charged alone through all this host until our horses died beneath us?"—he pointed to where Smoke and Flame lay with glazing eyes—"to have unhorsed Saladin and to have slain this prince in single combat?" and he turned to the body of the emir Hassan, which his servants were carrying away.

"You speak of me as wizard and murderer," he went on, "because some angel brought me understanding which, had you believed it, Templar, would have saved tens of thousands from a bloody death, the Christian kingdom from harm, and yonder holy thing from mockery." With a shudder he then glanced at the Rood, which its captors had set up upon a rock not far away with a dead knight tied to its black arms. "You, Sir Templar, are the murderer who by your madness and ambition have brought shame on the cause of Christ, as was foretold by the count Raymond."

"That other traitor who also has escaped," snarled the master.

Then Saracen guards dragged him away, and they were parted.

By now the pavilion was up and Saladin entered it, saying, "Bring before me the king of the Franks and Prince Arnat, he who is called Reginald of Chatillon."

Then a thought struck him, and he called to Godwin and Wulf, saying, "Sir Knights, you know our tongue; give up your swords to the officer—they shall be returned to you, and come, be my interpreters."

So the brethren followed him into the tent, where presently were brought the wretched king and the gray-haired Reginald de Chatillon, and with them a few other great knights who, even in the midst of their misery, stared at Godwin and Wulf in wonderment. Saladin read the look, and explained lest their presence should be misunderstood, "King and nobles, be not mistaken. These knights are my prisoners, as you are, and none have shown themselves braver today, or done me and mine more damage. Indeed, had it not been for my guards, within the hour I should have fallen beneath the sword of Sir Godwin. But as they know Arabic, I have asked them to render my words into your tongue. Do you accept them as interpreters? If not, others must be found."

When they had translated this, the king said that he accepted them, adding to Godwin, "Would that I had also accepted you two nights gone as an interpreter of the will of Heaven!"

The sultan told his captors to be seated and, seeing their terrible thirst, commanded slaves to bring a great bowl of sherbet made of rose-water cooled with snow, and with his own hand gave it to King Guy. He drank in great gulps, then passed the bowl to Reginald de Chatillon, whereon Saladin cried out to Godwin, "Say to the king it is he and not I who gives this man to drink. There is no bond of salt between me and the prince Arnat."

Godwin translated, sorrowfully enough, and Reginald, who knew the habits of the Saracens, answered, "No need to explain, Sir Knight, those words are my death warrant. Well, I never expected less."

Then Saladin spoke again.

"Prince Arnat, you strove to take the holy city of Mecca and to desecrate the tomb of the Prophet, and then I swore to kill you. Again, when in a time of peace a caravan came from Egypt and passed by Esh-Shobek, where you were, forgetting your oath, you fell upon them and slew them. They asked for mercy in the name of Allah, saying that there was truce between Saracen and Frank. But you mocked them, telling them to seek aid from Mahomet, in whom they trusted. Then for the second time I swore to kill you. Yet I give you one more chance. Will you subscribe the Koran and embrace the faith of Islam? Or will you die?"

Now the lips of Reginald turned pale, and for a moment he swayed upon his seat. Then his courage came back to him, and he answered in a strong voice, "Sultan, I will have none of your mercy at such a price, nor do I bow the knee to your dog of a false prophet, who perish in the faith of Christ, and, being weary of the world, am content to go to Him."

Saladin sprang to his feet, his very beard bristling with wrath and, drawing his saber, shouted aloud, "You scorn Mahomet! Behold! I avenge Mahomet upon you! Take him away!" And he struck him with the flat of his scimitar.

Then Mamelukes leapt upon the prince. Dragging him to the entrance of the tent, they forced him to his knees and there beheaded him in sight of the soldiers and of the other prisoners.

Thus, bravely enough, died Reginald de Chatillon, whom the Saracens called Prince Arnat. In the hush that followed this terrible deed King Guy said to Godwin, "Ask the sultan if it is my turn next."

"No," answered Saladin; "kings do not kill kings, but that truce-breaker and blasphemer has met with no more than his deserts."

Then came a scene still more dreadful. Saladin went to the door of his tent and, standing over the body of Reginald, bade them parade the captive Templars and Hospitallers before him. They were brought to the number of over two hundred, for it was easy to distinguish them by the red and white crosses on their breasts.

"These also are faith-breakers," he shouted, "and of their unclean tribes will I rid the world. Ho! my emirs and doctors of the law," and he turned to the great crowd of his captains about him, "take each of you one of them and kill him."

At this command the followers of Saladin hesitated, for though fanatics they were brave, and loved not this slaughter of defenseless men. Even the Mamelukes murmured aloud.

But Saladin cried again, "They are worthy of death, and he who disobeys my command shall himself be slain."

"Sultan," said Godwin, "we cannot witness such a crime; we ask that we may die with them."

"No," he answered; "you have eaten of my salt, and to kill you would be murder. Get you to the tent of the princess of Baalbec yonder, for there you will see nothing of the death of these Franks, your fellow worshippers."

So the brethren turned and, led by a Mameluke, fled aghast for the first time in their lives, past the long lines of Templars and Hospitallers, who in the last red light of the dying day knelt upon the sand and prayed, while the emirs came up to kill them.

They entered the tent, none forbidding them, and at the end of it saw two women crouched together on some cushions, who rose, clinging to each other. Then the women saw also and sprang forward with a cry of joy, saying, "So you live, you live!"

"Aye, Rosamund," answered Godwin, "to see this shame—would God that we did not—whilst others die. They murder the knights of the holy Orders. To your knees and pray for their passing souls."

So they knelt down and prayed till the tumult died away, and they knew that all was done.

"Oh, my cousins," said Rosamund, as she staggered to her feet, "what a hell of wickedness and bloodshed is this in which we dwell! Save me from it if you love me—I beseech you save me!"

"We will do our best," they answered; "but let us talk no more of these things which are the decree of God—lest we should go mad. Tell us your story."

But Rosamund had little to tell, except that she had been well treated, and always kept by the person of the sultan, marching to and fro with his army, for he awaited the fulfillment of his dream concerning her. Then they told her all that had happened to them; also of the dream of Godwin and its dreadful accomplishment, and of the death of Hassan beneath the sword of Wulf. At that story Rosamund wept and shrank from him a little, for though it was this prince who had stolen her from her home, she loved Hassan.

Wulf said humbly, "The fault is not mine; it was so fated. Would that I had died instead of this Saracen!"

Rosamund answered, "No, no; I am proud that you should have conquered."

But Wulf shook his head, and said, "I am not proud. Although weary with that awful battle, I was still the younger and stronger man, though at first he well-nigh mastered me by his skill and quickness. At least we parted friends. Look, he gave me this," and he showed her the great emerald badge which the dying prince had given him.

Masouda, who all this while had sat very quiet, came forward and looked at it.

"Do you know," she asked, "that this jewel is very famous, not only for its value, but because it is said to have belonged to one of the children of the Prophet, and to bring good fortune to its owner?"

Wulf smiled.

"It brought little to poor Hassan this day, when my grandsire's sword shore the Damascus steel as though it were wet clay."

"And sent him swiftly to Paradise, where he longed to be, at the hands of a gallant foe," answered Masouda. "Nay, all his life this emir was happy and beloved, by his sovereign, his wives, his fellows and his servants, nor do I think that he would have desired another end whose wish was to die in battle with the Franks. At least there is scarce a soldier in the sultan's army who would not give all he has for yonder trinket, which is known throughout the land as the Star of Hassan. So beware, Sir Wulf, lest you be robbed or murdered, although you have eaten the salt of Saladin."

"I remember the captain Abdullah looking at it greedily and lamenting that the Luck of the House of Hassan should pass to an unbeliever," said Wulf. "Well, enough of this jewel and its dangers; I think Godwin has words to say."

"Yes," said Godwin. "We are here in your tent through the order of Saladin, who did not wish us to witness the death of our comrades, but tomorrow we shall be separated again. Now if you are to escape —"

"I will escape! I must escape, even if I am recaptured and die for it," broke in Rosamund passionately.

"Speak low," said Masouda. "I saw the eunuch Mesrour pass the door of the tent, and he is a spy—they all are spies."

"If you are to escape," repeated Godwin in a whisper, "it must be within the next few weeks while the army is on the march. The risk is great to all of us—even to you, and we have no plan. But, Masouda, you are clever, make one, and tell it to us."

She lifted her head to speak, when suddenly a shadow fell upon them. It was that of the head eunuch, Mesrour, a fat, cunning-faced man, with a cringing air. Low he bowed before them, saying, "Your pardon, O Princess. A messenger has come from Saladin demanding the presence of these knights at the banquet that he has made ready for his noble prisoners."

"We obey," said Godwin and, rising, they bowed to Rosamund and to Masouda, then turned to go, leaving the star jewel where they had been seated.

Very skillfully Mesrour covered it with a fold of his robe, and under shelter of the fold slipped down his hand and grasped it, not knowing that although she seemed to be turned away, Masouda was watching him out of the corner of her eye. Waiting till the brethren reached the tent door, she called out, "Sir Wulf, are you already weary of the enchanted Star of Fortune, or would you bequeath it to us?

Now Wulf came back, saying mournfully, "I forgot the thing—who would not at such a time? Where is it? I left it on the cushion."

"Try the hand of Mesrour," said Masouda, at which point, with a very crooked smile, the eunuch produced it and said, "I wished to show you, Sir Knight, that you must be careful with such gems as these, especially in a camp where there are many dishonest persons."

"I thank you," answered Wulf as he took it; "you have shown me." Then, followed by the sound of Masouda's mocking laughter, they left the tent.

The sultan's messenger led them forward, across ground strewn with the bodies of the murdered Templars and Hospitallers. Over one of these corpses Godwin stumbled in the gloom, so heavily, that he fell to his knees. He searched the face in the starlight, to find it was that of a knight of the Hospitallers of whom he had made a friend at Jerusalem—a very good and gentle Frenchman, who had abandoned high station and large lands to join the order for the love of Christ and charity. Such was his reward on earth—to be struck down in cold blood, like an ox by its butcher. Then, issuing a prayer for the repose of this knight's soul, Godwin rose and, filled with horror, followed on to the royal pavilion.

Of all the strange feasts that they ever ate, the brethren found this the strangest and the saddest. Saladin was seated at the head of the table with guards and officers standing behind him, and as each dish was brought he tasted it and no more, to show that it was not poisoned. Not far from him sat the king of Jerusalem and his brother, and all down the board great captive nobles, to the number of fifty or more.

Sorry spectacles were these gallant knights in their hewn and blood-stained armor, pale-faced, too, with eyes set wide in horror at the dread deeds they had just seen done. Yet they ate, and ate ravenously, for now that their thirst was satisfied, they were filled with hunger. Thirty thousand Christians lay dead on the Horn and plain of Hattin; the kingdom of Jerusalem was broken, and its king a prisoner. The holy Rood was taken as a trophy. Two hundred knights of the sacred Orders lay within a few score yards of them, butchered cruelly by those very emirs and doctors of the law who stood behind their master's seat, at the express command of that merciless master. Defeated, shamed, bereaved—yet they ate, and, being human, could take comfort from the thought that having eaten, by the law of the Arabs, at least their lives were safe for a season.

Saladin called Godwin and Wulf to him that they might interpret for him, and gave them food, and they also ate who were compelled to it by hunger.

"Have you seen your cousin, the princess?" he asked; "and how found you her?" he continued between bites of food.

Then, remembering the events of the day, and looking at those miserable feasters, anger took hold of Godwin, and he answered boldly, "Sire, we found her sick with the sights and sounds of war and murder; shamed to know also that her uncle, the conquering sovereign of the East, had slaughtered over two hundred unarmed men."

Wulf trembled at his words, but Saladin listened and showed no anger.

"Doubtless," he answered, "she thinks me cruel, and you also think me cruel—a despot who delights in the death of his enemies. Yet it is not so, for I desire peace on terms that the laws of Allah can bless. It is you Christians who for nearly a hundred years have drenched these sands with blood, because you say that you wish to possess the land where your Prophet lived and died more than eleven centuries ago. How many Saracens have you slain? Moreover, with you peace is no peace. Those cursed

Templars that I destroyed tonight have broken it many times. Well, I will bear no more. Allah has given my army and me the victory, and I will take your cities and drive the Franks back into the sea. Let them seek their own lands and worship God there after their own fashion, and leave the East in quiet."

"No doubt," responded Godwin, "that there is some truth in what you say; yet you wish to ignore the fact that the growth of your religion in many parts of the world, including Europe, has come through violence and bloodshed. Deny if you can, O Sultan, that for over five centuries the sword of your people has seldom ceased to be at the throat of those who only seek peace to serve the Prince of Peace."

"I have no need or desire to speak further on such things," said Saladin. "The victory of my army speaks for itself. Now, Sir Godwin, tell these captives for me that tomorrow I send those of them who are unwounded to Damascus, there to await ransom while I besiege Jerusalem and the other Christian cities. Let them have no fear; I have emptied the cup of my anger; no more of them shall die, and a priest of their faith, the bishop of Nazareth, shall stay with their sick to minister to them after their own rites."

So Godwin rose and told them, and they answered not a word, who had lost all hope and courage.

Afterwards, he asked whether he and his brother were also to be sent to Damascus.

Saladin replied, "No." He would keep them for awhile to interpret, then they might go their ways without ransom.

The following day, therefore, the captives were sent to Damascus, and that day Saladin took the castle of Tiberias, setting at liberty Eschiva, the wife of Raymond, and her children. Then he moved on to Acre, which he took, relieving four thousand Moslem captives, and so on to other towns, all of which fell before him, till at length he came to Ascalon, which he besieged setting up his mangonels against its walls.

The night was dark outside of Ascalon, except when the flashes of lightning in the storm that rolled down from the mountains to the sea lit it up. This light revealed thousands of white tents set round the city, the walls and the sentries who watched them, the feathery palms set against the sky, and the mighty snow-crowned range of Lebanon. In a little open space near the garden of an empty house that stood without the walls, a man and a woman were talking, both of them wrapped in dark cloaks. They were Godwin and Masouda.

"Well," said Godwin eagerly, "is all ready?"

She nodded and answered, "In time, all. Tomorrow afternoon an assault will be made upon Ascalon, but even if it is taken the camp will not be moved that night. There will be great confusion, and Abdullah, who is somewhat sick, will be the captain of the guard over the princess's tent. He will allow the soldiers to slip away to assist in the sack of the city, nor will they betray him. At sunset but one eunuch will be on watch—Mesrour; and I will find means to put him to sleep. Abdullah will bring the princess to this garden disguised as his young son, and there you two and I shall meet them."

"What then?" asked Godwin.

"Do you remember the old Arab who brought you the horses Flame and Smoke, and took no payment for them, he who was named Son of the Sand? Well, as you know, he is my uncle, and he has more horses of that breed. I have seen him, and he is well pleased at the tale of Flame and Smoke and the knights who rode them, and more particularly at the way in which they came to their end, which he says has brought credit to their ancient blood. At the foot of this garden is a cave, which was once a sepulcher. There we shall find the horses—four of them—and with them my uncle, Son of the Sand, and by the morning light we will be a hundred miles away and lie hid with his tribe until we can slip to the coast and board a Christian ship. Does it please you?"

"Very well; but what is Abdullah's price?"

"One only—the enchanted star, the Luck of the House Hassan; for nothing else will he take such risks. Will Wulf give it?"

"Surely," answered Godwin with a laugh.

"Good. Then it must be done tonight. When I return I will send Abdullah to your tent. Fear not; if he takes the jewel he will give the price, since otherwise he thinks it will bring him ill fortune."

"Does the lady Rosamund know?" asked Godwin again.

She shook her head.

"No, she is anxious to escape; she thinks of little else. But what is the use of telling her till the time comes? The fewer that know such a plot the better, and if anything goes wrong, it is well that she should be innocent, for then—"

"Then death, and farewell to all things," said Godwin; "nor indeed should I grieve to say good-bye to them. But, Masouda, you risk much. Tell me now, honestly, why do you do this?"

As he spoke the lightning flashed and showed her face as she stood there against a background of green leaves and red lily flowers. There was a strange look upon it—a look that made Godwin feel afraid, although he knew not the reason.

"Why did I take you into my inn yonder in Beirut when you were the pilgrims Peter and John? Why did I find you the best horses in Syria and guide you to the Al-Jebal? Why did I often dare death by torment for you there? Why did I save the three of you? And why, for all this weary while, have I—who, after all, am nobly born—become the mock of soldiers and the serving woman of the princess of Baalbec?

"Shall I answer?" she went on, laughing. "Doubtless in the beginning because I was the agent of Sinan, charged to betray such knights as you are into his hands, and afterwards because my heart was filled with pity and love for—the lady Rosamund?"

Again the lightning flashed, and this time that strange look had spread from Masouda's face to the face of Godwin.

"Masouda," he said in a whisper, "Oh! Think me no vain fool, but since it is best perhaps that both should know surely, tell me, is it as I have sometimes—"

"Feared?" broke in Masouda with her little mocking laugh. "Sir Godwin, it is so. What does your faith teach—the faith in which I was bred, and lost, but that now is mine again—because it is yours. That men and women who are united in faith are free to be wed. Yet, even now we are not free. Was I free when first I saw your eyes and your spirit in Beirut, the spirit for which

I had been watching all my life? Indeed not, for this was but the beginning, for something came from you to me, and I the cast-off plaything of Sinan—loved you, loved you, loved you—to my own doom! Yes, and rejoiced that it was so, and still rejoice that it is so, and would choose no other fate, because in that love I learned that there is a meaning in this life beyond self. No, speak not. I know your oath, nor would I tempt you to its breaking. But, Sir Godwin, a woman such as the lady Rosamund cannot love two men," and as she spoke Masouda strove to search his face while the shaft went home.

But Godwin showed neither surprise nor pain.

"So you know what I have known for many days," he said, "so long that my sorrow is lost in the hope of my brother's joy. Moreover, it is well that she should have chosen the better knight."

"Sometimes," said Masouda reflectively, "sometimes I have watched the lady Rosamund, and said to myself, 'What do you lack? You are beautiful, you are highborn, you are learned, you are brave, and you are good.' Then I have answered, 'You lack wisdom and true sight, else you would not have chosen Wulf when you might have taken Godwin. Or perchance your eyes are blinded also.'"

"Speak not thus of one who is my better in all things, I pray you," said Godwin in a vexed voice.

"By which you mean, whose arm is perhaps a little stronger, and who at a pinch could cut down a few more Saracens. Well, it takes more than strength to make a man—you must add spirit."

"Masouda," went on Godwin, taking no note of her words, "although we may guess her mind, our lady has said nothing yet. Also, Wulf may fall, and then I fill his place as best I can. I am no free man, Masouda."

"The love-sick are never free," she answered.

"I have no right to love the woman who loves my brother; to her are due my friendship and my loyalty—no more."

"She has not declared that she loves your brother; we may guess wrongly in this matter. They are your words—not mine."

"And we may guess rightly. What then?" asked Godwin.

"Then," answered Masouda, "there are many knightly Orders, or monasteries, for those who desire such places—as you do in your heart. Please, talk no more of all these things that may or may not be. Back to your tent, Sir Godwin, where I will send Abdullah to you to receive the jewel. So, farewell, farewell."

He took her outstretched hand, hesitated a moment, then lifted it to his lips, and went. It was as cold as that of a corpse, and fell against her side again like the hand of a corpse. Masouda shrank back among the flowers of the garden as though to hide herself from him and all the world. When he had gone a few paces, eight or ten perhaps, Godwin turned and glanced behind him, and at that moment there came a great blaze of lightning. In its fierce and fiery glare he saw Masouda standing with outstretched arms, upturned face, closed eyes, and parted lips. Illumined by the ghastly sheen of the elements her face looked like that of one new dead, and the tall red lilies which climbed up her dark, pall-like robe to her throat—yes, they looked like streams of fresh-shed blood.

Godwin shuddered a little and went his way, but as she slowly slid into the black, embracing night, Masouda said to herself, "Had I played a little more upon his gentleness and pity, I think that he would have offered me his heart—after Rosamund had done with it, and in payment for my services. Nay, not his heart, for he has none on earth, but his hand and loyalty. And, being honorable, he would have kept his promise, and I, who have passed through the harem of Al-Jebal, might yet have become the lady D'Arcy, and so lived out my life and nursed his babes. This can come, Sir Godwin; when you love me—not before; and you will never love me—until I am dead."

Snatching a bloom of the lilies into her hand, the hand that he had kissed, Masouda pressed it convulsively against her chest, till the red juice ran from the crushed flower and stained her like a wound. Then she glided away and was lost in the storm and the darkness.

Chapter XX
The Luck of the Star of Hassan

An hour later, the captain Abdullah might have been seen walking carelessly towards the tent where the brethren slept. Also, had there been any who cared to watch, something else might have been seen in that low moonlight, for now the storm and the heavy rain which followed it had passed. Namely, the fat shape of the eunuch Mesrour, following after him wrapped in a dark camel-hair cloak, such as was commonly worn by camp followers. He took shelter cunningly behind every rock and shrub and rise of the ground. Hidden among some picketed dromedaries, he saw Abdullah enter the tent of the brethren, then, waiting till a cloud crossed the moon, Mesrour ran to it unseen and, throwing himself down on its shadowed side, lay there like a drunken man, and listened intently with his ears. But the thick canvas was heavy with moisture, nor would the ropes and the trench that was dug around permit him, who did not love to lie in the water, to place his head against it. Also, those within spoke low, and he could only hear single words, such as "garden," "the star," "princess."

So important did these seem to him, however, that Mesrour finally decided to crawl under the cords, and although he shuddered at its cold, drew his body into the trench of water. He then began, with the sharp point of his knife, to cut a little slit in the taut canvas. To this he set his eye, only to find that it served him nothing, for there was no light in the tent. Still, men were there who talked in the darkness.

"Good," said a voice—it was that of one of the brethren, but which he could not tell, for even to those who knew them best they seemed to be the same. "Good; then it is settled. Tomorrow, at the hour arranged, you bring the princess to the place agreed upon, disguised as you have said. In payment for this service I hand you the Luck of Hassan, which you covet. Take it; here it is, and swear to do your part, since otherwise it will bring no luck to you, for I will kill you the first time we meet—yes, and the other, also."

"I swear it by Allah and his prophet," answered Abdullah in a hoarse, trembling voice.

"It is enough; see that you keep the oath. And now away; it is not safe that you should tarry here."

Then came the sound of a man leaving the tent. Passing round it cautiously, he halted and, opening his hand, looked at its contents to make sure that no trick had been played upon him in the darkness. Mesrour screwed his head round to look also, and saw the light gleam faintly on the surface of the splendid jewel, which he, too, desired so eagerly. In so doing his foot struck a stone, and instantly Abdullah glanced down to see a dead or drunken man lying almost at his feet. With a swift movement he hid the jewel and wondered if he should walk away. He quickly determined that it would be wise to make sure that this fellow was dead or sleeping, so he turned and kicked the prostrate Mesrour upon the back with all his strength. Indeed, he did this three times, putting the eunuch through the greatest agony.

"I thought I saw him move," Abdullah muttered after the third kick; "it is best to make sure," and he drew his knife.

Now, had not terror paralyzed him, Mesrour would have cried out, but fortunately for himself, before he found his voice Abdullah had buried the knife three inches deep in his fat thigh. With an effort Mesrour endured this also, knowing that if he showed signs of life the next stroke would be in his heart. Then, satisfied that this fellow, whoever he might be, was either a corpse or insensible, Abdullah drew out the knife, wiped it on his victim's robe, and departed.

Not long afterwards Mesrour departed also, towards the sultan's house, bellowing with rage and pain and vowing vengeance.

It was not long delayed.

That very night Abdullah was seized and put to the question. In his suffering he confessed that he had been to the tent of the brethren and received from one of them the jewel, which was found upon him, as a bribe to bring the princess to a certain garden outside the camp. But he named the wrong garden. Further, when they asked which of the brethren it was who bribed him, he said he did not know, as their voices were alike, and their tent was in darkness; moreover, that he believed there was only one man in it, at least he heard or saw no other. He added that he was summoned to the tent by an Arab man whom he had never seen before, but who told him that if he wished for what he most desired and good fortune, he was to be there at a certain hour after sunset. Then he fainted and was put back in prison till the morning by the command of Saladin.

When the morning came, Abdullah was dead, who desired no more torments with doom at the end of them. But first he had scrawled upon the wall with a piece of charcoal:

"May that accursed Star of Hassan which tempted me bring better luck to others, and may hell receive the soul of Mesrour."

Thus died Abdullah, as trustworthy as he could be under pain of torture, since he had betrayed neither Masouda nor his son, both of whom were in the plot, and said that only one of the brethren was present in the tent, whereas he knew well that the two of them were there and which of these spoke and gave him the jewel.

Very early that morning the brethren, who were lying wakeful, heard sounds without their tent, and looking out saw that it was surrounded by Mamelukes.

"The plot is discovered," said Godwin to Wulf quietly, but with despair in his face. "Now, my brother, admit nothing, even under torture, lest others perish with us."

"Shall we fight?" asked Wulf as they threw on their mail.

But Godwin answered, "Nay, it would serve us nothing to kill a few brave men."

Then an officer entered the tent and commanded them to give up their swords and to follow him to Saladin to answer a charge that had been laid against them both, nor would he say any more. So they went as prisoners, and after waiting awhile, were ushered into a large room of the house where Saladin lodged, which was arranged as a court with a dais at one end. Before this they were placed, till the sultan entered through the further door, and with him certain of his emirs and secretaries. Also Rosamund, who looked very pale, was brought there, and in attendance on her Masouda, calm-faced as ever.

The brethren bowed to them, but Saladin, whose eyes were full of rage, took no notice of their salutation. For a moment there was silence, then Saladin bade a secretary read the charge, which was brief. It was that they had conspired to steal away the princess of Baalbec.

"Where is the evidence against us?" asked Godwin boldly. "The sultan is just, and convicts no man save on testimony."

Again Saladin motioned to the secretary, who read the words that had been taken down from the lips of the captain Abdullah. They demanded to be allowed to examine the captain Abdullah, and learned that he was already dead. Then the eunuch Mesrour was carried forward, for walk he could not, owing to the wound that Abdullah had given him. This witness told all his tale, how he had suspected Abdullah, and, following him, had heard him and one of the brethren speaking in the tent, and the words that passed. He also claimed to have seen Abdullah with the jewel in his hand.

When he had finished, Godwin asked which of them he had heard speaking with Abdullah, and he answered that he could not say, as their voices were so alike, but one voice only had spoken.

Then Rosamund was ordered to give her testimony, and said, truly enough, that she knew nothing of the plot and had no plan to leave. Masouda also swore that she now heard of it for the first time. After this the secretary announced that there was no more evidence and requested that the sultan give judgment in the matter.

"Against which of us," asked Godwin, "seeing that both the dead and the living witness declared they heard but one voice, and whose that voice was they did not know? According to your own law, you cannot condemn a man against whom there is no good testimony."

"There is testimony against one of you," answered Saladin sternly, "that of two witnesses, as is required, and, as I have warned you long ago, that man shall die. Indeed, both of you should die, for I am sure that both are guilty. Still, you have been put upon your trial according to the law, and as a just judge I will not twist the law against you. Let the guilty one die by beheading at sundown, the hour at which he planned to commit his crime. The other may go free with the citizens of Jerusalem who depart tonight, bearing my message to the Frankish leaders in that holy town."

"Which of us, then, is to die, and which to go free?" asked Godwin. "Tell us, that he who is doomed may prepare his soul."

"Say you, who know the truth," answered Saladin.

"We admit nothing," said Godwin; "yet, if one of us must die, I as the elder claim that right."

"And I claim it as the younger. The jewel was Hassan's gift to me; who else could give it to Abdullah?" added Wulf, speaking for the first time.

After this comment, all the Saracens there assembled, brave men who loved a knightly deed, murmured in admiration, and even Saladin said, "Well spoken, both of you. So it seems that both must die."

Then Rosamund stepped forward and threw herself upon her knees before him, exclaiming, "Sire, my uncle, such is not your justice, that two should be slain for the offence of one, if offence there be. If you know not which is guilty, spare them both, I beseech you."

He stretched out his hand and raised her from her knees; then thought awhile, and said, "No, plead not with me, for however much you love him the guilty man must suffer, as he deserves. But of this matter Allah alone knows the truth, therefore let it be decided by Allah," and he rested his head upon his hand, looking at Wulf and Godwin as though to read their souls.

Now behind Saladin stood that old and famous imam who had been with him and Hassan when he commanded the brethren to depart from Damascus. This religious leader had listened to everything that had passed with a sour smile. Leaning forward, he whispered in his master's ear, who considered a moment, then answered him, "It is good. Do so."

So the imam left the court and returned promptly carrying two small boxes of sandalwood tied with silk and sealed, so like each other that none could tell them apart, which boxes he passed continually from his right hand to his left and from his left hand to his right, then gave them to Saladin.

"In one of these," said the sultan, "is that jewel known as the enchanted Star and the Luck of the House of Hassan, which the prince presented to his conqueror on the day of Hattin, and for the desire of which my captain Abdullah became a traitor and was brought to death. In the other is a pebble of the same weight. Come, my niece, take you these boxes and give them to your kinsmen, to each the box you will. The jewel that is called the Star of Hassan is magical, and has virtue, so they say. Let it choose, therefore, which of these knights is ripe for death, and let him perish in whose box the Star is found."

"Now," whispered the imam into the ear of his master, "I wonder if we shall finally learn which it is of these two men that the lady loves."

"That is what I seek to know," answered Saladin in the same low voice.

As she heard this decree Rosamund looked round wildly and pleaded, "Oh! Be not so cruel. I beseech you spare me this task. Let it be another hand that is chosen to deal death to one of those of my own blood with whom I have dwelt since childhood. Let me not be the blind sword of fate that frees his spirit, lest it should haunt my dreams and turn all my world to woe. Spare me, I beseech you."

But Saladin looked at her very sternly and answered, "Princess, you know why I have brought you to the East and raised you to great honor here, why also I have made you my companion in these wars. Yet I am sure that you desire to escape, and plots are made to take you from me, though of these plots you say that you and your woman"—and he looked darkly at Masouda—"know nothing. But these men know, and it is right that you, for whose sake if not by whose command the thing was done, should mete out its reward, and that the blood of him whom you appoint, which is spilt for you, should be on your and no other head. Now do my bidding."

For a moment, Rosamund stared at the boxes, then suddenly she closed her eyes and, taking them up at hazard, stretched out her arms, leaning forward over the edge of the dais. Thereon, calmly enough, the brethren took, each of them, the box that was nearest to him, that in Rosamund's left hand falling to Godwin and that in her right to Wulf. Then she opened her eyes again, stood still, and watched.

"Cousin," said Godwin, "before we break this cord that is our chain of doom, know well that, whatever chances, we blame you not at all. It is God who acts through you, and you are as innocent of the death of either of us as of that plot whereof we stand accused."

Then he began to unknot the silk, which was around his box. Wulf, knowing that it would tell all the tale, did not trouble himself as yet, but looked around the room, thinking that, whether he lived or died, never would he see a stranger sight. Every eye in it was fixed upon the box in Godwin's hand; even Saladin stared as though it held his own destiny. No; not everyone, for those of the old imam were fixed upon the face of Rosamund, which was piteous to see, for all its beauty had left it, and even her parted lips were ashy. Masouda alone still stood upright and unmoved, as though she watched some play, but he noted that her rich-hued cheek grew pale and that beneath her robe her hand was pressed upon her heart. The silence also was intense, and broken only by the little grating noise of Godwin's nails as, having no knife to cut it, he patiently untied the silk.

"Trouble enough about one man's life in a land where lives are cheap!" exclaimed Wulf, thinking aloud, and at the sound of his voice all men started, as though it had thundered suddenly in a summer sky. Then with a laugh he tore the silk around his box with his strong fingers and, breaking the seal, shook out its contents. Lo! There on the floor before him, gleaming green and white with emerald and diamond, lay the enchanted Star of Hassan.

Masouda saw, and the color crept back to her cheek. Rosamund saw also, and nature was too strong for her, for in one bitter cry the truth broke from her lips at last, "Not Wulf! Not Wulf!" she wailed, and sank back senseless into Masouda's arms.

"Now, sire," said the old imam with a chuckle, "you know which of those two the lady loves. Being a woman, as usual she chooses badly, for the other has the finer spirit."

"Yes, I know now," said Saladin, "and I am glad to know, for the matter has vexed me much."

But Wulf, who had paled for a moment, flushed with joy as the truth came home to him, and he understood the end of all their doubts.

"This Star is well named 'The Luck,'" he said, as bending down he took it from the floor and fastened it to his cloak above his heart, "nor do I hold it dearly earned." Then he turned to his brother, who stood by him white and still, saying, "Forgive me, Godwin, but such is the fortune of love and war. Grudge it not to me, for when I am executed tonight this Luck—and all that hangs to it—will be yours."

So that strange scene ended.

The afternoon drew towards evening, and Godwin stood before Saladin in his private chamber.

"What seek you now?" said the Sultan sternly.

"A favor," answered Godwin. "My brother is doomed to die before nightfall. I ask to die instead of him."

"Why, Sir Godwin?"

"For two reasons, Sire. As you learned today, the riddle is finally answered. It is Wulf who is beloved of the lady Rosamund, and therefore to kill him would be a crime. Further, it is I and not he whom the eunuch heard bargaining with the captain Abdullah in the tent—I swear it. Take your vengeance upon me, and let him go to fulfill his fate."

Saladin pulled at his beard, then answered, "If this is to be so, time is short, Sir Godwin. What farewells have you to make? You say that you would speak with my niece Rosamund? No, the princess you shall not see, and indeed cannot, for she lies weeping in her chamber. Do you desire to meet your brother for the last time?"

"No, Sire, for then he might learn the truth and—"

"Refuse your sacrifice, Sir Godwin, which will scarcely be to his liking."

"I wish to say good-bye to Masouda, she who is waiting woman to the princess."

"That you cannot do, for, know, I mistrust this Masouda, and believe that she was at the bottom of your plot. I have dismissed her from the person of the princess and from my camp, which she is to leave—if she has not already left—with some Arabs who are her kin. Had it not been for her services in the land of the Assassins and afterwards, I would have put her to death."

"Then," said Godwin with a sigh, "I desire only to see Egbert the bishop, that he may prepare me according to our faith and make note of my last wishes."

"He shall be sent to you. I accept your statement that you are the guilty man and not Sir Wulf, and take your life for his. Leave me now, who have greater matters on my mind. The guard will seek you at the appointed time."

Godwin bowed and walked away with a steady step, while Saladin simply shook his head and stared at his vanishing form.

Two hours later, guards summoned Godwin from the place where he was kept, and, accompanied by the old bishop who had blessed him, he passed its door with a happy countenance, such as a bridegroom might have worn. In a fashion, indeed, he was happy, whose faith was the faith of a child, and who laid down his life for his friend and brother. They took him to a vault in the great house where Saladin was lodged—a large, rough place, lit with torches, in which waited the headsman and his assistants. Saladin soon entered, and, looking at him curiously, said, "Are you still of the same mind, Sir Godwin?"

"I am."

"Good. Yet I have changed mine. You shall say farewell to your cousin, as you desired. Let the princess of Baalbec be brought hither, sick or well, that she may see her work. Let her come alone."

"Sire," pleaded Godwin, "spare her such a sight."

But he pleaded in vain, for Saladin answered only, "I have said."

A while passed, and Godwin, hearing the sweep of robes, looked up, and saw the tall shape of a veiled woman standing in the corner of the vault where the shadow was so deep that the torchlight only glimmered faintly upon her royal ornaments.

"They told me that you were sick, princess, sick with sorrow, as well you may be, because the man you love was about to die for you," said Saladin in a slow voice. "Now I have had pity on your grief, and his life has been bought with another life, that of the knight who stands yonder."

The veiled form staggered some, then sank back against the wall.

"Rosamund," broke in Godwin, speaking in French, I beseech you, be silent and do not unnerve me with words or tears. It is best thus, and you know that it is best. Wulf you love as he loves you, and I believe that in time you will be brought together. Me you do not love, save as a friend, and never have. Moreover, I tell you this that it may ease your pain and my conscience; I no longer seek you as my wife, whose bride is death. I ask you, give Wulf my love and blessing, and to Masouda, that truest and most sweet woman, say, or write, that I offer her the homage of my heart; that I thought of her in my last moments, and that my prayer is we may meet again where all crooked paths are straightened. Rosamund, farewell; peace and joy go with you through many years, ay, and with your children's children. Of Godwin I only ask you to remember this, that he lived serving you, and so died."

She heard and stretched out her arms and, none forbidding him, Godwin walked to where she stood. Without lifting her veil she bent forward and kissed him, first upon the brow and next upon the lips; then with a low, moaning cry, she turned and fled from that gloomy place, nor did Saladin seek to stop her. Only to himself the sultan wondered how it came about that if it was Wulf whom Rosamund loved, she still kissed Godwin thus upon the lips.

As he walked back to the death-place Godwin wondered also, first that Rosamund should have spoken no single word, and secondly because she had kissed him thus, even in that hour. Why or wherefore he did not know, but there rose in his mind a memory of that wild ride down the mountain steeps at Beirut, and of lips which then had touched his cheek, and of the odor of hair that came before him. With a sigh he thrust the thought aside, blushing to think that such memories should come to him who had done with earth and its delights. He then knelt down before the headsman, and, turning to the bishop, said, "Bless me, Father, and bid them strike."

Then it was that he heard a well known footstep, and looked up to see Wulf staring at him.

"What do you here, Godwin?" asked Wulf. "Has yonder fox snared both of us?" and he nodded at Saladin.

"Let the fox speak," said the sultan with a smile. "Know, Sir Wulf, that your brother was about to die in your place, and of his own wish. But I refuse such sacrifice who yet have made use of it to teach my niece, the princess, that should she continue in her plotting to escape, or allow you to continue in them, certainly it will bring you to your deaths, and, if need be, her also. Knights, you are brave men whom I prefer to kill in war. Good horses stand without; take them as my gift, and ride with these foolish citizens of Jerusalem. We may meet again within its streets. No, thank me not. I thank you who have taught Saladin how strong a thing the love of brothers can be."

The brethren stood awhile bewildered, for the dark road they were on had suddenly turned again at its very edge, and ran forward through the familiar things of earth to some end unknown. They were brave, both of them, and accustomed to face death daily, yet since no man loves that journey, it was very sweet to know it was postponed for a while. Little wonder, then, that their brains swam, and their eyes grew dim, as they passed from the shadow to the light again. It was Wulf who spoke first.

"A noble deed, Godwin, yet one for which I should not have thanked you had it been accomplished, who then must have lived on by grace of your sacrifice. Sultan, we are grateful for your decision, though had you shed this innocent blood surely it would have stained your soul. May we bid farewell to our cousin Rosamund before we ride?"

"No," answered Saladin; "Sir Godwin has done that already—let it serve for both. Tomorrow she shall learn the truth of the story. Now go, and return no more."

"We go with heavy hearts," answered Godwin, and they bowed and went.

Outside that gloomy place of death their swords were given them, and two good horses, which they mounted. From this spot, guides led them to the assembly headed for Jerusalem that was already in the saddle, who were very glad to welcome two such knights to their company. Then, having bid farewell to the bishop Egbert, who wept for joy at their escape, escorted for a while by Saladin's soldiers, they rode away from Ascalon at nightfall.

Soon they had told each other all there was to tell. When he heard of the woe of Rosamund, Wulf nearly shed tears.

"We have our lives," he said, "but how shall we save her? While Masouda stayed with her there was some hope, but now I can see none."

"There is none, except in God," answered Godwin, "Who can do all things—even free Rosamund and make her your wife. Also, if Masouda is at liberty, we shall hear from her ere long; so let us keep a good heart."

But though he spoke bravely, the soul of Godwin was oppressed with a fear, which he could not understand. It seemed as though some great terror came very close to him, or to one who was near and dear. Deeper and deeper he sank into despair, until he could have cried aloud, and his brow was bathed with a sweat of anguish. Wulf saw his face in the moonlight and asked, "What ails you, Godwin? Have you some secret wound?"

"Yes, Brother," he answered, "a wound in my spirit. Ill fortune threatens us—great ill fortune."

"That is no new thing," said Wulf, "in this land of blood and sorrows. Let us meet it as we have met the rest."

"Alas! Brother," exclaimed Godwin, "I fear that Rosamund is in sore danger—Rosamund or another."

"Then," answered Wulf, turning pale, "since we cannot intercede, let us pray that some angel may deliver her."

"Aye," said Godwin, and as they rode through the desert sands beneath the silent stars, they prayed with all their strength. Yet the prayer availed not. Sharper and sharper grew Godwin's agony, till, as the slow hours went by, his very soul reeled beneath this spiritual burden.

The dawn was breaking, and at its first sign the escort of Saladin's soldiers had turned and left them, saying that now they were safe in their own country. All night they had ridden fast and far. The plain was behind them, and their road ran among hills. Suddenly it turned, and in the flaming lights of the new-born day showed them a sight so beautiful that for a moment all that little company drew rein to gaze. For before them, though far away as yet, throned upon her hills, stood the holy city of Jerusalem. There were her walls and towers, and there, stained red as though with the blood of its worshippers, soared the great cross upon the mosque of Omar—that cross which was soon to fall.

Yes, yonder was the city for which throughout the ages men had died by the millions and were now destined to die for once again. Saladin had offered to spare her citizens if they consented to surrender, but they would not. The leaders of the city had told him that they had sworn to perish with the holy places, and now, looking at it in its splendor, they knew that the hour was near, and groaned aloud.

Godwin groaned also, but not for Jerusalem. “Oh!” he said, “I know that I should have more faith, but I fear we will never see Rosamund again in the land of the living.”

“If so, we must join ourselves to the upcoming battle and make haste to follow her,” answered Wulf with a sob.

Chapter XXI
What Befell Godwin

At the village of Bittir, some seven miles from Jerusalem, the caravan dismounted to rest. After a brief rest, they pressed forward down the valley in the hope of reaching the Zion Gate before the mid-day heat was upon them. At the end of this valley swelled the shoulder of a hill from where the eye could view almost the entire region. On the crest of that shoulder, a man and woman suddenly appeared seated on beautiful horses. The company halted, fearing lest these might herald some attack and that the woman was a man disguised to deceive them. While they waited and wondered, the pair upon the hill turned their horses' heads and, notwithstanding its steepness, began to gallop towards them very swiftly. Wulf looked at them curiously and said to Godwin, "Now I am put in mind of a certain ride which once we took outside the walls of Beirut. Almost could I think that yonder Arab was he who sat behind my saddle, and yonder woman she who rode with you, and that those two horses were Flame and Smoke reborn. Note their whirlwind pace, and strength, and stride."

Just as he finished speaking the strangers pulled up their steeds in front of the company, to whom the man bowed his salutations. Then Godwin saw his face, and knew him at once as the old Arab called Son of the Sand, who had given them the horses Flame and Smoke.

"Sir," said the Arab to the leader of the caravan, "I have come to ask a favor of yonder knights who travel with you, which I think that they, who have ridden my horses, will not refuse me. This woman," and he pointed to the closely-veiled shape of his companion, "is a relative of mine whom I desire to deliver to friends in Jerusalem, but dare not do so myself because the hill-dwellers between here and there are hostile to my tribe. She is of the Christian faith and no spy, but cannot speak your language. Within the south gate she will be met by her relatives. I have spoken."

"Let the knights settle it," said the commander, shrugging his shoulders impatiently and spurring his horse.

"Surely we will take her," said Godwin, "though what we shall do with her if her friends fail to appear I do not know. Come, lady, ride between us."

She turned her head to the Arab as though in question, and he repeated the words, whereon she fell into the place that was shown to her between and a little behind the brethren.

"Perhaps," went on the Arab to Godwin, "by now you have learned more of our tongue than you knew when we met in past days at Beirut, and rode the mountain side on the good horses Flame and Smoke. Still, if so, I pray you of your knightly courtesy disturb not this woman with your words, nor ask her to unveil her face, since such is not the custom of her people. It is but an hour's journey to the city gate during which you will be troubled with her. This is the payment that I ask of you for the two good horses which, as I am told, served you well upon the Narrow Way and across plain and mountain when you fled from Sinan, also on the evil day of Hattin when you unhorsed Saladin and slew Hassan."

"It shall be as you wish," said Godwin; "and, Son of the Sand, we thank you for those horses."

"Good. When you want more, let it be known in the market places that you seek me," and he began to turn his horse's head.

"Stay," said Godwin. "What do you know of Masouda, your niece? Is she with you?"

"No," answered the Arab in a low voice, "but she asked me to meet her in a certain garden of which you have heard, near Ascalon, at an appointed hour, to take her away, as she is leaving the camp of Saladin. So now I go. Farewell." Then, with a reverence to the veiled lady, he shook his reins and departed like an arrow by the road along which they had come.

Godwin gave a sigh of relief. If Masouda had planned to meet her uncle the Arab, at least she must be safe. So it was no voice of hers, which seemed to whisper his name in the darkness of the night when terror had a hold of him—terror, born perhaps of all that he had endured and the shadow of death through which he had so recently passed. Then he looked up, to find Wulf staring back at the woman behind him, and reproved him, saying that he must keep to the spirit of the bargain as well as to the letter, and that if he might not speak he must not look, either.

"That is a pity," answered Wulf, "for though she is so tied up, she must be a tall and noble lady by the way she sits her horse. The horse, too, is noble, a probable cousin or brother to Smoke, I think. Perhaps she will sell it when we get to Jerusalem."

Then they rode on, and because they thought their honor in it, neither spoke nor looked more at the companion of this adventure, though, had they known it, she looked hard enough at them.

At length, they reached the gate of Jerusalem, which was crowded with folk awaiting the return of their ambassadors. They all passed through, and the caravan was escorted forward by the chief people. Most of the multitude following them wished to know if they brought news of peace or war.

Now Godwin and Wulf stared at each other, wondering where they were going and how they would find the relatives of their veiled companion, of whom they saw nothing. Out of the street opened an archway, and beyond this archway was a garden, which seemed to be deserted. They rode into it to take counsel, and their companion followed, but, as always, a little behind them.

"Jerusalem is reached, and we must speak to her now," said Wulf, "if only to ask her where she wishes to be taken."

Godwin nodded, and they wheeled their horses round.

"Lady," he said in Arabic, "we have fulfilled our charge. Be pleased to tell us where are those kindred to whom we must lead you."

"Here," answered a soft voice.

They stared around the deserted garden in which stones and sacks of earth had been stored ready for a siege and, finding no one, said, "We do not see them."

Then the lady let slip her cloak, though not her veil, revealing the robe beneath.

"By St. Peter!" said Godwin. "I know the broidery on that dress. Masouda! Say, is it you, Masouda?"

As he spoke the veil fell also, and lo! Before them was a woman like to Masouda and yet not Masouda. The hair was dressed like hers; the ornaments and the necklace made of the claws of the lion which Godwin killed were hers; the skin was of the same rich hue; there even was the tiny mole upon her cheek, but as the head was bent they could not see her eyes. Suddenly, with a little moan she lifted it, and looked at them.

"Rosamund! It is Rosamund herself!" gasped Wulf. "Rosamund disguised as Masouda!" And he fell rather than leapt from his saddle and ran to her, declaring, "God! I thank Thee!"

Now she seemed to faint and slid from her horse into his arms, and lay there a moment, while Godwin turned aside his head.

"Yes," said Rosamund, freeing herself, "it is I and no other, yet I rode with you all this way and neither of you knew me."

"Have we eyes that can pierce veils and woolen garments?" asked Wulf indignantly.

But Godwin said in a strange, strained voice, "You are Rosamund disguised as Masouda. Who, then, was that woman to whom I bade farewell before Saladin while the executioner awaited me; a veiled woman who wore the robes and gems of Rosamund?"

"I know not, Godwin," she answered, "unless it were Masouda clad in my garments before I left her. Nor do I know anything of this story of the executioner who awaited you. I thought—I thought it was for Wulf that he waited—oh! Heaven, I thought that."

"Tell us your tale," said Godwin hoarsely.

"It is short," she answered. "After the casting of the lot, of which I shall dream till my death-day, I fainted. When I found my senses again I thought that I must be mad, for there before me stood a woman dressed in my garments, whose face seemed like my face, yet not the same.

"'Have no fear,' she said; 'I am Masouda, who, amongst many other things, have learned how to play a part. Listen; there is no time to lose. I have been ordered to leave the camp; even now my uncle the Arab waits without, with two swift horses. You, Princess, will leave in my place. Look, you wear my robes and my face—almost; and are of my height, and the man who guides you will know no difference. I have seen to that, for although a soldier of Saladin, he is of my tribe. I will go with you to the door, and there bid you farewell before the eunuchs and the guards with weeping, and who will guess that Masouda is the princess of Baalbec and that the princess of Baalbec is Masouda?'

"'And whither shall I go?' I asked.

"'My uncle, Son of the Sand, will give you over to the caravan which rides to Jerusalem, or failing that, will take you to the city, or failing that, will hide you in the mountains among his own people. See, here is a letter that he must read so place it in your garment.'

"'And what of you, Masouda?' I asked again.

"'Of me? Oh! It is all planned, a plan that cannot fail,' she answered. 'Fear not; I escape tonight—I have no time to tell you how—and will join you in a day or two. Also, I think that you will find Sir Godwin, who will bring you home to England.'

"'But Wulf? What of Wulf?' I asked again. 'He is doomed to die, and I will not leave him.'

"'The living and the dead can keep no company,' she answered. 'Moreover, I have seen him, and all this is done by his most urgent order. If you love him, he bids that you will obey.'"

"I never saw Masouda! I never spoke such words! I knew nothing of this plot!" exclaimed Wulf, and the brethren looked at each other with white faces.

"Speak on," said Godwin; "afterwards we can debate."

"Moreover," continued Rosamund, bowing her head, "Masouda added these words, 'I think that Sir Wulf will escape his doom. If you would see him again, obey his word, for unless you obey you can never hope to look upon him living. Go, now, before we are both discovered, which would mean your death and mine."'

"How knew she that I would escape?" asked Wulf.

"She did not know it. She only said she knew how to force Rosamund away," answered Godwin in the same strained voice.

"And then?"

"And then—oh! Having Wulf's express commands, then I went, like one in a dream. I remember little of it. At the door we kissed and parted weeping, and while the guard bowed before her, she blessed me beneath her breath. A soldier stepped forward and said, 'Follow me, daughter of Sinan,' and I followed him, none taking any note, for at that hour, although perhaps you did not see it in your prisons, a strange shadow passed across the sun, of which all folk were afraid, thinking that it portended evil, either to Saladin or Ascalon.*

"In the gloom, we came to a place where was an old Arab among some trees, and with him two spare horses. The soldier spoke to the Arab, and I gave him Masouda's letter, which he read. Then he put me on one of the lead horses and the soldier mounted the other, and we departed at a gallop. All that evening and last night we rode hard, but in the darkness the soldier left us, and I do not know where he went. We eventually came to that mountain shoulder and waited there, resting the horses and eating food which the Arab brought with him. It was not long before we saw the caravan, and among them two tall knights.

"'See,' said the old Arab, 'yonder come the brethren whom you seek. See and give thanks to Masouda, who has not lied to you, and to whom I must now return.'

"Oh! My heart wept as though it would burst, and I wept in my joy—wept and blessed God and Masouda. But the Arab, Son of the Sand, told me that for my life's sake I must be silent and keep myself close veiled and disguised even from you until we reached Jerusalem, lest perhaps if they knew me the caravan might refuse escort to the princess of Baalbec and niece of Saladin, or even give me up to him.

---

*The eclipse, which overshadowed Palestine and caused much terror at Jerusalem, was on September 4, 1187, the day of the surrender of Ascalon.

"Then I promised and asked, 'What of Masouda?' He said that he rode back at speed to save her also, as had been arranged, and that was why he did not take me to Jerusalem himself. But how that was to be done he was not sure as yet; only he was sure that she was hidden away safely, and would find a way of escape when she wished it. And—and—you know the rest, and here, by the grace of God, we three are together again."

"Aye," said Godwin, "but where is Masouda, and what will happen to her who has dared to venture such a plot as this? Oh! Know you what this woman did? I was condemned to die in place of Wulf, how does not matter; you will learn it afterwards—and the princess of Baalbec was brought to say farewell to me. There, under the very eyes of Saladin, Masouda played her part and mimicked you so well that the sultan was deceived, and I, even I, was deceived. Yes, when for the first and last time I embraced her, I was deceived, although, it is true, I wondered. Also, since then a great fear has been with me, although here again I was deceived, for I thought I feared for you.

"Now, hark you, Wulf; take Rosamund and lodge her with some lady in this city, or, better still, place her in sanctuary with the nuns of the Holy Cross, whence none will dare to drag her, and let her don their habit. The abbess may remember you, for we have met her, and at least she will not refuse Rosamund a refuge."

"Yes, yes; we both may find refuge. But you? Where do you go, Godwin?" said his brother.

"I? I ride back to Ascalon to find Masouda."

"Why?" asked Wulf. "Cannot Masouda save herself, as she told her uncle, the Arab, she would do? And has he not already returned thither to take her away?"

"I do not know," answered Godwin; "but this I do know, that for the sake of Rosamund, and perhaps for my sake also, Masouda has run a fearful risk. Think now, what will be the mood of Saladin when he finds that she upon whom he had built such hopes has gone, leaving a waiting woman decked out in her attire."

"Oh!" broke in Rosamund. "I feared it, but I awoke to find myself disguised, and she persuaded me that all was well; also that this was done by the will of Wulf, whom she thought would escape."

"That is the worst of it," said Godwin. "To carry out her plan she held it necessary to lie, as I think she lied when she said that she believed we should both escape, though it is true that so it came about. I will tell you why she lied. It was that she might give her life to set you free to join me in Jerusalem."

Now Rosamund, who knew the secret of Masouda's heart, looked at him strangely, wondering within herself how it came about that, thinking Wulf dead or about to die, she should sacrifice herself that she, Rosamund, might be sent to the care of Godwin. Surely it could not be for love of her, although they loved each other well. From love of Godwin, then? How strange a way to show it!

Yet now she began to understand. So true and high was this great love of Masouda's that for Godwin's sake she was ready to hide herself in death, leaving him—now that, as she thought, his rival was removed—to live on with the lady whom he loved; aye, and at the price of her own life giving that lady to his arms. Oh! How noble must she be who could thus plan and act, and, whatever her past had been, how pure and high a gift! Surely, if she lived, earth had no grander woman; and if she were dead, the memory of her deeds would inspire many.

Rosamund looked at Godwin, and Godwin looked at Rosamund, and there was understanding in their eyes, for now both of them saw the truth in all its glory and all its horror.

"I think that I should go back, also," said Rosamund.

"That shall not be," answered Wulf. "Saladin would kill you for this flight, as he has sworn."

"That cannot be," added Godwin. "Shall the sacrifice of blood be offered in vain? Moreover, it is our duty to prevent you."

Rosamund looked at him again and stammered, "If— if— that dreadful thing has happened, Godwin—if the sacrifice—oh! What will it serve?"

"Rosamund, I know not what has actually happened; I go to see. I care not what may befall me; I go to meet it. Through life, through death, and if there be need, through all the fires of hell, I ride on till I find Masouda, and kneel to her in homage—"

"And in love," exclaimed Rosamund, as though the words broke from her lips against her will.

"That may well be," Godwin answered, speaking more to himself than to her.

Then, seeing the look upon his face, the set mouth and the flashing eyes, neither of them sought to stay him further.

"Farewell, my liege-lady and cousin Rosamund," Godwin said; "my part is played. Now I leave you in the keeping of the God of Heaven and of Wulf on earth. Should we meet no more, my counsel is that you two wed here in Jerusalem and travel back to Steeple, there to live in peace, if it may be so. Brother Wulf, fare you well, also. We part today for the first time, who from our birth have lived together and loved together and done many a deed together, some of which we can look back upon without shame. Go on your course rejoicing, taking the love and gladness that Heaven has given you. Live on as a good and Christian knight, mindful of the end which draws on apace, and of eternity beyond."

"Oh! Godwin, speak not thus," said Wulf, "for in truth it breaks my heart to hear such fateful words. Moreover, we need not part so easily. Our lady here will be safe enough among the nuns—more safe than I can keep her. Give me an hour, and I will set her there and join you. Both of us owe a debt to Masouda, and it is not right that it should be paid by you alone."

"I think not," answered Godwin; "look upon Rosamund, and think what is about to befall this city. Can you leave her at such a time?"

Then Wulf dropped his head and, trusting himself to speak no more words, Godwin mounted his horse, and, without so much as looking back, rode into the narrow street and out through the gateway, till rapidly he was lost in the distance and the desert.

Wulf and Rosamund watched him go in silence, for they were choked with tears.

"Little did I look to part with my brother thus," said Wulf at length in a thick and angry voice. "By God's wounds! I had more gladly died at his side in battle than leave him to meet his doom alone."

"And leave me to meet my doom alone," asserted Rosamund; then added, "Oh! I would that I was dead who have lived to bring all this woe upon you both, and upon that great heart, Masouda."

"Like enough the wish will be fulfilled before all is done," answered Wulf wearily, "only then I pray that I may be dead with you. For now, Rosamund, Godwin has gone, forever as I fear, and you alone are left to me. Come; let us cease complaining, since to dwell upon these grieves cannot help us, and be thankful that for a while, at least, we are free. God alone knows the end of our story. Follow me, Rosamund, and we will ride to this nunnery to find you shelter, if we may."

So they rode on through the narrow streets that were crowded with scared people, for now the news was spread that the ambassadors had rejected the terms of Saladin. He had offered to give the city food, and to permit the leaders to maintain control for a few months, as long as they were willing to hand over the city if no Christian forces arrived to relieve them by the end of the truce. The ambassadors of Jerusalem knew full well that no relief force would reach them in time so they answered that while they had life they would never abandon the place where their God had died.

So now war was before them—war to the end; and who were they that must bear its brunt? Their leaders were slain or captive, their king a prisoner, their soldiers skeletons on the field of Hattin. Only the women and children, the sick, the old, and the wounded remained—perhaps eighty thousand souls in all—but few of whom could bear arms. Yet these few must defend Jerusalem against the might of the victorious Saracen. Little wonder that they wailed in the streets till the cry of their despair went up to Heaven, for in their hearts all of them knew that the holy place was doomed.

Pushing their path through this sad multitude, who took little note of them, at length they came to the nunnery on the sacred Via Dolorosa, which Wulf had seen when Godwin and he were in Jerusalem after they had been dismissed by Saladin from Damascus. Its door stood in the shadow of that arch where the Roman Pilate had uttered to all generations the words "Behold the man!"

Here the porter told him that the nuns were at prayer in their chapel. Wulf replied that he must see the lady abbess upon a matter, which would not delay, and they were shown into a cool and lofty room. Presently the door opened, and through it came the abbess in her white robes—a tall and stately Englishwoman, of middle age, who looked at them curiously.

"Lady Abbess," said Wulf, bowing low, "my name is Wulf D'Arcy. Do you remember me?"

"Yes. We met in Jerusalem—before the Battle of Hattin," she answered. "Also, I know something of your story in this land—a very strange one."

"This lady," went on Wulf, "is the daughter and heiress of Sir Andrew D'Arcy, my dead uncle, and in Syria the princess of Baalbec and the niece of Saladin."

The abbess looked stunned and asked, "Is she, then, of their accursed faith, as her garb would seem to show?"

"Nay, mother," said Rosamund, "I am a Christian, if a sinful one, and I come here to seek sanctuary, lest when they know who I am and he clamors at their gates, my fellow Christians may surrender me to my uncle, the sultan."

"Tell me the story," said the abbess; and they told her briefly, while she listened, amazed. When they had finished, she said, "Alas! My daughter, how can we save you, whose own lives are at stake? That belongs to God alone. Still, what we can, we will do gladly, and here, at least, you may rest for some short while. At the most holy altar of our chapel you shall be given sanctuary, after which no Christian man dare lay a hand upon you, since to do so is a sacrilege that would cost him his soul. Moreover, I counsel that you be enrolled upon our books as a novice, and don our garb. Nay," she added with a smile, noting the look of alarm on the face of Wulf, "the lady Rosamund need not wear it always, unless such should be her wish. Not every novice proceeds to the final vows."

"Long have I been decked in gold-embroidered silks and priceless gems," answered Rosamund, "and now I seem to desire that white robe of yours more than anything on earth."

So they led Rosamund to the chapel, and in sight of all their order, and of the priests who had been summoned, they prayed over her and gave her sanctuary, and threw over her tired head the white veil of a novice. There, too, Wulf left her and, riding away, reported himself to Balian of Ibelin, the elected commander of the city, who was glad to welcome so stout a knight where knights were few.

Oh! Weary, weary was that ride of Godwin's beneath the sun, beneath the stars. Behind him, the brother who had been his companion and closest friend, and the woman whom he had loved in vain; and in front, he knew not what. What went he forth to seek? Another woman, who had risked her life for them all because she loved him. And if he found her, what then? Must he wed her, and did he wish this? And if he found her not, what then? Well, with his weary mind, the best plan he could think of was to give himself up to Saladin, who must think ill of them by whom he had dealt well, and tell him that of this plot they had no knowledge. Indeed, to him he would go first, if it were but to beg forgiveness for Masouda should she still be in his hands. Then—for he could not hope to be believed or pardoned a second time—then let death come, if it must.

It was evening, and Godwin's tired horse stumbled slowly through the great camp of the Saracens outside the walls of fallen Ascalon. None hindered him, for having been so long a prisoner he was known by many, while others thought that he was but one of the surrendered Christian knights. So he came to the great house where Saladin lodged, and bade the guard take his name to the sultan, saying that he craved audience of him. An hour later, he was admitted and found Saladin seated in council among his ministers.

"Sir Godwin," he said sternly, "seeing how you have dealt by me, what brings you back into my camp? I gave you brethren your lives, and you have robbed me of one whom I would not lose."

"We did not rob you, Sire," answered Godwin, "who knew nothing of this plot. Nevertheless, as I was sure that you would think thus, I am come from Jerusalem, leaving the princess and my brother there. I desire to tell the truth and to surrender myself to you, that I may bear in her place any punishment which you think fit to inflict upon the woman Masouda."

"Why should you bear it?" asked Saladin.

"Because, Sultan," answered Godwin sadly, and with bent head, "whatever she did, she did for love of me, though without my knowledge. Tell me, is she still here, or has she fled?"

"She is still here," answered Saladin shortly. "Would you wish to see her?"

Godwin breathed a sigh of relief. At least, Masouda still lived, and the terror that had struck him in the night was but an evil dream born of his own fears and sufferings.

"I do," he answered, "once, if no more. I have words to say to her."

"Doubtless she will be glad to learn how her plot prospered," said Saladin, with a grim smile. "In truth, it was well laid and boldly executed."

Calling to one of his council, that same old imam who had planned the casting of the lots, the sultan spoke with him aside. Then he said, "Let this knight be led to the woman Masouda. Tomorrow we will judge him."

Taking a silver lamp from the wall, the imam beckoned to Godwin, who bowed to the sultan and followed. As he passed wearily through the throng in the audience room, it seemed to Godwin that the emirs and captains gathered there looked at him with pity in their eyes. So strong was this feeling in him that he halted in his walk, and asked, "Tell me, lord, do I go to my death?"

"All of us go thither," answered Saladin in the silence, "but Allah has not written that death is yours tonight."

They passed down long passages; they came to a door, which the imam, who hobbled in front, unlocked.

"She is under ward, then?" said Godwin.

"Aye," was the answer, "under ward. Enter," and he handed him the lamp. "I remain without."

"Perchance she sleeps, and I shall disturb her," said Godwin, as he hesitated upon the threshold.

"Did you not say she loved you? Then doubtless, even if she sleeps, she, who has dwelt at Masyaf, will not take your visit ill, who have ridden so far to find her," said the imam with a sneering laugh. "Enter, I say."

So Godwin took the lamp and went in, and the door was shut behind him. Surely the place was familiar to him? He knew that arched roof and these rough, stone walls. Why, it was here that he had been brought to die, and through that very door the false Rosamund had come to bid him farewell, who now returned to greet her in this same darksome den. Well, it was empty—doubtless she would soon come, and he waited, looking at the door.

It did not stir; he heard no footsteps; nothing broke that utter silence. He turned again with his lamp and stared around him. Something glinted on the ground towards the end of the vault, just where he had knelt before the executioner. A shape lay there; doubtless it was Masouda, imprisoned and asleep.

"Masouda," he said, and the sounding echoes from the arched walls answered back, "Masouda!"

He must awaken her; there was no choice. Yes, it was she, asleep, and she still wore the royal robes of Rosamund, and a clasp of Rosamund's still glittered on her hair.

How sound Masouda slept! Would she never wake? He knelt down beside her and put out his hand to lift the long hair that hid her face.

It was only then that Godwin saw the blood and realized that she had been slain!

Then, with horror in his heart, Godwin held down the lamp and looked. Oh! Those robes were red, and those lips were ashen. It was Masouda, whose spirit had passed him in the desert; Masouda, slain by the headsman's sword! This was the evil jest that had been played upon him, and cruel and wicked were the hearts that fashioned it.

Godwin rose to his feet and stood over her still shape as a man stands in a horrible dream, while groans broke from his lips and a fountain in his heart was unsealed.

"Masouda," he whispered, "I know now that I love you and you only, henceforth and forever, O woman with a royal heart. Wait for me, Masouda, wherever you may dwell."

Then all was past and over, and he turned to see the old imam standing at his side.

"Did I not tell you that you would find her sleeping?" he said, with his bitter, chuckling laugh. "Call on her, Sir Knight; call on her! Love, they say, can bridge great gulfs—even that between severed neck and bosom."

With the silver lamp in his hand, Godwin smote, and the man went down like a felled ox, leaving him once more in silence and in darkness.

For a moment Godwin stood thus, till his brain was filled with fire, and he too fell—fell across the corpse of Masouda, and there lay still.

Chapter XXII
At Jerusalem

Godwin knew that he lay sick, but with the exception that Masouda seemed to tend him in his sickness he knew no more, for all the past was now beyond his recall. There she was always, clad in a white robe, and looking at him with eyes full of ineffable calm and love. He noted that round her neck ran a thin, red line, and wondered how it came there.

He knew, also, that he traveled while he was ill, for at dawn he would hear the camp break up with a mighty noise, and feel his litter lifted by slaves who bore him along for hours across the burning sand, till the evening came, and with a humming sound, like the sound of hiving bees, the great army set its bivouac. Then came the night and the pale moon floating like a boat upon the azure sea above, and everywhere the bright, eternal stars, to which went up the constant cry of "Allahu Akbar! Allahu Akbar! God is the greatest, there is none but he."

"It is a false god," he would say. "Tell them to cry upon the true Creator and Savior of the world."

At length, that journey was done, and there arose new noises as of the roar of battle. Orders were given and men marched out in thousands; then rose that roar, and they marched back again, mourning their dead.

At last came a day when, opening his eyes, Godwin turned to rest them on Masouda, and lo! She was gone. In her accustomed place there sat a man whom he knew well—Egbert, once bishop of Nazareth, who gave him to drink of sherbet cooled with snow. Yes, the woman had departed, and the priest was there.

"Where am I?" he asked.

"Outside the walls of Jerusalem, my son, a prisoner in the camp of Saladin," was the answer.

"And where is Masouda, who has sat by me all these days?"

"In Heaven, as I trust," came the gentle answer, "for she was a brave lady. It is I who have sat by you."

"Nay," said Godwin obstinately, "it was Masouda."

"If so," answered the bishop again, "it was her spirit, for I buried her and have prayed over her open grave—her spirit, which came to visit you from Heaven, and has gone back to Heaven now that you are of the earth again."

Then Godwin remembered the truth and, groaning, fell asleep. Afterwards, as he grew stronger, Egbert told him all the story. He learned that when he was found lying senseless on the body of Masouda the emirs wished Saladin to kill him, if for no other reason because he had dashed out the eye of the holy imam with a lamp. But the sultan, who had discovered the truth, would not, for he said that it was unworthy of the imam to have mocked his grief, and that Sir Godwin had dealt with him as he deserved. Also, that this Frank was one of the bravest of knights, who had returned to bear the punishment of a sin which he did not commit.

So the imam lost both his eye and his vengeance.

Thus it had come about that the bishop Egbert was ordered to nurse Godwin, and, if possible to save his life. When the time at last came to march towards Jerusalem, soldiers were chosen to bear his litter, and a good tent was set apart to cover him. Now the siege of the holy city had begun, and there was much slaughter on both sides.

"Will it fall?" asked Godwin.

"I fear so, unless the saints help them," answered Egbert. "Alas! I fear so."

"Will not Saladin be merciful?" he asked again.

"Why should he be merciful, my son? Saladin regards us as enemies who refuse to surrender and, indeed, we are his enemies! Nay, he has sworn that as Godfrey took the place nigh upon a hundred years ago and slaughtered the Muslims who dwelt there by thousands, men, women, and children together, so will he do to the Christians. Oh! They will lose Jerusalem! They will all die!" and, wringing his hands, Egbert left the tent.

Godwin lay still, wondering what the answer to this riddle might be. He could think of one, and one only. In Jerusalem was Rosamund, the sultan's niece, whom he surely desired to recapture, while he also intended to destroy the inhabitants of the Holy City.

In spite of his sickness and fatigue, Godwin sought for an opportunity to solve the dilemma that faced both Rosamund and the inhabitants of Jerusalem. Indeed, if Jerusalem were saved, would not tens of thousands of lives be saved, also? Oh! Surely here was the answer, and some angel had put it into his heart, and now he prayed for the strength and opportunity to plant it in the heart of Saladin.

The very next day, Godwin found the opportunity. As he lay dozing in his tent, being still too weak to rise, a shadow fell upon him and, opening his eyes, he saw the sultan himself standing alone by his bedside. He immediately tried to rise to salute him, but in a kind voice Saladin told him to lie still and, seating himself, began to talk.

"Sir Godwin," he said, "I am come to ask your pardon. When I sent you to visit that dead woman, who had suffered justly for her crime, I did an act unworthy of a king. But my heart was bitter against her and you. It was at this point that the imam, he whom you smote, put into my mind the trick that cost him his eye. I have spoken."

"I thank you, Sire, who have often acted nobly," answered Godwin.

"You say so. Yet I have done things to you and yours that you can scarcely hold as noble," said Saladin. "I stole your cousin from her home, as her mother had been stolen from mine, paying back ill with ill, which is against the law, and in his own hall my servants slew her father and your uncle, who was once my friend. Well, these things I did because a fate drove me on—the fate of a people who must conquer for Allah.

"Say, Sir Godwin, is that story which is heard in our camps true, that a dream came to you just before the Battle of Hattin? Is it also true that you warned the leaders of the Franks not to advance against me?"

"Yes, it is true," answered Godwin, and he told the dream, and of how he had sworn to it on the Rood.

"And what did they say to you?"

"They laughed at me, and hinted that I was a sorcerer, or a traitor in your pay, or both."

"Blind fools, who would not hear the truth when it was given to them," muttered Saladin. "Well, they paid the price, and I and my faith are the gainers. Do you wonder, then, Sir Godwin, that I also believe my vision, which came to me thrice in the night season, bringing with it the picture of the very face of my niece, the princess of Baalbec? It was she who was destined to lead me to victory."

"I do not wonder," answered Godwin.

"Do you wonder also that I was mad with rage when I learned that at last yonder brave dead woman had outwitted me and all my spies and guards, and this after I had spared your lives? Do you wonder that I am still so wroth, believing as I do that a great opportunity has been taken from me?"

"I do not wonder, but now, O Saladin, the princess Rosamund is in Jerusalem. She has been led to Jerusalem that you may spare it for her sake, and thus make an end of bloodshed and save the lives of folk uncounted."

"Never!" said the sultan, springing up. "They have rejected my mercy, and I have sworn to sweep them away, man, woman, and child, and be avenged upon all their unclean and faithless race."

"Is Rosamund unclean that you would be avenged upon her? Will her dead body bring you peace? If Jerusalem is put to the sword, she must perish, also."

"I will give orders that she is to be saved that she may be judged for her crime by me," he added grimly.

"How can she be saved when the stormers are drunk with slaughter, and she but one disguised woman among ten thousand others?"

"Then," he answered, stamping his foot, "she shall be brought or dragged out of Jerusalem before the slaughter begins."

"That, I think, will not happen while Wulf is there to protect her," said Godwin quietly.

"Yet I say that it must be so—it shall be so."

Then, without more words, Saladin left the tent with a troubled brow.

Within Jerusalem, all was misery and despair. There were crowded thousands and tens of thousands of fugitives, women and children, many of them, whose husbands and fathers had been slain at Hattin or elsewhere. The fighting men who were left had few commanders, and thus it came about that soon Wulf found himself the captain of very many of them.

First Saladin attacked from the west between the gates of Saint Stephen and of David, but here stood strong fortresses called the Castle of the Pisans and the Tower of Tancred. From these strongholds, the defenders made attacks upon him, driving back his stormers. So he determined to change his ground, and moved his army to the east, camping it near the valley of the Kedron. When they saw the tents being struck the Christians thought that he was abandoning the siege, and gave thanks to God in all their churches; but lo! Next morning the white array of these appeared again on the east, and they knew that their doom was sealed.

There were in the city many who desired to surrender to the sultan, and fierce grew the debates between them and those who swore that they would rather die. Eventually, it was agreed that a delegation should be sent. So it came under safe conduct, and was received by Saladin in the presence of his emirs and counselors. He asked them what was their wish, and they replied that they had come to discuss terms. Then he answered thus, "In Jerusalem is a certain lady, my niece, known among us as the princess of Baalbec, and among the Christians as Rosamund D'Arcy. She fled to you a while ago in the company of the knight, Sir Wulf D'Arcy, whom I have seen fighting bravely among your warriors. Let her be surrendered to me that I may deal with her as she deserves, and we will talk again. Till then I have no more to say."

Now most of the delegation knew nothing of this lady, but one or two said they thought that they had heard of her, but had no knowledge of where she was hidden.

"Then return and search her out," said Saladin, and so dismissed them.

Back came the envoys to the council and told what Saladin had said.

"At least," exclaimed Heraclius the Patriarch, "in this matter it is easy to satisfy the sultan. Let his niece be found and delivered to him. Where is she?"

One of the delegation members declared that the secret was known by the knight, Sir Wulf D'Arcy, with whom she had entered the city. So he was sent for, and came with armor rent and red sword in hand, for he had just beaten back an attack upon the barbican. Wulf asked what was their pleasure.

"We desire to know, Sir Wulf, said the patriarch, where you have hidden away the lady known as the princess of Baalbec, whom you stole from the sultan?"

"What is that to your Holiness?" asked Wulf shortly.

"A great deal, to me and to all, seeing that Saladin will not even talk with us until she is delivered to him."

"Does this council, then, propose to hand over a Christian lady to the Saracens against her will?" asked Wulf sternly.

"We must," answered Heraclius. "Moreover, she belongs to them."

"She does not belong," answered Wulf. "She was kidnapped from England by Saladin, and ever since has striven to escape from him."

"Waste not our time," exclaimed the patriarch impatiently. "We understand that you are this woman's lover, but however that may be, Saladin demands her, and to Saladin she must go. So tell us where she is without more ado, Sir Wulf."

"Discover that for yourself, Sir Patriarch," replied Wulf in fury. "Or, if you cannot, send one of your own women in her place."

Now there was a murmur in the council, but of wonder at his boldness rather than of indignation, for this patriarch was a very evil and unprincipled leader.

"I care not if you choose to bargain with Saladin," went on Wulf, "for it is known to all. Moreover, I tell this man that it is well for him that he is a priest, however shameful, for otherwise I would cleave his head in two who has dared to call the lady Rosamund my lover." Then, still shaking with wrath, the great knight turned and stalked from the council chamber.

"A dangerous man," said Heraclius, who was white to the lips; "a very dangerous man. I propose that he should be imprisoned."

"Aye," answered the lord Balian of Ibelin, who was in supreme command of the city, "a very dangerous man—to his foes, as I can testify. I saw him and his brother charge through the hosts of the Saracens at the Battle of Hattin, and I have seen him in the breach upon the wall. Would that we had more such dangerous men just now!"

"But he has insulted me," shouted the patriarch, "me and my holy office."

"The truth should be no insult," answered Balian with meaning. "At least, it is a private matter between you and him on account of which we cannot spare one of our few captains. Now as regards this lady, I like not the business—"

As he spoke, a messenger entered the room and said that the hiding place of Rosamund had been discovered. She had been admitted a novice into the community of the Virgins of the Holy Cross, who had their house by the arch on the Via Dolorosa.

"Now I like it still less," Balian went on, "for to touch her would be sacrilege."

"His Holiness, Heraclius, will give us absolution," said a mocking voice.

Then another leader rose—he was one of the party who desired peace—and pointed out that this was no time to stand on scruples, for the sultan would not listen to them or spare them unless the lady were delivered to him to be judged for her offence. Perhaps, being his own niece, she would, in fact, suffer no harm at his hands. Yet whether this were so or not, it was better that one should endure wrong, or even death, than many.

With such words he convinced most of them, so that in the end they rose and went to the convent of the Holy Cross, where the patriarch demanded admission for them, which, indeed, could not be refused. The stately abbess received them in the refectory, and asked their pleasure.

"Daughter," said the patriarch, "you have in your keeping a lady named Rosamund D'Arcy, with whom we desire to speak. Where is she?"

"The novice Rosamund," answered the abbess, "prays by the holy altar in the chapel."

"She has taken sanctuary," said one man.

The patriarch added, "Tell us, daughter, does she pray alone?"

"A knight guards her prayers," was the answer.

"Ah! As I thought, he has been beforehand with us. Also, daughter, surely your discipline is somewhat lax if you permit knights thus to invade your chapel. But lead us thither."

"The dangers of the times and of the lady must answer for it," the abbess replied boldly, as she obeyed.

The group soon arrived in the great, dim place, where the lamps burned day and night. There by the altar, built, it was said, upon the spot where the Lord stood to receive judgment, they saw a kneeling woman, who, clad in the robe of a novice, grasped the stonework with her hands. Outside the rails, also kneeling, was the knight Wulf, still as a statue on a sepulcher. Hearing them, he rose, turned him about, and drew his great sword.

"Sheathe that sword," commanded Heraclius.

"When I became a knight," answered Wulf, "I swore to defend the innocent from harm and the altars of God from sacrilege at the hands of wicked men. Therefore, I sheathe not my sword."

"Take no heed of him," said one; and Heraclius, standing back in the aisle, addressed Rosamund, "Daughter," he cried, "with bitter grief we are come to ask of you a sacrifice, that you should give yourself for the people, as our Master gave Himself for the people. Saladin demands you as a fugitive of his blood, and until you are delivered to him he will not bargain with us for the saving of the city. Come forth, then, we pray you."

Now Rosamund stood and faced them, with her hand resting upon the altar.

"I risked my life and I believe another gave her life," she said, "that I might escape from the power of the Muslims. I will not come forth to return to them."

"Then, our need being sore, we must take you," answered Heraclius confidently.

"What!" she cried. "You, the patriarch of this sacred city, would tear me from the sanctuary of its holiest altar? Oh! Then, indeed, shall the curse fall upon it and you. Hence, they say, our sweet Lord was haled to sacrifice by the command of an unjust judge, and thereafter Jerusalem was taken by the sword. Must I, too, be dragged from the spot that His feet have hallowed, and thrown as an offering to your foes, who will likely bid me choose between death and the Koran? If so, I say assuredly that offering will be made in vain, and assuredly your streets shall run red with the blood of those who tore me from my sanctuary."

Now they consulted together, some taking one side and some the other, but the most of them declared that she must be given up to Saladin.

"Come of your own will, I pray you," said the patriarch, "since we would not take you by force."

"By force only will you take me," answered Rosamund.

Then the abbess spoke.

"Sirs, will you commit so great a crime? Then I tell you that it cannot go without its punishment. With this lady I say"—and she drew up her tall shape—"that it shall be paid for in your blood, and perhaps in the blood of all of us. Remember my words when the Saracens have won the city, and are putting its children to the sword."

"I absolve you from the sin," shouted the patriarch, "if sin it is."

"Absolve yourself," broke in Wulf sternly, "and know this. I am but one man, but I have some strength and skill. If you seek but to lay a hand upon the novice Rosamund to hale her away to be slain by Saladin, as he has sworn that he would do should she dare to fly from him, before I die there are those among you who have looked the last upon the light."

Then, standing there before the altar rails, he lifted his great blade and settled the skull-blazoned shield upon his arm.

Now the patriarch raved and stormed, and one among them cried that they would fetch bows and shoot Wulf down from a distance.

"And thus," broke in Rosamund, "add murder to sacrilege! Oh! Sirs, bethink what you do—aye, and remember this, that you do it all in vain. Saladin has promised you nothing, except that if you deliver me to him, he will talk with you, and then you may find that you have sinned for nothing. Have pity on me and go your ways, leaving the issue in the hand of God."

"That is true," cried some. "Saladin made no promises."

Now Balian, the guardian of the city, who had followed them to the chapel and, standing in the background heard what passed there, stepped forward and said, "My lord patriarch, I pray you let this thing be, since from such a crime no good could come to us or any. That altar is the holiest and most noted place of sanctuary in all Jerusalem. Will you dare to tear a maiden from it whose only sin is that she, a Christian, has escaped the Saracens by whom she was stolen? Do you dare to give her back to them and death, for such will be her doom at the hands of Saladin? Surely that would be the act of cowards, and bring upon us the fate of cowards. Sir Wulf, put up your sword and fear nothing. If there is any safety in Jerusalem, your lady is safe. Abbess, lead her to her cell."

"Nay," answered the abbess with fine sarcasm, "it is not fitting that we should leave this place before his Holiness."

"Then you have not long to wait," shouted the patriarch in fury. "Is this a time for scruples about altars? Is this a time to listen to the prayers of a girl or to threats of a single knight, or the doubts of a superstitious captain? Well, have it your way and let your lives pay its cost. Yet I say that if Saladin asked for half the noble maidens in the city, it would be cheap to let him have them in payment for the blood of eighty thousand folk," and he stalked towards the door.

So they went away, all except Wulf, who stayed to make sure that they were gone, and the abbess, who came to Rosamund and embraced her, saying that for the while the danger was past, and she might rest quiet.

"Yes, mother," answered Rosamund with a sob, "but oh! Have I done right? Should I not have surrendered myself to the wrath of Saladin if the lives of so many hang upon it? Perhaps, after all, he would forget his oath and spare my life, though at best I should never be suffered to escape again while there is a castle in Baalbec or a guarded harem in Damascus. Moreover, it is hard to bid farewell to all one loves forever," and she glanced towards Wulf, who stood out of hearing.

"Yes," answered the abbess, "it is hard, as we nuns know well. But, daughter, that sore choice has not yet been thrust upon you. When Saladin says that he sets you against the lives of all this cityful, then you must judge."

"Aye," repeated Rosamund, "then I—must judge."

The siege went on; from terror to terror it went on. The mangonels hurled their stones unceasingly, the arrows flew in clouds so that none could stand upon the walls. Thousands of the cavalry of Saladin hovered round St. Stephen's Gate, while the engines poured fire and bolts upon the doomed town, and the Saracen miners worked their way beneath the barbican and the wall. The soldiers within could not attack because of the multitude of the watching horsemen; they could not show themselves, since whoever did so was at once destroyed by a thousand darts, and they, therefore, could no longer build up the breaches of the crumbling wall. As day was added to day, the despair grew ever deeper. In every street might be met long processions of monks bearing crosses and chanting penitential psalms and prayers, while inside each house women wailed to Christ for mercy. These same women held to their breasts the children which must so soon be given to death, or torn from them to serve some Muslim harem.

The commander Balian called the knights together in council, and showed them that Jerusalem was doomed.

"Then," said one of the leaders, "let us go out and die fighting in the midst of foes."

"Aye," added Heraclius, "and leave our children and our women to death and dishonor. Surrender is better, since there is some hope of succour."

"Nay," answered Balian, "we will not surrender. While God lives, there is hope."

"He lived on the day of Hattin, and permitted it," said Heraclius; and the council broke up, having decided nothing.

That afternoon, Balian stood once more before Saladin and implored him to spare the city.

Saladin led him to the door of the tent and pointed to his yellow banners floating here and there upon the wall, and to one that at that moment rose upon the breach itself.

"Why should I spare what I have already conquered, and what I have sworn to destroy?" he asked. "When I offered you mercy you would have none of it. Why do you ask it now?"

Then Balian answered him in those words that will ring through history forever, "For this reason, Sultan. Before God, if die we must, we will first slaughter our women and our little children, leaving you neither male nor female to enslave. We will burn the city and its wealth; we will grind the holy Rock to powder and make of the mosque el-Aksa, and the other sacred places, a heap of ruins. We will cut the throats of the five thousand followers of the Prophet who are in our power, and then, every man of us who can bear arms, we will sally out into the midst of you and fight on till we fall. So I think Jerusalem shall cost you dear."

The sultan stared at him and stroked his beard.

"Eighty thousand lives," he said slowly; "eighty thousand lives, besides those of my soldiers whom you will slay. A great slaughter—and the holy city destroyed forever."

Then Saladin sat still and thought a while, his head bowed upon his breast.

Chapter XXIII
Saint Rosamund

From the day when he spoke with Saladin, Godwin began to grow strong again, and as his health came back, so he fell to thinking. Rosamund was lost to him and Masouda was dead. Therefore, what more did his Maker desire for him to do with his life, which had been so full of sorrow, struggle, and bloodshed? Go back to England to live there upon his lands and wait until old age and death overtook him? The prospect would have pleased many, but it did not please Godwin. He understood that his days were not given to him for this purpose, and that while he lived he must also labor.

As he sat thinking thus, and was very unhappy, the aged bishop Egbert, who had nursed him so well, entered his tent, and, noting his face, asked, "What ails you, my son?"

"Would you wish to hear?" said Godwin.

"Am I not your confessor, with a right to hear?" answered the gentle old man. "Show me your trouble."

So Godwin began at the beginning and told it all—how as a lad he had secretly desired to enter the Church; how the old prior of the abbey at Stangate counseled him that he was too young to judge; how then the love of Rosamund had entered into his life with his manhood, and he had thought no more of religion. He told him also of the dream that he had dreamed when he lay wounded after the fight on Death Creek; of the vows which he and Wulf had vowed at the time of their knighting, and of how by degrees he had learned that Rosamund's love was not for him. Lastly, he told him of Masouda, but of her Egbert, who had observed her, knew already the details.

The bishop listened in silence till he had finished. Then he looked up, saying, "And now?"

"Now," answered Godwin, "I know not. Yet my heart longs to know the deep things of God and to walk in the paths of solitude, prayer, and charitable service."

"You are still young to talk thus, and though Rosamund be lost to you and Masouda dead, there are other women in the world," said Egbert.

Godwin shook his head.

"Not for me, my father."

"Then there are the knightly Orders, in which you might rise high."

Again he shook his head. "The Templars and the Hospitallers are crushed. Moreover, I watched them in Jerusalem and the field, and love not their tactics. Should they change their ways, or should I be needed to fight against the Infidel, I can join them by dispensation in days to come. But counsel me—what shall I do now?"

"Oh! My son," the old bishop said, his face lighting up, "if God calls you, come to God. He will show you the road."

"Yes, I will not rest until I find my rest in God," Godwin answered quietly. "I will come, and, unless the Cross should once more call me to follow it in war, I will strive to spend the time that is left to me in His service and that of men. For I think, my father, that to this end I was born."

Three days later, a special meeting took place between the head of the Jerusalem delegation and Saladin. The emissary Balian rode slowly toward the tent of the sultan and dismounted. Moments later, the two men approached each other. Saladin lifted his head and looked at Balian.

"Tell me," he said, "what of the princess of Baalbec, whom you know as the lady Rosamund D'Arcy? I told you that I would speak no more with you of the safety of Jerusalem until she was delivered to me for judgment. Yet, I see her not."

"Sultan," answered Balian, "we found this lady in the convent of the Holy Cross, wearing the robe of a novice of that order. She had taken the sanctuary there by the altar, which we deem so sacred and inviolable, and refused to come."

Saladin laughed.

"Cannot all your men-at-arms drag one maiden from an altar stone?—unless, indeed, the great knight Wulf stood before it with sword aloft," he added.

"So he stood," answered Balian, "but it was not of him that we thought, though assuredly he would have slain some of us. To do this thing would have been an awful crime, which we were sure must bring down the vengeance of our God upon us and upon the city."

"What of the vengeance of Saladin?"

"Sore as is our case, Sultan, we still fear God more than Saladin."

"I think that your city is about to fall," said Saladin, who again became silent and stroked his beard.

"Listen, now," he said at length. "Let the princess, my niece, come to me and ask it of my grace, and I think that I will grant you terms for which, in your plight, you may be thankful."

"Then we must dare the great sin and take her," answered Balian sadly, "while at the same time my servants slay the knight Wulf, who will not let her go while he is alive."

"No, Sir Balian, for that I would be sorry, nor will I permit it, for though a Christian he is a brave man and your servants dogs. This time I say 'Let her come to me,' not 'Let her be brought.' She must come of her own free will, to answer to me for her sin against me, understanding that I promise her nothing, who in the old days promised her much, and kept my word. Then she was the princess of Baalbec, with all the rights belonging to that great rank, to whom I had sworn that no husband should be forced upon her, nor any change of faith. Now I take back these oaths, and if she comes, she comes as an escaped Cross-worshipping slave, to whom I offer only the choice of Islam or a shameful death."

"What high-born lady would take such terms?" asked Balian in dismay. "Rather, I think, would she choose to die defending the walls of Jerusalem than by that of your hangman, since she can never abjure her faith."

"And thereby doom eighty thousand of her fellow Christians, who must accompany her to that death," answered Saladin sternly. "Know, Sir Balian, I swear it before Allah and for the last time, that if my niece Rosamund does not come, of her own free will, unforced by any, Jerusalem shall be put to sack."

"Then the fate of the holy city and all its inhabitants hangs upon the nobleness of a single woman?" stammered Balian.

"Aye, upon the nobleness of a single woman. If her spirit is high enough, Jerusalem may yet be saved. If it be baser than I thought, as well may chance, then assuredly with her it is doomed. I have no more to say, but my envoys shall ride with you bearing a letter, which with their own hands they must present to my niece, the princess of Baalbec. Then she can return with them to me, or she can bide where she is, when I shall know that I saw but a lying vision of victory flowing from her hands, and will press on this war to its bloody end."

Within an hour, Balian rode to the city under safe conduct, taking with him the envoys of Saladin and the letter, which they were charged to deliver to Rosamund.

It was night, and in their lamp-lit chapel the Virgins of the Holy Cross upon bended knees chanted the slow and solemn Miserere. From their hearts they sang, to whom death and dishonor were so near, praying their Lord and the merciful Mother of God to have pity, and to spare them and the inhabitants of the hallowed town where He had dwelt and suffered. They knew that the end was near, that the walls were tottering to their fall, that the defenders were exhausted, and that soon the wild soldiers of Saladin would be surging through the narrow streets.

Then would come the sack and the slaughter, either by the sword of the Saracens, or, perchance, if these found time and they were not forgotten, more mercifully at the hands of Christian men, who thus would save them from the worst.

Their dirge ended, the abbess rose and addressed them. Her bearing was still proud, but her voice quavered.

"'My daughters in the Lord," she said, "the doom is almost at our door, and we must brace our hearts to meet it. If the commanders of the city do what they have promised, they will send some here to behead us at the last, and so we shall pass happily to glory and be ever with the Lord. But perchance they will forget us, who are but a few among eighty thousand souls, of whom some fifty thousand must thus be killed. Or their arms may grow weary, or themselves they may fall before ever they reach this house—and what, my daughters, shall we do then?"

Now some of the nuns clung together and sobbed in their sorrow, and many were silent. Only Rosamund drew herself to her full height, and spoke proudly.

"My mother," she said, "I am a newcomer among you, but I have seen the slaughter of Hattin, and I know what befalls Christian women and children among the unbelievers. Therefore, I ask your leave to say my say."

"Speak," said the abbess.

"This is my counsel," went on Rosamund, "and it is short and plain. When we know that the Saracens are in the city, let us set fire to this convent and get us to our knees and so perish."

"Well spoken; it is best," muttered several. But the abbess answered with a sad smile, "High counsel indeed, such as might be looked for from high blood. Yet it may not be taken, since self-slaughter is a deadly sin."

"I accept your correction, Abbess," said Rosamund. "Those who engage in the murder of self shall not inherit the kingdom of Heaven. Yet, although for others I cannot judge, for myself I tell you that rather than fall into the hands of the Paynims, I will dare to fight with sword and shield though such an act may be but little better than self-slaughter."

And she laid her hand upon the dagger hilt that was hidden in her robe.

Then again the abbess spoke.

"To you, Daughter, I cannot forbid the deed, but to those who have fully sworn to obey me I do forbid it, and to them I show another if a more piteous way of escape from the last shame of womanhood. Some of us are old and withered, and have naught to fear but death, but others are still young and fair. To these I say, when the end is nigh, let them hide themselves in the cellar that stands here in this chapel. It is but a small place, but relief may yet come in weeks ahead."

Now a great groan of horror went up from those miserable women, who already saw themselves hideous to behold, there in the carved chairs of their choir, awaiting death by the swords of furious and savage men.

Yet one by one, except the aged among them, they came up to the abbess and swore that they would obey her in this as in everything, while the abbess assured them that she would lead them down that dreadful road of pain and humiliation.

Then again they got them to their knees and sang the Miserere.

At that moment, above their mournful chant, the sound of loud, insistent knockings echoed down the vaulted roofs. Some of the younger nuns sprang up screaming, "The Saracens are here! Give us knives! Give us knives!"

Rosamund drew her dagger from its sheath.

"Wait awhile," cried the abbess. "These may be friends, not foes. Sister Ursula, go to the door and seek tidings."

The sister, an aged woman, obeyed with tottering steps, and, reaching the massive portal, undid the guichet, or lattice, and asked with a quavering voice, "Who are you that knock?" while the nuns within held their breath and strained their ears to catch the answer.

Presently it came, in a woman's silvery tones, that sounded strangely still and small in the spaces of that tomb-like church.

"I am the queen Sybilla, with her ladies."

"And what would you with us, O Queen? The right of sanctuary?"

"Nay; I bring with me some envoys from Saladin, who would have speech with the lady named Rosamund D'Arcy, who is among you."

Now at these words Rosamund fled to the altar, and stood there, still holding the naked dagger in her hand.

"Let her not fear," went on the silvery voice, "for no harm shall come to her against her will. Admit us, Abbess, we beseech you in the name of Christ."

Then the abbess said, "Let us receive the queen with such dignity as we may." Motioning to the nuns to take their appointed seats in the choir she placed herself in the great chair at the head of them, while behind her at the raised altar stood Rosamund, the bare knife in her hand.

The door was opened, and through it swept a strange procession. First came the beauteous queen wearing her insignia of royalty, but with a black veil upon her head. Next followed ladies of her court—twelve of them—trembling with fright but splendidly appareled, and after these three stern and turbaned Saracens clad in mail, their jeweled scimitars at their sides. Then appeared a procession of women, most of them draped in mourning, and leading scared children by the hand; the wives, sisters, and widows of nobles, knights and burgesses of Jerusalem. Last of all marched a hundred or more of captains and warriors, among them Wulf, headed by Sir Balian and ended by the patriarch Heraclius in his gorgeous robes, with his attendant priests.

On swept the queen, up the length of the long church, and as she came the abbess and her nuns rose and bowed to her, while one offered her the chair of state that was set apart to be used by the bishop in his visitations. But she would have none of it.

"Nay," said the queen, "mock me with no honorable seat who come here as a humble suppliant, and will make my prayer upon my knees."

So down she went upon the marble floor, with all her ladies and the following women, while the solemn Saracens looked at her wondering, and the knights and nobles massed themselves behind.

"What can we give you, O Queen," asked the abbess, "who have nothing left save our treasure, to which you are most welcome, our honor, and our lives?"

"Alas!" answered the royal lady. "Alas, that I must say it! I come to ask the life of one of you."

"Of whom, O Queen?"

Sybilla lifted her head, and with her outstretched arm pointed to Rosamund, who stood above them all by the high altar.

For a moment Rosamund turned pale, then spoke in a steady voice, "Say, what service can my poor life be to you, O Queen, and by whom is it sought?"

Three times Sybilla strove to answer, and at last cried, "I cannot. Let the envoys give her the letter, if she is able to read their tongue."

"I am able," answered Rosamund, and a Saracen emir drew forth a roll and laid it against his forehead, then gave it to the abbess, who brought it to Rosamund. With her dagger blade she cut its silk, opened it, and read aloud, always in the same quiet voice, translating as she read:

"In the name of Allah the One, the All-merciful, to my niece, aforetime the princess of Baalbec, Rosamund D'Arcy by name, now a fugitive hidden in a convent of the Franks in the city el-Kuds Esh-sherif, the holy city of Jerusalem:

"Niece, —All my promises to you I have performed, and more, since for your sake I spared the lives of your cousins, the twin knights. But you have repaid me with ingratitude and trickery, after the manner of those of your false and accursed faith, and have fled from me. I promised you also, again and yet again, that if you attempted this thing, death should be your portion. No longer, therefore, are you the princess of Baalbec, but only an escaped Christian slave, and as such doomed to die whenever my sword reaches you.

"Of my vision concerning you, which caused me to bring you to the East from England, you know well. Repeat it in your heart before you answer. That vision told me that by your nobleness and sacrifice you should aid me on in my victorious quest. I demanded that you should be brought back to me, and the request was refused—why, it matters not. Now I understand the reason—that this was so ordained. I demand no more that force should be used against you. I demand that you shall come of your own free will, to suffer the bitter and shameful reward of your sin. Or, if you so desire, bide where you are of your own free will, and be dealt with as God shall decree.

"This hangs upon your judgment. If you come and ask it of me, I will consider the question of the sparing of Jerusalem and its inhabitants. If you refuse to come, I will certainly put every one of them to the sword, save such of the women and children as may be kept for slaves. Decide, then, Niece, and quickly, whether you will return with my envoys, or bide where they find you.—Yusuf Saladin."

Rosamund finished reading, and the letter fluttered from her hand down to the marble floor. Then the queen said, "Lady, we ask this sacrifice of you in the name of these and all their fellows," and she pointed to the women and the children behind her.

"And my life?" mused Rosamund aloud. "It is all I have. When I have paid it away I shall be beggared," and her eyes wandered to where the tall shape of Wulf stood by a pillar of the church.

"Perchance Saladin will be merciful," hazarded the queen.

"Why should he be merciful?" answered Rosamund, "who has always warned me that if I escaped from him and was recaptured, certainly I must die? Nay, he will offer me Islam, or death, which means—death by the rope—or in some worse fashion."

"But if you stay here you must die," pleaded the queen, "or at best fall into the hands of the soldiers. Oh! Lady, your life is but one life, and with it you can buy those of eighty thousand souls."

"Is that so sure?" asked Rosamund. "The sultan has made no promise; he says only that, if I ask it of him, he will consider the question of the sparing of Jerusalem."

"But—but," went on the queen, "he says also that if you do not come he will surely put Jerusalem to the sword, and to Sir Balian he said that if you gave yourself up he thought he might grant terms which we should be glad to take. Therefore, we dare to ask of you to give your life in payment for such a hope. Think—think what otherwise must be the lot of these"—and again she pointed to the women and children—"aye, and your own sisterhood and of all of us. Whereas, if you die, it will be with much honor, and your name shall be worshipped as a saint and martyr in every church in Christendom.

"Oh! Refuse not our prayer, but show that you indeed are great enough to step forward to meet the death which comes to every one of us, and thereby earn the blessings of half the world and make sure your place in Heaven, nigh to Him who also died for men. Plead with her, my sisters, plead with her!"

Then the women and the children threw themselves down before her, and with tears and sobbing pleaded that she would give up her life for theirs. Rosamund looked at them and smiled, then said in a clear voice, "What say you, my cousin and betrothed, Sir Wulf D'Arcy? Come hither, and, as is fitting in this strait, give me your counsel."

So the gray-eyed, war-worn Wulf strode up the aisle, and, standing by the altar rails, saluted her.

"You have heard," said Rosamund. "Your counsel. Would you have me die?"

"Alas!" he answered in a hoarse voice. "It is hard to speak. Yet, they are many—you are but one."

Now there was a murmur of applause. For it was known that this knight loved his lady dearly, and that but the other day he had stood there to defend her to the death against those who would give her up to Saladin.

Now Rosamund laughed out, and the sweet sound of her laughter was strange in that solemn place and hour.

"Ah, Wulf!" she said. "Wulf, who must ever speak the truth, even when it costs him dear. Well, I would not have it otherwise. Queen, and all you foolish people, I did but try your tempers. Could you, then, think me so base that I would spare to spend this poor life of mine, and to forego such few joys as God might have in store for me on earth, when those of tens of thousands may hang upon the issue? Nay, nay; it is far otherwise."

Then Rosamund sheathed the dagger that all this while she had held in her hand, and, lifting the letter from the floor, touched her brow with it in signal of obedience, saying in Arabic to the envoys, "I am the slave of Saladin, Commander of the Faithful. I am the small dust beneath his feet. Take notice, Emirs, that in presence of all here gathered, of my own free will I, Rosamund D'Arcy, aforetime princess and sovereign lady of Baalbec, determine to accompany you to the sultan's camp, there to make prayer for the sparing of the lives of the citizens of Jerusalem. In consequence of which, I will likely suffer the punishment of death in payment of my flight, according to my royal uncle's high decree. One request I make only, if he be pleased to grant it—that my body be brought back to Jerusalem for burial before this altar, where of my own act I lay down my life. Emirs, I am ready."

Now the envoys bowed before her in grave admiration, and the air grew thick with blessings. As Rosamund stepped down from the altar the queen threw her arms about her neck and kissed her, while lords and knights, women and children, pressed their lips upon her hands, upon the hem of her white robe, and even on her feet, calling her "Saint" and "Deliverer."

"Alas!" she answered, waving them back. "As yet I am neither of these things, though the latter of them I hope to be. Come; let us be going."

"Aye," echoed Wulf, stepping to her side, "let us be going."

Rosamund started at the words, and all there stared. "Listen, Queen, Emirs, and people," he went on. "I am this lady's kinsman and her betrothed knight, sworn to serve her to the end. If she be guilty of a crime against the sultan, I am more guilty, and on me also shall fall his vengeance. Let us be going."

"Wulf, Wulf," she said, "it shall not be. One life is asked—not both."

"Yet, lady, both shall be given that the measure of atonement may run over, and Saladin moved to mercy. Nay, forbid me not. I have lived for you, and for you I die. When I counseled you just now, I counseled myself, also. Surely you never dreamed that I would suffer you to go alone, when by sharing it I could make your doom easier."

"Oh, Wulf!" she cried. "You will but make it harder."

"No, no; faced hand in hand, death loses half its terrors. Moreover, Saladin is one whom I have been able to reason with in the past, and I also would plead with him for the people of Jerusalem."

Then he whispered in her ear, "Sweet Rosamund, deny me not, lest you should drive me to madness, who will have no more of earth without you."

Now, her eyes full of tears and shining with love, Rosamund murmured back, "You are too strong for me. Let it befall as God wills."

Nor did the others attempt to stop him any more.

Going to the abbess, Rosamund would have knelt before her, but it was the abbess who knelt and called her blessed, and kissed her. The sisters also kissed her one by one in farewell.

To the priest at the altar, first Rosamund and then Wulf made confession of their sins, receiving absolution and the sacrament in that form in which it was given to the dying; while, except the emirs, all in the church knelt and prayed as for souls that pass.

The solemn ritual was ended. They rose, and, followed by two of the envoys—for already the third had departed under escort to the court of Saladin to give him warning—the queen, her ladies, and all the company, walked from the church and through the convent halls out into the narrow Street of Woe. Here Wulf, as her kinsman, took Rosamund by the hand, leading her as a man leads his sister to her bridal. It was now evening with a bright moonlight, moonlight clear as day. By now, tidings of this strange story had spread through all Jerusalem, so that its narrow streets were crowded with spectators, who stood also upon every roof and at every window.

"The lady Rosamund!" they shouted. "The blessed Rosamund, who goes to a martyr's death to save us. The pure Saint Rosamund and her brave knight Wulf!" And they tore flowers and green leaves from the gardens and threw them in their path.

Down the long, winding streets, with bent heads and humble countenance, companioned ever by the multitude, through which soldiers cleared the way, they walked thus, while women held up their children to touch the robe of Rosamund or to look upon her face. At length, the gate was reached, and while it was unbarred they halted.

Then came forward Sir Balian of Ibelin, bareheaded, and said, "Lady, on behalf of the people of Jerusalem and of the whole of Christendom, I give you honor and thanks, and to you also, Sir Wulf D'Arcy, the bravest and most faithful of all knights."

A company of priests also, headed by a bishop, advanced chanting and swinging censers, and blessed them solemnly in the name of the Church and of Christ its Master.

"Give us not praise and thanks, but prayers," answered Rosamund; "prayers that we may succeed in our mission, to which we gladly offer up our lives, and afterwards, when we are dead, prayers for the welfare of our sinful souls. But should we fail, as it may chance, then remember of us only that we did our best. Oh! Good people, great sorrows have come upon this land, and the Cross of Christ is veiled with shame. Yet it shall shine forth once more, and to it through the ages shall all men bow the knee. Oh! May you live! May no more death come among you! It is our last petition, and with it, this—that when at length you die we may meet again in Heaven! Now fare you well."

Then they passed through the gate, and as the envoys declared that none might accompany them further, walked forward followed by the sound of the weeping of the multitude towards the camp of Saladin, two strange and lonesome figures in the moonlight.

At last these lamentations could be heard no more, and there, on the outskirts of the Saracen lines, an escort met them, and bearers with a litter.

But into this Rosamund would not enter, so they walked onwards up the hill, till they came to the great square in the center of the camp upon the Mount of Olives, beyond the gray trees of the Garden of Gethsemane. There, awaiting them at the head of the square, sat Saladin in state, while all about, rank upon rank, in thousands and tens of thousands, was gathered his vast army, who watched them pass in silence.

Thus they came into the presence of the sultan and knelt before him, Rosamund in her novice's white robe, and Wulf in his battered mail.

Chapter XXIV
The Dregs of the Cup

Saladin looked at them, but gave them no greeting. Then he spoke, "Woman, you have read my message. You know that your rank is taken from you, and that with it my promises are at an end; you know also that you come facing the death of a faithless woman. Is it so?"

"I know all these things, great Saladin," answered Rosamund.

"Tell me, then, do you come of your own free will, unforced by any, and why does the knight Sir Wulf, whose life I spared and do not seek, kneel at your side?"

"I come of my own free will, Saladin, as your emirs can tell you; ask them. For the rest, my kinsman must answer for himself."

"Sultan," said Wulf, "I counseled the lady Rosamund that she should come—not that she needed such counsel—and, having given it, I accompanied her by right of blood and of justice, since her offence against you is mine, also. Her fate is my fate."

"I have no quarrel against you whom I forgave, therefore you must take your own way to follow the path she goes."

"Doubtless," answered Wulf, "being a Christian among many sons of the Prophet, it will not be hard to find a friendly scimitar to help me on that road. I ask you to respect the duty which is mine to stand by her regardless of the cost."

"What!" said Saladin. "You are ready to die with her, although you are young and strong, and there are so many other women in the world?"

Wulf smiled and nodded his head.

"Good. Who am I that I should stand between a fool and his folly? I grant the favor. Your fate shall be her fate; Wulf D'Arcy, you shall drink of the cup of my slave Rosamund to its last bitterest dregs."

"I desire no less," said Wulf coolly.

Now Saladin looked at Rosamund and asked, "Woman, why have you come here to brave my vengeance? Speak on if you have a petition to make."

Then Rosamond rose from her knees, and, standing before him, said, "I am come, O Sultan, to plead for the people of Jerusalem, because it was told me that you would listen to no other voice than that of this your slave. See, many moons ago, you had a vision concerning me. Thrice you dreamed in the night that I, the niece whom you had never seen, by some act of mine should be the means of showing you victory and the way of peace. Therefore, you tore me from my home and brought my father to a bloody death, as you are about to bring his daughter; and after much suffering and danger I fell into your power, and was treated with great honor. Still I, who am a Christian, and who grew sick with the sight of the daily slaughter and outrage of my kin, strove to escape from you, although you had warned me that the price of this rebellion was death; and in the end, through the wit and sacrifice of another woman, I did escape.

"Now I return to pay that price, and behold! Your vision is fulfilled—or, at the least, you can fulfill it if God should touch your heart with the understanding to recognize that I have been brought into your path to help you save life, not to empower you to conquer without honor. I ask you, Saladin, to spare the city, and for its blood to accept mine as a token and an offering. Oh, as you are great, be merciful. What will it avail you in the day of your own judgment that you have added another eighty thousand to the tally of your slain, and with them many more thousands of your own folk, since the warriors of Jerusalem will not die unavenged? Give them their lives and let them go free, and win thereby the gratitude of mankind and the forbearance of God above."

So Rosamund spoke and, stretching out her arms towards him, was silent.

"These things I offered to them, and they were refused," answered Saladin. "Why should I grant them now that they are conquered?"

"Mighty Sultan," said Rosamund, "do you, who are so brave, blame yonder knights and soldiers because they fought on against desperate odds? Would you not have called them cowards if they had yielded up the city where their Savior died and struck no blow to save it? Oh! I am outworn! I can say no more; but once again, most humbly and on my knees, I beseech you speak the word of mercy, and let not your triumph be stained red with the blood of women and of little children."

Then, casting herself upon her face, Rosamund clasped the hem of his royal robe with her hands and pressed it to her forehead.

So for a while she lay there in the shimmering moonlight, while utter silence fell upon all that vast multitude of armed men as they waited for the decree of fate to be uttered by the conqueror's lips. But Saladin sat still as a statue, gazing at the domes and towers of Jerusalem outlined against the deep blue sky.

"Rise," he said at length, "and know, Niece, that you have played your part in a fashion worthy of my race, and that I, Saladin, am proud of you. Know also that I will weigh your petition as I have weighed that of none other who breathes upon the earth. Now I must take counsel with my own heart, and tomorrow it shall be granted—or refused. To you, who are doomed to die, and to the knight who chooses to die with you, according to the ancient law and custom, I offer the choice of Islam, and with it life and honor."

"We refuse," answered Rosamund and Wulf with one voice.

The sultan bowed his head as though he expected no other answer, and glanced round, as all thought to order the executioners to do their office. But he said only to a captain of his Mamelukes, "Take them; keep them under guard and separate them, till my word of death comes to you. Your life shall answer for their safety. Give them food and drink, and let no harm touch them until I bid you."

The Mameluke bowed and advanced with his company of soldiers. As they prepared to go with them, Rosamund asked, "Tell me of your grace, what of Masouda, my friend?"

"She died for you; seek her beyond the grave," answered Saladin, whereat Rosamund hid her face with her hands and sighed.

"And what of Godwin, my brother?" cried Wulf; but no answer was given him.

Now Rosamund turned; stretching out her arms towards Wulf, she fell upon his breast. There, then, in the presence of that countless army, they kissed their kiss of betrothal and farewell. They spoke no word, only before she went Rosamund lifted her hand and pointed upwards to the sky.

Then a murmur rose from the multitude, and the sound of it seemed to shape itself into one word: "Mercy!"

Still Saladin made no sign, and they were led away to their prisons.

Among the thousands who watched this strange and most thrilling scene were two men wrapped in long cloaks, Godwin and the bishop Egbert. Godwin tried several times to approach the throne. But it seemed that the soldiers around him had received orders, for they would not permit him to stir or speak; and when, as Rosamund passed, he strove to break away to her, they seized and held him. Yet as she went by he cried, "The blessing of Heaven be upon you, pure saint of God—on you and your true knight."

Catching the tones of that voice above the tumult, Rosamund stopped and looked around her, but saw no one, for the guard hemmed her in. So she went on, wondering if perchance it was Godwin's voice which she had heard, or whether it was an angel, or only some Frankish prisoner that had spoken.

Godwin stood wringing his hands while the bishop strove to comfort him, saying that he should not grieve, since such deaths as those of Rosamund and Wulf were most glorious, and more to be desired than a hundred lives.

"Aye, aye," answered Godwin, "would that I could go with them!"

"Their work is done, but not yours," said the bishop gently. "Come to our tent and let us to our knees. God is more powerful than the sultan, and perhaps He will yet find a way to save them. If they are still alive tomorrow at the dawn we will seek audience of Saladin to plead with him."

So they entered the tent and prayed there, as the inhabitants of Jerusalem prayed behind their shattered walls, that the heart of Saladin might be moved to spare them all. While they knelt thus, the curtain of the tent was drawn aside, and an emir stood before them.

"Rise," he said, "both of you, and follow me. The sultan commands your presence."

Egbert and Godwin went, wondering, and were led through the pavilion to the royal sleeping place, which guards closed behind them. On a silken couch reclined Saladin, the light from the lamp falling on his bronzed and thoughtful face.

"I have sent for you two Franks," he said, "that you may bear a message from me to Sir Balian of Ibelin and the inhabitants of Jerusalem. This is the message:—Let the Holy City surrender tomorrow and all its population acknowledge themselves my prisoners. Then for forty days I will hold them to ransom, during which time none shall be harmed. Every man who pays ten pieces of gold shall go free, and two women or ten children shall be counted as one man at a like price. Of the poor, seven thousand shall be set free also, on payment of thirty thousand bezants. Such who remain or have no money for their ransom—and there is still much gold in Jerusalem—shall become my slaves. These are my terms, which I grant at the dying prayer of my niece, the lady Rosamund, and to her prayer alone. Deliver them to Sir Balian, and bid him wait on me at the dawn with his chief notables, and answer whether he is willing to accept them on behalf of the people. If not, the assault goes on until the city is a heap of ruins covering the bones of its children."

"We bless you for this mercy," said the bishop Egbert, and we hasten to obey. But tell us, Sultan, what shall we do? Return to the camp with Sir Balian?"

"If he accepts my terms, no, for in Jerusalem you will be safe, and I give you your freedom without ransom."

"Sire," said Godwin, "ere I go, grant me leave to bid farewell to my brother and my cousin Rosamund."

"That for the third time you may plot their escape from my vengeance?" said Saladin. "No, bide in Jerusalem and await my word; you shall meet them at the last, no more."

"Sire," pleaded Godwin, "of your mercy spare them, for they have played a noble part. It is hard that they should die who love each other and are so young and fair and brave."

"Aye," answered Saladin, "a noble part; never have I seen one more noble. Well, it fits them the better for Heaven, if Cross-worshippers enter there. Have done; their doom is written and my purpose cannot be turned, nor shall you see them till the last, as I have said. But if it pleases you to write them a letter of farewell and to send it back by the embassy, it shall be delivered to them. Now go, for greater matters are afoot than this punishment of a pair of lovers. A guard awaits you."

So they went, and within an hour stood before Sir Balian and gave him the message of Saladin, whereat he rose and blessed the name of Rosamund. While he called his counselors from their sleep and ordered his servants to saddle horses, Godwin found pen and parchment, and wrote hurriedly:

"To Wulf, my brother, and Rosamund, my cousin and his betrothed,—I live, though I nearly died by the cold body of Masouda—Jesus rest her gallant and most beloved soul! Saladin will not suffer me to see you, though he has promised that I shall be with you at the last, so watch for me then. I still dare to hope that it may please God to change the sultan's heart and spare you. If so, this is my prayer and desire—that you two should wed as soon as may be, and get home to England, where, if I live, I hope to visit you in years to come. Till then seek me not, who would be lonely a while. But if it should unfold otherwise, then when my time and work for God are done I will seek you among the saints in Heaven.

"The embassy rides. I have no time for more, though there is much to say. Farewell.—Godwin."

The surrender terms of Saladin were accepted with little protest. With rejoicing because their lives were spared, but with woe and lamentation because the holy city had fallen again into the hands of the heathen, the people of Jerusalem made ready to leave the streets and seek new homes elsewhere. The great golden cross was torn from the mosque el-Aksa, and on every tower and wall floated the yellow banners of Saladin. All who had money paid their ransoms, and those who had none begged and borrowed it as they could and, if they could not, they gave themselves over to despair and slavery. Only the patriarch Heraclius, forgetting the misery of these wretched ones, carried off his own great wealth and the gold plate of the churches.

Then Saladin showed his mercy, for he freed all the aged without charge, and from his own treasure paid the ransom of hundreds of ladies whose husbands and fathers had fallen in battle, or lay in prison in other cities.

So for forty days, headed by Queen Sybilla and her ladies, that sad procession of the vanquished marched through the gates. Many of them who fled the city, as they passed the conqueror seated in state, halted to make a petition to him for those who were left behind. A few also who remembered Rosamund, and that it was because of her sacrifice that they continued to look upon the sun, implored him that if they were not already dead, that he would spare her and the brave knight.

At the end of forty days it was over, and Saladin took full possession of the city. Having purged the Great Mosque, washing it with rose-water, he worshipped in it after his own fashion. He then distributed the remnant of the people who could pay no ransom as slaves among his emirs and followers. Thus did the Crescent triumph over the Cross in Jerusalem, not in a sea of blood, as ninety years before the Cross had triumphed over the Crescent within its walls, for the inhabitants of Jerusalem who named Christ had enough sense to surrender before things had gone too far.

Thus did Almighty God use the heathen Saracens to chasten the wayward and ignorant leaders of the Crusades who seldom understood why the Lord would refuse to bless their carnal plans for extending the Kingdom of Christ.

During all those forty days Rosamund and Wulf lay in their separate prisons, awaiting their death. The letter of Godwin was brought to Wulf, who read it and rejoiced to learn that his brother lived. Then it was taken from him to Rosamund, who, although she rejoiced also, wept over it, and wondered a little what it might mean. Of one thing she was sure from its wording, that they had no hope of life.

They knew that Jerusalem had fallen, for they heard the shouts of triumph by the Muslims. From far away, through their prison bars, they could see the endless multitude of fugitives passing the ancient gates laden with baggage, leading their children by the hand, to seek refuge in the cities of the coast. At this sight, although it was so sad, Rosamund was content, knowing also that now she would not die in vain.

After some time, the camp broke up, Saladin and many of the soldiers entering Jerusalem; but still the pair was left languishing in their dismal cells, which were fashioned from old tombs. One evening, while Rosamund was kneeling at prayer before she sought her bed, the door of the place was opened, and there appeared a glittering captain and a guard of soldiers, who saluted her and bade her follow him.

"Is it the end?" she asked.

"Lady," he answered, "it is the end." So she bowed her head meekly and followed. They placed her in a litter and bore her through the bright moonlight into the city of Jerusalem and along the Way of Sorrrow, till they halted at a great door, which she knew well, for by it stood the ancient arch.

"They have brought me back to the Convent of the Holy Cross to kill me where I asked that I might be buried," she murmured to herself as she descended from the litter.

Then the doors were thrown open, and she entered the great courtyard of the convent, and saw that it was decorated as though for a festival, for about it and in the cloisters round hung many lamps. Around these cloisters and in the space in front of them were crowded Saracen lords, wearing their robes of state, while yonder sat Saladin and his court.

"They would make a brave show of my death," thought Rosamund again. Then a little cry broke from her lips, for there, in front of the throne of Saladin, the moonlight and the lamp-blaze shining on his armor, stood a tall Christian knight. At that cry he turned his head, and she grew sure that it was Wulf, wasted somewhat and grown pale, but still Wulf.

"So we are to die together," she whispered to herself, then walked forward with a proud step amidst the deep silence, and, having bowed to Saladin, took the hand of Wulf and held it.

The sultan looked at them and said, "However long it may be delayed, the day of fate must break at last. Say, Franks, are you prepared to drink the dregs of that cup I promised you?"

"We are prepared," they answered with one voice.

"Do you grieve now that you laid down your lives to save those of all Jerusalem?" he asked again.

"Nay," Rosamund answered, glancing at Wulf's face; "we rejoice exceedingly that God has been so good to us."

"I, too, rejoice," said Saladin; "and I, too, thank Allah who in bygone days sent me that vision which I so little understand which has given me back the holy city of Jerusalem without excess bloodshed. Now all is accomplished as it was fated. Lead them away."

For a moment they clung together, then emirs took Wulf to the right and Rosamund to the left, and she went with a pale face and high head to meet her executioner, wondering if she would see Godwin before she died. They led her to a chamber where women waited but no swordsman that she could see, and shut the door upon her.

"Perchance I am to be strangled by these women," thought Rosamund, as they came towards her, "so that the blood royal may not be shed."

Yet it was not so, for with gentle hands, but in silence, they unrobed her, and washed her with scented waters and braided her hair, twisting it up with pearls and gems. Then they clad her in fine linen, and put over it gorgeous, broidered garments, and a royal mantle of purple, and her own jewels which she had worn in bygone days, and with them others still more splendid, and threw about her head a gauzy veil worked with golden stars. It was just such a veil as Wulf's gift, which she had worn on the night when Hassan dragged her from her home at Steeple. She noted it and smiled at the sad omen, then said, "Ladies, why should I mock my doom with these bright garments?"

"It is the sultan's will," they answered; "nor shall you rest tonight less happily because of them."

Now all was ready, and the door opened and she stepped through it, a radiant thing, glittering in the lamplight. Then trumpets blew and a herald cried: "Way! Way there! Way for the high sovereign lady and princess of Baalbec!"

Thus, followed by the train of honorable women who attended her, Rosamund glided forward to the courtyard, and once more bent the knee to Saladin, then stood still, lost in wonder.

Again the trumpets blew, and on the right a herald cried, "Way! Way there! Way for the brave and noble Frankish knight, Sir Wulf D'Arcy!"

Lo! Attended by emirs and notables, Wulf came forth, clad in splendid armor inlaid with gold, wearing on his shoulder a mantel set with gems, and on his breast the gleaming Star of the Luck of Hassan. To Rosamund he strode and stood by her, his hands resting on the hilt of his long sword.

"Princess," said Saladin, "I give you back your rank and titles, because you have shown a noble heart; and you, Sir Wulf, I honor also as best I may, but to my decree I hold. Let them go together to the drinking of the cup of their destiny as to a bridal bed."

Again the trumpets blew and the heralds called, and they led them to the doors of the chapel, which at their knocking were thrown wide. From within came the sound of women's voices singing, but it was no sad song they sang.

"The sisters of the Order are still there," said Rosamund to Wulf, "and would cheer us on our road to Heaven."

"Very odd," he answered. "I understand not. I am in very truth amazed."

At the door, the company of Muslims left them, but they crowded round the entrance as though to watch what passed. Now down the long aisle walked a single white-robed figure. It was the abbess.

"What shall we do, mother?" said Rosamund to her.

"Follow me, both of you," she said, and, they followed her through the nave to the altar rails, and at a sign from her knelt down.

Now they saw that before the altar stood a Christian priest. The priest—it was the bishop Egbert—came forward and began to read over them the marriage service of their faith.

"They'd wed us ere we die," whispered Rosamund to Wulf.

"So be it," he answered; "I am glad."

"And I also, beloved," she whispered back.

The service went on—as in a dream, the service went on, while the white-robed sisters sat in their carven chairs and watched. The rings that were handed to them had been interchanged; Wulf had taken Rosamund to wife, Rosamund had taken Wulf to husband, till death did them part.

Then the old bishop withdrew to the altar, and called upon a lay brother to come forward to say the benediction. The hooded friar came forward and bellowed out the benediction in a deep and sonorous voice, which stirred their hearts most strangely, as though some echo reached them from beyond the grave. He held his hands above them in blessing and looked upwards, so that his hood fell back, and the light of the altar lamp fell upon his face.

It was the face of Godwin, and on his head was the tonsure of a monk.

Once more they stood before Saladin, and now their train was swelled by the abbess and sisters of the Holy Cross.

"Sir Wulf D'Arcy," said the sultan, "and you, Rosamund, my niece, princess of Baalbec, the dregs of your cup, sweet or bitter, or bitter-sweet, are drunk; the doom which I decreed for you is accomplished, and, according to your own rites, you are man and wife till Allah sends upon you that death which I withhold. Because you showed mercy upon those doomed to die and were the means of mercy, I also give you mercy, and with it honor. Now bide here if you will in my freedom, and enjoy your rank and wealth, or go hence if you will, and live out your lives across the sea. The blessing of Allah be upon you, and turn your souls to light. This is the decree of Yusuf Saladin, Commander of the Faithful, Conqueror and Caliph of the East."

Trembling, full of joy and wonder, they bowed before him and kissed his hand. Then, after a few swift words between them, Rosamund spoke.

"Sire, may the God that we serve, the God of all the world, have mercy on your soul and reward you for this royal deed. Yet listen to our petition. It may be that many of our faith still lie unransomed in Jerusalem. Take my lands and gems, and let them be valued, and their price given to pay for the liberty of some poor slaves. It is our marriage offering. As for us, we will get us to our own country."

"So be it," answered Saladin. "The lands I will take and devote the sum of them as you desire—yes, to the last bezant. The jewels also shall be valued, but I give them back to you as my wedding dower. To these nuns further I grant permission to remain here in Jerusalem to nurse the Christian sick, unharmed and unmolested, if so they will, and this because they sheltered you. Ho! Minstrels and heralds lead this new-wed pair to the place that has been prepared for them."

Still trembling and bewildered, they turned to go, when lo! Godwin stood before them smiling, and kissed them both upon the cheek, calling them "Beloved brother and sister."

"And you, Godwin?" stammered Rosamund.

"I, Rosamund, have also found my bride, and she is named the Church of Christ. My calling now is to pull down the strongholds of Satan by forsaking worldly ambition and office so that I might comfort the poor and needy. Having fought the good fight as a knight, I now turn my heart to the greater battle in the spiritual realm that will ultimately conquer the hearts of men in ways that are beyond the reach of the sword."

"Do you then, return to England, Brother?" asked Wulf.

"Nay," Godwin answered, in a fierce whisper and with flashing eyes, "the Cross is down, because we have had a zeal to serve God that is not according to knowledge. The cause of Christ, however, will not be down forever, dear brother. It is well reported that good King Richard of England, and many others of good will, may pick up the battle in the days ahead. Therefore, Wulf, before our lives are done, we may meet again in time of war—yet, in the next struggle against the enemies of God, I have determined to wield the weapons of Christian charity and compassion. Till then, farewell."

So spoke Godwin, who, after embracing his friends was gone.